RELUCTANT INTERN

A NOVEL BY BILL YANCEY

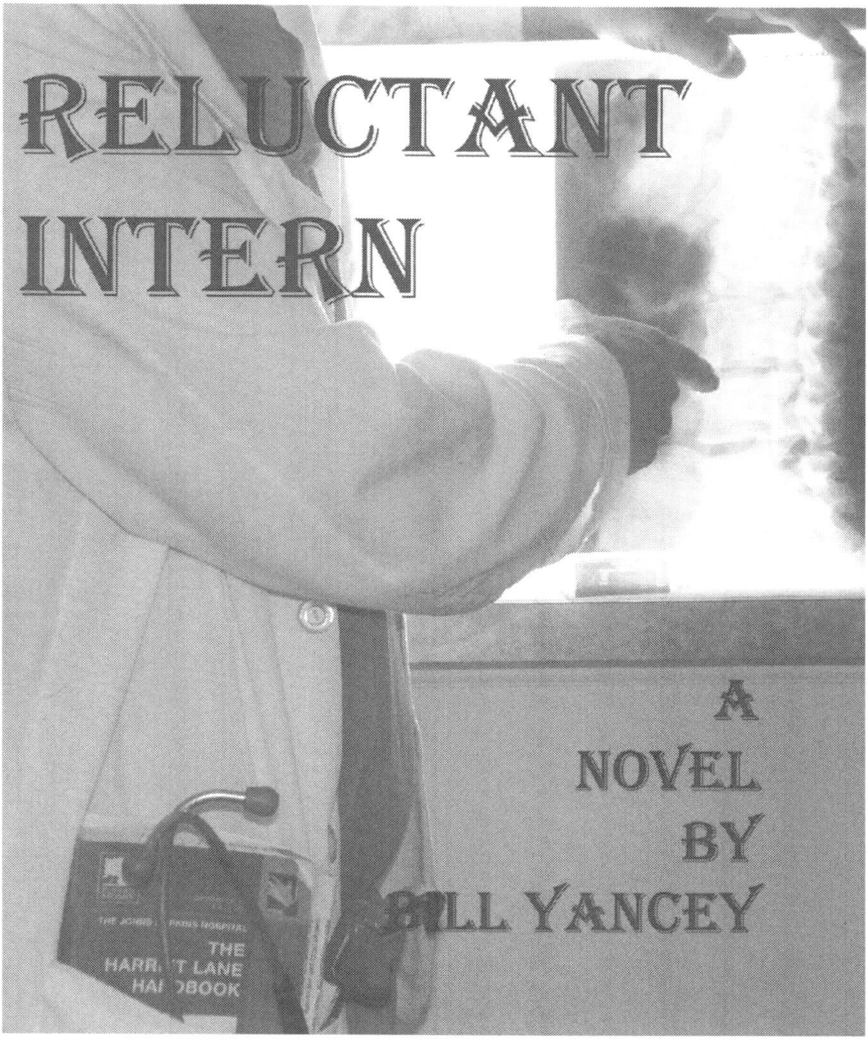

Reluctant Intern

by

Bill Yancey

Reluctant Intern
Bill Yancey

ISBN: 1496070046
ISBN-13: 978-1496070043

Dedication

This book is dedicated to the patients, interns, residents, attending physicians; and the administrative, medical, and house staff at University (now UF Health Shands) Hospital in Jacksonville, Florida, past, present, and future. This is especially true for those who have given or devoted their lives to furthering the education of physicians. From you I learned a lot, although sometimes the lessons were not obvious until much later. I apologize if my responses were not what you expected.

It is also dedicated to the memory of two physicians:

Robert P. Turk, M.D.

was a fine surgeon and educator. Without Bob's encouragement I might not have survived my own internship at WPAFB Medical Center in 1976-77. He was an extraordinary human being and will be missed by many, many people.

Michael D. Blackburn, M.D.

was an Emergency Medicine resident classmate of mine. Mike's good humor and intelligence made being an emergency medicine resident and physician a worthwhile occupation. Stricken at a young age by Alzheimer 's disease, Mike is also missed by many.

Acknowledgements

Many friends and some of my family read the rough draft of this novel and offered insightful criticisms. I would like to thank Pat Aller; Bryan Baker; Esther Gayoba, PA; Pete Grimm; Jane Helwig, MD; George Kamajian, DO; Larry Kerr; Frank Snyder, MD; Barbara Turner; Jerry Anne Yancey and Tom Yancey, for their suggestions and for taking the time out of their busy lives to help me. Any remaining typographical errors, punctuation mistakes, or other blunders, however, are mine.

Also by Bill Yancey

Elvis Saves

No One Lives Forever

The Last Day

What Your Doctor Won't Tell You About Your Lower Back

Invictus

Multidimensional Man

A Dog Named Fridge

Author's Statement

I have not asked my family or friends to read this book and put inflated reviews on the internet. I would appreciate it if you would put an honest review (good or bad) on the internet when you finish reading it. Also, my email address is on the last page of the book and you can direct comments or criticisms to me at that address. Thank you for spending your money and taking the time to read this novel. I hope you got your money's worth.

Bill Yancey

Praise for *Elvis Saves* by Bill Yancey

"The novel reads well, with sufficient suspense and ambiguity to keep the reader turning pages. It is an entertaining extension of all the rumor mongering that makes the supermarket tabloids all the time—those about Elvis being sighted in cellars or cornfields—or films such as *Finding Graceland*...in which the purpose is to convince the other characters in the story and the audience that Elvis could actually still be among the living."

Joseph Meigs, Western Carolina University, author of *Tenure Track; Mountain Laurel Magazine*

"If you like Elvis fiction, you'll surely enjoy *Elvis Saves*; if you've never ventured into Elvis fiction, then *Elvis Saves* is a good place to start."

David Neale; *Elvis in Print*

"Yancey has written a ... good book. It is good because of the plot, characters and fascinating details.... The author's obvious familiarity with details about the real Elvis Presley helps him to create B.J. Nottingham, a plausible and engaging Elvis impersonator who is the fulcrum on which the story balances nicely. Lomax hires Nottingham to create fake Elvis sightings. When Nottingham disappears, his feisty girlfriend hires a weather-beaten private detective to find him, and Lomax hires thugs to do the same. *Elvis Saves* is a fun read."

A.K. Williams; *Roanoke Times*

Table of Contents

Prologue

Addison Wolfe dreamed. He knew he dreamt. He knew what would happen next. It was an old dream, a recurrent dream. That made it no less terrifying.

A television hung from the ceiling in the corner of the residents' on-call sleep room. Prior to its renovation, the room had been a semi-private patients' room with a bathroom including shower. One television had been left, the second removed. There were now five beds for the residents to sleep in while on call. Each had a bedside table and lamp.

On the television, the local Jacksonville news team from WJXT, Channel 4, a man and a woman, presented the day's local news. He sat on the left of the screen; his face was green. She sat on the right, face pink to purple. The middle of the picture appeared to be normal tones at times, so when the cameraman zoomed in for a close-up the reporters appeared normal color, except for their ears.

"In local news today," the man said, "state and federal authorities are in the process of taking into custody the entire intern class at University Hospital in Jacksonville. Officials cited the number of deaths attributed to this class as the reason. It seems that wrong doses of medications, inappropriate surgeries, failure to diagnose lethal conditions, and other mistakes have led to hundreds of deaths...."

Propped up in bed on several pillows, Wolfe watched video of men in blue windbreakers with FBI or JSO (Jacksonville Sheriff's Office) in large yellow letters on the back escort interns in handcuffs from the ambulance entrance of University Hospital. Each tried to hide his or her face from the camera. Not wanting to undergo the same fate, Wolfe leapt from bed. Pulling off his scrub shirt and scrub pants, he searched under the bed for civilian clothes. He left his name tag and photo ID on the bed with the scrub suit. Dressed in corduroy pants, a knit short-sleeved shirt and in Nike running shoes, he ran down the hallway to the rear fire escape and stairway. Literally flying down the stairs, his feet never hit the steps or landings.

On the ground floor, he had a choice of exiting the stairwell into the hospital or into the parking lot. He chose to go outside. Forcing himself to walk slowly, he made his way to his car, unlocked it, and drove slowly out of the parking lot. At the exit to the parking lot, a Mercedes sedan waited. Wolfe recognized the driver, Dr. Ramon Figueroa. Another automobile sat behind the first, a convertible. In it sat Drs. Nick Robinson, and Samantha Joiner. Both had gray hair and appeared much older than he remembered them from internship.

Hoping not to be recognized, Wolfe ducked low and stomped on the accelerator. His vehicle lurched forward, leaving a squeal and black tire marks in its wake. Figueroa followed. So did Robinson and Joiner. Through the city of Jacksonville the chase continued. Wolfe dodged other vehicles, made sharp turns, went the wrong way on one way streets. Both cars stayed glued to his tail.

Wolfe raced through red lights, turned more sharply then he should have, narrowly missing pedestrians and lifting the automobile onto two wheels. The *Greaseman* on WAPE blared at him through the car radio. As he approached the Mathews Bridge, he sped up until the vehicle reached ninety miles per hour. In the Fiat Spider, Robinson and Joiner easily passed Figueroa. They pulled alongside Wolfe. Turning his head, he saw the two doctors laughing, and then Robinson rammed his car into the passenger side of Wolfe's car.

Wolfe lost control of his vehicle. It crossed into the oncoming traffic lanes. He turned the steering wheel sharply to the left to avoid an approaching truck. His car tore through the guard rail at the top of the bridge. As it fell, it rotated, the doors opened, and Wolfe fell out of the automobile. *Forgot the seatbelt. Being thrown clear*, he thought. In his dream he fell and fell and fell. It was a long way to the St. Johns River from the top of the Mathews. The vehicle hit the water before he did. A huge splash from his car buoyed him upward and Wolfe woke up. He sat bolt upright in the bed, sweat pouring from his face, heart pounding, and short of breath.

His wife rolled over and spoke to him, "Same dream?" she asked.

"Yeah," Wolfe said.

"You need to see a shrink," his wife said, burying her head under the pillow.

"Nah," Wolfe said. "I know it's stress induced. But it sure is nice to be awake and have to deal only with O'Bama Care, ICD-10, pay for performance, patients I have sent to hospitalists, meaningful use and electronic health records, staff turnover, what my patients read on the internet yesterday, where my daughter and son are with our grandchildren, and whether I can play golf this weekend. God. Things were so much simpler during my internship."

"That's not the way I remember it," she said.

Addendum

Chapter 1

Bay Two had been cleared for a resuscitation: A twenty-something year-old white male with massive bleeding from a lacerated brachial artery, according to the EMT on the ambulance.

The doors to the ER banged open. Two paramedics rushed the stretcher to the middle of the bay.

"Cut his clothes off," the senior emergency resident instructed his charges. Turning to the police officer who followed the rescue squad members into the ER, the resident asked, "Why is he handcuffed to the stretcher? I need access to all his arteries and veins."

The cop leaned over the unconscious pale white patient and unlocked the cuffs. "Guess he can't run too far without any blood. Don't let him out of your sight, though. He's under arrest for attempted murder."

The senior resident turned and took a clôser look at the patient. "Shit," he said. "It's Wolfe. Who did he try to kill?"

The officer pulled a small pad from his shirt pocket. He flipped a page and read a name. "Some guy named Figueroa. A B&E apparently gone bad."

Eleven months earlier:

A tall, imposing, heavily built, muscular man stood in front of the small auditorium. He wore a long white coat over a pinstriped shirt,

at the sides of the auditorium and two more on the third floor behind the projection booth. Behind the lectern and the man in the white coat were a complex collection of sliding projection screens, white boards, and chalk boards, all on rails. A green chalk board was exposed at present. A large triangle had been drawn in the middle of it, looking like one view of an Egyptian pyramid.

Scattered throughout the auditorium sat about fifty young men and women. The women were a small minority of three, one black, one Asian, and one blonde with frizzy hair and freckles. The men ranged in color from black to brown to yellow to white. Some had a lot of hair, some were nearly bald. Hair color and length varied.

A massive hand reached out and tapped the microphone on the lectern with its index finger. The loud *thunk* emanated in stereo from a dozen speakers hidden in the ceiling tiles.

"Okay, we need to get started," the big man said. "I'll give you one minute to fill in the seats in the front rows. Fifty-seven people do not need to spread out in this space. Get closer. Meet your new classmates. Most of you graduated from medical school in the last two months, May or June, 1976. There are some '75s, and one '74. You are all the new University Hospital Intern Class of 1977. Some of you are in residencies already. Provided you do well during your internship that will continue. The rest of you are in the rotating internship. With luck, over the next twelve months you will figure out what you want to be when you grow up.

"Anyone farther back than the third row one minute from now will be on call for the entire month of July. You people in the first three rows move to the middle; give the others some room up front." He smiled at the flurry of moving bodies. People collected books, papers, jackets, purses and other personal belongings. Wolfe slipped out of one row and into another. The interns converged on the front of the amphitheater. Those already in the first three rows moved toward the middle, vacating their seats.

"Okay. You guys comfy? Cozy? Get used to it. Take a good look at the people on either side of you. You will see a lot more of most of them over the next year. I say most, because one or two of you will not be here at the end of your internship year." The man paused and let that sink in.

"July first is six days away. Your formal training begins at 7 a.m. on Thursday, July 1st. Between now and then, you have a lot to learn: the layout of the hospital, how to use the phone system, and what the loud speaker codes are for cardiac arrests, fire, and danger, etc. My staff is going to present all that information to you over the next six hours. I suggest that if you want to get your meals, have a place to sleep while on call, need to know where the bathrooms are, where to park your cars, and more, that you listen very carefully. They can also help those of you who have not found places to live yet.

"I also suggest that you show my staff every courtesy. They have the power to make you more comfortable and less miserable during your internship. You don't want to have your meager paycheck tied up in a bureaucratic snafu. You don't want your car towed, or your beeper going off 24 hours a day. Be nice to my staff and they will return the favor. They will begin presenting information to you in a few minutes, starting with filling out W-4s. Expect to be here a while.

"Before I start with my presentation, do any of you have any emergencies that need to be addressed today? Been arrested? Break a bone? In the wrong hospital? Anything?"

A hand shot up in the second row. A curly headed, well-tanned individual blurted, "I need a pair of glasses."

Face placid, the big man responded, "Let me see. You are a college and medical school graduate. You are myopic and have been since third grade. You have worn glasses for approximately fifteen years. How is it that you urgently need glasses now? Leave them in a bar last night? Or some whore make off with them and your wallet? Float away while you were swimming at Jax Beach?"

"Uh, no, sir. I sat on them," the intern said. He held up a twisted metal frame from which hung one lens with a large crack into it. The other lens was missing.

"No back-up pair?"

"This is my back up pair. My girlfriend drove over my good ones before I left Camden."

The man in the long white coat studied briefly the list he held in his meaty hand. Finding one name associated with Camden, N.J., Figueroa asked, "So, Doctor Abrahms, you will find it difficult to recognize your patients and colleagues, or drive to work, correct?"

Blushing, the young man nodded. "Yes, sir," he whispered.

"Miss Barbara Sutton will be in to speak to you and your fellow interns. She is in charge of setting up your group health insurance. It becomes active today. Since we have an ophthalmology department that will accept your health insurance, she will help you get an appointment today to see one of the residents. You will have two pair of glasses in three days. One of you people please give Dr. Abrahms a ride home and back tomorrow. We don't want him dead in an MVA because he can't see. That would mean extra call for his fellow interns. Any other emergency issues?"

The quiet group remained silent. No one else volunteered to be flayed alive. "Okay, good. Let me introduce myself. I am Doctor Ramon Figueroa. As most of you may have recognized, I am not the person who interviewed you for the matching program, nor am I the guy who invited you to participate in one of our internship programs. Pity, that.

"They don't let me choose who comes here. I only decide who

gets to finish, and move on. I am the Director of Medical Education for University Hospital, this institution. There is some history you need to be aware of. For those of you who don't know, this is a county hospital. The county is Duval County, Florida. Geographically, Jacksonville, Florida is in Duval County. Jacksonville has incorporated all of the county, making Jacksonville one of the largest, if not the largest, cities in the USA.

"As a county hospital, we take care of a mainly indigent population. People who have no money. In many cases, also no education. We are overwhelmed by this responsibility, but we excel at it anyway. The only busier hospital in the entire state of Florida is Jackson Memorial in Miami. They are beleaguered, too.

"I know that this was the first choice for residency for a very few of you." Snickers and some hoots, along with chuckles rippled quietly through the group. Figueroa scowled. The murmuring stopped. Dead quiet filled the auditorium. "I will decide what is funny," he said.

"Those few idealists who came here on purpose will soon be hardened against social medicine. There is some competition for the Emergency Medicine Residency, since there are only five in the country at this time. The rest of you, the majority, are here because you didn't get your first, or second, or third choice during the match. You are here because no one else wanted you. Did you hear me? No one else wanted you. And you did not want to be here.

"What that means is that we have something to show the world. We have to show them that they made a mistake. That you are better than they thought. That you are smarter than they thought. That you can be better physicians than they thought. But, don't take the reverse to be true. This hospital does not have to prove to you that it is better than other hospitals. University Hospital will throw pathology at you, physical, psychological, and social, so fast that you will either adapt or drown in it. You are going to get a master course in medicine like no other on the planet, if you can tolerate it.

"Behind me on the chalk board I have drawn a pyramid. At one time you were at the top of that pyramid. In high school, you were the smartest and went to university. In college, you were the smartest and went to medical school. In medical school you were mediocre compared to your classmates and ended up here. You now rest at the base of that pyramid, maybe below the base. There is a lot to learn here.

"One thing we pride ourselves on at University Hospital is differential diagnosis." Figueroa picked up a piece of chalk. "Give me ten signs or symptoms. Just call them out."

After a pause, someone said, "Chest Pain." Figueroa wrote the symptom on the board and drew a line under it.

Followed by, "Fever." To the right and at the same level as Chest Pain, Figueroa printed the sign on the board, underlining it also.

"Vomiting."

"Icterus."

"Dysuria."

"Rash."

"Alopecia."

"Blindness."

"Itching."

"We'll say pruritis," Figueroa intoned. "You can say itching to the patients, if you want."

"Let's see, one, two, three, four, five, six, seven, eight, nine. Give me one more."

"Joint pain."

"Okay, watch." Figueroa quickly wrote down the ten most common causes of each sign or symptom below each, from most frequent to least common.

With his back to the interns, he drew circles around the causes that were the same in each list. "Black, white, or Hispanic?" he asked.

"Hispanic," someone said.

"Male or female?"

"Female." Another voice suggested.

When finished, he turned to them and said, "I would guess this patient has an autoimmune disease, like Lupus, maybe cholecystitis, or if really unlucky a cancer like Hodgkin's lymphoma. By the time you finish your internships, you will all be able to do this." He beamed, evidently expecting the young physicians to be impressed with his skills in differential diagnosis. He continued, "You have to play mental games; stereotype the patient. Men don't get pregnant; black women usually don't have osteoporosis; a lot of Hispanic women have gall bladder problems; American Indians can't hold their liquor. Etc. None of that is absolute, but the more you know the better you can narrow your choices."

To Addison Wolfe's right a ripple of laughter expanded outward. He glanced in the direction of the gigglers but couldn't decide who had started it. Figueroa scowled, then blushed slightly. "Something amusing?" he asked. There was no response. Figueroa stared at a well tanned young man with shoulder length, obviously bleached, blond hair. He then looked briefly at his list. You, Dr. Robinson, I believe. Please tell us all what is so funny."

Caught, Robinson shrugged. He stood and in a clear loud voice stated, "I was betting on syphilis. Sir." Nervously, the rest of the audience tittered, with hands over mouths.

Figueroa's forehead wrinkled, eyebrows narrowing. He stared at Robinson for a long time in silence. Slowly, he cracked a thin smile, not reflected in his eyes. "Sir William Osler, the great diagnostician, did call syphilis the great imitator, Dr. Robinson. Thank you for reminding me. You may be seated." Figueroa coughed into his hand. He wiped his face and hand on a handkerchief that he replaced in his white coat pocket. Then he continued.

"One of our brighter internal medicine interns last year had a diagnostic dilemma during his first month," Figueroa said. "A patient who looked terrible came into Primary Care, sent by his wife. The intern asked the man how he felt. The patient said he had never felt better. In fact, he felt great. The intern spent an hour examining the man. Later he reviewed lab work and x-rays. He consulted with several textbooks over the week and when the patient returned to the Internal Medicine Clinic for a follow-up appointment, he told the man that he had found the diagnosis. Great, the patient said. Tell me, so I can tell my wife and get her off my back. You have *vagina*, the intern announced. What does that mean? The patient asked. Is it terminal? I don't know, the intern said. It was the only thing in the books I could find that looked terrible but felt great."

The majority of the interns in the room exploded in laughter, including Wolfe. Behind him a woman's voice spoke clearly and disgustedly, although drowned out by the others. "Men are such pigs." Wolfe turned to see who had spoken. Behind him sat a black woman, a woman with white blonde hair, more curly than that of the black intern, and a woman who appeared to be Chinese. All three had looks of disgust on their faces. That was how he met Latesha Marks, Samantha Joiner, and Charlene Wu. They sat together, likely for protection, surrounded by a sea of testosterone.

Smile on his face he held his right hand out to each. "Oink. Call me Addy," he said while shaking their hands. Reluctantly, they all smiled.

"I decide what's funny," Figueroa said from the rostrum. "Take fifteen minutes to find your social security numbers and some coffee.

Then meet back here. My staff has a lot of paperwork for you."

"So, for the 200th anniversary of our country's independence, we all become indentured servants," someone said, as the group rose to its feet.

"I hope they free us before the 200th anniversary of the Emancipation Proclamation," another intern said. Addy chuckled.

Chapter 2

Addison Wolfe didn't grow up wanting to be a doctor, unlike many of his classmates. Some had made their wishes known at very young ages, before grade school even. A few had survived nasty medical issues: cerebral palsy, leukemia, polio, severe trauma. Having benefited from modern medical care, they then dedicated their lives to helping others postpone the inevitable.

Some classmates were the privileged off-spring of physicians, even generations of physicians. From birth they had been expected to be physicians when they entered the work force. Many of these classmates already understood the intricacies of medical care, medical education, the politics of hospital work, and the hierarchies of medical societies. They also understood the tremendous financial advantage one acquired by being a physician. Well aware of the long hours surgeons or general practitioners spent working, they were eager to avoid those, but still enjoy the prestige and income that came from practicing medicine. These medical students wanted to become radiologists, dermatologists, pathologists, ophthalmologists, and psychiatrists, or medical researchers, MD/PhDs, if they were smart enough. They also knew in advance that the number of residencies for those types of positions were limited. The competition among those students thus aware was cutthroat for those slots.

A few of the others, Wolfe included, had no idea what they

were getting into when they applied to medical school. Wolfe didn't think he was totally ignorant of the society of medicine, but he was wrong. There had been some nurses in his family. His father's mother needed to support her family after her father abandoned her mother and his two daughters. She went to nursing school immediately after high school. On a French battlefield in WWI, she met Wolfe's grandfather. They subsequently married. Afterward, she only practiced nursing on him, much to his chagrin.

Unfortunately, no one understood the devastating effects tobacco could have on a person's heart and lungs at the turn of the previous century. Wolfe's grandfather died at 65 of heart disease, despite the continued nursing (nagging, Grampa called it) ministrations from his wife: margarine instead of butter (which he hated) and other useless pre-WWII treatments for heart disease: treating angina and heart attacks with strict bed rest, and avoiding physical and emotional distress. Wolfe's grandmother and all her children, including his father, also smoked. They suffered with emphysema and COPD at the ends of their lives.

His father's oldest sister was a nurse in WWII, where she kept up the family tradition of finding a soldier on the battlefield, then marrying him. She also never nursed again except unto her husband. Medicinal alcohol was that side of the family's cure for most distress. Instead of lung disease they passed on from cirrhosis. Wolfe's youngest aunt also trained as a nurse, then left the profession to have two children by an army officer. She was too young to serve in WWII and effectively retired from the profession by the time of the Korean War.

So, Wolfe had little practical knowledge of political or practical medicine to which to refer prior to starting medical school. He hadn't wanted to be a doctor anyway, so he probably would have ignored any information his aunts or grandmother might have passed on to him.

Wolfe had two reasons for deciding to become a doctor, at the grand age of 27. He had been in the Navy in Vietnam. There, he served on an aircraft carrier, the USS Oriskany. The Oriskany had been on station in the Gulf of Tonkin when another aircraft carrier, the USS Forrestal, attempted suicide. During that fire, he helped load fire-fighting equipment onto the helicopters. They flew the hoses and foam to the Forrestal. Upon the choppers return to the Oriskany, he unloaded the injured and burned sailors and helped carry them to sick bay for treatment. At some point during this mass casualty operation he surmised he would have better served the injured had he been a doctor.

It was a fleeting thought.

The next time he gave serious thought to being a physician was when he re-enrolled in college after discharge from the navy. He had been an engineering student until thermodynamics and some advanced calculus knocked him out of the program. Wolfe couldn't see repeating that mistake. He wanted to get a degree, become a pilot, then an astronaut, but his vision was terrible. This was about the time NASA started collecting astronauts who were engineers, doctors, and scientists to fly on the space shuttle in the *shirt sleeve environment* as mission specialists, with glasses if they needed them. Not wanting to or being able to afford to spend 10 years earning a PhD, Wolfe looked at the pre-requisites for medical school and chose a degree at a university that allowed him to fill those requirements. Being more mature than during his first attempt, the second time around Wolfe did much better in college. The Virginia Tech chapter of Phi Kappa Phi gave him a pin. He also apparently did well on the Medical College Admission Test. Despite one medical school dean's opinion that he was too old, he found himself accepted to two medical schools. Wolfe chose the least expensive, a state university, the Medical College of Virginia.

The first two years of medical school in the 1970s were a forty hour a week job, with overtime at home. Wolfe sat in class from 8a-5p, Monday through Friday, along with 144 of his newest close friends. Then he went home and tried to make heads or tails of what the professors had lectured.

Third year was less book study, more practical stuff, but the hours were still long. The fourth year allowed him to cut back to forty hour weeks and take some electives, like the USAF Aerospace Medicine course in San Antonio, Texas. He also spent six weeks at NASA in Houston learning what the scientists would do on the space shuttle.

During the four years of medical school, Wolfe had spent as little time in the hospital as he could manage. He didn't plan on practicing medicine, despised hospitals, and was always behind in his studying. His undergraduate degree had been in General Science. The curriculum had been designed for middle school science teachers. It required a major in one science of some 40 hours, a minor in another science of 30 hours, and at least one year of every other science offered. Wolfe's major was math; he got credit for all the engineering math he had passed and he took some other math courses to accumulate enough hours. He couldn't believe what passed for a math course at the university level: genetics, statistics, computer science, astronomy, etc. That was tough, but he put in the hours and did well enough: As and Bs.

Because a medical school applicant had to have taken organic chemistry to fill the prerequisites for medical school, he made chemistry his minor. He did well in inorganic, organic, and physical chemistry. In addition to the usual English, history, and various humanity courses, he had been required to take a two semester course in every other science offered by the university. Not many pre-med students knew what he knew about geology, physics, oceanography, meteorology, or astronomy. They knew a hell of a lot more than he did about biology, though. He had had only two semesters of that before medical school – the reason for his always playing catch-up. Some of his classmates had studied gross anatomy. Most also had a course in microbiology, leaving him gasping for air when they took those courses. The professors wouldn't slow down for him.

As everyone knows, they still call the guy who graduates last in his medical school class *Doctor*; just like everyone else in the class. Wolfe wasn't last, but he surely wasn't first. Once he had his diploma in hand in the middle of May, 1976, he sent a copy to NASA. He asked if they would consider him for the next astronaut class. Wolfe figured there weren't too many physicians willing to give up their cushy lives and high income to take risks as civilian astronauts at government wages.

Wolfe received a nice letter back from some administrator. Wolfe was more naive about the politics of space travel than he was about medical politics. The essence of the reply was NASA had had so many applicants for the physician-astronaut position that they had decided to raise the requirements in order to winnow out the underachievers, like him. They wanted only physicians who had more to offer than an MD degree. In addition to an MD degree, a PhD in a hard science or engineering was now required. The bureaucrat included a synopsis of Story Musgrave's resume for perusal: Enlisted Marine Korea War veteran as a flight mechanic and aircrewman, skydiver, PhD in mathematical sciences, MD, accepted into neurosurgery residency, commercial pilot with instrument rating, plus more. "We are looking for 10 more guys like Musgrave," he wrote. *Major bummer.*

As a lark, Wolfe had participated in the age-old tradition of *Matching*. Senior medical students visited multiple residency programs they thought might suit them in terms of sleep deprivation, future specialty, and lack of income. The programs' directors interviewed the medical students and tried to impress upon them how much more money the student could make or how much more prestigious it would be if his credentials included graduating from their residency program, despite the lack of time off and the low pay. Both the students and the directors of the programs wrote down their choices, from most desired to least desired.

The medical school sent that information to the National Resident Matching Program, where a giant computer, probably an IBM 360, crunched the numbers, and *matched* students with programs. Not everyone who wanted to be a neurosurgeon, or plastic surgeon, or internist, or radiologist, or ophthalmologist, got his first choice. Many of Wolfe's classmates moaned when they opened their acceptance letters. Budding orthopedic surgeons learned that they had matched with their last choice: Urology or Ob-gyn. Pseudo-dermatologists found out they would have to become Family Practitioners. Hoped-for Anesthesiologists learned they would become Internists. Students wishing to do surgery in Miami ended up in Buffalo. Of course, the students could have opted to skip the internship offered. They could then look for an opening in a residency somewhere else that had not matched or had been turned down. Or, they could sit out a year and try again the following year.

Wolfe had played the game, but honestly. He had told everyone with whom he interviewed that he wasn't really interested in their program. He was going to be going to NASA. He wanted to do research in the hostile environment of outer space. The directors all smiled and took notes. Wolfe didn't even open the letter he got back from the Matching Program. He had a hell of a time finding the damned thing after NASA turned him down. He seriously thought about going back into the navy as an officer, but the Navy recruiter said he would be working as a hospital administrator or physician because of his education. The Air Force and Army said similar things. He changed his mind.

Wolfe spent the four weeks from the middle of May until the middle of June going over his options. He sat in a bar in Richmond, Virginia. He couldn't go home and admit to his family that he would not be going to NASA. Over the previous four years he had stated that as a fact so many times that he had believed it. He didn't want to hang around the medical school waving good-bye to all his disappointed classmates, who for the most part had chosen to get on with their lives and accept their matches. Those classmates who had gotten their first choices were insufferable. He avoided them. Those winning their second choices were nearly as bad. Wolfe felt safe in the bar, even if he was not sober.

"There are lots of different types of doctors," the barkeep said one day. "Maybe you can find yourself a quiet little niche? Make lots of money? Raise a family?"

"I don't want to be a doctor," Wolfe said, tongue semi paralyzed with alcohol. He sounded like a dental patient with a full dose of Novocain. "I want to be an astronaut."

Chapter 3

The alarm rang noisily. Wolfe had placed it on the bureau at the opposite end of the small bedroom, knowing he would otherwise slap it to turn it off. After thirty seconds of the piercing, high-pitched, shrill ring, one of his new roommates in the next room pounded on the wall next to the head of his bed. “All right, all right,” Wolfe growled, throwing the sheets off and climbing unsteadily out of bed. Sleepily, he groped for the clock and switched it off. Standing in his underwear, he peeked at the mirror on top of the dresser.

A woman with a blonde afro sat upright in his bed staring at him. When he turned to face her, she said, “If you expect me to spend much time here, that thing has to go.”

“I thought you said you weren’t interested in a relationship, just sex occasionally. Something about a fiancé in Boston, I think.” He pulled a bathrobe off a door hook and wrapped himself in it. From the top of the dresser, he found his shaving kit. Pulling a bath towel off a second door hook, he reached for the doorknob. “Need a shower. We’re supposed to observe the Morbidity and Mortality Conference today, all the new interns. You going?”

“Maybe. Haven’t decided,” she said, as she picked up a pack of cigarettes, withdrew one daintily, and lit it. Left arm crossed over her chest, right hand held the cigarette out, she remained under the covers. For some reason her pose reminded Wolfe of the Statue of Liberty.

Maybe it was her Long Island accent. A smoke ring floated in his direction. When it reached him, the smell was reminiscent of the bar the night before.

"You don't want to piss off Figueroa the first week, do you?" Wolfe asked. He could feel the robe starting to elevate in front of him, levered by his short member as it came to life.

"That's exactly who I'd like to piss off. The man is an asshole." She stared at his robe. "Are you happy to see me or is there a cobra in your pocket?"

Wolfe blushed. Medical school hadn't left him much time to pursue the fairer sex. He kept waiting for the rush of women who should have thrown themselves at his feet because he would some day be a rich doctor, but the crowd of sex-starved women had never appeared. He liked to think it was because they were shallow, but likely they had no interest in a shy bookworm who didn't drink alcohol often and had limited sexual experience. "We could put the cobra to work," he suggested. "We have time for a quickie, if you are interested."

"Maybe later," Samantha Joiner said, rising nude from between the sheets. She sauntered toward him and put both arms around his neck. Holding the cigarette away from his head, she planted a heavy wet kiss on his lips. She tasted of Marlboro Lights. His pupils dilated and so did his lower member. Deftly she slipped the bath towel out of his hands and wrapped it around herself, dodging the protrusion. "Fix us some breakfast while I shower, will you?" She opened the door and slipped out before he remembered he had been on the way to take a shower.

The trip to the hospital from Jacksonville Beach in another intern's Volkswagen Beetle took thirty-five minutes. The bug's owner, Ignatius Harrison, Iggy or Harry, depending on how well you knew him, was an orthopedic surgery intern. He had also come from the Medical College of Virginia in Richmond, Virginia. He and his wife shared the apartment with Wolfe. They got the master bedroom with adjoining bathroom. A Jacksonville University senior history major got the next largest bedroom. After all it was his apartment. He sublet to Iggy and Wolfe in order to pay his rent. Wolfe got the smallest room, but it cost $25 less per month than the master. Downside was sharing the bathroom with the JU student, if he was around. He spent most of his time in his girlfriend's apartment.

"Janice find a job?" Wolfe asked Iggy. Iggy's wife was a dental assistant. Dental assistants were uniformly the best looking collection of women on the medical school campus. Wolfe had never been able to figure out how that worked. Nursing students at the medical college seemed to have the same percentage of good looking, plain, or ugly women as the general population, but the DAs were always knockouts. He finally decided the committee that chose applicants was made up of a bunch of randy old goats, and/or they took bribes from the dental school instructors.

And the DAs always seemed to marry money. They seemed to be able to smell the future income of the men they dated. Wolfe had had a single date with one DA student. He mentioned she was gorgeous one too many times and she never went out with him again. Either that was the reason, or she didn't smell money in his future. Janice had never given up her sister student's secret. Iggy had been a college All American football player, tight end at the University of Virginia. Smart ex-jocks in medical school tended to gravitate toward orthopedics. There was something about wanting to find out what their orthopedic surgeons had done to them, and if their career was really over when they blew out their knees, or their elbows if they had been pitchers.

"Yeah. There's a small dental practice in Neptune Beach. Older guy. His wife was his assistant, but she recently died. He's looking to retire in the next three or four years."

"Sounds perfect," Wolfe said. "She won't be leaving anyone high and dry when you finish residency."

"My thinking, exactly, and hers. She can walk to work, too. That'll save some money."

"Let's hope the rich, old, dentist doesn't make her his trophy wife," Sam laughed in the back seat. "Wouldn't be the first time that has happened."

Iggy laughed. "Not a chance," he said. Wolfe noticed the back of Iggy's neck turned red anyway.

"Do you think living at the beach will be a problem for you guys?" Samantha asked no one in particular. "I think Arlington is a better choice. Roll out of bed, cross the Mathews Bridge, and you are at University Hospital. Ten minutes, max."

"You'll miss the beach, Sam," Iggy said. "It's a lot easier to get there when it's a five minute walk, rather than a thirty to forty minute drive with all the other tourists who want to see it."

"Maybe," she said, stubbing out her cigarette in the tiny ashtray in the back seat, "but you never know when those crazy Arabs will squeeze the flow of oil again. And I'll get thirty minutes more sleep than you guys will."

"Interns don't sleep. I did pay 63 cents a gallon yesterday," Iggy said. "but as long as they don't go back to rationing, I think we'll be alright. Don't miss Tricky Dick or rationing."

"Or Vietnam, or shoeing horses," Wolfe said with a grin.

"Might take a horse to get to the hospital," Samantha intoned, and added, "Maybe Tricky Dick could teach Cobra something."

"Who's Cobra?" Iggy asked.

"Inside joke," Wolfe said, shaking his head.

Samantha winked at him.

Chapter 4

By the time Wolfe, Sam, and Iggy had seats in the back of the same auditorium in which they had had their introduction to University Hospital, Iggy had let on that in addition to Addy, Wolfe was also known as the *Old Man*. Having spent four years in the navy, he was five years older than most of his classmates – those who had sailed through college without side trips to a warmer, hostile environment, or Canada. Still, he was not the oldest student to graduate in the class of 1976 from the Medical College of Virginia. The oldest student had a PhD in microbiology. Until she had joined their class during sophomore year, she had been one of their professors as freshmen medical students. The second oldest had taught Iggy organic chemistry at the University of Virginia. "Creeped me out to have Dr. Harper be one of my gross anatomy lab partners," he told Sam. "They grouped us alphabetically. Kept calling him *sir*, until he cut me with the scalpel. What a klutz."

"What did you call him after that?" Sam asked, idly watching the junior and senior residents set up the slide projector and screen for the conference.

Iggy held up his left fist so Samantha could see the back of his hand. A thin, white Z-shaped scar adorned it from knuckles to wrist. Iggy laughed, "Zorro. Took thirty sutures to close the wound. Could have been worse; missed all the tendons. He stained another classmate with gentian violet in microbiology. I think she still has a purple hand.

Fortunately they assigned partners randomly in micro."

Before Wolfe could add any more to the anecdote, Dr. Ramon Figueroa stood in front of one of the four chairs on the dais, strode to the rostrum, and tapped on the microphone. *Thunk, thunk.*

"It's going to be a long year if I have to see him every day," Sam said under her breath.

"Gentlemen," Figueroa said, "please find yourselves a seat. There are four hundred plus seats in here and only about two hundred of you, plus ten or so staff." The rustling gradually came to a standstill and the conversations abated. "Senior residents," he started again, "this is your last Morbidity and Mortality conference at this institution. For their entertainment and enlightenment, I have invited the new intern class to observe. If you could give them a round of applause in welcome...."

The boisterous chorus of boos and jeers surprised Wolfe. An occasional catcall of "Good luck, suckers," and, "You'll be sorry," worried him. Then he realized the seniors were all laughing. He relaxed a little, until he studied the faces of the other residents. Those who apparently filled the ranks between intern and senior – their designations varied: sophomores, 3rd, 4th, and some 5th year juniors, depending on how long their residencies were – did not seem amused, however. Wolfe's anxiety increased again.

"Okay, okay. Calm down you guys. We have a lot to cover." Figueroa led them through a fairly routine M&M conference. They discussed the junior ER resident's short comings when reading neck x-rays. He had missed several transverse process fractures of the cervical spine. They weren't easy to see. Luckily, they also were not lethal. His only excuse had been that he had been distracted by the patient's constant screaming for pain medications. "You can't let the patient distract you," Figueroa stated at the end of the presentation. "If you get angry at him, you'll miss stuff. While we're on the subject, how you feel when interviewing a patient usually reflects how the patient feels. If you are angry, he probably is, too. If you are anxious or intimidated, that is probably the result of his anxiety or defensiveness. Don't forget that."

"If you feel paranoid, or schizophrenic...." drifted to Wolfe's ears from somewhere. He smiled. Sam laughed.

The residents discussed a rare case of measles on the pediatric ward, and immunizations. Someone mentioned the local population's almost uniform dread of needles. The Duval County Public Health Department feared a measles epidemic if they could not increase the percentage of immunized children in the county. Parents were known to keep their children out of school in order to avoid the injections.

A senior orthopedic resident presented a case of back pain. After a very brief exam, an intern had ordered a lumbar spine x-ray. Figueroa leaped to his feet. "You better have a good reason for that," he declared. Turning to the audience he bemoaned the amount of money wasted on unnecessary x-rays, "Although, it gives our radiology residents practice in reading normal films," he added. "Skull and lumber films for pain are routinely a waste of time and money, not to mention you expose the patient to excess radiation for no good reason. Generally, I don't order x-rays for back pain on the first visit unless the patient has a neurological deficit."

He turned back to the resident. "Did this patient have a deficit?"

The senior resident smiled. "No, sir," he said. Flicking a finger toward the projectionist, the resident challenged Figueroa by saying, "Doctor Figueroa, maybe you could pick someone to read this x-ray."

The black and white image of a lumbar spine from mid-pelvis upward to the lower thoracic spine filled the wall in front of the audience, eight feet tall and almost four feet wide. Figueroa stared at the image for about 30 seconds. "Looks normal to me," he said, "but if you brought this case to M&M, I'd be foolish to assume that." He paused, right elbow in left hand, right hand stroking his chin. "Dr. Zhao," he called out without looking at the audience. "What am I missing? Just for you interns, one of the things you will need to learn while you are here is intradepartmental co-operation. No one, not even the attending physicians, has a monopoly on knowledge. For those of you who haven't met Dr. Zhao, he will be a senior radiology resident starting next week."

An Asian resident stood in the third row. "The image could be clearer...."

Figueroa laughed, "And *clinical correlation is suggested*," he said, quoting the most frequent cop-out cited by the radiologists. "Do you see an obvious abnormality?"

"No sir, I don't. Maybe if I could compare this with an older image?"

"There aren't any older images," the orthopedic resident stated. "And if you are interested, the radiology attending missed the abnormality, also."

"Okay, we'll open this to the audience," Figueroa said. "Anyone see anything abnormal?" For several minutes there were murmurings in the audience, but no *eureka*, until an intern spoke up.

A voice from the last row called out, "Dr. Figueroa, may the new interns participate?"

"Absolutely," Figueroa said. "Never too soon to show your ignorance." Many of the residents in the room laughed, knowing only too well how much Figueroa enjoyed rubbing a resident's nose in a mistake.

The voice continued, clearer when he stood. Wolfe noticed it belonged to the tan, long-haired blond, he had dubbed *surfer* at the introduction. *Robertson? No, Robinson.* "If you will look closely at the bowel gas pattern in the right abdomen, near the right side of the L3 vertebra, you will see what appears to be gas is actually the absence of the right one-third of L3. That's probably an osteolytic lesion, likely from hematogenous spread of metastatic prostate cancer. Or, that would be my guess."

Even with the abnormality and its location described, most of the audience had trouble seeing it. "Well?" Figueroa asked the senior orthopedic resident.

"He nailed it."

"Who found it the first time?"

"A rotating intern. On physical exam in Primary Care, the patient had a poker spine, straight as a flag pole, even when he bent over at the hips. The intern thought he was going to see ankylosing spondylitis on the x-ray. When he didn't, he searched the film until he found the abnormality."

"Great job," Figueroa said. "Who was the intern?"

"He's no longer in the program," the senior orthopedic resident said quietly.

"Okay. Let's move on," Figueroa suggested.

They then talked about an intern, who would have been a sophomore in a four year Ob-gyn program in a couple days. He missed pre-eclampsia, hypertension of pregnancy, in a young black woman. The result had been the death of the fetus and the near-death of the pregnant woman. "He has voluntarily resigned. Depression and guilt, I suspect. I believe he plans to do a rotating internship on the west coast next year," Figueroa said.

"Bastard," a young man in front of Wolfe said.

"The intern?" asked Wolfe.

"No," the young man said quietly without turning his head to look at Wolfe, Iggy, or Sam. "There were no attending physicians on call that night. The senior resident was delivering babies right and left by himself. The poor intern was taking care of the entire obstetric ward alone and missed the blood pressure because of someone's handwriting. He's a good guy. He got screwed by that bastard." The young doctor pointed the end of a pencil at Figueroa. "Sacrificial lamb."

"Where was the attending?" Sam asked.

"End of the year bash for all the attendings. Drunk as a skunk. Thirty miles away, even though he was on call."

"He got canned, too?" Iggy asked.

At that the young man turned his head swiftly in the threesome's direction. "They've got no money to hire real attendings. They can only afford a couple full time docs. They rely on part-time volunteers, for whom they supplement their incomes a little. They can't afford to fire him. It would shut down the residency." Just as swiftly, he returned to facing the front and slunk down in his seat, appearing to hide from any observers.

Stunned the three interns sat silently. The conference had proceeded to the finale, another Emergency Residency case. The senior resident started his description, "EMS responded to a report of a cardiac arrest at 1:07 a.m. in Junior's Topless Bar, on East Bay Street...."

Figueroa again jumped to his feet. "What is this, a bad joke?" he asked. "Two EMTs walk into a bar.... Let's be realistic, guys. The most likely reason for needing a paramedic in a bar at 1 a.m. is a knifing or a gun shot wound, not a heart attack."

The senior resident presenting the case took a long, cool look at the junior resident standing next to him, and then proceeded to tell the story complete with autopsy results. The EMTs had responded to a man who had collapsed from his bar stool onto the floor. They worked the cardiac arrest for ten minutes on scene, and then decamped to the University Hospital ER via ambulance. The junior emergency resident had continued with intubation, central lines, cardiac massage, and every cardiac drug available for twenty minutes. A senior surgical resident was available in house, so the junior emergency resident prevailed upon him to open the man's chest. They proceeded with open cardiac massage for another twenty minutes before calling the code off and pronouncing the cardiac arrest patient dead.

The autopsy and x-rays were condemning. The thirty-nine year old, black male had no history of heart disease. No medical history of any kind. He did have a bullet entrance wound to the back of his head, with no exit, bullet still in his brain. Someone had walked behind him in the noisy establishment and popped him as he sat on the barstool drinking a beer. Jacksonville Sheriff's Office investigated after the autopsy, but the crime scene had been mopped and polished. No witnesses were forthcoming. The perfect crime.

"I guess you thought the blood on the pillow was from hitting his head on the floor when he collapsed during his heart attack?" Figueroa asked. The rhetorical question bounced off the blushing resident. "I'm not saying every patient should be stripped naked and re-assessed," Figueroa continued, "but you might think about it if your treatment isn't working as planned. You are all dismissed. Except, Dr. Robinson. Nick? If I could talk with you for a minute?" Figueroa held his hand out to the tall, tan man with long blond hair, beckoning him forward.

Chapter 5

Wolfe's first day of internship, Thursday, July 1st, 1976, started with a bang, or actually a Code Blue. Code Blue was the designation for a resuscitation, for whatever reason, in the Intensive Care Unit of the Emergency Room. As instructed, Wolfe had arrived at 7 a.m. for his introduction to his first rotation, the ER. Ideally, a resident would like to have that rotation be the last of his internship, after he had learned all the hospital terminology, and more about trauma, heart attacks, and death. Not every intern could be last, though; someone had to be first. Wolfe found himself sitting in the ER director's office at 6:55 a.m. with two other interns: George Harding, from internal medicine, and Ravi Gupta from general surgery.

The three had introduced themselves and started an idle conversation. At 7:01, the office door flung open and a very large black nurse dressed in an immaculate white uniform said in a drill instructor's voice, "Ain't got time for no chit-chat. Get your asses out on the floor." She turned and marched into the ICU, "Follow me," she said, "I'll show you where to go, what to do." Intimidated, they followed.

The wing they entered had two stretchers in a large bay. On one stretcher lay a woman covered to her waist with a bloody sheet. A thin black woman with large breasts that hung limply to either side of her chest, she stared blankly at the ceiling with pale blue eyes. A large swollen bruise to the left and above her umbilicus oozed dark blood from a nickel-sized hole. From past experience, visits to the busy ER at the Medical College of Virginia as a student, Wolfe knew she was dead from a gunshot wound. Two EMTs or medical assistants in green scrubs talked quietly as they clipped intravenous lines and taped them in place. The endotracheal tube was secured to the dead woman's face with more tape. The two cleansed the body, in preparation for wrapping it and sending it to the morgue for autopsy.

"You," the nurse pointed to George Harding, who stared wide-eyed at the corpse. "You can't help her. Bullet hit Big Red."

"Big Red?" Wolfe asked.

"The aorta," the nurse explained. "Big Blue is the vena cava. Bleed out quickly from wounds in Big Red or Big Blue. Faster than we can put blood into you." She again pointed to Harding, "Take the ambubag from the EMT and start pumping air into this guy."

Wolfe turned his attention to the second patient. An obese man, protuberant belly, skin a mottled blue color from his chest to his face, lay face up on the stretcher. No sheets covered him. His legs had been spread and two men in scrubs and short white coats had latex glove covered fingers on his inguinal pulses. An older, white female nurse held the large man's more than adequate genitalia up and out of the way, bored look on her face. Each of the men held a large bore needle in one hand. One, a man with a short goatee, spoke to the other. "Bet I get a line in before you."

"You're on," said the second.

"You two," the heavy nurse repeated, pointing to Gupta and Wolfe. "You are going to relieve the nurse doing chest compressions. One of you stand on that foot stool," she pointed to the empty chrome stool with back rubber mat on it at the patient's right side, "and take over for Dorothy. She's beat. You do know how to do CPR, right?" Gupta nodded, stepping onto the stool. Without the stool, he would have been too low to adequately compress the patient's chest.

"When Dorothy turns CPR over to that intern," the black nurse continued to Wolfe, "she'll step down from her stool. You go to the other side and take her place. Then you and your friend alternate compressions. Got it?"

Wolfe nodded, silently. He took his place on the stool. The well-built, red-haired nurse who glided gracefully from the stool left behind a fragrance of perfume and hospital alcohol that seared Wolfe's nose and olfactory nerves all the way to his brain.

"Jesus, an intern," one of the men in white coats searching for a femoral pulse said. "Someone show him how to compress the chest, I just lost the pulse."

A thin, short, black nurse kicked another step stool next to Gupta's stool. She stood next to him. "Lock your fingers like this. Wait. Stop and find the xyphoid process and sternal notch. Now, place the heel of one hand halfway between on the sternum. In the middle, not to the side. Otherwise you'll break his ribs."

"I need a pulse!" the second physician yelled.

Calmly the nurse continued, "Push down about 3 inches. Keep your hand on the chest when you relax."

"Finally. A pulse. Don't these interns know anything?"

"Shut up Nichols," the heavy black nurse said. "You were an intern until ten minutes ago."

"Yeah, I guess I was," Nichols said, smiling.

"I'm in," the other man said. "Give me a line." The thin black nurse stepped off the stool and handed the goateed doctor the tip of an intravenous line. "Epi. 1 milligram. Quickly." He held his hand out, not looking at the nurses, watching the femoral line. Deftly, she found the medication on top of a red cart next to the bed and handed the syringe to the young doctor, plunger first. He squirted the medication into the line, then opened the stopcock from the intravenous bag of fluids and let it run full bore into the patient. "Pump that around for a while," he told Wolfe, who had taken over from a sweating Gupta.

"No pulse!" Nichols yelled, eyes on the cardiac monitor, hand in the patient's crotch. "Good complexes, but no pulse. Are you pushing hard enough, intern?"

The thin black nurse appeared at Wolfe's side. "Find the sternal notch and xyphoid. Lock your fingers. Press down about three inches. Don't let your hands come off the chest," she instructed in measured tones.

"I feel a pulse. Stop compressions," Nichols ordered.

The nurse placed her hands on top of Wolfe's. "Stop," she said quietly. Wolfe had been concentrating on technique and hadn't heard the order to stop.

"No pulse. V. Fib. Start compressions again. Charge the defibrillator. Get me some more epi and 2 grams of calcium."

The delicate black hands pushed down on Wolfe's hands. "Go," she said.

Over the next thirty-five minutes Gupta and Wolfe alternated chest compressions. Gradually, their vision expanded from the man's chest. They became aware of the choreographed struggle around them. The other intern squeezed the ambubag forcing oxygen down the man's trachea to his lungs. He timed his bag compression to fit between their chest compressions. The defibrillator was charged and current was sent through the victim's chest several times. A portable x-ray machine stood nearby. Someone took arterial blood for blood gases. Multiple cardiac drugs were flushed into the man in an attempt to save his life. All to no avail.

"Well, I guess we have to call it," the senior ER resident eventually said, looking at a large clock overhead. "Time of death: 7:43 a.m." The staff within several feet of the dead man exhaled collectively. Gupta and Wolfe stepped from their stools. Both were drenched in sweat. Wolfe looked around for a towel to mop his face, finally settling on a green procedure towel from a cut-down tray.

The large black nurse appeared. "Dr. Singhal," she said to the older man who had stood at the head of the bed and watched the resuscitation quietly, "Primary Care is going to open in ten minutes and no one has briefed the new interns." She pointed to Wolfe, Gupta, and Harding.

"Oh, quite right," the dark skinned, balding man answered with a slight British accent. "Nichols, Gentry. You did an excellent job."

Nichols smiled. "Resuscitation a success. Only the patient died." He held his hand out to Gupta, then Harding and Wolfe. "John Nichols. We try to learn from every attempt. Less than ten per cent of patients survive a full cardiac arrest. Less than one percent leave the hospital. Lowers your odds a bit when the rescue squad puts the ET tube in the esophagus and fills the stomach instead of the lungs with oxygen. Hence the subcutaneous emphysema. Notice the blue? That was the crunchy feeling you felt while doing CPR. We'll talk with the EMTs later."

"Except in Seattle," Gentry added, also shaking the new interns' hands. "Bob Gentry. Nice to have you here. You'll learn a lot more before the rotation is over. Believe me."

"Why Seattle?" Gupta asked.

Singhal replied. "I'll explain. Please come with me to my office. I have a lot to go over with you and not much time. Nichols, please go talk with the family." The three followed him to his office.

"No family," Nichols said to no one in particular. "He had the arrest in his mistress's bed. Joan," he said to the ward clerk as he pointed a finger toward the closed conference room door. "when I finish in here, we'll have to talk to his wife by phone. He flipped the patient's wallet onto the counter. I think you'll find her somewhere in Connecticut. He and his secretary were here for a cable TV conference, whatever that is."

Chapter 6

Finished in his office, Dr. Singhal led the three interns to another large wing in the Emergency Room. "This is trauma," he said. Within the room, there were nine stretchers in a row. Each stretcher held a patient, either seated with legs hanging over one side or the other, or lying down. Curtains hung from the ceiling. Potentially, they could be pulled to protect a patient's privacy. The staff rarely did so, not having the luxury of time. "Gupta, you will spend the month here, unless there is a code. During resuscitations, all you interns will help out in the ER ICU. Between codes, the nurses will put the patients in these stretchers. They'll help you move people through. They will all be in need of x-rays or sutures, or have suffered recent trauma. Your second month will be in Primary Care. Wolfe will be here then. Harding only spends a month here. He'll be back in the spring for his trauma rotation. Any questions?"

Gupta surveyed the room. Most of the staff wore well-used, stained scrubs. Family members of the patients milled around the stretchers, waiting for a doctor to examine their loved ones. With Indian calm and acceptance, Gupta shrugged. "No, sir," he said.

"Dr. Gupta," the same slim, short black nurse who had instructed him and Wolfe in CPR technique said, "if you would come down here to bed number one we can start. It's a young man with a swollen ankle."

"Gentlemen," Dr. Singhal said to Wolfe and Harding. He led the way to the third wing of the ER. Six exam rooms ringed a nurse's station in the middle of the smallest wing. "You see the patients in order. One rotates through rooms 1 to 3; the other does 4 to 6. When you finish the first three, you start over. It never ends. There are at least a hundred patients in the waiting room already. They started signing in at 6 a.m. At 5 p.m. the nurse stops putting patients in the rooms. When you finish with those patients, your day ends. In general, you will see thirty to forty patients in a day and leave at about 7 p.m., plus or minus. Whenever you hear a Code Blue called, you will stop what you are doing and go to the ER ICU. As the month progresses, you will be doing more and more during the codes, starting lines, intubating, giving drugs. July is a tough month to get to do procedures. The new senior and junior ER residents covet them. But you'll get your chances."

"What about the other 40 patients?" Harding asked.

Singhal looked at Harding. "What other 40 patients?"

"You said there were 100 in the waiting room. If we each see thirty, who sees the other 40?"

Singhal shook his head. "If there are no codes, the junior and senior residents see some in the ER ICU. If the patients don't get seen today, they come back the next morning, Monday through Friday. First come, first serve. The sickest are triaged to ER ICU. Oh, you get a half hour for lunch. If there isn't a code going on, the junior resident will fill in for you. The junior and senior residents work 12 on, 12 off, like you, but 2 days on, 2 days off, then 2 nights on. You guys work 12 hour shifts, 7 a.m. 'til approximately 7 p.m., Monday through Friday. If you have any questions, talk with the nurses first, the junior and senior resident, as needed. Questions?"

What did I do to deserve this? Wolfe asked himself. "No, sir," he said.

Harding shook his head. "I'll take 4, 5, and 6, Addison." Wolfe nodded. He pulled a chart out of the clear plastic box on the wall next to room 1. "Back pain for three months," the Chief Complaint stated. *God, I hope he doesn't have a poker spine,* he thought.

Upon Wolfe's return from a brief lunch, cut short by another Code Blue, he caught a glimpse of a familiar profile partially hidden behind the high desk of the small nurses' station in Primary Care. Figueroa took no notice of him, perhaps did not see him at all. The attending physician evidently leafed quickly through patients' charts on the nurses' desk. Wolfe thought about asking him if he were going to help out, since they were backed up. He thought better of the idea when he remembered that Figueroa had no sense of humor.

Instead, he pulled a chart from the holder and slipped unobtrusively into an exam room. By the time he finished with the patient, Figueroa had disappeared. As casually as he could, he asked the medical assistant if there had been a problem with one of the patients he or Harding had seen that morning

"I don't think so," the EMT said. "Why do you ask?"

"I saw Dr. Figueroa looking at charts. Thought he might be gathering materials for an M&M conference."

"His visits down here rarely have anything to do with M&M," she said. "He checks up on all the interns' work, almost daily. Takes his position very seriously." She took the chart from Wolfe's hands.

***

Wolfe sat in the lounge chair, holding a bowl of cereal. Cartoons played silently on WTLV-TV Channel 12 in front of him. He had not wanted to disturb his roommates. Behind him the master bedroom door opened. Janice, barefoot and wearing one of Iggy's old football jerseys, the orange and blue of the U.Va. Wahoos, strode into the kitchen. "Oh," she said, startled by Wolfe's presence. "What are you doing here, Addy?"

Exhausted after only two days of the constant interaction with the dying, severely injured, very sick, mildly sick, psychotic, and hypochondriacal, Wolfe could only smile lamely as he stared at the beautiful dental assistant. Eventually, his mind cleared. "I only have to work Monday through Friday, 7 a.m. to 7 p.m. Primary Care is closed on weekends. How's Iggy doing?"

"I don't know," she said, sitting on the hide-a-bed couch that completed the living room furniture collection. She put a cup of coffee on the battered end table next to the couch. Pointing to it she asked, "Want some?" Wolfe shook his head. "Iggy had a long day Thursday, you guys' first day. He went to work Friday morning, yesterday, and was on call last night. I guess they kept him busy all night. I didn't hear from him at all. So, I expect him home any time. Probably have morning rounds and then come get some sleep. Looks like he will have at least one day off on the weekends this first month."

"Only a hundred hour work week. That's good," Wolfe said. He wished he could be enthusiastic about his projected 60-70 hour week. "I think they are paying us about $2.13 an hour." He laughed weakly.

Janice studied Wolfe's face. "Tough couple of days, huh?"

"The pervasiveness of their poverty, the depths of their ignorance about medicine," Wolfe started. "It's overwhelming. And our, the interns, response to it. It's crushing."

"It must have been just as hard for the second year residents, I mean last year when they first started," Janice offered. "Tell me about it. I don't think Iggy will share. He keeps everything inside."

"Do you know why they call internists fleas?" Wolfe asked her.

"Something about being nitpickers?"

"Yeah. They want to know every little detail. They ask every patient a thousand questions. They want to have every little fact at their fingertips. They want to cull the differential diagnosis from a hundred possibilities down to ten, then three. Then with x-rays or tests to prove beyond a doubt what is wrong with the patient."

Wolfe stared at the cartoons as he spoke. Wylie E. Coyote was being hammered into the ground by an anvil meant for the Roadrunner. "That could be me," he said, pointing to the cartoon. "Or Harding. He's an internal medicine intern working with me in Primary Care. On Thursday, he started out taking an hour long history on each patient. By noon, he was down to thirty minutes. The nurses kept harassing him, telling him to speed up. Hell, even the patients harassed us. 'Worse day of the year to get sick,' one guy said. 'July fust; we all gone die.'"

Wolfe stretched, placing the empty bowl on the end table closest to him. Then he leaned back in the seat and stared at the cartoons. "By the time we finished last night, George was walking into the exam rooms saying, 'Don't say a word; you'll just confuse me.'"

Janice laughed. "That's quite a change, Addy. How about you?"

"My differential list was never more than three diseases long. While George looked for Zebras, I was looking for horses. The trifecta. Most of the time I was happy with mules, even. They told us about an intern from another year. Want to hear about it?"

Janice looked at her watch. "I've got time, unless Iggy shows up."

"This poor guy was in over his head. His first day he examined a patient with right abdominal pain. He listened to his story about vomiting, fever, muscle aches, brown urine, etc. Then he examined him and found a swollen liver, yellow eyes, needle marks on his arms. But he was so rattled by the pressure he couldn't figure out what the guy had."

"Even I know that he probably had hepatitis," Janice said.

"I'm impressed," Wolfe said.

"Better than being oppressed, depressed, compressed,

suppressed, or just pressed," Janice laughed, repeating one of Iggy's favorite sayings. "So what happened to the intern?"

"No one knows. He never came back the second day. That was five years ago."

"Really?"

"I think it's a myth. A story to scare the new interns," Wolfe said. He stood to return his bowl to the kitchen. "Can I get you anything?"

"One hundred thousand dollars, small bills, brown paper bag, non-sequential numbers, US currency only, and no dye pack," she said with a smile on her face – another of Iggy's favorite expressions.

"If I had that, I would disappear, too," Wolfe said, placing the bowl in the sink and turning on the water.

The door to the apartment opened and Iggy stumbled in, glassy-eyed. He glared at Janice and Wolfe. "Need some sleep," he mumbled and stumbled into the master bedroom. Janice looked at Wolfe and shrugged. She followed him into the bedroom. "Poor baby," was all he heard before the door closed behind them.

Chapter 7

"Dr. Addison Wolfe," the secretary barked loudly, without looking up from her typewriter.

"Yes, ma'am," Wolfe said, standing from the row of chairs in the hallway in which he and several interns sat outside the door to the Office of Medical Education. He stepped into the outer office.

"Dr. Figueroa will see you now," she continued. From the top of a large stack of manila folders on her sideboard, she slid a folder with his name on it into his hands. "Return this to me when you leave. Do not take it with you, and do not lose it." He had heard her give the same instructions to the three interns who had preceded him into the office.

"Yes, ma'am," he said. He walked toward the open door. The frosted glass that made up the top half of the door had *Ramon Figueroa, DO,* painted on it.

The Director of Medical Education looked up from some papers he filled out when Wolfe entered the office. "Dr. Wolfe," he said pleasantly. "Have a seat. Be with you in a second."

Wolfe sat in the straight back wooden chair directly in front of Figueroa, the only empty seat in the room. The wall behind the director was covered with diplomas, awards, photos of the director and others.

Eventually Figueroa finished scribbling and laid the paper on a stack on his desk. He gazed at Wolfe for several uncomfortable seconds and asked, "Do you know the difference between a DO and an MD,

Wolfe?"

"You mean do I know the difference between a Doctor of Medicine and a Doctor of Osteopathic Medicine?" Wolfe asked.

"Yes. I am a DO. You are an MD. Do you know the difference?"

"Can't say I have ever given it much thought, sir," Wolfe said. In fact, he had known of only one DO until he started the internship. "I assume they are equal as far as the state authorities are concerned. There seem to be a lot of them, DOs that is, here. Are there more in Florida than in other states?" Figueroa's eyes bored into him, a penetrating stare Wolfe had difficulty facing. He looked out the window behind Figueroa.

Intimidated by the stare, Wolfe confessed, in hopes that Figueroa would be empathetic, "You know, I'm not sure I want to be a physician. Research in hostile environments was my first choice after medical school. I don't really understand hospital politics at all. A doc is a doc to me. I'll bet to most of the patients in this hospital feel the same way. I could be blue, and have the letters ABC after my name. If I took the time to talk to them and try to help them, they would be thankful."

Figueroa's stare intensified. Wolfe thought he could see the director's lips begin to curl. "About one third of your rotating internship classmates are DOs. About half of all the interns and residents here are DOs. I applaud you for your candidness, but you have to realize, son, the DOs in this environment are going to eat your lunch. They are hungry to prove something to the world."

Wolfe thought about the statement, but could not understand what point Figueroa was trying to make. "If you say so...."

"I'll make a comparison for you, Wolfe," Figueroa interrupted. He stood behind his desk and started to pace back and forth. "DOs are considered inferior to MDs by a lot of MDs and some of the public – though they have had the same training. John Q. doesn't know the difference. Did you know that? It almost mirrors the divide between whites and blacks. DOs are not smart enough to get into real medical schools, or to study certain specialties, some say. Did you know that?"

"Sir," Wolfe started, "I think the flight surgeon on my carrier might have been a DO. He seemed like a competent physician to me. In the middle of the Forrestal fire, he was doing everything; saved a lot of lives. I knew almost nothing about medical politics before I went to medical school. I still don't know much, other than interns are on the low end of the totem pole. All the docs I have worked with seem to be good, unprejudiced people: racially, politically, and medical education wise. But then I have only been here a month. I have lots to learn."

"Well, that's true," Figueroa said, losing his bluster slightly. He returned to his seat and picked up a single sheet of paper. "Your first month's evaluation has some interesting remarks. You seem to be pretty fast at seeing patients in Primary Care, although your work-ups are rather thin. You need to work on your diagnostic skills, Dr. Wolfe."

"I think if I made the differential diagnosis lists longer, then I would need more time, to do more lab tests and x-rays to rule out rare conditions. Doesn't appear to be much time in Primary Care. Too many patients," Wolfe said.

Figueroa stiffened, interrupted. "You need to do both. List more possibilities, but eliminate them by physical exam and thinking more clearly and more quickly." He stopped and studied the ceiling briefly, then continued, "Your next rotation is in ER Trauma. Doesn't take much thought there. People come in with cuts, bumps, bruises, and fractures. You fix them and move on. Occasionally there will be a complicated case, a domestic dispute or a child abuse, but those are rare. And the nurses will find them before you will. Anyway, I want you to spend more time with a good internal medicine book on differential diagnosis in the evenings and on weekends. You appear to be weak in that department. When you get to your two months of internal medicine, that shortcoming may hurt you. Understand?"

Wolfe nodded, less willing to argue. He recognized a losing cause when he saw one. "Yes, sir," he said.

Figueroa sat staring at Wolfe for several more seconds. "You may go, young man," he finally said, pointing a hand full of papers at the door. "Thank you for your honesty about your ambitions."

Or lack thereof, Wolfe thought. "Did you want this folder?" He offered Figueroa the folder the secretary had given him.

"No. Some interns offer to resign after their evaluations. Then I need the folder." Wolfe swallowed hard. Had the secretary known something, or was everyone given a folder for appearances sake? "Give that back to Miss Jackson. And Wolfe? Don't be a stick in the mud. By that, I mean don't be one-dimensional. I don't want you working all day and studying all night every night. Get out, learn some things other than medicine during your internship, understand?"

Wolfe shook his head, "Yes, sir. Study differential diagnosis rigorously, and don't be one dimensional."

Apparently unaware of the paradox, Figueroa leaned forward to sign a paper and waved a hand over his head as Wolfe left the office.

Wolfe dropped his folder on the secretary's desk as he passed by. "Dr. Bartholomew Howard," she bellowed, loud enough to be heard in the hallway.

***

Iggy and Janice joined Wolfe at the beach the afternoon of the third Sunday in July. Iggy had the afternoon and evening off. Wolfe was beat from working all week in Primary Care, and not looking forward to starting Trauma in a week. On the weekend the ER interns were relieved by the junior ER residents who were doing cushy rotations. To keep up their skills, they spent eight hours in the trauma room stitching and splinting and going to Code Blues. Monday through Friday, they worked on other skills, reading EKGs in cardiology, starting intravenous lines in or intubating surgical patients in anesthesiology, setting up ventilators on the pulmonary ward, etc.

"Where's Samantha?" Janice asked Wolfe, who lay supine on a blanket, head on a rolled up beach towel, facing the Atlantic Ocean, beer can in hand. Mirrored sunglasses reflected Janice and Iggy's images as they stood between him and the ocean.

"Don't ask? I hope you wore some sandals or flip-flops. There must be a thousand pop-tops on the beach." He lifted his foot toward them. "Got cut already."

"Welcome to Jax Beach," Iggy said, laughing. "Better hurry on down to the ER."

"Not even if the great white shark from *Jaws* took off a leg would I go to University Hospital ER," Wolfe said. "Sit. Sit. There's more beer in the cooler. And wine. Also some cheese and crackers."

Janice collapsed on the corner of the large blanket. Iggy spotted two guys near the pier throwing a football around. "I'm going to check that out," he told Janice and jogged away.

Flat on his back, not needing to see what Iggy had spotted, Wolfe said. "He saw the guys with the football, didn't he?"

"Yep." Janice smoothed out the corner of the blanket and lay down parallel to Wolfe, but several feet away. "He wouldn't be here if he hadn't blown out his knee. He can't give it up. He'll be back in thirty minutes with a sore, swollen knee."

"I know. During intramural football at MCV, we wouldn't let him run. The only position we let him play was quarterback. I can still remember his favorite phrase, 'Addy, go long.' I'd run as far and as fast as I could and he'd still throw it twenty yards over my head. And I lettered in track, was a sprinter in high school. What an arm. It's as big and strong as my leg. He must have been a monster at tight end."

"Yep. But he was an even better quarterback in high school." They lay in silence for a long time, admiring the sugar like beach.

"Mind if I join you?" A deep voice asked.

Wolfe looked up and behind him into the sun working its way downward over the stucco homes west of the beach. A well-tanned or dark-skinned individual stood behind him. The sun cast a shadow on his face, which seemed to carry a full beard.

"Sure," Janice said, sitting up. "Make yourself at home. I'm Janice Harrison. This is...."

"Addison Wolfe," the stranger finished for her. "We are in the same intern class, with your husband, Ignatius." Wolfe stared at the young man. Never having had a memory for faces and names, he struggled to place the intern.

A smile creased the man's face and his eyes twinkled. "It's the beard, Addy. I didn't have a beard at the M&M conference. I'm Kervork Torrosian, remember?"

"Ah," Wolfe exclaimed, "the pilot's son." He reached up; Torrosian bent to shake hands. To Janice, Wolfe said, "Kervork's father flew PBYs in WWII. My father was a pilot, too. Also flew seaplanes in the navy, but in Korea," he explained to Janice. "Your testosterone level must be in the 99th percentile. That's quite a beard after only four weeks."

"It's an Armenian thing. Unfortunately our women can also do it." Torrosian chuckled, as did Janice and Wolfe. "Your dad flew Albatrosses, right?"

"What's a PBY?" Janice asked. "I know what an albatross is, an almost extinct bird, right?"

A large body collapsed suddenly onto the blanket between the seated Janice and Kervork on one side and the lying Wolfe on the other. Iggy sweated profusely. "Crap," he said. He rolled onto his back. "Have any ice in that thing?" he pointed to Wolfe's cooler.

Wolfe pulled out the remains of a plastic bag of melting ice. "Your knee?" he asked.

"Poor baby," Janice said, taking the bag of ice and squeezing the water out of it. She tied a knot in the open end, and then wrapped one of their towels around it. Carefully, she placed it on her husband's right knee. "Better?" He nodded.

Iggy looked around and recognized Kervork. "Hey, buddy. Nice beard. How's it going? You live at the beach, too?"

Torrosian nodded. "Up the street. Was out jogging when I spotted Addy and your wife. Bad knee?"

"Old football injury."

"Keep you out of the OR?"

"No way," Iggy answered. "Just wrap a long leg splint around it and I'm good for 10-12 hours."

Torrosian grimaced. "Don't let Figueroa know about it. I hear he bounced an orthopedic resident with a trick knee a couple years ago."

"Not a problem," Iggy said. "I'm on his good side. He already asked me for an autographed vanity shot."

"A what?" Torrosian asked.

"U.Va. gave me a hundred color 8 x 10s when they were pushing the press to name me to the All-American team. I signed most of them and gave them to sports writers, but I still have ten or twelve. He wanted one. 'To my favorite mentor, Dr. Ramon Figueroa. Signed Iggy Harrison, #81, U.Va, All-American Tight End.' He eats that stuff up. On the wall behind his desk, he has one signed by Steve Spurrier during one of his Gator Bowl appearances. He treasures sports memorabilia." Iggy smiled.

"You didn't really do that, did you?" Wolfe asked. "That man is a maniac. He wanted me to weigh in on hospital politics between DOs and MDs."

"What does he have against DOs?" Torrosian asked. "He's a DO. So am I."

"I don't know. He seems a little insecure; that's all. A lot of bluster."

"Does he have something against MDs?" Janice asked.

"I think he's paranoid," Wolfe said. "He's obviously a smart guy, smarter than me."

"Everyone is smarter than you, Addy," Iggy said. Wolfe slapped Iggy's bad knee. "Ow!"

"Well, I did hear some negative things about the Fig from the junior residents," Torrosian admitted.

"Like what?" Janice asked.

"They call him *the proctologist* behind his back. He's constantly ripping new assholes for people." Torrosian laughed. Wolfe offered him a can of beer. "Another nickname is AA."

"Alcoholics Anonymous?" Iggy asked.

"No. *Attending Asshole*. Like Addy said, he's damned smart, but he tends to be an intellectual bully. Intimidates people for sport, it seems." Torrosian downed the beer in two gulps. "A little dehydrated from the run I guess. Back to Figueroa. If you get on his bad side, you're toast. He has a lot of political power. None of the attending physicians like him, either. He is not above pointing out their deficiencies, too."

"Then why don't they get rid of him?" Iggy asked.

Janice had taken a number of psychology courses as an undergrad. "Who would take the job? The other attendings probably don't want it." she said. "It's a thankless position. Not rewarding at all. He probably has to defend every decision."

"Unless he makes his own rewards by entertaining himself at others' expense. At least it seems he is an equal opportunity asshole. Well, almost equal opportunity; he picks on everyone except jocks," Wolfe suggested. In response, Iggy belched loudly enough to be heard at the pier. Wolfe passed out more beer. If they didn't drink it soon, it would warm quickly without the ice. He offered the cheese and crackers to each of his friends.

Chapter 8

"Code Blue, ER ICU, Code…."

"Excuse me, please," Wolfe told the young woman. "Someone is trying to die next door. He opened the door to the exam room and placed her chart in the plastic box next to the door. Walking as swiftly as he could without actually breaking into a run, he followed Harding into the corridor. Directly behind Gupta, they filed into the ER ICU while pulling on the latex exam gloves they kept in their white coat pockets. On the way to the ER ICU, Wolfe glanced out one of the doors that led to the parking lot. A wall of water obscured everything outside the glass door. He hadn't seen rain like that since he had been in the navy transit barracks in Subic Bay in the Philippines. *Monsoon-like*, he thought. He should have been used to it by then, because for the past week, it had poured every afternoon for about an hour. *Just like P.I.*

In the ER ICU, the senior and junior ER residents stood near the head of one of the code stretchers. The senior, Gentry, struggled with the patient, trying to put a nasal cannula around his ears and position the prongs in his nose. Obviously very agitated, but weak, the patient shook his head. Nichols slapped EKG monitor leads on the patient's bare chest. A flannel shirt hung unbuttoned from the man; his undershirt had been pulled up to his neck. When Nichols found the cardiac rhythm on the CRT, he slipped an elastic tourniquet around the patient's thin black arm and began looking for a vein in which to start an intravenous.

Knowing their station in the pecking order, the three interns took position at the foot of the bed, out of the way of the nurses, waiting for direction. "Get his clothes off," Nichols said. "He's in V.tach." Three intern heads turned as one toward the monitor. The patient was indeed in ventricular tachycardia, a rhythm that heralded loss of blood flow, followed by cardiac arrest and death. Wolfe reached for the patient's pants, only to be pushed out of the way by a nurse who had a pair of heavy duty scissors. She cut through the patient's belt, and both sides of the patient's trousers and underwear in a practiced motion, down one side and up the other. Then she continued up one side of his shirts and down the other. One swift pull by another nurse and the patient lay naked before them and God, wearing only a ragged pair of combat boots.

"Charge the defibrillator. Set to sync," Gentry said. A nurse reached for the Lifepack 5 and hit a button. The Lifepack 5 whined loudly as the capacitor charged. "Gel," Gentry commanded. One of the nurses squirted a lubricant that conducted electricity onto one of the paddles. Gentry rubbed the two paddles together, making certain both were lubricated. At the same time, the patient gave up his struggle and slipped into unconsciousness. He collapsed on the stretcher. His body fought on, making a loud gasp, taking in a large breath in an attempt to oxygenate itself. "Clear," Gentry said.

"Clear," everyone around the bed repeated automatically, as they stepped back several inches.

Gentry placed the paddles firmly on the tall, thin man's left anterior and left lateral chest, and pushed the triggers.

Blam! Synchronized with one of the electrical complexes in the patient's heart rhythm, 300 joules of electrical energy discharged from one of the paddles through the patient and into the second paddle, completing a circuit through the man's heart. Every muscle in his body tried to flex at the same time, lifting him three to four inches off the bed. He fell back to the stretcher, still unconscious, but moaning. Nichols looked at the monitor. "Nice job, Bob, he's in sinus rhythm. Do we have a pulse?"

A nurse's hand shot to the man's femoral area. "Good pulse."

"I.v. in?" Gentry asked. "Good. Push a milligram of epi. Turn up the oxygen to 100%. Is he breathing on his own? Get me an i.v. with theophylline in it. Need some aerosol Albuterol, too. Is the respiratory tech around?"

Another nurse listened in several locations over the man's

chest. "He's moving air. He's not even wheezing very much, Dr. Nichols."

"Good. He's still unconscious, though. We need to protect his airway, but I don't want to intubate him. You, intern, put an oral airway in him," Gentry said to Wolfe. Nervously, Wolfe moved to the head of the bed. He picked up the middle oral airway from the three lying on the crash cart. "Get the one that is the same length as the distance from the corner of his mouth to his ear. That's the one you want." Gentry pointed. Wolfe put down the medium sized oral airway and picked up the largest one. Laying it against the man's cheek, he measured its length. A perfect length. He attempted to insert it in the man's mouth.

Gentry continued. "Open his mouth with your thumb and middle finger, like you are snapping your fingers. Turn the airway upside down. Shove it gently between his hard palate and tongue, and then rotate it so it holds his tongue out of the way. Second intern, you," Gentry pointed to Gupta, "get me a set of gases from the radial artery. Third intern, use the ambubag and hyperventilate him while we wait for the arterial blood gas results."

Nichols added, "Someone cover him up. Wolfe, make sure his airway stays in place and keep your finger on his carotid pulse. I want to know if his heart stops again. The cardiac monitor won't tell you that. It only shows electrical activity, not what the heart muscle is actually doing. Got it?"

Wolfe nodded. He rested two fingers on the man's airway until the ambubag covered the patient's mouth. He placed his thumb on the carotid artery. "What happened?" he asked Gentry.

"Near respiratory arrest," Gentry said. "Who's the triage nurse? Couldn't she see this coming?"

"New girl," one of the nurses said.

"Jesus," Nichols said. "Everyone else knows James. What happened?"

The charge nurse summarized the events that led to the arrest for the doctors. "James is an asthmatic. His triggers include cat dander and mold, but his biggest trigger is psychological. He comes in wheezing frequently, usually three or four times a week when it rains heavily. The mold grows in his shack. If you tell him he is next to be seen and a shot of epinephrine is being drawn up, he calms down. Almost doesn't need the shot to open his lungs."

"But," the second nurse continued, "the new triage nurse doesn't know him. She probably said, 'You don't sound so bad. Have a seat. There are a lot of people ahead of you.'"

Nichols finished, "So James's asthma, driven by his anxiety got so bad he almost stopped exchanging CO^2 and O^2 when his bronchial tree went into spasm, followed shortly thereafter by ventricular tachycardia. Fortunately, he didn't have a complete pulmonary or cardiac arrest."

"Blood gases look good," Gupta said returning from the pulmonary lab. He handed the hand written slip to Gentry, who looked at it critically, then handed the piece of paper to Nichols.

"You're Harding, right?" Gentry asked. Harding nodded. "You are internal medicine, correct?" Harding nodded again. ""Do you know who's on call today for your guys?"

"Senior resident on call today is Prescott."

"Crap. Well, someone page the bastard. James has to be admitted."

James sat up on the stretcher pushing away the ambubag and spitting out the oral airway. "I ain't staying. No one to feed my dogs." He reached for the intravenous and began to pull on the tape that held it in his arm. Wolfe grabbed his arm to prevent him from pulling the plastic tubing out.

"Sorry, James. People who have heart attacks have to spend at least one night in the hospital. Especially if they've got no clothes to wear home. It's a rule," Gentry said.

"I wouldn't have had no heart attack if that stuck up nurse had just given me my shot." James looked down and realized his clothing had been destroyed. "At least you left me the boots," he said. "Good boots is hard to find. Been breaking these in for six months."

"You can bet she'll get you right back next time," Nichols said, laughing. "Hang tight James. I'll get social services to get one of your neighbors to feed your dogs and bring you some clothing."

"Make sure whoever it is don't steal nothing from my shack," James said.

The ER residents wandered over to the nurses' station, Gentry scribbling madly to finish the chart before the senior internal medicine resident arrived. Prescott waited for them, seated behind the high desk. They had not seen him. "So, the internal medicine service doesn't have enough work to do?" Prescott asked. "The ER docs are now causing cardiac arrests. You guys in the fifth best Emergency Medicine Residency, out of five mind you, need the practice? My intern'll shit when she hears about this abortion. It will be her fourth admission today, and it's only 11:27 a.m."

"Nice to see you too, Rick," Nichols said. "That was quick. Were you hiding in the ER? You get to decide, of course, but I think he'll be a short stay for observation in a monitored bed."

"I was down the hall in radiology talking with Dr. Figueroa when I heard the Code Blue. Came to watch you goof-offs try to kill someone. If we run out of cardiac monitors, can I borrow one of your interns to keep tabs on a couple pulses? With his thumbs? Even EMTs know to use their index and middle fingers." Wolfe blushed.

Aggravated, Nichols asked. "If you don't like patients, Rick, why in the name of God did you go to medical school?"

Prescott quoted Charles M. Schulz and Linus from Peanuts, "'*I love mankind. It's* people *I can't stand.'* Medical training is a *tradition* in my family. We do it for the financial rewards," then chuckled. He scanned the chart Gentry handed him. "Jesus, can anyone read your handwriting, Bob?"

Gentry shrugged. "The first day of medical school, they broke all our fingers. It's a *tradition* where I went to school."

Chapter 9

Wolfe eventually learned the names of some of the ER staff. They rotated in all the departments of the ER. He occasionally saw the nurses who had done triage or put patients in Primary Care exam rooms in the trauma department. And they all went to the codes, unless they had been designated to remain in their department for crowd control. Patients sometimes expressed their displeasure by getting rowdy when the doctors left them hanging to attend a dying patient.

Staff members were a mixture of races. They worked a variety of shifts, meaning he might see the same person three days in a row and then not for a week. It took him a long time to remember their names. The names of patients and diseases kept intruding on his short term memory.

Jada Thomas was the short, black nurse who had showed him and Gupta the proper chest compression technique. A single mother of two young sons, her schedule was the most erratic. Grade school teacher meetings and ill children at home meant she missed a lot of work. Other nurses were compassionate about her circumstances but resented being called to fill in for her. Wolfe learned there was yet another aspect to hospital politics.

Dorothy Salak was the statuesque, redheaded nurse he had relieved doing chest compressions the first day. The daughter of a wealthy banker in town, she sometimes found herself at the wrong end of barbed comments from her colleagues. They could not understand why she worked in a public hospital when the private hospitals paid more. A lot of the comments suggested she trolled for a rich resident to marry and change those circumstances. The truth was she qualified to work in any hospital in Jacksonville. She did not need the money, so chose to work for the pittance paid at University Hospital as a donation to society. Of course, she didn't close her eyes to the possibility of finding a rich doctor to marry. For that, she dated the residents at more prestigious hospitals, like Shands Hospital at the University of Florida in Gainesville, however. She knew the score about this batch of interns and the residents in general. Finding a diamond among the quartz and glass here would not be easy.

The ER charge nurse worked the day shift, Monday to Friday. A large black woman, Emilou Jones's favorite expression was, "We ain't got time for that foolishness." She ran a tight ship. The racial, sexual mixture of nurses, EMTs, LPNs, nursing assistants, and doctors paid attention to what she said, or they found other places to work. However, when she was not in the department, evenings and weekends, the assistant charge nurses could be much more lax, especially if the ER pace slowed for any reason.

Manuel Navarra, one of the rotating evening charge nurses, had been a linebacker at the University of Miami until he ticked off the coaches one too many times and lost his scholarship. Back home in Defuniak Springs, the Puerto Rican joined a volunteer rescue squad, became an EMT, then a paramedic. Eventually he put himself through nursing school. 6' 3" tall and muscular, his presence helped calm some of the agitated patients in the ER. His best friend, Joe O'Malley, a black EMT, whose family took the name of their slave owner in 1865, was about the same size. The pair worked the same schedule and together restrained many a drunk or patient strung out on PCP. They occasionally had their differences, however. Rarely, they would get into boisterous arguments, especially if the ER was quiet and there were new interns who needed impressing.

"Mine's at least 3 inches longer," Navarra shouted at O'Malley, just feet away behind the nurses' station.

O'Malley rose to the bait, and his feet. He pushed himself past Wolfe. "'Scuse me, doc," he said. Face to face with Navarra, he said, "I doubt it's longer, and I'll bet you it's old and moth eaten. Won't be surprised if it didn't have dry rot from lack of use."

"That right?" Navarra confronted O'Malley. "It's seen more use than yours. That's why it's longer. Yours is shriveled up from inattention."

Voices increasing in volume almost loud enough to be heard in the waiting room O'Malley challenged Navarra, "Okay, pull that brown sucker out and we'll see which is longer."

"You pull that old black thing out and we'll compare. Side by side. You man enough to do that with all these nurses around?"

O'Malley snarled, "No problem, farm boy." He reached for his pants.

Thoroughly taken in by the argument, Wolfe stepped between the two men. He had to look up at them. Both had determined looks on their faces. They stared at one another, attempting to ignore the intern. At the same time, they undid their belts. "Hey, guys," Wolfe said. "This is not a good idea. You've got quite an audien..."

"On three, sucker," Navarra challenged. "One, two...."

"You really should think about the consequences," Wolfe suggested.

"...three." Each man pulled the belt out of his pants. Holding both belts up, they compared the two dangling side by side. The brown one held by Navarra was indeed three inches longer than the black one held by O'Malley.

"Manny, you need to get back on your diet," O'Malley said, as he re-threaded his belt through the loops on his pants. Behind the nurses' station, a dozen nurses and techs had gathered to witness the ritual harassment of a new intern. They clapped, cheered, and laughed. Wolfe knew he had been had. He smiled congenially. "Oh, I get it," he finally said.

O'Malley elbowed him in the ribs. "We only do that to physicians we like, Doc." He smiled and shook Wolfe's hand, as did Navarra, who also slapped him on the back. Navarra pointed to a row of gauze dolls sitting on the top of the nurses' desk. They were crude constructions, made from Popsicle sticks and roller gauze. Each had an official black plastic name tag with white letters engraved into the top layer. Wolfe read the names of the last two: Robert Gentry and John Nichols. "The guys we like the most get the *Wizard of Gauze* award from us at the end of their internship. It's a singular award. You are in the running, pal."

"Uh, thanks. I think," Wolfe said. Navarra laughed.

ER Trauma was similar to Primary Care in that the pace was never ending. As soon as Wolfe finished suturing a patient, the nurses asked him to write a brief note. They finished with the patient's dressings and escorted him out. Wolfe rolled his stool to the next stretcher and started over with the next patient. By the time he finished the nine stretchers, ordering x-rays, suturing, splinting, ordering ace wraps and crutches, they were filled again.

With his first trauma patient he learned a valuable lesson. The patient had a swollen ankle. Wolfe tried to slip the man's boot off, but when he tried it didn't move. A loud scream emanated from the patient. The ankle and foot were so swollen that any motion sent pain shooting up the man's leg. "Touch that, again, white boy, and you may die today," the black man on the stretcher said.

Jada stepped between Wolfe and the patient. "You see that man over there?" she asked the patient. He nodded, seeing O'Malley. "You threaten this doctor one more time and he will deposit your ass in the parking lot. Got that?" Before the man could answer, Jada used her heavy duty scissors and cut the boot and sock off. She then split the man's pants to his knee.

"Jesus," the man complained, "those boots cost ten bucks at Goodwill."

Jada ignored him. "Sorry, Doc," she said. "We should have had that stuff off before you got here. See these?" She held up the scissors. "We call them penny-cutters, because you really can cut through copper with them if you want. Get yourself a pair. They'll save you some aggravation."

"Uh, thanks, Jada," Wolfe said. He looked at the man's foot. It was twice normal size and the blue-green color of the deep ocean from mid shin to great toe. "What happened to your foot?" Wolfe asked.

"A car ran over it."

"When?"

"Three days ago."

"Where have you been?" Wolfe asked. "Surely you didn't walk on it."

The man pointed to a tree branch he had whittled into a cane. "I spent three days sitting out front waiting to be seen," he said. "They never called my name. Limped home each night. It didn't hurt so bad in the boot. That is unless some honky-ass intern tried to pull it off."

Jada said, "Joe." O'Malley took two steps toward the stretcher.

The man on the stretcher held up his hands. "Sorry. Sorry, Doc. It's just painful. Can you fix it?"

"It's okay, Joe," Wolfe said. O'Malley went back to the nurses' station. Wolfe spoke to the patient, "First we have to figure out how badly broken it is." Risking the patient's displeasure, again, he palpated the ankle and foot. He also checked for pulses and sensation. "Jada, he needs a foot film."

"You want an ankle x-ray, too?" she asked.

"Naw, his ankle's fine," Wolfe said. "Besides, according to Iggy, Figueroa gave someone in orthopedics a hard time about not knowing if the foot or ankle needed imaging the other day when he ordered both films on a single extremity." Wolfe's patient had four fractured metatarsals. Iggy came down from the floor to admit him to the orthopedic service. The patient required surgery to pin three of the unstable fractures.

Wolfe learned lessons with almost every patient over the month. The second patient on the first day had two small lacerations that had required only cleansing and dressings. As he struggled to find the ends of a Band Aid wrapper to open it, the charge nurse, Emilou Jones, tapped him on the shoulder. He swiveled on his rolling stool away from the patient and looked up. In a deft motion she tore the paper wrapper in half. The Band Aid fell into Wolfe's hand. "We ain't got time for that foolishness. This is quicker," she said and walked away.

Chapter 10

On one of the few nights Wolfe found himself in the apartment for a reasonable night sleep, he tossed and turned fitfully. In his third month and on pediatrics, his mind raced. Nightmares about holding children for spinal taps, on the pediatric ward, in the pediatric ER, in the lab, at his parents' home, even in gas stations and convenience stores, intruded on his REM sleep. A loud blast from a car horn startled him and he rolled out of bed, landing on the clothing he had stripped and dropped before climbing into the sack. The horn sounded again.

He quickly pulled his trousers over his underpants. Barefoot, in a scrub shirt and the corduroy pants, he looked out his window into the apartment parking lot for the source of the noise. The street lights illuminated a man sitting in a dark convertible. Behind the convertible sat a trailer on which sat a catamaran sailboat. Large bold letters on the side of one of the hulls proclaimed, *HOBIE*.

A young blonde woman leaned into the passenger side of the convertible screaming unintelligible anger at the long-haired, young man. Wolfe eventually recognized the two as Nick Robinson and Samantha Joiner, two of his internship classmates. Nick appeared to be the calmer of the two, nodding his head, and trying to calm Sam with the motion of his right hand. Wolfe thought he could hear Nick say, “Okay, Sam. Okay.”

As quietly as he could, Wolfe let himself out of the apartment and slipped down two flights of stairs. His flip-flops clopped a weird Morse code on the cement steps, as he hurried to reach the pair. Warm humid air and the smell of the ocean smothered him as he exited the building.

"You can take this cata-whatever and shove it up your ass," Sam yelled as Wolfe stepped from the curb, headed toward the convertible.

Nick said, "Whatever you say, Sam. Now go with Addy and get some rest. You have to be on rounds in a few hours."

"Addy?" she asked, lisping her words. "Who cares about Addy?"

Ignoring her remark, Wolfe put his hand on her shoulder. Surprised, by his touch, she jumped and spun, swinging a fist slowly, which he easy avoided. Gently grabbing both her wrists, he crossed her arms in front of her while holding her from behind. He held her tightly, the way he learned from Manny Navarra in the ER when subduing drunks. Head next to hers and looking over her left shoulder, he spoke to Nick. "Lovers' quarrel?"

"Something like that," Nick responded. "I can't see the point in involving myself with a woman with a fiancé."

"You're probably homosexual," Sam spat. "Pretty boy peroxide hair, tan, Fiat convertible, surfboard, and HobieCat. A real Californian queer."

Nick laughed. "No, that would be Justin Murcheson, if that sort of relationship interests you." He looked at Wolfe. "Addy, she says you two have some sort of connection. I didn't want to leave her drunk and angry at *Sailors' Liberty*. Too many rough characters, if you know what I mean. And she wasn't capable of driving. She won't tell me where she lives. Can you get her home?"

Sam twisted in Wolfe's arms, squirming in an attempt to free herself. "I'll take care of her, Nick," he said.

"Thanks. See you later." He stepped on the accelerator and eased the Fiat Spider and boat out of the parking lot without running over the sidewalk or grass.

"Now, see what you've done?" Sam asked him. Robinson's car and boat disappeared into the night, turning from Hopkins down 3rd Street, aka State Route A1A. Wolfe slackened his grip on her wrists and let her arms drop to her side. He let loose of her and took one step back, just as she launched her right hand at his face in an attempt to slap him. She missed by several feet. Bending at the waist, hands on her knees, she began to sob. "That stupid son of a bitch," she said. "That stupid son of a bitch!"

Wolfe took her by the hand and led her up the stairs and into the apartment. Janice met them at the door. "You two okay?" she asked.

"No," Sam said.

"Yes," Wolfe corrected her. "We're going to get a couple hours of sleep before we go to the hospital. Sorry we woke you."

"It's okay," Janice said. "Iggy never heard a thing. Sleeps like the dead." She dead-bolted the door and returned to the master bedroom, closing the door quietly behind her.

Wolfe waited outside the bathroom for Sam, and then led her into his room. He slipped off her outer clothes and pushed her under the sheet and blanket. Half asleep already, she mumbled drunkenly, "Let's play with your dead leprechaun, Addy."

Wolfe ignored her. He took a pillow and lay in his comforter on the floor next to the bed. "Get some sleep," he said, "we'll talk in the morning."

"Let's see that little stiff," Sam said. She laughed intoxicatedly. Drifting to sleep, she muttered more that Wolfe could not interpret.

Wolfe left her at the house she rented with two roommates on Townsend Boulevard in Arlington when he drove to the hospital. She said she would eventually make it to work, but he did not see her the remainder of the day. Their paths rarely crossed that month. He took care of munchkins and rug rats on the floor and occasionally visited the ER to admit one, being on call every other night. She kept bankers' hours on the psychiatric rotation, her one elective for the internship year.

"Addy, how many spinal taps have you done?" pediatric attending Benjamin Rose asked.

"Held three," Wolfe responded, hoping to avoid any more.

Rose laughed. "Around here it's: see one; do one; teach one. You are falling behind in your education. Why are you so reluctant to do lumbar punctures?"

"It seems barbaric," Wolfe said, defending his lack of participation. Any time he examined a child with a high fever, he prayed to himself that he would find an obvious source, a strep throat, an ear infection, a pneumonia, a urinary infection, anything that kept the child from being labeled as having an FUO: fever of unknown origin. If the resident and attending also could not find a source of the fever, the child usually underwent a spinal tap in an effort to prove he did not need high doses of antibiotics for meningitis.

"Not so barbaric as letting a child die from *H. flu* meningitis," Rose countered. "Come with me. One of the children on the floor has an otitis media that isn't responding to antibiotics. In fact, I think you tried to admit him."

"The blond three-year-old with the ear infection and *really soft meningeal signs*, as the second year resident said?" Wolfe asked. He had seen a child with a temperature of 105, who had a slightly red eardrum. When Wolfe lifted his head off the bed, the child bent his knees, but did not cry out. The second year pediatric resident had decided to treat him with intramuscular antibiotic injections. After his temperature dropped to normal, he sent the boy home to be seen in clinic in 48 hours for follow-up. Clinic rechecks tended to be iffy propositions. The hospital population, being mainly indigent, had little access to transportation. Many parents could not afford antibiotics, either, which was the reason for the injections. However, this child's grandmother, given custody by the court because of her daughter's inability to stay off drugs, took her duties seriously. The child returned, fever recurrent.

"Yeah, he's back. No improvement, except that slight blush of his left tympanic membrane is gone," Rose said. "Needs a tap. You get to do it. You have to perform a minimum of six to pass the rotation. We prefer you do at least ten."

"Shouldn't be a problem," Wolfe said, knowing they did an average of five per day on the pediatric service, including both the ward and ER. He didn't realize that made him sound confident to Rose.

"Good. The other residents are tied up. You and I will do this one. I'll hold; you will put the needle in."

With Rose positioning the patient, Wolfe had no trouble pushing the needle into the meningeal space surrounding the child's spinal cord. The attending physician curled the boy into a tight ball and thus opened the spaces between the lumbar vertebrae. Rose also coached Wolfe well. "Don't identify with the patient, identify with the pathologist. He wants a good sample. No bloody specimens. Stay midline. Keep the needle horizontal, but aim cephalad slightly to get between the posterior spinous processes. Check the opening pressure. Good. Get three tubes of fluid. Need glucose, protein, etc. Also need an uncontaminated sample for microscopic studies and cultures. Know why you want glucose and protein?"

"Bacteria increase protein and decrease glucose," Wolfe tried to remember the assigned reading. "The first and third samples are for cell counts, in case there is blood. Decreased red blood cell counts indicate blood in the needle. Increasing or steady red blood count indicates central nervous system bleeding. Do you want a tube for fungal cultures?"

"Naw. Kids don't have a lot spinal fluid or frequent fungal infections. As it is, he's going to have a hell of a headache already," Rose said. "Adults have more to give."

"Wouldn't you expect a child with meningitis to already have a headache?" Wolfe asked.

Rose nodded. "Problem is they can't tell you about it," he said. "This is veterinary medicine. Don't forget that."

"One of my colleagues has been telling adult patients, 'Don't say anything, you will just confuse me,'" Wolfe said.

Rose laughed. "That's too direct, but I sometimes think I would like to gag the parents. They have too many theories about cause and effect."

There were a few white cells in the child's spinal fluid when the report returned. Either he had a viral meningitis, or the antibiotic was doing its job. Rose changed it to a more powerful broad spectrum antibiotic and told Wolfe they would wait on the cultures or the patient's response to the change in medications over the next twenty-four hours.

About 1 a.m. Wolfe finally finished working up the admissions for the day and went to the residents' sleeping room on the fifth floor. A silent color television played in the room throwing ever changing shadows across the furniture. Wolfe saw a clip of presidential candidate Jimmy Carter shaking hands with someone. Three of the beds were already occupied. He had barely sat on the bed when his beeper went off. As one, three hands reached from under the covers, flicked on small lights, looked at beepers, turned off the lights, and went back under the blankets. *Wonder if they even woke up?* Wolfe asked himself.

He silenced his beeper and stepped into the hallway, where a phone hung on the wall. Picking up the receiver, he dialed the pediatric ER. "Wolfe here," he said. "Be right there."

The child lay on the ER stretcher. A pediatric resident stood at the head of the bed using an ambubag to push air into the baby's lungs through the tiny intubation tube. Wolfe recognized the raccoon eyes and Battle's sign, bilateral black eyes and bruised areas behind the child's ears. "Head injury?" he asked.

The junior pediatric resident nodded slowly. An anesthesia

resident worked on making an intravenous cutdown on the child's ankle. "This is secure," she said, taping it to the child's leg. "Where is the neurosurgical resident?"

The nurse held a clipboard. "He's waiting in the operating room."

"What do you want me to do?" Wolfe asked.

The anesthesiologist said, "I need someone to monitor his vitals from this point on. If he survives, he'll be a joint admission to pediatrics and neurosurgery. He'll need an admission physical."

"Okay. Someone talking to his parents?" Wolfe asked, taking out his reflex hammer and starting the physical.

"Mom's in JSO's psychiatric jail unit for drug abuse. The sheriff's office is talking with her live-in boy friend. They think he did this," the nurse said.

The attending, Rose, eventually arrived from home having been beeped at the same time as Wolfe. Before the child went to the operating room, Rose did another complete examination of the child. As Wolfe watched and listened, Rose pointed out the signs Wolfe did not recognize, could not explain, or had missed completely. "Both clavicles have been broken in the past. They are deformed. There are cigarette burns on his hands, thighs, and buttocks. All the burns are approximately the same circumference, in different stages of healing. The bruises on his arms and shins are multiple ages, one week, two weeks and three weeks old. See the color variation, purple to green to yellow. Of course, the skull fracture can be from 12 to 24 hours old. There is blood behind both tympanic membranes. Both pupils are fixed and dilated. I don't think he will survive the surgery. You go with him, Addy. I'll talk with the cops."

Chapter 11

Preparing to leave the hospital the next night, having been awake for almost thirty-five hours, Wolfe was approached by one of the attending physicians. "Wolfe. Where are you going?" Cheryl King asked.

There were more female pediatricians than female attending physicians in other specialties. Figueroa had expressed his feelings clearly at M&M one month before. If there had to be female physicians, they might as well be pediatricians, a motherly role. Wolfe had tried to suppress those thoughts, but King had a way of making Wolfe wish there were no female physicians, at least no Dr. King. She never asked politely; she demanded. Also, she never allowed that someone might have a good reason for declining her requests. Resigned to his fate, he replied, "Well, I was going home for some sleep, Dr. King. But what can I do for you?"

"You wanted to be an astronaut, right?" How she knew that, Wolfe did not want to know. "Well, a helicopter is going to land in the parking lot in a couple minutes. There's a three-year-old in Lake City with asthma and pneumonia that needs to be transported here. Shands Hospital in Gainesville can't take her. They are in the midst of a severe cold front, thunderstorms with tornado warnings. The child has to come here. Think of it as an orbital flight."

"Sounds like a real pediatrician should go, not an int...."

She interrupted him. "You are expendable. Everyone else is tied up. You completed the ER rotation. Besides, the child is stable right now, according to the ER doc at Lake Shore Hospital. You haven't got much time. Get down to the parking lot."

Wolfe arrived as the chopper set down, sand blasting every car within fifty yards with the dirt and trash that normally collected in the lot. A flight nurse dressed in a blue flight suit ducked under the main rotor blades and walked briskly toward him and the security guards standing between the helicopter and the hospital entrance. "You Dr. Wolfe?" she shouted over the roar of the jet engine spinning at idle." He nodded.

She took him by the hand to the front of the helicopter and opened the front left door, shoving him into the seat. Wolfe eyed the pilot in a tan flight suit, head covered by a white plastic helmet. He sat in the right hand seat, already belted in. Grim mustached face glanced at Wolfe and nodded, then resumed scanning his instruments. After snapping on and tightening his seat and shoulder belts for him, the nurse fit a set of ear phones over Wolfe's head. The screech of the helicopter's turbine moderated slightly. Pointing to the switch in the cable, she mouthed, "Push to talk." Slamming the door, she disappeared.

The pilot held his cable in one hand in front of Wolfe. He pushed the button, "You the doc?"

Wolfe pushed his button. "Yep. You the pilot?" The pilot laughed. Eyes gleamed. Wolfe had flown in navy helicopters while on the aircraft carrier, so seeing the pilot in the *passenger seat* didn't fool him. "How long is the flight?" he asked.

"'Bout twenty minutes each way. We have to be back here in less than ninety minutes. That front in Gainesville will pass through here and Lake City in about two hours. They've already had three tornadoes touch down near Inverness and Ocala. More expected."

Wolfe saw the pilot's lips move, but didn't hear the words. He had released the intercom button and spoken with air traffic control. "Everyone strapped down?" the pilot asked, again pressing the button.

Two voices echoed in Wolfe's ears. "Yo," one said.

"Roger," said the other.

The pilot tapped Wolfe on the shoulder and held a thumb up in front of his face. Wolfe nodded. The helicopters in the navy had used the aircraft carrier's speed to take off. Basically they added a little lift to the thirty knot speed supplied by the carrier and rose sedately into the air. Even though the military prided itself on its hot-shot pilots, the air space around a carrier was strictly controlled. There were too many ways to die when the jets, propeller aircraft, and helos converged near the deck. No wild antics allowed.

Expecting a controlled take-off, Wolfe left his stomach and heart in the parking lot when the pilot launched the helicopter skyward. It seemed to Wolfe that the aircraft barely cleared the top of the hospital, flying almost in terrain-following mode. In the distance to the west and south lightning flashed frequently illuminating billowing, dark, storm clouds. He didn't think the helicopter ever got more than 1000' above the ground before slamming into the landing pad, a bright red cross in a white circle painted on a cement slab next to Lake Shore Hospital in Lake City.

The nurse pulled him out of the chopper and through the automatic doors into the ER. A blue flight-suited EMT followed, pushing a helicopter stretcher loaded with an orange crash box and medical supplies. "Jesus, where did he learn to fly?" Wolfe asked the nurse when they could no longer hear the screech of the jet engine.

"Vietnam. Occasionally, he has flashbacks. Probably the lightning. Looks a lot like an artillery battle tonight," she said.

"How would you know that?" Wolfe asked.

"I spent a year flying with a MASH unit in Vietnam," she said.

"Oh," Wolfe said.

The child needing transport underwent evaluation by the nurse and helicopter EMT. "We shouldn't transport her in this condition," the nurse told the Lake Shore ER physician.

"What?" the physician responded. "Why not?" Wolfe looked around the small ER. It was evident the ER doc had been extremely busy. The residue of at least one Code Blue still littered the nearest stretcher. All six other beds held what appeared to be extremely ill or injured patients. The waiting room had looked full when they walked past it. "I can't take care of her here. We don't have a pediatrician on call tonight. I'm up to my ears in alligators." He waved a hand at the confusion surrounding him.

"She's not stable to transport. If you want us to take her, she'll have to be intubated and sedated," the nurse responded. "She needs a stable airway. We can't intubate or resuscitate her in flight. She has to be intubated or trached before we can take off. And we only have ten minutes before we need to leave. There's a storm coming."

"I've never intubated a child, or trached anyone," the doctor said. "If you leave her here, she'll likely die. We don't have the facilities to care for her. The ambulance service refused to transport her to Gainesville."

The child's mother wailed loudly on hearing the argument. "Please save my baby," she cried.

"Likely for the same reason," the nurse said. She turned to Wolfe. "Can you intubate her, doctor?"

Wolfe suppressed an urge to urinate in his pants. "Maybe," he said. He chose a pediatric intubation tube and measured it against the child's little finger. The ER nurse handed him a laryngoscope. He put it on the stretcher. "Not going to need that," he said.

"Are you going to sedate her?" the flight nurse asked. "You have done this before?"

"I have seen this technique done, but never used it myself," Wolfe replied. With his right hand, he clamped the child's mouth shut and closed her right nostril with his thumb. Slipping the well lubricated endotracheal tube into her left nostril, he waited. The child struggled against his hand. The ER nurse reached for his hand and attempted to peel it off the child's face. *Breathe!* Wolfe commanded silently. Suddenly rewarded by the child's attempt to inhale, Wolfe felt the ET tube pulled through his fingers. The child sucked it into her trachea by inhaling forcefully through the only opening available, her left nostril.

Wolfe ignored the ER nurse clawing at his right hand. "Tape," he said. "Listen to her lungs. Are we in good position?" He attached the ambubag to the ET tube. "You said she's about 20 kilos?" The ER nurse nodded, releasing his hand from her grip. "Then give her one milligram of Valium through the i.v. over the next four or five minutes," he commanded.

Five minutes later, the nurse and EMT strapped the sedated child onto the helicopter stretcher. The flight back to University Hospital mirrored the outgoing flight. Wolfe sat in his seat behind the Plexiglas bubble with his eyes closed. It seemed like a hundred years since the Vietnam War had ended for him with his discharge from the navy in May, 1969. He knew the war hadn't really ended for the country until the evacuation of Saigon in April, 1975, a little more than a year before. For the pilot, the war probably never had ended. The pilot laughed and cackled while guiding the chopper on a low level flight, tilting left and right, avoiding ground fire from the Viet Cong.

Dr. King and the on-call intern met the helicopter in the parking lot. Wolfe listened briefly to the nurse's report, and then headed for his car wondering if there were any paint left on it.

Chapter 12

Of course Wolfe had to present the abused child's death at the next M&M conference. Rose let him identify the physical findings associated with child abuse on the color slides. He struggled to keep his emotions in check, nearly choking-up in outrage over the youngster's death. The pediatric attending then led the discussion through the autopsy results, displayed in vivid color and giant size on the projection screen in the auditorium. Finding an abused child was only half the battle, however.

Rose pointed out that the reporting of suspected child neglect or abuse was the law, one of the few times the state intruded in the patient-doctor relationship. There were hazards with reporting. Arguments were given for and against telling the parents that they would be investigated. A few parents understood the physician was trying to protect the child. Others felt it was an invasion of their privacy, or worse, an unjust accusation. Most parents who had injured a child were just frustrated with the child and didn't know their own strength, or possessed bad tempers and had over-reacted. A few, though, were truly malicious, especially if the child were not their off-spring. Physicians had been injured by parents who reacted poorly to the suggestion that they might have injured their child on purpose: child abuse vs. accidental injury, termed child neglect. Rose returned the floor to Figueroa.

Figueroa was strangely silent about the death of the child. Although his countenance showed anger and sadness, he said little about the child's death apparently feeling the macabre case spoke for itself. Wolfe felt relieved to not have been grilled. Other presenters were not so lucky.

A surgical intern and a second year ER resident suffered through the description of their faux pas. An eight-year-old girl had come into the ER Trauma unit complaining of eye pain. Careful history taking by the intern revealed that she and her brother had been throwing scissors into the air and that once the pair of scissors had hit her in the eye. The patient exhibited 20/40 vision in each eye before having her eye stained with fluorescein, a dye that glowed under ultraviolet light revealing corneal or scleral abrasions. The fluorescein showed a small scratch on the globe, in the white area just above the pupil, but no corneal damage.

Uncomfortable with discharging the child without an ophthalmologist's exam, the intern had talked to the junior ER resident. The resident congratulated him on the work-up to that point, but insisted the intern check the pressure in the globe to rule out a puncture before bothering the ophthalmology resident. He had been chastened for calling them unnecessarily in the past. No tonometer to measure globe pressure could be found in the ER. The ophthalmology residents, who had access to a tonometer in the ophthalmology clinic, did not pull call in the hospital. So, the ER resident told the intern to (and he stressed this point) very carefully press on the good eye to get an idea of how that felt, and then to very, very carefully and gently touch the injured eye. If there were any difference at all in pressure, the intern was to put a metal guard on the eye and call the ophthalmology resident. There had been a huge difference in the way the eyes felt to even a very light touch. The intern taped the metal guard over the child's eye.

At surgery to repair the punctured globe, the ophthalmology attending physician found part of the patient's iris poking through the hole in her globe, a result of the increased pressure caused by pushing on the globe. Per protocol, any portion of the iris outside the globe had to be sacrificed to cut down on the chance of serious eye infection and subsequent loss of the eye to infection. The patient would have an irregularly shaped iris and perhaps, but not certain, decreased visual acuity for the rest of her life.

The ophthalmology attending physician complained to the ER

attending, who added the case to the M&M conference. The teaching points were obvious: never touch a possibly violated globe without obtaining a pressure first. And, enough pressure would have forced the entire contents of the globe, iris, lens, and vitreous humor out of the eye through the tiny slit, like the inside of a grape squirting out if someone pinched the skin. Wolfe envisioned an aircraft depressurizing through a small opening in the wall with the aircraft at high altitude, all of the passengers squeezed through the tiny opening.

Figueroa lost all semblance of self-control upon hearing about the potential outcome. He instructed the attending physicians present for the M&M conference, "You will have a tonometer available in the ER at all times. All residents, ER and ophthalmology, will be trained in its use. Do you realize what the lifetime loss of vision is worth to a lawyer if this child should lose sight in her eye? I'm thinking 1-2 million dollars. Tonometers cost what, $50-100?"

The ophthalmology attending physician, Dr. Jason Ferris and no friend of Figueroa, took issue with the statement. "It's likely that using the tonometer would have had the same result. We just wanted the residents to be aware of the possible catastrophic results of even lightly touching a penetrated globe. No need to go off the deep end, Fig."

Taking exception to the remark, Figueroa stated, "Any resident who eviscerates an eye, or anyone who practices *tonometer by thumb*, will no longer be a resident at University Hospital." The two physicians stared at one another, animosity visible, while the auditorium collectively held its breath. "Whatever," Ferris finally said.

In another case, an intern had not reviewed a patient's chart when it was presented to him by a nurse, before he signed an order to give the patient an aspirin. The patient was a massively obese woman who complained of a headache. The intern knew only that she was complaining of a headache and had requested aspirin. Extremely busy, and assuming the nurse would let him know if it were not a good idea to give the patient aspirin, he quickly flipped to the order page and signed the order that had been written by the nurse. Figueroa asked the intern if he had talked with the patient. No. Had he examined the patient? No. Had he even skimmed the chart? He had not. He asked if he knew what allergies the patient had. The intern did not know. At the time he approved the order for aspirin, did he realize the patient was on warfarin, another clotting inhibitor? No. Did he know that aspirin also inhibited platelets and clot formation? Yes. Did he know the patient had a history of blood clots? No. Did he suppose that a blood clot in someone's brain or a ruptured berry aneurysm in the same area might cause headaches? Yes, he knew that. The autopsy pictures revealed stenosed carotid arteries, two small clots in the patient's brain, and massive bleeding from a ruptured berry aneurysm. "A cerebral *hat trick*!" Figueroa crowed. The aspirin had not killed the patient, but it certainly added to the anti-clotting effects of the warfarin and the intracerebral bleeding, which had. With nowhere to drain, the bleeding inside the skull had increased the intracranial pressure and squashed the patient's brain like roadkill.

Figueroa declared what then became Intern Rule #1 for the class of 1977: "No intern will write an order for a medication for a patient, unless said intern has taken a history from the patient, examined the patient in person, and reviewed the chart for allergies and contraindications." The pronouncement saved innumerable lives from that point forward, but not the woman who had received the aspirin.

Continuing in the same vein, Figueroa asked John Nichols, the junior ER resident, what he would do if an adult or child presented to the ER with one large pupil. Smart, and quick on his feet, Nichols told the audience that such a presentation after head trauma, or with a bleeding aneurysm, and without a history or diabetes or previous eye trauma might mean bleeding inside the skull. The increased intracranial pressure might squeeze the brain as it had with the previous patient. That would cause herniation of the brain stem into the foramen magnum, trapping the third cranial nerve and causing dilation of the pupil. He supposed his response would be to find a bone drill and drill a hole in the temporal bone, since most traumatic bleeds occurred after fracture of the temporal bone and rupture of the temporal artery. If there were blue colored meninges, he would cut the meninges and let out the blood, lowering the intracranial pressure.

"On which side would you drill?" Figueroa asked.

Nichols continued his lecture, "The standard thinking is the bleeding on the left side of the brain would trap the right third nerve, and vice versa. One might think to drill on the side opposite of the blown pupil. However, there have been cases in which the entrapment was on the same side. So, I'd drill both."

"You'd drill both sides?" Figueroa asked, trying to sound incredulous and not succeeding.

"Yeah," Nichols answered, "but not through the same hole. Tends to cut down on survival, if you know what I mean." Almost everyone paying attention to the exchange laughed. The others had to hear second hand that Nichols had told Figueroa that drilling straight through a patient's head was a bad idea. Figueroa blushed.

Drolly, he said, "Thanks for that insight. Why not take an x-ray first?"

"X-rays are great for showing you bone, the skull, etc.," Nichols said. "But you'll never see the brain. At the most you might see a fracture or a calcified pineal gland. Helpful if it is in the midline. Suggests herniation if it is not, but hardly definitive. Would waste a lot of time, too. The patient might die in radiology."

A smile appeared on Figueroa's face. Evidently, he had more teaching in mind, a chance to show off his education and preparation. "Dr. Robinson, are you here?" His eyes searched the audience for the intern.

"Yes, sir," Robinson replied from the middle of the lecture theater.

"Good. For those of you who don't know, Nick was a radiology resident in California, but decided he wanted a broader education. So, he came here as an ER intern this year," Figueroa said, big smile on his face. "Perhaps he can enlighten us on this. Is there a way to see the brain and whether or not it is herniating, before drilling holes in the patient's head? Before doing an autopsy?"

"Yes, sir," Robinson said. "There are two new techniques that will be available soon: CAT scan, computer aided tomography, a powerful x-ray technique and less developed at this point. And MRI, magnetic resonate imaging. That involves no x-rays, just the magnetic properties of protons within the various tissues of the body. The images are similar to cross sections done by pathologists but don't require killing the patient."

"Any downside to this MRI?" Figueroa asked, apparently having read up on the new imaging technique.

"None that damages the patient. Just his wallet. It's going to be very expensive, at least at first. The machines cost 2-5 million dollars to make."

An Ob-gyn resident asked, "Any harm to the fetus in a pregnant woman?"

Robinson smiled and repeated a joke he had heard in California, "Just a tendency for the newborn to rotate toward magnetic north after delivery if you place him in a swing,"

The auditorium erupted in laughter bringing the conference to a close. Wolfe noticed the glower on Figueroa's face. Once again,

Figueroa motioned for Robinson to meet him on the dais as the others filed out of the room.

Chapter 13

Iggy sat with legs dangling over the end of the long, padded, orthopedic exam table in the exam room on the orthopedic floor. He wore a green scrub shirt and a pair of U.Va. gym shorts. The rotating interns on the orthopedic service, Wolfe and Latesha Marks, stood at the foot of the table listening to the senior orthopedic resident, Mike Dixon, explain the knee exam.

"It's very important that you are capable of doing a complete exam quickly, especially in the ER and busy orthopedic clinics. There isn't much time between patients," the mustachioed resident said. Obvious to Wolfe, Dixon was also an ex-jock. Smaller than Iggy, still muscular and thin, the orthopedist moved like an athlete. Wolfe thought Dixon might have been a runner, or maybe a soccer or lacrosse player. Dixon continued. "It's best to undress the patient from the waist down. You want to watch him walk, too. Note any limps or abnormal gait. We'll assume Iggy limped in here dragging a swollen right knee."

"Not an uncommon occurrence," Iggy said.

Dixon slapped Iggy's right knee. "It's nice that Iggy has some pathology, so you guys can see it." He sat on a rolling stool and began to palpate the knee. "Compare both knees. After checking for swelling and motion of the knee and patella, you want to feel for tenderness in the joint spaces and posteriorly. Here, feel this." He stood and relinquished the stool to Marks.

She sat and put her thumbs on Iggy's right knee and squeezed the space behind his knee. "He's got a mass in the popliteal fossa. Baker's cyst?"

"Gold star for you, Latesha. Baker's cysts develop in knees that have old meniscus trauma. Okay, Iggy, flat on your back," Dixon said. Iggy slipped backward on the table and lay flat. Dixon bent the right knee, then straightened it, twisting it in several directions. With his fingers in the joint spaces, he applied stress in several directions looking for laxity of the lateral and medial ligaments. He then bent the knee and sat on Iggy's foot. Pulling forward on Iggy's tibia, he said, "Yep. It's still there. Wolfe try this."

Wolfe sat on Iggy's right foot and placed both hands behind Iggy's tibia with thumbs in front. He pushed backward and pulled forward. The tibia did not move backward, but came forward about half an inch. "Do that on the left knee," Dixon said.

Wolfe bent Iggy's left knee and sat on his left foot. When he pushed and pulled the tibia, it didn't move in either direction. "Wow," he said. "There's a big difference."

"Know why?" Dixon asked. "Did you do that reading I gave you?"

"Sorry. I was up all night doing pre-ops. Didn't get a chance to read the AJO articles," Wolfe said, referencing the xeroxed copies of articles from the American Journal of Orthopedics that were still folded in half widthwise and stuffed into his white coat pocket. "I assume Iggy has torn his medial and lateral collateral ligaments, though, with that much laxity."

Dixon shook his head. "Actually, the varus and valgus stress tests I applied to his knee show his collaterals are intact, strong as a horse's. Latesha? You weren't doing pre-ops last night. Do you know?"

"Both articles were about the ACL and PCL. I'll guess he tore his anterior cruciate ligament, since the tibia moves forward," She said.

"Two gold stars. Wolfe, you better get on the stick. Latesha is going to make you look bad," Dixon said. "For a long time we didn't know what the Anterior or Posterior Cruciate Ligaments did. Now we know they keep the tibia positioned directly under the femur. It's especially important for changing direction. Lose one or the other, and anytime you plant your foot and change directions your knee will buckle."

Dixon straightened Iggy's knees positioning both legs flat on the table. "It takes a lot of strength to do an anterior drawer test, especially in big athletes, like Iggy. There's a new test called a Lachman. Even small women can do it on large patients. Relax your quads, Iggy. Watch." He placed one hand under Iggy's right femur and one under his tibia, thumbs on top and bent the knee about thirty degrees. "With a gentle pull, you can see Iggy's tibia move forward. Doesn't happen on the other knee. Try it Latesha. You can put your knee under his thigh if you don't feel strong enough to elevate his leg." Without much difficulty, in spite of Iggy's leg size and weight, Marks demonstrated the positive Lachman.

"Can you show us McMurray's test, again?" Wolfe asked, throwing in the only knee trivia he knew in an attempt to look not so stupid, "You should feel a click with loose cartilage, right?"

"Meniscus tears, as we call them," Dixon said. "Sure, but I don't think Iggy has a torn meniscus at the moment, so the test will likely be negative." He lifted Iggy's bad knee, placing his right index finger and thumb in the lateral and medial joint spaces. His left hand held Iggy's foot at the heel. Carefully, he rotated the foot inward and outward as he flexed and extended Iggy's knee feeling for clicks. "Whoops," he said. Wolfe noticed Iggy wince in discomfort. "Guess I was wrong about whether he has a torn meniscus. It's locked, Iggy."

"What does that mean?" Wolfe asked.

Dixon struggled to straighten Iggy's knee. It would not extend past thirty degrees flexion, and it would not flex more than 90 degrees. "It's mechanically locked. There's a piece of meniscus stuck in the joint."

Iggy began to be concerned. "Okay, Mike, fix that so I can get back to work."

"I can't, Iggy." Dixon shrugged and blushed.

Losing his temper, Iggy raised his voice. "What do you men you can't?"

"Evidently, you have a loose chunk of cartilage. It's what the McMurray's is designed to find. The only way to fix it is to surgically remove it."

"Oh, shit, are you kidding me? Figueroa will bounce me from the residency if he finds out I need surgery."

Dixon thought for a minute. "Maybe not. Let's get you to the landing on the stairs between here and the third floor."

Iggy lay on the landing for almost an hour before the inevitable call from the ER sent Latesha and Wolfe running down the same flight of stairs to work up the new orthopedic admission. When they came across Iggy, lying in pain, they reported that he had been with them, running down the stairs, taking the steps two and three at a time. When he hit a wet spot on the landing, a coffee conveniently spilled there by Dixon, he slipped and his leg collapsed, they said. It took Dixon plus two EMTs to carry Iggy back to the clinic. There Dixon confirmed that Iggy's knee was locked and he would need surgery the next morning.

Marks finished the pre-op exam on Iggy quickly. The orders had no sooner been written than Figueroa appeared on the floor wanting to know the details. He apparently left mollified.

Two days later, very early in the morning, Wolfe returned, having been given most of the previous afternoon off to catch up on his sleep and studies. Making intern rounds by himself, without Marks who had worked all night, or the junior or senior resident, or the attending physician, he found Iggy with Janice in a semi-private room. "So, how's the cripple?" Wolfe asked.

"Just great, traitor." Iggy said, frown on his face. "Did you really need to see the McMurray's test?"

Wolfe blushed, "Just trying to make brownie points with the senior resident. I'm sorry."

"Is *Sorry* your first or last name, moron?" Iggy asked.

Janice sat next to Iggy holding his hand. "He didn't get much sleep last night, Addy. They didn't realize how much pain medicine he needed. Apparently he built up quite a tolerance while taking narcotics for sports injuries over the years."

Wolfe pulled back the sheet and began to change the dressing on Iggy's right knee. Intern rounds consisted of gathering any x-rays and labs, and checking wounds for infection, before the real orthopedists arrived. "Let's see the incision," he said, pulling on the paper-like adhesive tape to remove several blood-soaked layers of gauze 4 x 4 bandages. "Didn't drain much. No pus. Does it still hurt?" Iggy now sported two parallel six inch incisions, slightly tilted off the vertical on the medial side of his knee. "Jesus. Those are long incisions. What did they do?"

"Well, thanks to my buddy, Addison Wolfe, MD and moron, they totally removed the medial meniscus. They took a good look at the ACL. It's totally destroyed."

"Did they fix it?"

"Can't, so they say." Iggy looked at the ceiling. "There are some experimental surgeries now. Implanted nylon straps, animal grafts, cadaver grafts, whatever. But, unless you are Bert Jones and play quarterback for the Colts, or have a lot of money, no one is going to do that to a human, yet. They said maybe in ten years."

"Career's really over," Janice said. "That's what bothers him the most."

"No good news at all?" Wolfe asked.

"They told him to keep his quads strong and he could do whatever he wanted, if he wore a knee brace. They're going to fit him for that tomorrow. He'll likely have arthritis in the knee sooner than later."

Iggy brightened a little. "Actually, Addy, I have to thank you. The meniscus tear was initially small. Every time I'd cut, it got bigger. That's what caused the pain and swelling, like at the beach. At least that's over. Can't do anything about the ACL. And that's not your fault." He smiled briefly. "At least Figueroa can't throw me out of the residency because of my knee without thinking I might sue the hospital. That's a win."

"One of the nurses said he visited you in the recovery room," Wolfe said.

Iggy blushed. "Jesus. I forgot about that. Hope I didn't say anything stupid coming out of anesthesia."

"You were fine with him," Janice said. She had stayed with him the whole time. "You did upset the hematologist, though."

"He deserved it," Iggy explained. "Asshole came into recovery and started harassing me because he didn't like the way I worked up a patient with anemia before surgery. Good thing he isn't one of my attendings."

"I think the orthopedic attendings liked what you said to him," Wolfe said. "Yesterday, I heard them talking about how you had taken him down a peg. They said you offered to take him outside and put on the boxing gloves. Don't do it again, though, if you see him. He was a Golden Gloves boxer in college."

"Thanks for the warning," Iggy said. Under the influence of his pain medication, his head sagged into the pillow and he fell asleep.

"Tough night," Janice said.

Wolfe redressed the incisions, pulled the sheet up, and left quietly.

A week later, Wolfe found Iggy in the apartment wearing gym shorts. The long leg splint he had been instructed to wear leaned against the kitchen table. "Come with me," Iggy said, standing.

"You going to put that on?" Wolfe asked, pointing to the splint.

"Nah. No cane either."

The two friends walked in silence to the beach, about 400 yards across A1A. "Watch this," Iggy said. He started to jog gingerly on the hard packed sand.

"You sure you should be doing that?" Wolfe asked. "Doesn't it hurt?"

"All pain, like all bleeding, stops eventually." Iggy said. "And the surgeon said I could do what ever I could tolerate."

"Going back to work tomorrow?"

"Yep."

Chapter 14

Wolfe's last evening on orthopedics he spent in the emergency room. The Jacksonville Chapter of the Knife and Gun Club didn't usually hold celebrations on Sundays, but this Sunday coincided with Halloween. The local population came to the ER in droves: gunshot wounds, stabbings, poisoning, bar fights, people who wanted their kids' candy x-rayed for needles and razor blades. Wolfe could only thank the ER gods that a full moon was still a week away. Not that he believed that myth, but everyone who worked in the ER did. Their belief just slowed them down. They spent more time comparing the patient load to previous full moons than working. Knowing he would be on the Ob-gyn service for the next full moon calmed him somewhat.

Pulling a rolling stool next to one of the stretchers in the ER Trauma wing, he sat in front of a young man who had shattered his ankle jumping from a second story window when his girlfriend's father returned home unexpectedly. Wolfe held the acetate of the x-ray up to the fluorescent lights, not wanting to take the time to walk to the x-ray view box. The comminuted fracture appeared as large splinters inside the swollen leg. The senior resident had already scheduled the patient for surgery in the morning. He told Wolfe to make the patient comfortable before leaving for the night. Latesha Marks, the intern on call for orthopedics that evening, had a full slate of pre-op physical exams awaiting her on the ward. In an effort to lessen her work load,

Wolfe decided to splint the ankle, do the physical, and order the necessary labs for Latesha. For that reason, he was still in the ER when an orderly pushed another patient into the trauma room in a wheel chair.

"GSW to left thigh," the orderly announced, locking the wheels of the wheelchair. He then turned, shoes squeaking on the recently waxed terrazzo floor, and departed the room. By himself, Wolfe continued to work on splinting the ankle fracture. No free hands were available to help. Having been in ER Trauma for a month, he had learned to do everything by himself and not to expect help when the staff could not keep up with the flow. He rolled his patient onto his stomach, gently supporting the shattered leg to diminish the patient's pain. Slipping the stockinet over the leg, he wrapped it in cotton batting, to protect the skin from the plaster. The patient maintained his ankle in the air by keeping his knee bent. Wolfe soaked a thick collection of plaster strips in a bucket of water and laid them along the back of the patient's leg from knee to toes. He wrapped the leg tightly with an ace wrap. Gently, he straightened the leg, laying it on the stretcher, toes over the end.

"That will get warm," he told the patient. "Don't move. Keep your toes at ninety degrees. They should feel like they are pointed at your knee. The plaster will get hard in about ten minutes. Then I'll loosen the ace wraps. Tell me if it gets too tight or too hot." Wolfe looked at his new watch. Red, LED numerals stared back at him. He pressed a button on the side and the stopwatch function started at 0:00. The numbers flashed: 0:00, 0:01, 0:02....

The man in the wheelchair said, "Hey doc, how long until I see someone," when he realized Wolfe stood idly waiting for the plaster to harden.

Turning to face the man, Wolfe observed blood dripping from the wheelchair onto the terrazzo floor, pooling in a dark red puddle. Slowly, the pool of blood enlarged, a dark red amoeba swallowing the polished marble chips in the floor. "What happened to you?" he asked the man.

"Shot in the leg."

"Who did it?" Wolfe asked, knowing the answer ahead of time. It was always, *a friend*.

"A friend."

"No doubt," Wolfe replied, casually searching the trauma room for a nurse or EMT to attend the man. To make conversation, Wolfe asked, "What did he shoot you with?"

"This," the patient said. He leaned forward and reached under his left buttock with his left hand. From under him he pulled the largest, chrome-plated, .45 caliber pistol Wolfe had ever seen.

"Whoa," Wolfe said, eying the weapon. "Mind if I take that?"

"No problem, man," the patient said. "I don't think it's loaded."

Once Wolfe had the gun in hand, he released the clip into his other hand and checked the chamber. He had had a brief introduction to the weapon in the navy. After assuring himself it was not loaded and the safety was on, he called quietly to the unit clerk, "Unloaded weapon. Get security." He held the weapon above his head, high in the air, by the barrel, waiting for the rapid, loud footsteps of the ER security guard.

"May I have that," the obese rent-a-cop asked when he arrived.

"By all means," Wolfe said. He handed the weapon handle first to the guard, and then looked at his watch. Speaking to the man with the thigh wound, he said, "I think you'll get some attention now." Turning to his original patient, Wolfe rapped the plaster splint with his knuckles. The sound he produced sounded like someone knocking on the door. The ten minutes had flown. "Knock, knock," he said.

"Who's there?" the patient asked. The pain medication had begun to take effect.

"Atlas. Feel that?" Wolfe asked after loosening the ace wrap around the splint. He checked for pulses and sensation, and then re-wrapped the leg more loosely.

"Ouch! Yeah, I feel that. Atlas who?"

"Atlas, I can go home," Wolfe said. "Dr. Latesha Marks will take care of you on the floor tonight. Your surgery will be in the morning."

"Ooh, bad joke. Thanks, Doc."

"Don't mention it. Good night." Wolfe went to the floor and collected his books, papers, and jacket. He got in his car and drove back to the apartment, arriving about the same time as his roommates and some friends returned from Trick or Treating. He went to bed exhausted; he never said one word to any of them.

***

Wolfe had not looked forward to the month on Ob-gyn. If there were two things he hated, they were dealing with screaming women or trying to comfort crying children. Ob-gyn meant both. True to University Hospital standards, he saw a delivery, and then did one. The attending physicians were available during the day, with the junior or senior, 3rd or 4th year, residents available during the day and at night. There were two clinics, in addition to the patients on two wards and the occasional ER patient. Obstetric clinic dealt with pregnancies and admitted to the OB maternity ward; Gynecology clinic dealt with gynecological disease and admitted to the GYN ward.

Wolfe gradually learned about sexually transmitted diseases, their prognoses, and their treatment. Gynecological diseases came in many other forms, also. He spent hours standing in one operating room or another, freezing his ass off in the overly air conditioned environment while the surgeons worked up a sweat wearing heavy gowns. They removed tumors, explored abdomens, and did other procedures on women who sometimes weighed less than a hundred pounds to occasionally more than the anesthesiologist and surgeon combined.

Obstetric clinic had its own challenges. Just wearing the bone conduction stethoscope that fitted over his forehead, made Wolfe self-conscious. He rarely heard the fetal heart beats the nurses routinely documented, although he spent hours trying. Occasionally he could tell which direction a fetus lay, but that talent took more than a month to develop, also. He was pretty good with a tape measure, though, and could tell how big around a patient was at her naval, and if that matched her supposed delivery date.

Unable to correlate a teenager's dates with her size, he stopped the third year resident in the hall. “She's only 32 weeks along, but big enough to have delivered already. What does that mean?” Wolfe asked the Ob-gyn resident.

“It means she just bought herself an ultrasound,” Myra Johnston said. “Delivery dates are guesses. She's probably farther along than we think, or there is a rare chance of some pathology, something that might increase the size of the fetus, like diabetes. Write the order; I'll see it gets done. You have a new admission to work up in the ER.”

Wolfe told the unwed mother-to-be and her aunt that she would need to stay for the test. When both women began to cry, he assured them that the test was just a formality, that maybe her pregnancy would be over sooner than they had planned. “Be nice to finish early, right?” They both nodded.

Back in the ER, Wolfe found his next gynecology/oncology patient on a stretcher in the ER ICU. She had been seen initially in Primary Care by Samantha Joiner, who stood next to the woman. “Sam,” Wolfe exclaimed. “Didn't expect to see you here.” He hadn't seen her since her tiff with Nick Robinson.

"All rotating interns have to work in Primary Care," she said, brushing her blonde, tightly curled hair backward with the back of her left hand. "Mrs. Walsh, here, has a left breast mass." She nodded toward the black woman with very short white curly hair. "I need to show Dr. Wolfe your mass, Mazie. Okay?"

The black woman lay in a stretcher with the head elevated so she sat almost upright. The right side rail was up and she leaned on that with her right elbow, chin in hand, lips pushed together in the characteristic fashion of someone who had no teeth. She nodded, not looking at either Wolfe or Joiner. To Wolfe, Joiner said, "Ten people must have seen it, already." Sam pulled the sheet down and then pulled the hospital gown forward. The patient did not have her arm through the short sleeve because the gown had been up and down all day. Sam also removed a large gauze bandage that lay across the breast.

Wolfe was not prepared for the sight that greeted him. A large mass enveloped the entire lateral, upper left breast. It looked like a large bag of worms, except the surface had numerous sores in various stages of healing or decomposition. Pus and blood filled innumerable pockets within the mass. The fetid smell burnt his nostrils. "How long?" Wolfe choked.

"At least two years," Sam answered. "No health insurance or money. I ordered some blood work and x-rays, but they haven't been done yet. I didn't want her stuck twice. Got to go back to PC." She turned toward the patient. "Mazie, Addy is good people. He'll take care of you." Sam left them alone.

Mazie Walsh answered all of Wolfe's questions with, "Yep, nope," or "Don't know." Wolfe did a complete physical on her while waiting for the hospital transportation orderly to get her out of the ER. When the orderly arrived to take her to radiology and then the floor, she said nothing to Wolfe, although he said, "See you in a little bit."

About to leave the ER ICU, Wolfe noticed a large group of physicians and staff standing around the second code stretcher. They were conspicuous for their silence. Obviously, no resuscitation took place. Having thought to go to Primary Care and talk with Sam, he sauntered over to the bed. The emergency residents stood with eyes on the floor but looked up as Wolfe approached. ER residents, Bob Sandoval and Art Lynch, recognized Wolfe. Sandoval, the senior resident, held a finger to his lips while looking at Wolfe.

Wolfe caught the tail end of the advice being given to the patient who lay on the stretcher. Dr. Pierre Thibodeaux, spoke in his

French Canadian accented English. The attending neurosurgeon leaned over the stretcher, face close to the patient. An imposing man, well over six feet tall, with a curly full black beard and frontal balding, he spoke quietly and earnestly to the young man. “Your spinal cord has been severed. When your forehead hit the bottom of the pool, your neck broke; the bones sliced through the cord. I can't fix that. No one on Earth can fix it, my friend. The most I can offer you is being a quadriplegic the rest of your life. I am willing to take you to surgery and stabilize your neck. You will spend the rest of you life on a respirator, a machine that puts oxygen in your lungs, kind of like this tech is doing now. Blink twice if you understand.”

Neck encased in a hard cervical collar, with an endotracheal tube in his throat, the patient could not speak. Had his vocal cords been free to move, being paralyzed from the neck down and powerless to move his diaphragm, he was incapable of moving air through them. Barry Johnson, a pulmonary technician, squeezed the ambubag rhythmically supplying air to the patient. After a brief hesitation, the patient on the stretcher blinked twice, exaggerating the eyes closed portion of the blinks. “Now, blink twice if you want to be on a respirator the rest of your life. Blink once if you would prefer to die in the next couple minutes.” The young man could not have been more than twenty-five years-old. Wolfe didn't think anyone that young would choose to die; he certainly would not have. *Wasn't it a doctor's obligation to save every life? A patient would maintain hope against all odds, wouldn't he?* The patient blinked once, holding his eyes closed longer than usual. He opened his eyes and stared at the neurosurgeon. “Are you sure?” the attending asked. “Blink once for yes, twice for no.”

Once again, the patient blinked. This time he blinked only once.

“Stop bagging him,” Dr. Thibodeaux ordered the respiratory technician.

“No,” Johnson said.

Sandoval placed both hands over the technician's. He attempted to take the ambubag from the man. “I'll do this, Barry,” he said quietly to the technician. Both men continued to squeeze the bag rhythmically. “You can go back to pulmonary clinic. We'll beep you if we need you.”

Defeated, Barry let his hands fall from the bag. He turned and walked toward the elevators, not looking back. When he had turned the corner in the hallway and could no longer be seen, Sandoval stopped squeezing the bag. No one moved. No one breathed. The patient's eyelids widened, and then gradually closed. Eventually the cardiac monitor ran through a dozen arrhythmias, then flatlined. “Time of death: 3:37 p.m.,” Sandoval said.

Forgetting about talking to Samantha, Wolfe walked numbly to the hallway. The respiratory technician stood facing the bank of elevators. “That son of a bitch. *My friend*?” he repeated to himself, almost inaudibly. “That son of a bitch. *My friend*?”

Chapter 15

At least Wolfe had not been required to deliver the bad news to Barbie Nichols, the unmarried, sixteen-year-old, near-term pregnant girl. The fetus she carried had caused the increase in girth that Wolfe had found on physical exam. Normally, the fetus swallowed some of the amniotic fluid, and processed it, decreasing the amount in the uterus. Her child could not swallow. Her child had no brain. Strictly speaking, it had a small brain; it was anencephalic. It had a midbrain, but no cerebellar lobes. After delivery, its life expectancy would be measured in minutes.

"I want you to deliver my baby," Nichols begged Wolfe on her next clinic visit. "You are so much nicer than the other doctors."

Knowing his kindness had really been only his insecurity, Wolfe tried to remain poker faced. Less intimidating to patients because he was less knowledgeable than the Ob-gyn residents, Wolfe was less inclined to present the bluster they did. He had limited experience delivering normal babies; he did not know what would be expected of him when delivering an abnormal child. "I'm only an intern," he said. "I don't know if they would let me...."

"They said you could if you agreed," Nichols's aunt said quietly, holding Wolfe's hand. "It would mean a lot to us. Help the child out," she said. Wolfe nodded, knowing she meant her niece, not the fetus.

The senior resident managed the induction of labor with

intravenous medication. Wolfe had only to catch the child as he squirted from his mother's vagina; no episiotomy required. He was smaller than Wolfe expected. Holding the child head down in his left arm, with fingers around his neck, he gently cleared the nostrils and mouth with the bulb syringe. The flattened sunken skull on the baby ended at the eyebrows. A full head of hair masked the deformity somewhat. The nurse tied off and cut the umbilical cord. Wiping the baby's face, he handed him to the nurse, who quickly cleansed him more thoroughly and laid him in his mother's arms. The sixteen-year-old cradled the child, “My baby,” she cooed, “my poor baby.”

The infant gurgled, took a single breath, and died in his mother's arms. “I am so, so sorry,” Wolfe told the teenager, watching the tears roll down her cheeks. He left the delivery room when the nurses took charge of the mother and infant.

Nichols's aunt stopped him in the waiting room. “It’s better this way,” she said. “Maybe Barbie will get more serious about school after this experience.” Wolfe nodded, wiping moisture from his eyes.

***

“Jesus, this will be a cluster fuck,” said an attending physician Wolfe did not recognize, when Wolfe joined the group with the laboratory reports he had been sent to collect. The small group of Ob-gyn physicians stood outside the ward looking over charts before entering.

“What?” asked a junior resident.

The attending flipped through the patient's chart. “The next patient has had no prenatal care. Admitted from the ER today. She's 35 weeks, with twins. Looks like she'll deliver tonight or early in the morning. The newborns will be premature, of course. Do you know why, Wolfe?”

Something in his reading had alluded to twins almost always arriving early, and presenting smaller and immaturely. They frequently needed extra support, sometimes resuscitation and maintenance in incubators for weeks. He tried to articulate those thoughts to the attending.

“Close enough,” the attending physician said, “for a rotating intern. Look, Jim,” he said to the senior resident, “you'll have to find two portable incubators and an ambulance crew to take these kids and the mother to Gainesville tonight if she delivers.” The resident nodded, making notes on white 3 x 5 index cards. “A junior or senior resident will have to go in the ambulance. And you might as well let pediatrics know, because one of them will have to go, too. Start working on that as soon as we finish rounds."

"Why Gainesville?" Wolfe asked.

The resident answered. "They have the closest neonatal intensive care unit for indigent patients."

"Okay," the attending said, "let's make rounds." He turned and pushed on the door to the ward.

Innocently, Wolfe said, "Too bad she didn't drive herself there, but I guess she doesn't have a car."

Stunned, the attending stopped suddenly in mid-stride. The resident walked into him. "Sorry," he said.

"Wolfe," the attending exclaimed, "that's brilliant. We should have at least three hours before she delivers. Jim, round up an ambulance. Do it now, and notify Gainesville they have an incoming patient who might deliver on their doorstep. There's no better incubator than the mother's womb, Wolfe. Great idea."

Blushing, Wolfe said nothing. The attending continued. "Of course, you'll have to ride along. You did want to be an astronaut, didn't you? Think of this as a mission." *Who told these guys about NASA?* Wolfe asked himself. *And why do they all equate ambulance rides with trips into outer space?*

"You have a watch with a second hand?" the attending asked Wolfe. Wolfe held up the new LED watch and showed him the stop watch function. "Good. You should have no trouble timing the contractions. I don't expect her to deliver, but she might. We'll give you two delivery kits and we'll heat up some blankets in the autoclave. Remember, if she does deliver, you need to keep the babies warm."

A half hour later, Wolfe found himself in the dark, in the back of an ambulance rolling north on I-95 at 55 mph, the national speed limit following the Arab oil boycott. In addition to Wolfe, the patient, and all the gear sent by the obstetrics department, an EMT sat in the second jump seat. Through the windows, Wolfe watched the tall buildings in downtown Jacksonville roll by, illuminated by the flashing lights of the ambulance. The doctors had decided that using the siren on the ambulance would affect the three patients, mother and two fetuses, more than other motorists. It remained silent.

Holding his hand the 32 year-old black woman moaned. "Mrs. White," Wolfe said, "another contraction?" She nodded silently. Wolfe looked at his watch. *Nine minutes apart. Piece of cake,* he thought.

When the ambulance left Jacksonville behind after taking the ramp to I-10 West, the driver shouted that he would increase his speed to 65 or 70 miles per hour. Wolfe nodded. The road noise increased measurably with the increase in speed, rendering them essentially deaf. The contractions increased in rapidity, also. By the time the driver reached US 301 and turned south toward Gainesville, the contractions were 4 minutes apart. Wolfe had one hand under the sheet on the patient's abdomen. To him the contractions seemed more intense. He reset the stopwatch with each contraction. White began to breathe like *The Little Engine Who Could* with each contraction. Her puffing increased Wolfe's anxiety, although he tried not to show it.

The ambulance slowed to 60 miles per hour through Waldo, "Most famous speed trap in Florida," the second ambulance attendant shouted to Wolfe. "Go 1 mph over the limit here and you will get a ticket. Unless, of course, you are in an ambulance with the lights on." They saw no evidence of the radar or any police cars. The van veered to the west onto State Route 24 toward Gainesville.

When they entered the Gainesville town limits, the driver shouted at the second EMT. "Okay, where's the hospital?"

"I thought you knew," the man in the jump seat said. "Doc, do you know?"

Wolfe had never been to Gainesville, much less Shands Hospital. White's grip on his hand tightened. The next contraction followed the previous one by only two minutes. As calmly as he could, Wolfe suggested. "Use the radio."

"We're on a different frequency," the EMT said, "and too far to contact Jacksonville for directions."

Shaking his head, Wolfe said, "Next police car you see, flash your headlights to get his attention and ask for directions." The ambulance slowed to the speed limit as the driver searched for a police car.

"Never one around when you need a policeman," White said, gritting her teeth and puffing through the next contraction, 90 seconds after the previous.

"Got one," the driver said. Wolfe looked up and saw the ambulance's high beams flash intermittently. Pulling next to the police car, the driver relayed the need for directions. The police officer told the driver to follow him. Racing ahead, the officer turned on his siren. Wolfe wasn't sure if the siren had any effect on White, but by the time they pulled into the ER driveway at Shands Hospital on Archer Road, the contractions were down to 45 seconds apart.

Fortunately, the neonatal ICU nurses waited inside the automatic doors. The stretcher carrying White disappeared into the bowels of the huge hospital with only a wave of her hand on top of an elevated arm. Wolfe climbed back into the ambulance. "Don't you guys carry maps?" he asked.

By the time they returned to Jacksonville, he had formulated a plan to have ambulance maps made up of plastic cue cards that the driver flipped over at every intersection where the ambulance made a turn, like in the automobile touring races held in Europe or flight demonstrations at air shows. There would be a map for every hospital in the state, and a collection each for every ambulance. *I'll be rich*, he thought. The idea disappeared by morning, after three deliveries and the admission of a rape patient from the ER.

Chapter 16

Janice and Iggy invited as many of the new interns as they could to Thanksgiving dinner at the apartment on the 25th. Few of the interns were married. Fewer were off that day. None were able to go to their home towns. Several made it to the apartment, if not for the whole celebration, at least part of it. Wolfe arrived in the early evening to find Iggy, Janice, Samantha Joiner, and Nick Robinson seated around the table in the kitchen. He dropped his coat on his bed and joined them, sitting next to Nick.

"Happy SHIT day," Nick said.

"So Happy It's Thursday?" Wolfe asked.

"No," Sam explained. "It's Nick's last day in Jacksonville."

Wolfe had seen Nick's Fiat Spider and boat parked on the road in front of the apartment and wondered why Nick would be boating in the chilly waters this time of the year.

"What do you mean?" Wolfe asked.

"I've been fired by that asshole, Figueroa," Robinson said.

"Why? How? Can he do that?" Wolfe asked.

"Can and did. Got my walking papers from Dr. Singhal this morning," Nick said, not looking Wolfe in the eyes, but allowing his eyes to roam around the apartment. "Dr. Figueroa and the administration don't think I'm a good fit here."

"Jesus," Wolfe said. "You're one of the smartest interns we

have. Singhal couldn't have agreed with Fig. What happened?"

"Singhal says Figueroa has too much political clout. He can't reverse the decision, and Chancellor Scoggins and the board either agree with everything he says, or are afraid of him for some reason."

"Maybe he knows where some skeletons are buried," Wolfe suggested. "What got you canned, Nick? We don't want to make the same mistake."

"Well, all of you are smarter than he is, so you'll have to watch how you address him. He has a severe inferiority complex. The final insult, though, as Figueroa put it, was the suggestion campaign. I suggested they cut off the hot water in all the patient and visitor bathrooms. As any surgeon will tell you, you can't get the water hot enough to kill bacteria and not burn your hands. Mechanical scrubbing is more important. Surgeons don't use hot water, destroys their skin if they do."

Wolfe nodded. "Well, yeah, we all learned that in medical school. Why was that a problem?"

"The jerks promised a $100 for the best suggestions," Samantha said. "Then they refused to pay him. That suggestion alone will probably save them thousands of dollars a year."

"I still don't understand how that led to your dismissal," Wolfe said.

"The suggestion didn't," Robinson admitted. "My response to them refusing to pay me did. They offered me a check for $25, saying they couldn't afford to pay the $100 they had promised. I tore the check in half and sent it back. Wrote a note that their stinginess wouldn't affect me, but it certainly would affect the staff with as little as they were paid. And, I told them to shove the check up their asses."

"But the real reason Figueroa cut him loose was that Nick kept making him look bad at M&M conferences," Iggy said. "He couldn't say that, though."

"That bastard," Wolfe said. "What are you going to do, Nick?"

"I took a leave of absence from the radiology residency for a year in order to do this internship. If I did well, I was going to continue in the ER residency. Looks like I'll be forced to go back to California and surf and sail for six months. I need a vacation."

"We all do," Sam said.

A knock sounded at the door. Iggy got up and answered it. Justin Murcheson, the gay ER intern, stepped inside the apartment. "Oh, Janice, that smells so good," he said. "I hope you saved some for me."

He shook hands all around the table. “Happy Thanksgiving, everyone,” he said. Noting the gloom, he added, “Sorry to be the bearer of glad tidings. What's going on?”

After he had been informed, he nodded. “Sorry, Nick. We'll miss you.”

Nick held up a glass for a toast, “To Figueroa. May he get a large tube of Anusol HC for Christmas.”

“Waste of time,” Justin said. “I realize what you are saying is he is an asshole, but Figueroa is a surgeon. Anusol HC is used for hemorrhoids, but surgeons don't have hemorrhoids. As we all know, they are all perfect assholes.”

Nick glared at Justin. “Know what they call a man with a one inch penis?”

“What?” asked Sam

“Just-in,” Nick laughed. Justin glowered intently in return and then smiled, understanding Nick's state of mind.

“Don't feel too upset, Nick,” Justin said. “Everyone knows Figueroa is not much of a physician. They gave him this job to keep him away from the patients.”

“What do you mean?” Iggy asked, reaching for his beer.

“When he was a surgery intern here, he scheduled a man with a very large sebaceous cyst on his chest for exploratory chest surgery. He was convinced it was a cancerous mass. As a senior resident on the thoracic surgery rotation, he biopsied a spleen. He was supposed to be closing the patient at the end of a case. The attending physicians usually leave that to the senior residents. The attending left the operating room. Figueroa saw what he thought was a blue mass poking through the diaphragm. The patient almost bled to death before they could stop the bleeding.”

“No,” Sam said. “No attending is stupid enough to leave that moron with an open surgical patient. Why would they leave him alone?”

“He's so arrogant he sounds smart,” Murcheson said. “As a surgery attending, he sent home an appendicitis one of the pediatric interns had found. The kid had classic pain, but no fever. Also, in Figueroa's favor, he had a normal white count.”

“A lot of appendicitises do,” Iggy said. “My surgical attending physician says that if half of your surgical appendix specimens aren't normal, then you are missing some hot appendices. Until we get one of Nick's MRIs in every hospital, there is no way to see inflamed or infected soft tissue inside the body. It's all guess work.”

"The intern had the last laugh, kind of," Murcheson said. "The kid's parents brought him back about twelve hours later, throwing up. White count was up then, still no fever. Another surgical attending took the boy to the OR. Inside his belly they found a normal looking appendix. But the surgeon couldn't believe it, so he cut it open. Inside the appendix they found a broken half toothpick poking into the walls of the appendix. The surgeon put the appendix in a bottle of formalin and sent it to the pathology lab. On its way to the lab, the toothpick floated out of the appendix. The pathologist apparently decanted the toothpick along with the formalin. He reported the appendix as normal. Figueroa maintains to this day that the kid had the stomach flu."

Everyone laughed. Noticing Janice had not participated in the conversation and not wanting to exclude her, Justin asked, "So, Janice, what do you think?"

She stood and started collecting dishes, "Not much, not often, and never deeply. Get you something to drink while I'm up, Justin?"

"I'd like some 2% milk if you have it," Justin said. "Otherwise, I'll take a glass of water."

"Ooh, yuck," Iggy said. "We don't have any 2% milk. I can't stand the stuff."

"Water then, thanks," Justin told Janice.

"No, that's fine, Justin," Janice said. "We have some 2% milk. And don't listen to Iggy, he's been drinking 2% for the last month. He didn't know it, though. I mixed larger and larger amounts of it with his real milk. He never noticed. I have used the same old whole milk carton for weeks."

"You did what?" Iggy asked. "Get me a glass of milk, too," he ordered Janice. Glass in hand, he gulped down the milk. "No. That's real milk," he said.

Justin downed his more slowly. "Hate to disagree with you, Iggy, but that's 2%."

Holding a carton of 2% milk in her hand, Janice asked, "More, Iggy?" He frowned. Everyone else laughed. There was another knock at the door.

"I'll get it," Nick said. "I've got some more good-byes to say." He opened the door to Latesha Marks and bade her and the group good-bye.

Letting herself in, Latesha closed the door. She dropped her coat on the couch with the others and took Nick's seat next to Sam. "Hey, everyone. Iggy, how's the knee?"

Iggy pointed to the cane leaning against the wall in the corner. "Don't use that any more," he said. "Don't tell anyone, but I can jog a mile, when I am not exhausted."

Latersha sucked in a deep breath through her nose, vacuuming in the turkey aroma. "This looks delicious, Janice. Sorry, I'm late," she said, licking her lips in anticipation.

"Take as much as you want, Latesha," Janice said. "Iggy doesn't like leftovers." She passed the mashed potatoes to Marks.

The need to report the latest from the ER got the best of Marks. "You guys aren't going to believe the latest dump," she said, picking up a fork to place turkey on her plate.

Iggy tried to forget his embarrassment over the milk, "Would you like some milk, Latesha?" he asked the newcomer.

"I'm only drinking 2%, Iggy, and I know you don't like the stuff." Howls of laughter greeted her statement.

Wolfe asked, more seriously, "What hospital tried to dump an indigent patient on University this time?"

Marks took the glass of milk from Janice. "Thanks," she said. "The one down the street, "Beaches. They stuffed a sixty-year-old rape victim in the back of a police car and sent her to University. She was bleeding heavily, so the cop radioed us in the ER. He wanted know what to do. Nichols said go to the nearest hospital and have the patient stabilized, then have the ER doc call the Ob-gyn service to make the transfer."

"Sounds right," Sam said.

"Yeah," Marks said, "except the cop was still sitting in the parking lot at Beaches Hospital."

"What did he do?"

"He took her back inside Beaches ER. They packed her vagina and put in two i.v. lines. Too bad they didn't give her some blood, though," Marks explained, not bothered by the fact that she was eating during the conversation. "Six hours later they called us on Ob-gyn and requested permission to transfer. She lost so much blood that she had a heart attack. But it looks like she'll survive. Figueroa is bent out of shape. He's talking about getting Nichols canned."

"That arrogant asshole," Sam said. "We've got to do something about that guy before he destroys any more careers. Nichols likely saved that lady's life. She might have bled to death in the back of the police cruiser."

"What do we know about him that we can use against him?"

Wolfe asked. “The only thing I've heard is that he never touches a patient, relies entirely on lab results and x-rays to make diagnoses.”

“Why won't he touch a patient?” Janice asked.

“Don't know,” Wolfe said. “Maybe he thinks they’re dirty.”

“Or thinks they are beneath him,” Sam said.

“Probably thinks it's unnecessary,” Iggy said. “He's so much of an intellectual that he can make the diagnosis with history and labs or x-rays only.”

“I heard it was because he got sued for assault and battery after examining a patient,” Marks said. “Malpractice doesn't cover civil liability or unlawful acts. He eventually prevailed, but he had to pay legal fees himself and it was very expensive.”

“I don't think there is anything the interns can do to him,” Janice said. “Politically, he's out of your league. The best thing to do is avoid him if possible, and make as few mistakes as possible. Nick brought on his dismissal by being outspoken. You need to steer clear of that.”

Grumbling, the interns agreed. Over the next several hours, they dispersed, after watching the Detroit Lions beat the inept Buffalo Bills 27-14, despite O.J. Simpson's record-setting 273 yards for the Bills. “They'd fix his ACL if he tore it,” Iggy said about O.J.

Samantha and Wolfe retired to his room, when Janice and Iggy went to theirs. “You going to stay over?” Wolfe asked, dropping his car keys and wallet next to the portable typewriter on the bedside stand.

“Unless you've forgotten how,” she said. “What’s the typewriter for?”

“Never forget how,” Wolfe said. “It's like riding a biped.” He crawled onto the bed lying next to her, admiring her body. “I’ve started on the paper Figueroa wants each of us to write. Show you later what I have so far.”

Sam lay with her head on Wolfe’s chest, hand stroking the short hair on his head. “You certainly gave Justin a hard time, tonight. Are you homophobic?” she asked.

Wolfe thought for a long time. “Not a *hard* time, a *difficult* time. I’m going to give you the *hard* time. I don’t fear homosexuals, so in that sense no. Justin is bright, has a good sense of humor, works hard, is honest, I guess all the things you want in a friend.”

“You sound like a racist saying, ‘Some of my best friends are black.’”

“Probably,” Wolfe agreed, “but what I am trying to say is I like

Justin for his intellect. I just have a difficult time with the penis in the mouth bit. Turns me off; hard to swallow, if you want a pun."

"Hmmm," Sam hummed. "Bet you won't have a problem if I don't have any qualms with that." She laughed and began pulling the blanket and sheets back on the bed. "Do you have a condom? Come on, lover boy" she said, "you can't start a fire rubbing just one stick together."

Wolfe pulled a latex glove out of the pocket of the white coat hanging on the corner post of his bed. He brandished it in her direction. "I learned you could use this as a condom in medical school."

"Yeah?," Sam said. " Does Wolfie fit in the thumb or pinkie finger?"

"Yeah," Wolfe grinned, ignoring the remark. "A friend of mine had his car broken into in the parking deck, lost a side window. So, after that he left it unlocked. Later he found a bunch of used condoms and latex gloves that had been used as condoms in his back seat."

"Look in my purse," Sam said. "I carry a couple spares for emergencies."

Chapter 17

"I've never felt anything like that," Wolfe said to the obstetric nurse. He had his arm, seemingly up to his elbow inside a large black woman's vagina. His hand rested on the dilated cervix of her pregnant uterus, through which he could feel a pulsating mass. "You've been doing this for twenty years. Have an idea?"

Talking quietly and with an assured tone, she shook her head, no, while saying, "Happens all the time, doc. That's the umbilical cord. It's trying to come through first. You just have to keep pushing the baby up, into the uterus, so his head can't squeeze the cord against the pelvis and cut off the blood supply."

"Ooh!" the mother-to-be screamed and started to pant. "Oh! Oh! Oh!"

"Breathe. Slowly. Puff. Concentrate," the nurse said to the patient.

Wolfe spread his fingers, pushing the fetus's skull and body upward and back into the woman's uterus. The umbilical cord ran between his spread index and middle fingers. The woman's contraction threatened to push the baby, the cord, and Wolfe out. She was a big woman, in excess of two hundred fifty pounds, and a good bit of that weight was muscle.

"Call Rivers," Wolfe said. "Tell him the senior resident is delivering like a pizza delivery boy tonight and we need to do a C-section. Since I'm already in here, I'll maintain the baby's position. You guys will have to schedule the OR, get the intravenous started, find the pediatric resident, etc."

Ten minutes later Wolfe walked alongside the rolling hospital bed, hand in the woman's vagina. The obstetric nurse steered the bed. The transport orderly supplied the muscle power to move it along. The hospital bed weighed four times what a stretcher weighed, but they had decided it was too risky to transfer the mother and fetus to a stretcher. Wolfe turned his head to say something to the nurse. As he did the glass intravenous bottle flew by his face, erasing the thought. The i.v. pole had caught on the door jamb, bent back about two feet and then snapped forward as the bed passed through the door to the OR. The bottle missed Wolfe by inches. It shattered when it hit the floor in the operating room.

"Shit!" Wolfe, the nurse, and the anesthesiologist who waited for them in the OR all said in unison.

"Sorry," the orderly said. "Didn't have time to warn you. We were moving too fast."

"Get something to clean that up with," the anesthesiologist said. "Can't have broken glass on the floor while we operate." Turning, the orderly went in search of a broom and dustpan. After replacing the intravenous bottle with another, the nurse pumped the hospital bed upward until it was even with the operating room table. The anesthesiologist and nurse each grabbed an end to the sheet on which the woman lay. They had her inch her way across the bed to the OR table, while pulling the sheet in the same direction. Wolfe managed to crawl backwards over the operating room table and help slide the woman from the bed to the table, all the while maintaining the fetus above the umbilical cord. The pulsations continued suggesting the head had not compressed the cord and blood still flowed to the fetus, although that was not guaranteed. The mother might still have maintained a pulse in the cord where Wolfe could feel it, but the fetus might have compressed it beyond Wolfe's reach.

Quickly, the anesthesiologist reviewed the patient's chart. Between contractions, he asked her several questions about medications and allergies. He then induced anesthesia. The force of her contractions eased immediately. "Do you need me to relieve you?" the nurse asked.

Wolfe shook his head. "I'm good, now that she's asleep. How long until Rivers gets here?" On cue, the OR door banged open and

Rivers and the orderly entered the room.

"I'm here," he said. "Actually, Dr. Thigpen and I are both here." He referred to another part-time attending physician, his partner in private practice. He smiled. "The pediatric resident is on his way. You know, Addy, you ruined a perfectly nice cocktail party."

"Sorry," Wolfe said. "Just didn't want to be addressing Dr. Figueroa in M&M conference next week."

The orderly said, "I think I got most of it," referring to the broken glass. He mopped up the i.v. solution with antiseptic liquid and several sterile towels, also picking up more tiny glass fragments.

"Okay. Get out of here. Thanks," the anesthesiologist said.

Wolfe had to stay in the OR until Rivers and Thigpen removed the child through the Cesarian incision. That meant he had to be draped like furniture with a sterile drape. Given the usual chill maintained in the OR, Wolfe did not complain about the drape; it kept him warmer than usual. His hand was beginning to cramp when he felt the child's head move quickly away from his fingertips.

"Looks like a healthy boy," Rivers said. "Cord was around his neck as well as prolapsed. Good job, Addison." Wolfe heard the child wail. *He sounded healthy, too,* Wolfe thought. "Addison," Rivers continued, "back out of the drape, but don't touch anything. You aren't sterile. I'd invite you to watch the rest of the procedure, but it's crowded in here." He pointed to Dr. Thigpen, the nurse, and the senior pediatric resident. "Go give the obstetric resident a hand."

"My pleasure," Wolfe said.

Chapter 18

Wednesday, the first day of December, as on the first work day of every month, Brenda Jackson ignored the interns seated in the hallway. She typed steadily at her desk. Either she was a very good typist, or she faked it well. Wolfe thought at times that the IBM Selectric buzzed like a chain saw or machine gun. The steady drone of the typewriter had almost lulled him to sleep when she called his name.

Well drilled in the proper procedure during the first four evaluations, Wolfe picked up the folder with his name on it and strode into Figueroa's office. He placed the manila folder on Figueroa's desk and sat rigidly in front of the Director of Medical Education.

Standing behind his desk, leaning on his hands, peering down on Wolfe, Figueroa said, “Well?”

Confused, Wolfe asked, “Well, what, sir?”

“What do you have to say for yourself?”

“About what?” Wolfe asked, still perplexed.

Figueroa shook his head. “Dr. Wolfe, if someone had said what I said about you in your last review, I think I would at least make a comment in my own defense.”

“I don't know what you said in the review,” Wolfe said. “If you sent me a copy, I didn't receive it.”

Smiling, Figueroa nodded to the manila folder on the desk. “It's in the folder. Are you telling me you have not read it?”

Wolfe shook his head. "No one said I could look in the folder, just to bring it into your office."

Pursing his lips, Figueroa blew slowly through them. *As if he is thinking it will be a long day, or I am an idiot, or both,* Wolfe thought. "That explains your lack of response to your previous evaluations, too, I suppose. Read it now. I'll wait."

Wolfe pulled the manila folder into his lap and opened it. Inside he found large folding metal prongs holding several sheets of paper to the back cover of the folder. The first sheet had his name and demographics on it. The following sheets contained his evaluations from ER Primary Care, ER Trauma, Pediatrics, Orthopedics, and finally, Ob-gyn. His face reddened as he quickly scanned the first four sheets. All his grades had been average, or slightly worse. On the Ob-gyn page, he had received all substandard grades. Under the remarks section, Figueroa had written, "It is likely that Dr. Wolfe will need remedial training, in order to complete his internship."

Wolfe swallowed with difficulty, his mouth having become drier than the Gobi Desert while scanning the pages. As he flipped the pages, he noticed there were other grades on the back sides, but he did not think it wise to take the time to turn over the pages and read that information, too. He assumed they were also universally negative.

"What does remedial training mean?" Wolfe asked when he could finally speak.

"We find that some interns progress more slowly than others in their training," Figueroa spoke in a haughty tone of voice. "The education committee might require you to do an extra three to six months of internship. If they allow you to stay at all. Some interns are dismissed without completing their training. If the committee feels your performance is uniformly substandard, you can be released at any time."

"You wrote this?" Wolfe asked quietly, waving the folder in the air.

"In conjunction with the attending physician on each of your rotations," Figueroa said. "So, now, do you have a comment to make?"

Wolfe thought, shaking his head. No one on the rotations had led him to believe his performance had been less than good to excellent. *Ambushed*, he thought. *Why would they not tell me I wasn't performing up to expectations?* He finally put together a response in his head, but had difficulty articulating what he wanted to say. "I wish someone had said something to me before now," he said. "I certainly do not want to have remedial training."

"Then you better improve your performance," Figueroa said. Abruptly, he waved his hand toward the door behind Wolfe. "Go, now. Get back to work. Take copies of those evaluations and work on your deficiencies."

"Yes, sir," Wolfe said, leaving.

At Jackson's desk, he asked if he could use the copier. Wordlessly, Jackson pointed with her chin to the machine sitting on the credenza near the window. The rat-a-tat-tat of the keyboard never slowed. When he finished copying both sides of each evaluation and putting the folder back together, he dropped it on her desk. By then, another intern who Wolfe did not know well exited from Figueroa's office. He also asked to use the copy machine. A wordless flip of Brenda Jackson's chin answered his request also.

Following his first day on the pathology rotation, Wolfe met with Ob-gyn attending, Dr. Rivers, in his private office on Merrill Road in Arlington. The obstetrician's busy practice kept him seeing patients until well after 7 p.m. Wolfe sat in the waiting room, reading women's magazines and alternately getting weird looks from younger women who probably wondered what a guy was doing there, and adoring looks from older women who likely thought how nice it was that a young husband would accompany his wife to the obstetrician's office.

Finally escorted back to Rivers's office, Wolfe found the physician hiding behind a desk piled high with charts. He had to stand directly in front of Rivers to see portions of the man while they talked. The whole conversation was punctuated with Rivers alternately opening charts, dictating snippets of history or exam, and then slamming charts closed and dropping them to the floor. "Sorry," he said. The palm-sized recorder clicked and snapped with each snippet of dictation. "-Starting second trimester and doing well.- I'm behind in my clinic charting and they have again threatened my privileges. -Gravida three, para two.- Did you want to do Ob-gyn after you finished your rotating internship, Addison? You did a hell of a job for us. The ride in the ambulance to Gainesville was a brilliant idea, and catching that prolapsed cord...."

"The nurse actually found that," Wolfe confessed.

"Really? She said you did. -Nulliparous, overweight black female.- And delivering the anencephalic. You had one hell of a rotation, Addison. Learned a lot, I think."

"Well, I found it. She knew what it was. Combined discovery, I guess," Wolfe said. "I really don't want to be an obstetrician, though,

Dr. Rivers. Do you know why I got such low marks on the evaluation? You say I did well. From Dr. Figueroa's report, it sounds like you would have been better off if a chimpanzee had done the rotation."

"Fig's an ass. We've had more complaints than ever from the interns this year about his heavy-handed grading and bullying," Rivers snorted. "Unfortunately, he has too much political power. I haven't been around long enough to understand his grading system, but I wouldn't worry if I were you. I think it's all done on a curve and a guy as bright as you will be at the head of the class at the end of the year."

"I don't suppose you would intercede with him for me?" Wolfe asked.

"I'd like to, and, in fact, if you declared you wanted a space in our residency, I'd fight tooth and nail for you, son. We just have limited political capital and we have to pick our battles. Sorry. -Ultrasound reveals twins.-"

"Well, thanks, anyway," Wolfe said. He did not wait to hear the remainder of the report.

In pediatrics the next day, the response by the attending physicians mirrored that of the obstetricians. "If you'd like to be a pediatrician, we'll get those evaluations rewritten. No problem. Don't worry about his grading. We don't pay much attention to it. All the interns complain bitterly about his attitude and harsh words." Wolfe had no interest in pediatrics either. His willingness to ride in the helicopter and the intubation of the child had impressed the pediatricians and the flight nurse. She had written that even though it may have appeared barbaric or inhumane, the nasal intubation probably saved the child's life because it allowed them to transport her to University Hospital. Figueroa had harped on *inhumane and barbaric*. He suggested that Wolfe might need more intern time in the ER to learn proper technique.

Dr. Singhal, Director of the Emergency Medicine Residency program, also invited Wolfe to join his residency as a second year resident. "We were impressed with your quick thinking and diagnostic skills, as well as your ability to learn new procedures promptly," Singhal said. "Your time in Primary Care showed what a hard worker you are. If you want to be an ER physician, let me know. I can't take on Figueroa now, but I will have more influence after Dr. Jacobi retires in June. I can use that if you change your mind."

"But your evaluations on the backside of this page were so much higher than Figueroa's," Wolfe moaned. "I don't understand.

You're the attending. Shouldn't your opinion carry more weight?"

"Unfortunately, our evaluations are treated as suggestions. The Director of Medical Education's evaluations are what counts. He has final say. As I told you, I may be able to reverse some of the bad marks, but only if you choose to join the Emergency Medicine Residency. I already have one hole to fill. You heard Nick Robinson left, didn't you? There may be others; lots of residents are looking for other positions in other institutions because of that man. Think on it, Addison."

"Yes, sir," Wolfe said, nodding. His head hung low as he left Dr. Singhal's office.

***

Wolfe and another intern, Philip von Hoffman, whispered while watching Chief Pathologist, Joseph Rubel, talk quietly with two senior pathology residents. The three stood at the head of the stainless steel table in the autopsy suite. The body of a young, white or Hispanic, woman lay supine on the table. Her face obscured by the flap of scalp pulled over it, race could not be determined by Wolfe. With her arms by her side, a wide-opened Y incision started near her shoulders. The arms of the incision met at the xyphoid process below the sternum and proceeded to the pubic bone in the pelvis. A transverse incision had been made above her breasts. The chest plate, heart and lungs had been removed, as had most of her organs. These sat in various stainless steel pans on the counter on the opposite side of the table. Thoracic and abdominal cavities lay opened wide and nearly empty.

Needle tracks decorated her antecubital fossae, the depressions inside her elbows. The chart revealed the patient had been a known epileptic patient on barbiturates to prevent seizures, a prostitute, and a drug user. Cause of death was suspected barbiturate overdose. She had been found two blocks from the hospital on the evening of January 20th, following record low temperatures the night before. The same weather system also produced snow fall in Pensacola and Tampa. The cold snap generated one of the rare overnight hard freezes Jacksonville experienced during the winter. Pronounced dead after resuscitation efforts at the scene and in the ER, her body had been sent to the morgue and placed in the large cooler. The resident pathologists arrived in the morning to perform an autopsy to determine the exact cause of death.

After removing her organs and sectioning them for further study, the two residents had begun to use the bone saw on the patient's skull to remove her brain for examination. With every advance of the saw, the woman's legs and arms flailed. Confused, the residents turned off the saw and called Dr. Rubel.

At the time, Rubel had been in his office explaining the pathology rotation to Wolfe and von Hoffman. They would participate in all three branches of pathology during their one month stint in the Pathology Department. They would be expected to participate in all forensic necropsies, from 1-5 per day depending on how active the knife and gun club had been the day before. Second, they would assist him in surgical pathology, collecting specimens from surgery and reviewing slides of tumors and other surgical specimens. Lastly, they would spend any time left over in clinical pathology, learning how chemistries, immunology, hematology, cultures and microbiology were accomplished in a large hospital.

The two interns followed the short, white haired, elder *Dean of Pathology* as he seemingly trundled from the third floor to the basement. The three walked through the long corridor to the morgue, situated in the basement of another building connected by an underground tunnel to the main hospital.

Rubel and the residents held their whispered conversation at the head of the autopsy table. Standing to the side at the far end of the table, Wolfe and von Hoffman quietly discussed their most recent evaluations. "Did anyone get good reports?" Wolfe asked von Hoffman.

"Two of the guys I think are the biggest fuck-ups, Harville and Daniels. Harville went to medical school in the Caribbean and Daniels went to Mexico. Neither has any practical experience although they can speak Spanish like the Cisco Kid and Poncho," von Hoffman said. "Their skills are way behind the guys who trained in the States. You can see they're damned smart, just never had a chance to practice procedures or physical exams. They'll be good one day. Anyway, they got good to excellent reviews across the board."

"Gentlemen," Rubel beckoned the two interns from behind the skull of the woman. Her hair and scalp had been peeled forward over her face, so that after the brain had been removed, the incision in the skull could be hidden. The bone saw left a deep red gash across a third of the skull. "We have chemistries to run and slides to review." He strode out the dual swinging doors into the hallway that led to the nearest elevator inside the building that housed the morgue.

Wolfe pushed the button for the elevator. Von Hoffman saw Dr. Rubel remove his glasses and wipe a tear from his cheek. "Are you okay, Dr. Rubel?" von Hoffman asked.

"Sure, sure," the old man said, replacing his glasses. "Such a sad case, that was." He rubbed the small white mustache under his prominent Middle Eastern nose.

"The overdose?" Wolfe asked.

"Yes," Rubel replied, "that will be her legal cause of death, of course. The real cause of death was the autopsy. Barbiturate overdose, followed by refrigeration outside and then here in pathology, slowed her metabolism down. She was actually alive when they started the autopsy. The flexing of her limbs when the saw touched her brain happened because of nerve conduction, brain to extremities. But it is too late; we cannot put her back together. A hard lesson for those poor boys to learn. You, too, gentlemen. It is also true for those who are clinically dead from exposure or drowning. Remember this: a patient is never dead until he is warm and dead. Don't forget that!"

After waiting ten minutes for the elevator, von Hoffman said, "Looks like we'll have to walk. O-cubed." He turned and headed up the tunnel to the main bank of hospital elevators nearly a hundred yards away.

"O-cubed?" Rubel asked Wolfe as they followed.

"Out Of Order," Wolfe said. *Like the rest of my life. And that young woman. All the Kings horses and all the Kings men could not put Humpty Dumpty or the young woman back together again....*

Chapter 19

Figueroa gave an impassioned speech at the beginning of the next M&M conference about safety, especially pertaining to weapons. Unless they were actively undergoing resuscitation, all gunshot and knifing victims and their families were henceforth to be searched for weapons before being admitted to the ER. If resuscitation were on-going, they would undergo a search at the conclusion of resuscitation. He called on Wolfe to explain the presence of the .45 caliber pistol, and thanked him for having the good sense not to pull the trigger. Wolfe blushed, said nothing more.

A case presented by the orthopedic residents showed what appeared to be a normal wrist x-ray, even in a specific carpal navicular view. The senior resident, Mike Dixon, explained that tenderness over the navicular bone meant a possible fracture, even without x-ray evidence of a fracture. A special *thumb-up* splint needed to be constructed to protect the navicular bone until an orthopedic surgeon could evaluate the patient. He explained how to place such a splint. The area over the navicular bone at the base of the thumb was known as the anatomical snuff box. Snuff users had placed their finely ground tobacco into it before inhaling it into their nostrils. “Snuff box pain should guarantee the patient a splint,” Dixon said, “or this will happen.”

The second x-ray film showed the result of not splinting the same wrist in a thumb-up position for a suspected fracture. The distal end of the navicular bone had floated free from the proximal portion. "This is a problem," Dixon told all present, "because the blood supply for the entire navicular comes from the distal end and consists of a single artery. The proximal portion of the bone has lost its blood supply and is now at risk for dying."

The third x-ray showed the disappearance of the proximal half of the navicular bone by reabsorption after its blood supply had been interrupted and the bone died. "This individual will have wrist pain and arthritis in this area for the rest of her life," Dixon said.

The senior resident then showed another x-ray of a different navicular. "If you look very closely at this film, you will see a tiny crack across the waist of the navicular bone. This fracture was missed by both the radiologist and the orthopedic attending. It was seen by an intern, though."

"Who was that?" Figueroa asked.

Unaware Robinson had been dropped from the emergency medicine program, Dixon called his name, "Nick. Nick Robinson. Stand up. Take a bow." To Figueroa, he continued, "You know, Dr. Figueroa, Robinson's a bright young doctor. Nick? Are you here? Guess not."

Figueroa glowered. "He's not here today," he said under his breath.

Cheerfully, the senior resident said, "Well, when you see him, tell him he did well."

Figueroa ignored the remark. "Our next case involves a man who complained of chest pain and collapsed in front of the judge in the 4th Circuit Court at the courthouse. He arrived by ambulance, supposedly in a coma, eyes clenched shut. He refused to respond to attempts at questioning. Anyone have an idea how to decide if a patient is malingering?"

"Rub on his sternum with your knuckles," someone said.

"It was done," Figueroa said. "No obvious response."

"Hold his hand over his face and let go. If it drops to the side, he's faking it."

"Done. His arm fell to the side, missing his face. But he still refused to answer questions or open his eyes," Figueroa said.

"Put a pencil between his fingers and squeeze."

"Not tried, but not a bad idea," Figueroa said. "I'll save you the trouble of guessing further. I need a volunteer. Dr. Joiner, would you please join me on stage?" Samantha rose from her seat in the front row. "Please sit in one of the three chairs. In fact lie down across the three of them. Feet toward the board. Don't want any of your colleagues peeking under your skirt, do we?" He leered at the audience.

Sam scowled at Figueroa, but said nothing. She lay on her back, feet toward the board, blonde curls hung to one side. "Now close your eyes and pretend you are unconscious," Figueroa said. Sam closed her eyes. Figueroa waited a minute for effect, and then said, "Okay, now I'm going to go over there and pick her up by her pubic hair."

"Oh, no, you're not!" Sam yelled. She bolted out of the chairs and stood, fists clenched, facing Figueroa.

The amphitheater broke out in laughter. Of course, all but a very small minority of the doctors in the auditorium were male. "And that's how you find out if someone is faking unconsciousness without hurting them. Suggest you will hurt them," Figueroa said.

"And if that doesn't work?" a resident asked.

"I find that holding a reflex hammer by the head and slapping the bottom of a patient's feet two or three times with the flat metal end is more painful than most malingerers can tolerate. If they don't wake up then, they are either really unconscious or psychotic," Figueroa said. "This is, in fact, what the senior ER resident did. The patient sat up in the stretcher, jumped out of it and attempted to chase down the resident. Fortunately, he was handcuffed to the stretcher. He overturned it and dragged it some ways down the ER ICU. The deputy accompanying him had no trouble subduing the man. You can step down, Dr. Joiner." Still frowning, Sam stepped off the dais.

The weekly heart attack death report made little impression on Figueroa. His only comment, "If you need motivation to exercise, then jog in a cemetery," had almost no effect on the young doctors. None had the time or energy to jog, and they all understood they should.

The last case involved a fifteen-year-old who suffered a C-5 fracture as a passenger in a TransAm that her boyfriend drove into a Hart Bridge abutment at high speed. He died at the scene. The girl's parents arrived. They hysterically demanded everything be done to save her life and so it was. "Was that a good thing?" Figueroa asked. "She has a broken neck and can't feel or move anything from her shoulders down. By the way, her foot was slapped with a reflex hammer, because of how casually she told the junior ER resident that she was numb and could not move her arms. Turns out she was very intoxicated. She didn't panic until later."

"Better than letting her die in the ER," Wolfe said, memory of the young man who chose to die vivid in his mind. "They may have only temporarily saved her life, but she would at least have the chance to say good-bye to her family."

"And not make a final decision while obviously in a depressed state," a psychiatry resident said.

"She might be suffering from a cord contusion rather than a transection," a neurosurgical resident offered. "That early, no one could say how much function she would regain,"

"What about the enormous cost of maintaining a quadriplegic for the rest of her life?" Figueroa asked. "Her parents have no insurance and are indigent. The state and the federal governments pay out millions of dollars for surgeries, ventilators, special housing, even transportation for quadriplegics. Don't you think they should suffer the consequences of their actions?"

"What fifteen-year-old understands the consequences of her actions?" Samantha asked. "Why do you think we see so many teen pregnancies and sexually transmitted diseases? That any one of us is sitting here just means we were lucky and survived our own stupidity until now."

"Valid point, Dr. Joiner," Figueroa said. "But a lifetime of support is expensive. Can the country afford it?"

"Two responses to that," Iggy said. "If the government can pour billions of dollars into a black hole like Vietnam for no return, it can damn well afford to help widows and injured children. And, number two, who says this is a lifetime problem? Just because there is no easy treatment now doesn't mean there won't be in the near future. Research into cord repair is ongoing."

"Yeah, and someday there will be a cure for sickle cell disease, too," a sarcastic comment came from the audience. "For that to happen, someone is going to have to invent a way to repair DNA. Three chances of that in our lifetime: slim, fat, and no." The sorrowful chuckles that followed rang hollow.

"Continue your discussion among yourselves throughout the week. I don't think there is an obvious good answer," Figueroa said. He ended the debate, "That's all I have for you at this time." As the residents and attending physicians left the auditorium, he motioned to Dr. Joiner to again join him on stage.

Chapter 20

If any part of the internship could be considered a vacation, the Pathology rotation fit the description. Wolfe had only to arrive before Dr. Rubel and leave after he left. Being in his late 70s and a volunteer attending physician who received only $1 per year in salary, Rubel worked banker's hours. Over the years, several assistants had offered to take over the supervision of the interns and residents, but he steadfastly refused their meddling. After practicing medicine for over fifty years, he was not going to let someone else do the part he liked the most – teaching. He also felt that University Hospital, indeed most training hospitals in the United States, looked upon their residents as chattel and overworked them. A chance to rest and to learn some practical pathology gave them a chance to recharge their batteries, he believed.

Wolfe's only complaint about the pathology rotation became the traffic. Under normal circumstances, he would arrive at the hospital long before the rush to work happened each morning. The drive from the Beaches to 8th Street at 8:30 a.m. looked much different from that at 6:00 a.m., or earlier.

"Nice car," Wolfe screamed at the slow driver in front of him. "Next time buy the model with a speedometer in it!" With the windows closed to the December chill, no one could hear him. People who zoned out, who were totally unaware of their surroundings or how they affected other people, drove Wolfe nuts. When he told the other interns about his plight, they nodded unsympathetically in their drowsy state and told him to be patient. "Your patience tries my patience," Wolfe would say, or, "I have lots of patients on pathology, but they're all dead."

Depending on the traffic, Wolfe would arrive either on time or a half hour early. He gave himself lots of cushion. Occasionally, he saw Dr. Figueroa skulking around the hospital. In general, Wolfe managed to avoid the man by slipping into a patient's room or the nearest stairwell. Figueroa carried a clipboard with him, rarely smiled, and walked head down and hurriedly as if always late for his next appointment.

One morning Wolfe found no way to evade Figueroa. The Director of Medical Education sat in the phlebotomy chair in the hospital pathology clinical laboratory. The phlebotomist had taken seven tubes of blood with various different colored rubber stoppers from Figueroa's arm. After removing the tourniquet and needle from his arm, she placed a cotton ball on the puncture wound, bent his elbow, and said, "Hold this. I'll be right back."

"I've told you a hundred times," Figueroa said to the diminutive Filipina, "it's best to put direct pressure on the wound without flexing the elbow. If you bend the patient's arm, he gets a larger hematoma."

"Suit yourself," she said, tearing the cover off a Band Aid and placing it over the cotton ball.

Figueroa grumbled and held his arm out straight pushing on the cotton ball. He noticed Wolfe observing him. A smile crossed his lips; his eyes bored into Wolfe. "So, Dr. Wolfe, how is your pathology rotation progressing?"

Possibly too upbeat with Christmas approaching, Wolfe answered flippantly, "Pretty good, I think, but I guess I'll have to wait on your interpretation of Dr. Rubel's evaluation." He immediately regretted the remark.

The smile disappeared from Figueroa's face. "That's right," he said. "And don't you forget it." Figueroa spun on his heels and left the laboratory.

After he left, Mary, the phlebotomist, said, "I don't like that man. I never have. You take care, Dr. Wolfe, not to get on his bad side. He has a temper. And he can be vindictive."

Wolfe shook his head. "Don't I know it," he said.

Wolfe found von Hoffman instructing one of the lab workers in the proper spelling of his name, "It's always a lower case *v*," he told the woman. That means royalty in the old Prussian states. Don't ever put an upper case *V* in my name."

The woman replied, "Well, you certainly are a *royal* pain in the ass, Dr. von Hoffman." Fortunately, she laughed when she said it.

Von Hoffman eventually chuckled. "Merry X-mas to you, too," he said.

"Let's keep Christ in Christmas," a voice in one of the back rooms suggested.

"Or, let's keep Malcolm in X-mas," Wolfe offered, "as in Malcolm X."

"Dr. Wolfe, are you a racist?" the black laboratory supervisor asked.

"No. Sorry," Wolfe said. "It was just a joke. A bad joke, I admit."

"Actually, I thought it was mildly funny," the supervisor said. "I'm a Muslim and generally I don't like jokes about Malcolm X, but I think even he would have appreciated that one. Besides, I don't celebrate Christmas any longer; I am following a new tradition, Kwanzaa. It started in California after the Watts riots. It's a way to bring all black people together."

Wolfe shook his head. "Well, when you figure out a way to bring everyone together, black, white, red, brown, yellow, green, and blue, let me know."

"I've got the answer for that," von Hoffman said. "We are due in the autopsy suite in ten minutes. Everyone is the same lying on a slab in the morgue. Can't get more together than in death. Addison, Dr. Rubel wants us to pick up the body in the ER on our way."

Bob Gentry, the nerdy senior ER resident, stopped Wolfe and von Hoffman when they reached the ER. "The body's not quite ready," he said, pointing to the end of the room where the curtains had been pulled around the last stretcher in the ER ICU.

"How long will it be?" Wolfe asked.

"Some of the interns are practicing central lines and intubating," Gentry said. "Go to the cafeteria and get a cup of coffee. They'll be done by the time you get back."

Dr. Rubel finished the autopsy, required for any suspicious death, in about two hours. He practiced as the hospital's forensic pathologist, in addition to being Chief of Pathology. Two Jacksonville Sheriff's Office deputies stood at the table, in addition to one of the senior pathology residents, Wolfe, and von Hoffman. Rubel explained the patient had exsanguinated from a ruptured spleen. He also had suffered a liver laceration and multiple fractured ribs leading to lung and heart contusions. “There were no extremity or facial injuries, so the beating was likely delivered in this fashion in an attempt to hide it. All the injuries were survivable had he been given blood and undergone a splenectomy soon enough,” Rubel said. “Who assaulted him?”

Initially, neither of the officers answered. They averted their gaze from Dr. Rubel to the floor. One finally said, “That’s under investigation, Doc. Thanks for your help,” without looking at Rubel.

Rubel continued his lecture. “When he arrived in the ER, multiple intravenous lines were established and he was intubated. From the number of puncture wounds in his body, I would say they had difficulty starting the lines.” He pointed to the central lines that had been clipped and taped down, and also to the extra central line punctures without intravenous tubing.

“Also,” he continued, “the intubation tube is in his esophagus, so they had difficulty giving him oxygen. He didn’t have much blood circulating in any case. It was all in his abdomen, and unable to carry oxygen to his heart and brain. After we see the toxicology report, I’ll be able to tell you about drugs and alcohol. I have sections of his kidneys, brain, and other organs, but I don’t think they will reveal anything else.”

The JSO officers thanked Rubel, put on their hats, and left through the large swinging doors. When they were out of ear shot, von Hoffman spoke. “Dr. Rubel, I think some of those intravenous punctures were posthumously.”

“And the ET tube was likely left in the esophagus by an intern,” Wolfe added. “They were practicing on this guy when we went to get the body. They made us wait for ten or fifteen minutes while they did some training.”

Rubel’s eyes got large. He took a deep breath. “I’ve asked them to refrain from doing that,” he said. “Now I have to look at each puncture wound under the microscope and decide if it happened ante- or postmortem. Unfortunately, the autopsy report will have to reflect the ET tube being in his stomach rather than lungs. I’ll have to suggest they did not resuscitate him correctly and that may have contributed to his death. Some day a smart lawyer is going to use that in his client’s defense. ‘The perpetrator only wounded the victim,’ he’ll say. ‘The ER docs killed him.’” He sighed.

“Who is he?” von Hoffman asked, pointing to the cadaver.

“He was a prisoner in police custody,” Rubel said. “They probably waited too long to transport him to the hospital. Jailers don’t have much empathy. They tend to ignore prisoners who complain. After they lose a large sum of money in a personal injury lawsuit, that will change I believe. More lessons, boys. JSO can be brutal. Never give them cause to arrest you. There is a chance that he was beaten by the police and not his *friends*, although JSO usually assaults miscreants with their nightsticks. I have seen welts on bodies where the capillaries are ruptured in parallel lines two inches apart and two inches deep, all from the force of a single nightstick blow. If you see long, linear, parallel bruises on a patient, you can assume someone hit him very hard with a long, narrow object of some kind."

After the autopsy and once back in the clinical lab, Wolfe tracked down Mary. He coaxed her into the back room and made sure they were alone. "Why did you draw Figueroa's blood?" he asked. "Is he sick?" *I can only hope he's dying,* he thought guiltily, *or maybe he'll need a medical retirement before my internship ends.*

"No. He's not sick," Mary said. "But he is a bit of a hypochondriac and a cheapskate. Rather than see a private doctor or go to a private lab, he comes here and orders every test we do. I guess he interprets them himself." She excused herself, "I have to get back to work. The electrolyte analyzer has broken down and the technician who is going to fix it just arrived."

"You know what they say about *analyze*?" Wolfe said, starting the well-worn chemistry laboratory joke.

"Like *harass, analyze* is really two words: *anal* and *lies.*" She laughed.

Von Hoffman and Wolfe spent the remainder of the day in the biological laboratory plating and reading cultures.

"I think watching autopsies is affecting my mind," von Hoffman said, as they restacked urine culture plates in the incubator.

"How's that?" Wolfe asked.

Von Hoffman paused for a minute for effect, then said, "I have spent days designing a line of furniture called Urniture. Every piece is hollow. You can put the remains of your loved one inside after cremation." He chuckled.

"That's just sick," Wolfe said, not knowing if von Hoffman were joking.

"Told you this rotation has warped me. I like the name for my sofa-bed best: *Sleep With Me Forever Hide-a-bed*."

"Sick. Sick. Sick." Wolfe started laughing and couldn't stop.

Chapter 21

Wolfe left the pathology rotation on December 31st. Internship half over, he started the anesthesiology rotation on January 1, 1977, unfortunately a Saturday. That meant he had to work through the weekend. Iggy, just starting his rotation through pathology along with Latesha Marks, got to stay home that weekend, a fortunate occurrence. Although Janice had been pregnant when the internship started, she had kept that fact hidden fearing it would affect her employment. Her figure gave away her secret by mid October. Estimated due date for Iggy's *Next Great Quarterback* had been scheduled for January 9, 1977. Iggy thought that was great because the NFL had scheduled Super Bowl XI for the same day and everyone knew due dates were never accurate. He would be able to watch the Super Bowl, scheduled to be played in Pasadena, California, between the Minnesota Vikings and the Oakland Raiders. Not a big fan of either team, he was certain Minnesota would crush the Raiders. Like most pro football fans, he considered AFC teams, the old American Football League for the most part, to be much weaker than the NFC teams.

As Janice and Iggy would recall for Wolfe when he visited them in the maternity ward the following Monday, while they were preparing for bed on Saturday, January 1st, Janice mentioned casually that she thought her water had broken.

"When?" Iggy asked.

"Just before lunch," Janice said, climbing into bed.

"Up!" Iggy said. "If you ruptured your membranes, then the baby needs to be delivered within twelve hours."

Janice stayed in bed. "I'm not having any contractions," she said.

Iggy knew from his rotation on Ob-gyn the month before that there would be a significant increase in postpartum infection and infant mortality if the child did not deliver within hours.

"Get dressed," he said. "I'll call the hospital." After making the call, Iggy fetched the suitcase Janice had pre-packed. He carried it to the VW bug. Leaving the car running in order to warm it up, as well as could be expected for an air-cooled engined vehicle, he returned to the apartment and escorted Janice to the car.

"You know this means I'll miss the Sugar Bowl game tomorrow between Pittsburgh and Georgia, don't you?" Iggy joked nervously while driving.

"Then take me home," Janice said. "I don't think *Little Q*, their nickname for the *Next Great Quarterback*, is ready anyway." Iggy had been a high school quarterback. He grew six inches and gained sixty pounds his freshman year at U. Va., and migrated to tight end.

"He's ready," Iggy said, "I just hope your obstetrician is also."

Iggy held a reserve commission in the navy and expected to go on active duty at the end of residency. Even though he had been excused from monthly drills, he still had military privileges at any military installation. The obstetricians at the Jacksonville Naval Air Station Hospital had been following Janice's pregnancy.

After delivering Janice to the care of the nurses on the maternity ward, Iggy parked the VW in the huge lot in front of the hospital and returned to the ward. He stopped the first corpsman he saw and asked, "Has Dr. Jackson been notified?"

The corpsman recognized Iggy as the pending father and said, "Lieutenant, you'll have to talk with the nurse, Lt. Commander Dasinger."

"Fine. Where is Renee?" Iggy knew the charge nurse from previous visits.

"Here," Dasinger said from behind him. "Iggy, you and I need to talk. In private." She took him by the arm and led him to the patient conference room. Iggy suddenly felt lightheaded remembering Wolfe's delivery of the anencephalic fetus. He followed Dasinger into the room. She motioned for him to sit, while she secured the door.

"Is Janice okay? The baby?" Iggy asked.

"Oh, they're fine," Dasinger smiled. "It's just Dr. Jackson."

Relieved, Iggy, sighed. He took a minute to think about what Dasinger said, then asked, "What's up with Captain Jackson? Is he sick?"

Dasinger sat in front of Iggy on the cushioned chair, crossing her long legs in the tight white nurse's uniform. She pulled out a rumpled package of cigarettes from her hip pocket, looked at it a long time, thought better of lighting up, and then put it away. "Dr. Jackson's intoxicated."

"What?"

"It's not his night to be on call. He's also a flight surgeon. As such, he and some of the P-3 pilots went to the officers' club, I guess to celebrate the one month anniversary of the end of hurricane season. In any case, they are all rip-roaring drunk. He's aware your wife is here. Being the chief of the department and her chosen obstetrician, he wants to deliver your son."

Iggy snorted indignantly. "While drunk?" he asked.

"No. He's stopped drinking. Started with some black coffee. He thinks he'll be sober by the time she's ready to deliver. If she begins having hard contractions before he's ready, he thinks the family practice intern can handle the delivery."

"It's January 1st," Iggy said. "Even I know the intern is spending his first day on this rotation. How many deliveries has he made? Janice's membranes ruptured almost twelve hours ago. How long can we wait?"

"If there appears to be any pending complications before Dr. Jackson has recovered, he wants the on-call doctor, Commander Norenberg, to deliver your son."

"Where's he? How many deliveries has the intern done?" Iggy asked.

"Norenberg's at home. He lives close to the Naval Air Station. We'll call him when your wife goes into active labor." She smiled. "You'll see; everything will work out."

"How many deliveries has the intern made?"

"As you surmised, this is his first night on OB. He made a delivery this morning. In addition to your wife, one more woman is in labor, so he could have two under his belt before your wife. The senior family practice resident is in the hospital ICU tonight, also. He's made ten or fifteen deliveries each year during his residency."

Iggy took a deep breath. "Okay, listen to this, Commander. I just finished the Ob-gyn rotation at University Hospital. I delivered twenty-seven children, most of those by myself, with no attending. If Dr. Jackson isn't sober by the time Janice goes into labor, I will deliver my son and your intern can assist. If there are complications because we are forced to wait an excess amount of time, then I may have her shipped to another hospital."

"Are you sure that's wise, Doctor?" she asked. "After all, you are personally involved with the patient."

"Damned right I am," he said. He left the nurse in the conference room. She pulled out the cigarettes as he left.

Iggy found his wife. The family practice intern had just finished evaluating her and putting on the fetal monitor, clipping the electrode to the child's scalp. He watched the fetal heart monitor with his hand on Janice's abdomen. Iggy noted the betadine stained gloves the intern had discarded. "Thanks for keeping him sterile," he said, nodding at the procedure tray. He repeated what he had told Dasinger about who would deliver his son.

The intern said, "Thanks. I'm glad you're here. This is my first day. Shouldn't be a problem, though. Contractions are almost non-existent."

"See? I told you so," Janice said. "Let's go home and come back later."

"Oh, no," the intern said. "Protocol dictates that once your membranes have ruptured you can't leave the hospital. Too much chance of infection."

"See? I told *you* so," Iggy told his wife. She stuck her tongue out at him.

Iggy sat in the chair next to the bed holding his wife's hand. She fell asleep. He cat-napped through the night. About 3 a.m. she had some mild pain with contractions waking them both. The alarm went off on the fetal heart monitor, but the readings were actually normal. Iggy reset it. The contractions subsided. Janice went back to sleep.

About 7 a.m., a bedraggled Dr. Jackson, unshaven, in civilian clothes, stumbled into the room. "How are we doing?" he asked, waking Janice and Iggy.

Iggy stood and shook the captain's hand. He smiled after surveying the physician's appearance. "Quite possibly better than you. Looks like you need some more coffee."

"Yeah," Jackson said, watching the monitor absently. "I'll finish making rounds. If she hasn't gone into labor by the time I have a shower and shave, say ten-hundred hours, we'll induce her. Twenty-four hours is as long as I want the uterus open to the outside world without delivering."

At the appointed hour, the corpsmen and orderly rolled Janice into the delivery suite, where a cleanly shaven, bright-eyed Captain Jackson in fresh scrubs oversaw a perfectly normal delivery. "You are welcome to stay," he told Iggy at the start of the procedure, turning up the medication in Janice's intravenous. "You are a physician. I wouldn't let just anyone stay. Can you imagine what a disaster it would be to have almost anybody in the delivery room? Next thing you know they'd be taking pictures with their Polaroids."

"Can't imagine that." Iggy agreed.

A very healthy, seven pound, eight ounce, baby girl arrived at eleven minutes after one p.m., 1311 hours, in navy parlance. The ultrasound interpretation had been wrong about the gender of the child. "That's alright, honey. She'll be the first female NFL quarterback," Janice told the heartbroken Iggy. "We'll have more; won't quit until we have at least one boy."

Iggy left Janice in the hospital and returned to the apartment, where he slept through the tail end of the Sugar Bowl. Pittsburgh Panthers and Tony Dorsette thrashed the Georgia Bulldogs to gain the national collegiate football title. He then showered, ate supper and went to bed. He called Dr. Figueroa on Monday morning and begged out of his monthly review. Leniently, Figueroa allowed Iggy to secure a day off to visit Janice and the baby.

"Let's called her Nova," Iggy said to Janice when he returned to the maternity ward. They had spent no time choosing a girl's name thinking she would be a boy.

Janice still fumed over her treatment by the female corpsman who ran the ward. She wanted no part of picking a name. "That can wait," she said. "That woman was like a marine drill sergeant. 'Up and at'em,' she called at 0545. Eat now, then get cleaned up. The babies will be here at 0630. Move it!'"

Iggy laughed. "It'll be alright. How's the baby?"

"It will *not* be alright," Janice said. "They want me to spend three more days here. I'm not going to listen to that marionette for the next three days."

"Okay, I'll talk to Jackson," Iggy said. "Maybe we can get a reduction in your sentence."

Janice and the baby left the hospital the next morning. Iggy drove, but he had to leave Janice alone in the apartment. Figueroa was on the warpath about him missing pathology. When he reported to Dr. Rubel, the kindly pathologist handed him a book, *Neonatology: Pathophysiology and Management of the Newborn* by Gordon B. Avery. Rubel told him, “This is your independent study assignment. Take it home and read it. You’re not going to get much sleep over the next month. I don’t want to see you back here before next Monday. Got it?”

Iggy hefted the thousand page book, and looked at the title. He smiled and said, “Yes, sir. Thank you, sir.”

Janice and Iggy settled on Nancy Rose for their daughter’s name, a combination of their mothers’ names. They spent hours filling in Wolfe on the adventure. By June, Janice was willing to think about having another child, “In four to five years, or when Iggy finishes training, whichever happens first.”

Chapter 22

The Anesthesia rotation exhausted Wolfe. The Chief of Anesthesiology assigned him to two senior anesthesiology residents. Whenever they pulled call, so did he. Since there were six anesthesiology residents who rotated call every sixth night, Wolfe found himself on call every third night.

Tasked at first with starting intravenous lines, he quickly progressed to doing pre- and post-op evaluations and the collection of laboratory work, x-rays, and EKGs. His new friends in the clinical pathology laboratory came in handy. In addition, having Iggy doing the same rotation right behind him made finding lost lab results easier. Kervork Torrosian supplied him with EKGs from the cardiology and internal medicine rotation. Justin Murcheson's location in radiology gave him a contact there.

Doing the scut work for the anesthesiologists proved interesting, if not educational. In turn, they gave him tips on starting i.v.s, (arm down, squeeze extra blood into it before placing the tourniquet, and lots of alcohol to highlight the veins) and intubating (sniffing position, straight blade on the laryngoscope instead of the curved one, and lift away from the table without hitting the patient's teeth).

Wolfe's only complaint was with one of the attending physicians he assisted, R. Wilson Tibbs, MD. The man knew absolutely everything.

There existed no subject on which he was not an expert and could not expound upon for hours. He pulled a bookmark from one of Wolfe's manuals. The slim piece of cardboard had a painting of a Jaguar XKE on it. "No such car," the anesthesiologist said.

"What?" Wolfe asked.

"I know every model of Jaguar ever made. That car never existed," Tibbs insisted.

"It's just a draw..."

"Doesn't matter," the anesthesiologist interrupted. "It never existed."

Patients found it difficult to get along with him, also. One thanked Wolfe for opening the stopcock on the intravenous to allow the anesthetic to put him to sleep. "Now, I won't have to listen to that bag of wind," he said, drifting off to never, never, land. "I hope his isn't the last voice I'll ever hear." Sadly, it was. The patient died of a ruptured aortic aneurysm before the surgeons could repair it.

His death precipitated a fight between the surgeons and Tibbs over the cause of death. "You didn't relax him enough," the surgeon shouted at the anesthesiologist. "His blood pressure was way too high."

"My ass," the anesthesiologist responded. "He didn't have enough blood volume to give him more anesthesia. He would have stroked out had I lowered his pressure any more. You guys worked so slowly he bled to death."

Wolfe left them in the recovery room, arguing whether the man had died in the operating room or in the recovery room. He went to do the pre-operative physical on another patient.

"Tibbs is absolooney tune," Wolfe told Iggy that night, as Iggy practiced feeding the baby with a bottle of previously harvested breast milk.

"According to an article I read, one in four anesthesiologists is addicted to drugs. Sounds like he could be one of them. Either that or he's psychotic. Manic-depressive would be my guess," Iggy said. He looked at the small bottle in his large hand. "I think Janice is grooming me to get up nights to feed the baby."

Tibbs's rants continued. With another patient, one who received an anesthetic block prior to having his shattered distal tibia and fibula fixed with pins, the patient complained of pain when the surgeon began to work. Tibbs had decided the elderly man could not live through general anesthesia; he had undergone a spinal. Both legs should have been numb, insensate to any pain. "Ow!" the man cried when the surgeon tested the block by poking him with a needle.

"Let's give the anesthetic a couple more minutes to work," the anesthesiologist said. When the second test proved as painful as the first, Tibbs lost his temper with the patient. "Can you really feel that?"

"Yes."

"And it is really very painful, not just pressure?"

"It hurts like hell," the man said.

"You're just a wimp," Tibbs told him. He proceeded to argue with the surgeon about what to do next. Losing his temper completely, he stormed out of the operating room.

Several minutes later the orthopedic surgeon followed him out the door after pulling off his latex gloves. He threw them into the kick bucket near the table and cursed under his breath. Wolfe sat on the stool at the head of the table waiting, freezing in the air conditioning. Eventually, the Chief of Anesthesia came into the room. Several minutes later the orthopedic surgeon returned, rescrubbed, with new gloves.

The Head of the Department, Dr. Husam Khouri, reviewed the patient's chart. "I think we can use general anesthesia safely on Mr. Stewart," he said. "We must not take too long, however." Within minutes the patient lay paralyzed and insensate. The orthopedic surgeons repaired the ankle quickly, in less than forty-five minutes. Stewart woke up in the recovery room thankful for Dr. Khouri's intervention.

Halfway through the January rotation, Wolfe received a call to return to the hospital for an emergency exploratory laparotomy. An elderly man apparently had an obstructed and ruptured small intestine. When Wolfe arrived outside the operating room, R. Wilson Tibbs, MD had not arrived yet. Wolfe set up the usual intravenous lines, attached the leads to the cardiac monitor, and checked the gas lines.

With Tibbs still absent, he did a brief physical on the elderly man with the distended abdomen. The patient's blood pressure was low and his heart rate high. A unit of blood ran into one arm and a bag of Lactated Ringers intravenous solution ran into the other. The portable heart monitor sat on the stretcher between the man's legs, beeping merrily at a rate of 120 beats per minute. On high doses of pain medication, the patient slumbered supine, head to one side, mouth open and drooling on his pillow. The transport orderly leaned over the nearest nurses' station reading a magazine.

"Where is everyone?" Wolfe asked him.

The orderly looked up and shrugged. "The surgeon is in the

office calling for the anesthesiologist," he said, pointing.

Wolfe walked to the door of the office. On the way, he passed flat and upright abdomen x-rays he presumed belonged to the drooling patient. Except for a small intestine that looked like a stack of coins, the flat film looked okay. However, the upright film showed a lot of free air under the diaphragm, a sure sign that gas was escaping from a hole in the man's intestines. Fluid collected in loops of bowel. A man in green scrubs with paper booties over his shoes and a crumpled paper hat in one hand leaned on the desk, telephone receiver in the other hand.

"I need an anesthesiologist and I need him ten minutes ago," the surgeon said into the phone. "I don't care who is on call. This man will die if not operated on soon. You get me one of your residents now, or you come in yourself if you can't find Tibbs." He slammed down the phone. Wolfe watched him stomp off to the scrub station and begin to wash his hands and forearms in one of the large sinks with knee controls and foot pedals for the faucets. Most surgeons took fifteen minutes to finish the ritual, involving betadine soap, and a surgical scrub brush and nail cleaner.

Wolfe followed him to the sinks. "I'm the rotating intern on anesthesiology, sir."

"Ever put anyone under?" the surgeon asked.

"No, sir."

"Well if an anesthesiologist or anesthesiology resident doesn't show up soon, you and I are going to. For twenty years, I have been telling myself these assholes are over rated." He tied a surgical cap on his head, and placed a mask on his face. As he started his scrubbing routine, he added, "And if the surgical nurse doesn't show up quickly, you are going to learn how to pass instruments. Got it?"

"Yes, sir."

The surgical nurse arrived a minute later. "Sorry, I had to buy gas. Drifted into the service station on fumes. Husband used the car and forgot to refill it," she said. She disappeared into the OR, beckoning the transport orderly to help her move the patient on the stretcher.

As Wolfe prepared to open the stopcock on the mixture of anesthesia the surgeon had him put together, the door to the OR opened and Dr. Khouri entered. He placed his hand around Wolfe's. "Let me do that," he said. He pulled the bag of fluid off the i.v. pole, disconnected it from the patient's intravenous line, and dropped it into the kick bucket. "Mind if I use my own concoction, Dr. Stephens?" he asked the surgeon.

"Okay with me, if you are quick about it," the surgeon said.

The patient had a rough post-op course. He spent three days in intensive care and two weeks on the general surgery floor. He survived. R. Wilson Tibbs, MD, anesthesiologist, did not. The anesthesiologist had given himself an overdose of medication, likely by accident. JSO found his body and a cache of stolen narcotics and anesthetics in his apartment. For days the conversation in the anesthesiology department centered on how they had been unable to recognize the personality changes in Tibbs that should have been an obvious give away to his drug addiction.

Chapter 23

In late afternoon of the last Sunday of January, Iggy and Wolfe sat in the apartment, bemoaning the end of the collegiate and NFL football seasons. Janice had taken the baby for a walk along the beach in the second hand stroller Iggy had found for sale in the newspaper.

Iggy lounged on the couch, in gym shorts and one of his U. Va. jerseys. He held a beer in one hand. Wolfe's T-shirt said, *Virginia Tech: Non-Athletic Department*. "You look refreshed after your nap," Wolfe told Iggy. "Up last night with the baby?"

"I didn't take that nap," Iggy corrected. "It took me, wrestled me down and pinned me to the mattress. I was lucky to escape."

Only half interested, they watched a professional basketball game on the television. Although rarely off at the same time, the friends avoided talking about their respective internships, not wanting to raise their own anxiety levels. "Football is much more exciting," Iggy said. "Where else can a team make a comeback, after being behind by twenty-one points?"

"This is pretty damned boring," Wolfe said. "And the last two minutes of the game will take an hour to play with all the purposeful fouls and the time-outs."

Iggy thought for a minute. "You're right. They should cut to the chase: give each team a hundred points and three time-outs. Then set the clock to two minutes."

A knock sounded at the front door. Wolfe, being closest to the door, stood and opened it. "Sam," he said, "how's internal medicine going? Come in. Didn't expect to see you today." He leaned forward to put a peck on her cheek.

Joiner brushed past him. "Sit down, Addy. Don't get your testicles in an uproar. This is not a conjugal visit," she said. "Hi, Iggy. Glad you are here. Is Janice around?"

Iggy sat upright, making a space for Sam on the couch. "Hi, Sam. Janice and the baby are taking a walk. Do you need to speak with her? I know where I can find her."

"No that's just as well," Sam said. "I have something I want you and Addy to hear. I would probably ask her to leave if she were present."

"Must be pretty serious if you didn't want Janice to hear about it," Iggy suggested. "Do you really want Addy to stay?" He poked Wolfe in the ribs.

"It is serious. And, yes, I want you both to listen to it. I'm in big trouble with that sexist asshole, Figueroa," Sam said. Exhaustedly, she plopped down across from the couch on the wobbly wooden chair that normally sat in the kitchen. She faced Wolfe and Iggy over the stained coffee table with peeling veneer. "Is your landlord here?"

"Never," Wolfe said.

"Okay, then. Do you remember when Figueroa had me pretend I was unconscious and then made the remarks about looking up my skirt and pulling on my pubic hair?"

"Sure," Iggy said, "and after the Morbidity and Mortality conference, I saw him call you up front. What was that all about?"

"He said he wanted to apologize. Realized he had overstepped some boundary," Sam said. "He invited me to his office later in the week. When I went in, he told me he would like to take me to dinner to apologize. I could pick the restaurant, any place I wanted."

"Generous," Wolfe said.

"More like suspicious," Iggy said. "What did you do?"

"I had no compunction about taking the man's money. The more he paid, the better he would remember to be a gentleman in the future, I figured," Sam said. "I decided on O'Steen's Restaurant, the seafood place in St. Augustine. It didn't make much sense to take two cars, so I drove to his house in Arlington, near Ft. Caroline. He drove to O'Steen's in his Mercedes. The whole evening he was a perfect gentleman. He told stories on himself; his humor was self-deprecating. I got the impression that he's really, really brilliant. I think he'd give you the shirt off his back if he believed you needed it, but not the time of day if he thought you were an idiot."

"You are being too magnanimous," Wolfe said. "Everyone's an idiot in his book."

"You didn't fall for that line of crap, did you Sam?" Iggy asked.

"Almost," Sam said and blushed. "When he drove me back to his place to get my car, he asked if I'd like a glass of wine. 'We could make a toast and bury the hatchet, in private,' he said. That made me suspicious again." She took a pocket recorder out of her purse, the type all the residents used for dictating charts. She pushed a button and the lid opened. From her jeans pocket, she pulled a mini tape and slipped it into the recorder. Fast forwarding a small amount until chipmunk voices could be heard, she stopped the tape and rewound it a short ways.

"I turned this on in my purse after he got out of the car," she said. Wolfe and Iggy heard the car door slam, the jingle of keys, and the front door to Figueroa's house open and close.

"White or red?" Figueroa asked, voice quiet, muffled by the purse.

"White, if that's alright," Sam replied. The pop of a cork and the clink of glasses and bottle followed.

"Please, sit," Figueroa invited. "The large couch is most comfortable."

"I'll bet," Iggy said.

"Shhh!" Sam said, "You'll miss it." A hand apparently slapped the leather couch.

"Now, Dr. Joiner, I hope I have proved to you that I'm no ogre," Figueroa said, "Do you agree?"

"So far, you have been perfectly genteel," Sam's disembodied voice replied.

"Well, I have a proposal for you – doctor to doctor."

"And that is?" Sam asked.

"I have become aware that you believe in the free love philosophy, if you know what I mean. You have a fiancé in the northeast, yet you have managed to have a number of liaisons here in Jacksonville with..."

"That's none of your business!" Sam interrupted.

"Ah, but it is," Figueroa said. "As Director of Medical Education, I am responsible for the well-being of all the interns: moral, physical, and educational."

"Right," Sam said, sarcastically.

Figueroa continued, "Your internship, so far, has been less than stellar, if you catch my drift. There is a chance you could lose your place here. You were not guaranteed placement in any of our residencies when you were accepted for the rotating internship. You could even leave early from the internship. Of course, that's only if your performance does not improve."

The pitch of her voice and volume rising, Sam asked, "And what would I need to do to improve my performance, Dr. Figueroa?"

"Since the death of my wife, obtaining sexual fulfillment has proven difficult for me," Figueroa said. "I think if you extended your sexual favors to me occasionally, then your evaluations might improve dramatically."

"And if not, one of those excellent interns, like Harville the foreign medical graduate, will take my place in whatever residency I want?"

"Oh, no, silly girl," Figueroa chuckled. "Menendez, Daniels, Harville, all those FMGs and some American medical school graduates get good evaluations so other institutions will recruit them. They're worthless to us at University Hospital. We don't have the time or resources to complete their educations. They are too far behind, having no practical experience like the American students. The people we want to protect from being stolen by other hospital residencies get low grades. I certainly don't want another institution to know how good they are; they might recruit them. Dr. Wolfe, for instance, would make an excellent resident, but I'm not about to let him know that."

"You just did, asshole," Wolfe said.

Sam stopped the tape and rewound it a little. "Quiet, Addy," she said, restarting the tape.

"Of course, there are a certain few whose lower grades are factual, like Nick Robinson, as you already know," Figueroa finished his thought.

"That's bullshit and you know it," Sam said. "Nick is brilliant. You got rid of him because he frequently made you look bad."

"As you also know, we can't have residents who disagree with their mentors. Education is from the top down, not bottom up or peer-to-peer, my young lady. Now, if you will consider my proposal...."

Only the squeaking of the minitape and the tiny wheels on the recorder turning interrupted the silence. Sam reached over and shut off the tape. "That's it," she said, "The batteries died."

"What did you tell him?" Wolfe asked.

"I told him I was on my monthly, and I'd have to think about his proposal," Sam said. "That was a lie. With my birth control pills I can adjust my menstrual cycle any way I like. Haven't had a period since Thanksgiving. Won't have another until my pathology rotation, when I have weekends off again and can choose the right one."

"That's only a temporary solution to your problem. He's going to keep asking, or get rid of you," Iggy said.

"I know," Sam said. "That's why I'm here. I need your help, Iggy. He likes you. You're a star athlete."

"He still got mad at me for missing some of pathology," Iggy said. "Don't know that I'm in his good graces at this point. Addy, any ideas?"

"Actually, I have one. It might not only solve Sam's problem, but rid us of Figueroa altogether, at least temporarily," Wolfe said. "First, you can't lose that tape, Sam. In fact you should make several copies and give one to Iggy for safe keeping."

"I can do that," Sam said. "What else?"

"When I was on pathology, Figueroa came in for blood tests. He's a hypochondriac. Mary says he has blood drawn almost every month. Most of the results have to be transcribed by hand after the machines spit them out. Eventually computers and teletype machines will do the job, but not yet. Anyway, I took the liberty of raising his alkaline phosphatase by a considerable amount, from 79 to over a thousand. He came back and had his blood drawn again, and ordered a lot more tests. I think the guys on radiology said he had some films taken, too. I'm sure he didn't believe the second result."

Sam interrupted. "You know, Doctor Latin Lover also mentioned that no one knew how long they would be around for, that everyone should live for the moment. He hinted at a family history of Paget's disease, too. I thought he was just trying to push my empathy buttons, but now I think he was generally worried.

"How does this help Sam, Addy?" Iggy asked.

"Well, he was really concerned about the ALP, even though his repeat test came back normal. Several interns later told me that he had asked them for the differential diagnosis of an increased alkaline phosphatase during their evaluation reviews. Obviously, he was picking their brains, too, while making it look like a pop quiz. Maybe, if we can get the other interns on pathology to help out, we can trigger some paranoid reaction. Or, perhaps he'll take a medical leave of absence to get a complete work-up and leave us all alone. Dr. Rubel likes to teach. Possibly he'd take the job."

"Why copy the tape?" Sam asked.

"As a last resort, we use it to blackmail him. Send copies to the board of directors. Something. It's a nasty solution, but they could ask for his resignation and review his work," Wolfe said. "I think they'll want more than Sam's word that the tape isn't a hoax, though."

"Okay," Iggy said, "I think Kervork Torrosian takes my place in pathology on Tuesday. I'll speak with him. What tests should we mess with?"

"Let's get Harrison's internal medicine text book and find some rare diseases," Sam suggested.

Sam did spend the night, but as far from Wolfe as she could get in the double bed. Her anger prevented any type of romantic interlude. Early the next morning, however, Wolfe felt her reach for his hand. She began to rub his fingers, squeezing them seductively. Eventually, he was awake enough to talk. "What's up?" she asked.

"Nothing, yet," Wolfe replied.

"Could have sworn I had a *Wolfie* sighting," she said, referencing her nickname for his male member. She gently kissed him on the lips.

"More like a Wolfie watch," Wolfe said, harking back to the U.S. Weather Service alerts for tornados. "Whoops. Looks like we're now experiencing a Wolfie warning."

Sam laughed and rolled him onto his back. "Yep, I think you're right," she said, crawling on top of him and pinning him to the bed.

Chapter 24

The Internal Medicine rotation for the rotating interns consisted of a week or so at a time in sub-specialties, as well as time in general internal medicine. Wolfe spent his first week of the rotation on cardiology, along with Iggy. There he met a number of memorable patients. One day Wolfe opened the door to the exam room and found a stunningly beautiful, young black woman seated on the exam table facing him. She wore a navy blue pair of slacks and high heels, and nothing else. Flustered, he said, "Good morning." He quickly glanced at the chart in his hand and added, "Miss Howard."

Miss Howard had a generous brown bosom with firm breasts displaying large areolae and protruding firm nipples. Her chest was marred only by a long, thin, white scar that ran from her sternal notch to her xyphoid process. "I'm Dr. Wolfe," he said fishing his stethoscope out of his white coat pocket and placing the ear pieces around his neck. "Dr. Delaney wants me to listen to your heart murmur."

Miss Howard leaned forward and grabbed the business end of Wolfe's stethoscope. She casually placed it on her chest. Eyes wide, Wolfe watched as she moved the diaphragm and then the bell of the stethoscope around her chest, under her left breast to the apex of her heart, and then to the base of her heart, closer to the sternum. "Hear that?" she asked. Wolfe nodded, although all he heard was a faint clicking, which he could not place.

"There are two murmurs," she said, "a III/VI systolic ejection murmur and a less intense diastolic murmur. The late systolic/early diastolic click is the tilting disk, artificial heart valve seating. Hear that?" Wolfe nodded again, solemnly, eyes fixed on her breasts. He heard nothing but that irritating, distant clicking.

"Oh, silly me," Miss Howard said, with a chuckle. "Of course you can't hear the murmur and click." She dropped the diaphragm of the stethoscope. It swung into Wolfe's belt buckle and bounced off. With both hands, she reached forward and spread the ear pieces to the stethoscope, lifting them from his neck and fitting them into Wolfe's ears. Again she grabbed the diaphragm of the stethoscope and positioned it under her left breast. The clang of the artificial heart valve disk slamming into its housing rang in Wolfe's ears. It sounded remarkably like the annoying click but much louder. That was followed by the diastolic and systolic murmurs.

Taking a deep breath, Wolfe said, "Yeah, that's better." His face reddened.

"Are we done here, Sugar?" Howard asked after tracing again all the interesting points of her cardiac exam and explaining them in detail to Wolfe. "Hear the S2 heart sound split when I take a deep breath? I have to get back to work. If you or your friends are ever celebrating near Blanding Boulevard, come by the Gentlemen's Bar and Grill and look me up." Howard pulled her blouse and jacket from the chair in the room. She slipped them on and departed before Wolfe could respond. He sat at the small desk to write down the exam's finer points. In the hallway, he heard several people laugh and hoped to God it wasn't about him.

Greg Delaney, the Chief of Cardiology entered the room before Wolfe could finish writing. "Cynthia gone?" he asked.

Wolfe looked at the chart. Howard's first name was Cynthia, followed by, in quotes, *Desiree*. "Uh, yes, sir," he said. "Interesting murmur, though. You could almost hear the valve without a stethoscope it was so loud."

"You know, she's been through so many heart exams, I think she could teach auscultation," Delaney said. Ever cerebral, Delaney looked at his watch. He added, "After you've listened to hearts as long as I have, *everyone*, even normal people, have interesting murmurs. It's all I can do to avoid writing them down on the charts. But who'd believe a 0.3 over 6 diastolic murmur? None of the family practice docs would be able to hear it."

"No sir," Wolfe said, almost thankful to have suffered mild hearing loss from running around on the aircraft carrier listening to screaming jet engines all day. He rarely heard any but the loudest murmurs. He certainly wouldn't be aggravating family practitioners by reporting murmurs they could not hear.

***

"That's got to be a Wenckebach," Wolfe told Iggy the name of the arrhythmia, as they sat at the table reviewing EKGs. "See here, no P wave after the fifth QRS complex."

"Well aren't you spatial?" Iggy said. "Not special, spatial. As in, what planet are you from? If it can't be fixed with cold, hard, sharp steel, I don't see what difference it makes what kind of block it is."

"Typical surgeon," Wolfe said.

The first hour of every morning, the interns sat in the cardiology back office at a large table. There, they looked at every EKG done in the hospital over the previous twenty-four hours, usually more than one hundred. 99% of the job was mindless rubber stamping of other residents' interpretations. 1% proved fascinating. The electrical activity of peoples' hearts varied as much as the personalities of the people who depended upon those hearts for life itself. No two abnormal EKGs were the same, although they fell into many interesting groups: atrial fibrillation; 1st, 2nd, and 3rd degree blocks, the Wenckebach, ventricular tachycardia, ventricular fibrillation, etc. And then there were the heart attacks, how the electrical activity changed because of dead or dying heart muscle: inferior, lateral, even posterior myocardial infarctions. All had their own signatures.

For short periods of time Wolfe thought the EKGs fascinating. After about the 50th of each type, he began to understand why the cardiology attending physicians let the interns and residents read them. Sooner or later they would be using trained chimps. Occasionally, even the cardiologists disagreed on what cardiac rhythm had been traced by the EKG machine. Sometimes that required the placement of special electrical leads to sort out. Sometimes the technicians had placed the leads in the wrong places.

"Okay, guys," Dr. Delaney called out. "Put the tough EKGs in the box for the cardiology fellow to explain to you this afternoon. We have a consult to do in the ICU."

The patient in the intensive care unit was 105 years-old, soon to be 106. He had been born in Georgia just after the Civil War ended. His parents had moved to Florida with all their children shortly thereafter, because northern Florida had been under Federal control during the War Between the States and they feared the South might really rise again.

"Okay," Delaney said, after they reviewed the man's chart. "Here's his EKG, Addison. What's his rhythm and what's the cure?"

Wolfe knew right away that the patient was in third degree block. His P waves had no connection to his R waves. Each marched to the beat of his own drummer. The man's ventricular heart rate on the rhythm strip approached 24 beats per minute, much too slow to sustain life. A temporary pacemaker had been placed through a central line in the ER. "He's in complete heart block," Wolfe said. "If he were 65 years-old, I'd say he needs a pacemaker. I don't know what you do for a 105 year-old. He needs a new heart, but I doubt he qualifies to be on a transplant list."

"Absolutely correct," Delaney said.

"You're on a roll, buddy," Iggy said. "Got those cardiac blocks down cold."

"Kaiser, sesame seed, or cinnamon?" Wolfe asked.

Delaney chuckled. "Girls, girls. Don't go knocking the oldsters. Let's see how with it he is."

Delaney, Iggy, and Wolfe spent thirty minutes in the ICU room of the 105 year-old man, talking about politics – he didn't trust Gerald Ford any more than he did Tricky Dick. And he thought the Cincinnati Reds had done a bang up job sweeping the Yankees in the World Series.

"See," Delaney said, after they left the man's room, "His quality of life will be excellent with his heart rate adjusted. If he can perfuse his brain and the rest of his body, there's no telling how long he will live."

"Or, he could die tomorrow," Iggy said.

"Or, he could die tomorrow," Delaney agreed. "Though, we don't want to make that a self-fulfilling prophesy by *not* giving him the pacemaker."

Unfortunately the patient's body could not withstand the rigors of opening his chest and placing the permanent pacemaker under the pectoralis muscle. Infection set in. Four days later his kidneys stopped working and he became comatose. The family decided against dialysis and the 105 year old man died, one day short of living 106 years.

Wolfe and Iggy were tasked with retrieving the almost new pacemaker from the man's body while it was in the autopsy suite. Iggy pushed the portable EKG machine into the morgue. They were met by a young, black attendant, an orderly in green scrubs who was obviously uncomfortable being there. "This is one scary place," he said to Wolfe. "I'm only here temporarily and it's my first day. The usual orderly had a heart attack. He's upstairs in the ICU. They say a ghost scared him so much his heart stopped beating."

"We won't be but a minute or two," Wolfe told the young man. "I just need to see Jon Brown, recently deceased from complications after heart surgery."

The orderly opened the door to one of the refrigerated trays and slid out the body of the late Mr. Brown. "What are you going to do?" he asked Iggy.

"Just check to see if the pacemaker is still working and then retrieve it if it is," Iggy said. "They're too expensive to bury with the patient."

Wolfe put the leads from the EKG machine on the patient and turned it on. The paper rolled and the needle burned a beautiful line of pacer spikes along the EKG tracing. All that was absent was the electrical and mechanical response from Mr. Brown's heart. The orderly saw the needle move on the EKG machine. Not knowing the difference between a pacer EKG and a paced heart EKG, he assumed the man had returned from the dead. "Oh my God!" was all Iggy or Wolfe heard. By the time they turned around the swinging doors were closing. The orderly was no where to be seen.

Chapter 25

The routine for general internal medicine, when not on one of the specialties, cardiology, neurology, immunology, etc. for a week at a time, sometimes put Wolfe to sleep. He awoke sitting in a chair one morning during chart review while Dr. Raymond Scott, chief of the department rattled on about how tired everyone looked and how they should do what he did, take power naps. “I find a ten minute nap in the middle of the day, after lunch, refreshes me as much as a whole night’s sleep,” he said.

“If I only had the *power* to wake up again after I fell asleep,” Iggy whispered. Wolfe nodded, then began to nod off again, head bobbing and eyes closing as he tried to will himself awake. Everything happened in cartoon-like fashion. Wolfe saw Dr. Scott stand. He missed a few frames of the action. Scott appeared in front of the blackboard, where they had written patient names, pending tests, and possible differential diagnoses. In the next frame, Wolfe saw Scott posed as a pitcher delivering a baseball to a batter.

When the chalk hit the desk and exploded in front of him, Wolfe spilled over backward, taking the chair with him. Everyone in the room laughed, except for him and Dr. Scott. “Dr. Wolfe,” Scott said, “I expect you to stay awake for these chart reviews. Important decisions are made here, life and death decisions in fact. Understand?” Wolfe nodded. “If you are that tired, stand in the back of the room. That goes for the rest of you slackers, too."

Scott sat again behind his desk. "Since you are now wide awake, Dr. Wolfe, and because you missed most of the discussion about the patients on the wards, I guess you should take the first new admission for the day." Scott picked up a 3 x 5 index card, on which had been stamped the identification of a patient to be found in the ER. "Go on."

Embarrassed and worried about how the incident would play for Figueroa, Wolfe picked up his papers and shuffled out of the meeting room. Shortly thereafter, he found himself in the ER, talking to Chauncey Z. Brown. Chauncey Z. Brown weighed 450 pounds, approximately, because the ER scale stopped at 300 pounds. His diagnoses included Type II Diabetes, congestive heart failure, decreased renal function, and blindness. How he had survived for twenty-eight years, no one knew. Wolfe only knew that Chauncey would not die on his rotation. The resident who allowed Chauncey Z. Brown to die would live in infamy, forever. Fortunately, Wolfe had help. The brilliant third year internal medicine resident on call, Hiram Myers, stood next to Brown's stretcher. He called to Wolfe, "Hey, Addy, meet Chauncey Brown. Chauncey, this is Dr. Wolfe. He's a bright new intern. He and I are going to get you through this admission. First thing I want you to do is tell Dr. Wolfe why you are here. What did you do wrong?"

Brown, a huge black man who hung over both sides of the ER stretcher, chuckled. "It was my birthday, Doc. I didn't want my family to feel bad about giving me presents."

"I know, Chauncey," Myers said, "but tell Dr. Wolfe."

"I ate too much birthday cake," Brown admitted.

"And?" Myers pressed.

"Two large bottles of Coca-cola. And a whole lot of chocolate chip cookies," Brown added.

"His serum glucose was 550. He didn't get into keto-acidosis, but we have an intravenous drip of insulin going after the bolus we gave him. Problem is keeping him in fluid balance. His kidneys don't function well. He's on oxygen to help with the congestive heart failure. He'll be a great learning case for you," Myers said. "Everything that can go wrong with the human body as a result of diabetes, Chauncey manifests to one degree or another." Myers handed Wolfe a clipboard holding the admission forms. He pointed to the nurses' desk, upon which sat three manila charts, each two to three inches thick. "Those are volumes I, III, and IV of Chauncey's chart. Medical records can't find II. I'll see you on the ward in about two hours."

While Wolfe took Brown's medical history, family history, social history, and did a complete physical exam, including prostate check, the ER ICU overflowed with patients. Three codes and four serious injuries from motor vehicle accidents filled the beds. From past experience on Primary Care, Wolfe knew the patients in the waiting room were not being seen, and likely their tempers were beginning to boil over. The interns and ER residents barely had time to breathe between crises. Finally finished with Brown's admission – the patient remained chipper and friendly throughout the work-up – Wolfe gathered all the charts from the nurses' desk.

"If Volume II should show up, could you send it to the ward?" he asked Jada, the ER nurse.

"If you'll do me a favor, Dr. Wolfe," Jada said.

Very much in Jada's debt for her kindness, intelligence, and her tips on how to move patients quickly and exist in the milieu of the ER, Wolfe acquiesced easily. "Anything," he said.

"There's a patient out front who is on the verge of causing a big scene. I don't want her to start a riot. We've been tied up with serious injuries and codes all morning," Jada said. "The interns still aren't back in Primary Care. Could you see her for me?"

Wolfe swallowed hard, thinking he may have obligated himself too quickly. "What's wrong with her?" he asked.

"I don't know that anything is wrong with her," Jada said. "She wants a note to return to work. Would you mind?"

Wolfe had spent hours trying to convince people they were well enough to go back to work. The pervasive ambiance of entitlement proved difficult to reverse with the hospital's indigent population. People who saw their neighbors on welfare, driving nice cars, partying, or spending money unwisely often wondered why they should work so hard for a few dollars, when Workers Compensation could make their burdens so much lighter. To have someone actually want to go back to work surprised Wolfe. "Put her in room one in Primary Care," Wolfe said, assuming the visit would take only a minute.

When Wolfe entered the room, he found surprises on many levels. The patient was white. Only ten percent of his patients had been white. She was dressed as an airline stewardess; she had a well-paying, glamorous job. And she was beautiful: brunette, high cheek bones, tall, and good looking with an attractive build.

"H-h-how can I help you, Miss?" he stammered, forgetting to look at the chart for her name.

"Get me out of here," the flight attendant said. "What a zoo. All I want is a note to return to work."

"Why are you off work?" Wolfe asked.

"Does it matter?" she asked. She thrust an 8½" x 11" pink sheet of paper into his hands. "Just check the box on the bottom, sign it, and stamp it with your name or hospital stamp."

"I'd like to," Wolfe said, "but I can't put Typhoid Mary on a plane. If you have a serious contagious disease, I would be doing your passengers a disservice, and getting myself in trouble with the FAA and your bosses. Why are you off work? And why would you come here, rather than go to a private physician's office?"

"I came here because it is close to the airport. My flight takes off at noon. We landed late last night and there were no doctors available. No one will see me in their office today on short notice. They're all too busy. I had ear pain when we landed last night. Got dizzy. Had to be carried off the plane. That's when they gave me the pink slip. Had a date with the co-pilot, but had to cancel when I started vomiting."

Wolfe patted on the middle of the well worn exam table. "Have a seat," he said. "Let me look in your ears, nose, and throat and listen to your lungs."

"I don't have time for this," the stewardess raised her voice.

"You are so close to either getting out of here, or getting back in line to be seen," Wolfe said, beginning to dislike her attitude. "Either you do as I ask, or I go back to the wards and you wait for the intern who is supposed to see you to return from wherever he is. Okay?"

The woman climbed onto the table, pulled off her uniform coat and pulled her blouse from her skirt. Her face remained grim, determined to live through the experience. Wolfe listened to her heart and lungs through the blouse. He then checked her cranial nerves, looked in her mouth, and put the otoscope speculum into her ears. "Do your ears hurt right now?" he asked. "And how is your hearing?" Both eardrums were candy apple red, and bulging. They reminded him of volcanoes preparing to erupt, instead of the flat, tan colored tympanic membranes he usually saw.

"Ears hurt like hell, and sounds are muffled," she said. "But I have to be on that flight today."

"Well, I don't know if you lucked out when you got to see me, or whether it was bad luck, but I can't sign that note," Wolfe said. "I am probably the only doctor in this hospital to have completed the USAF's Aerospace Medicine course as a medical student. I can almost guarantee your ear drums will rupture if you fly in this condition. This is called barotitis media, if you want to know. I'm guessing you have allergies or a cold and flew anyway. I'll write you some prescriptions and have you buy some Afrin over the counter, but you can't fly like this. If you rupture your eardrums, you'll be out of work for four to six more weeks, maybe longer. As it is, you probably will not be able to fly for a week or two."

"Can't anything be done?"

"In the old days, we used to use a sterile needle and poke a hole in bulging ear drums to let the fluid and pressure out, but a certain percentage of patients lost their hearing as a result. German pilots in WWII did the same, so they could change altitude quickly in their unpressurized aircraft without having incapacitating ear pain or vertigo. Your pain will be so bad that you'd be useless on any flight you took today without narcotics on board. Pain medicine would sedate you and make you worthless, too."

"You mean I wasted my morning here?" she asked.

"Not exactly," Wolfe said handing her the prescriptions and a written reminder to buy Afrin.

"I have no place to stay for a week. My cheating boy friend will be on that airplane with those other harlot stewardesses. Thanks a lot, Doc." Tears began to seep from her tear ducts.

Wolfe let her anger spill over him. He had gotten used to patients' rage and verbal abuse when they did not get their way. For some reason, he felt a lot more empathy for her, though, than other patients. He scribbled Samantha's name, address, and phone number on the back of a blank prescription slip. "This is the name of a friend of mine," he said. "She's a doctor here, too. Call her. Use my name. She'll have a place you can stay. One of her roommates is out of town for a month. And when your ears are better, she'll sign that note."

The stewardess stood. She laid the papers on the exam table and pulled on her coat and tucked in her blouse. Once dressed, she deliberately held the prescriptions in front of Wolfe's face and tore them into fourths. Not seeing the trash can, she shoved the scraps of paper into a coat pocket and marched out of the exam room.

"You're welcome," Wolfe said.

Jada stood outside the door. "I heard. Sorry, Doc."

After he finished writing, Wolfe scanned the file for the patient's name: Lisa Johannsen. He handed the chart to Jada.

Chapter 26

"When I was in the air force," Dr. Scott reminisced at morning chart review. Wolfe wished he could fall asleep, but the memory of Ms. Johannsen had had a surprising effect on him. Any time he tried to sleep, the recollection of her face, her perfume, and her anger welled up out of his subconscious, to haunt him. He realized he was well on his way to becoming obsessed with the stewardess, also that he would never see her again. As a child, Wolfe had gone through these obsessions, too. He had an undying crush on a neighbor. She was 12; he was nine. She stopped talking to him when she realized he followed her around. He still played with her little brother; they were buddies. And her mother, kind soul, chided him about his love for her daughter, while giving him chocolate chip cookies and advice. Wolfe was heartsick for a month. Magically, the heartbreak gradually disappeared after months.

In eighth grade, it happened again. Only Cherie Winslow's father was in the Army. They moved away after school let out for the year. Wolfe spent an entire summer in the doldrums. He had repeat attacks in high school, fortunately short-lived and infrequent. There had been casual female acquaintances in the navy; no special love, except maybe the girl from San Mateo. And when he decided to go to medical school, he forswore any interest in women or close personal relationships, believing they would interfere with school. But the nurse from California who later went on missions to an Indian reservation and Africa certainly made studying for exams difficult during one pathology course.

Then, Lisa Johannsen entered his life. Wolfe knew the feeling would not last forever. He also knew he was going to be miserable for at least a month, possibly three. Until his mind wrote over her memory with newer, less painful memories, he was stuck.

"...Kenneth Cooper, you know the aerobics guy, was one of my docs. The guy he wrote about in his first book, the guy with chest pain and a heart attack? Hell, we all knew him. He didn't have a myocardial infarction; he had pericarditis. Jogging didn't make him well. When the inflammation went away, he would have gotten better if he had jogged or done nothing at all. It's all hokum," Scott said. He sent the interns and residents to the wards, but asked Wolfe to remain in the classroom.

Wolfe stood by Scott's desk, waiting for the physician to punish him for whatever he had done wrong. Scott pulled a sheaf of papers from his briefcase. "I read your paper," he said.

"Yes, sir?" Wolfe said. He expected some criticism. Scott's specialty was criticism. All interns had been required to author an article for a medical journal as part of the internship. He had never written a medical paper before and expected he had not done a very good job of it. Figueroa had pushed them to choose a subject quickly and have the paper written by January. Most interns picked a subject from their first rotation. Being in the ER, Wolfe had chosen intubation as his subject. He had asked Dr. Scott to review it.

"This is actually not a bad paper," Scott said, stunning Wolfe. "I don't think you need some of the statistics or background you put into the paper, however."

"I copied the format other people had used in the Journal of the American College of Emergency Physicians," Wolfe explained.

"JACEP's standards are a bit lower than our journal, the Journal of the American Medical Association," Scott said. "You have to remember, there is no real national board of Emergency Medicine, yet. And there may never be one. It's a composite board, made up of people who are not ER docs: family practice, surgery, internal medicine, etc. I don't know if it will ever be a real board. A lot of us don't think ER docs are genuine docs. They don't have enough in-depth knowledge about the diseases they treat."

"I thought the idea was for them to keep the patient alive long enough for the specialists to take over," Wolfe said.

"Yeah, yeah," Scott said. "I've heard all the arguments. Know a little bit about a lot of things versus knowing everything about a small subject. These guys may be only the fifth ER residency in the US, but they may also be the last. A lot of ER guys in the real world are just losers. Can't run a private practice on their own. If you want to be a *real* doctor, Wolfe, you want to complete a real residency."

"Like an internist?" Wolfe asked.

"Surgeons are just technicians doing what the internists tell them to do," Scott explained his point of view. "Sub-specialists, like neurologists, dermatologists, and immunologists, are looking for a soft life. The general internist is the best equipped physician there is. Don't forget it." He handed Wolfe the paper. "I made some remarks in the margins, things I think make it a better paper. But you do what you want. Give it to Figueroa by next week. It would be nice to have it accepted by a journal before your internship ends. Of course, it won't be published for 18 to 24 months after it is accepted. Too much trash out there today. Hard to keep up with all the journals now." Scott waved Wolfe out of the classroom, pulling a chart toward himself to review.

"Yes, sir," Wolfe said, leaving the room. He leafed through the paper and his illustrations on the way to the wards. *Hell*, he thought, *Scott marked on every page*. Wolfe did not touch-type. Each page had been re-typed at least three times to make it as perfect as possible. He would have to do them all again. *Maybe someday, someone will figure out a way to use a computer to make corrections*, he thought.

Prior to entering the female ward, Wolfe was stopped by an elderly man, one he recognized as the husband to an elderly woman who suffered from severe rheumatoid arthritis. "Dr. Wolfe," the old man called, "may I have a word with you?"

Wolfe did not remember the man's last name, or his wife's first name. He had gotten into the habit of remembering patients by their diseases and locations. This man was the husband of the rheumatoid arthritis in the third bed on the female general medical ward. Given a minute, he could pick her card out of the stack of fifty 3 x 5 cards in his breast pocket, but a name from memory? No way. "Yes, sir?" he said.

"Do you suppose you could get me the last name of my wife's evening nurse and her phone number?"

"I don't think the nurse expects you to give her a gift or a special thank you," Wolfe said, completely misinterpreting the man's intentions.

"Oh, no," the man said. "It's not that. You see, Doctor, my wife has a serious case of rheumatoid arthritis. She has been unwilling and unable to have sex for a decade. She doesn't know, because I tell her

I'm no longer interested, but I've had a number of sexual partners over the years. I am attracted to the young woman who took care of her last evening. I think she is attracted to me, also."

Wolfe eyed the old man carefully. He seemed to be in his late sixties. *Did people in their sixties have sex?* He remembered reading they did. He had heard jokes about younger folks finding their parents or grandparents in compromising positions and places, but couldn't imagine this old man doing it with a young nurse. Wolf grinned at the thought. "I don't think I can help you, sir."

Offended by Wolfe's grin, the elderly man snapped, "Young man, I want you to know that my partners have always been very satisfied."

"Yes, sir," Wolfe replied. *I wish I could say the same*. He walked away shaking his head. *Now I have to pimp for these people, too?*

Chapter 27

Toward the end of February and while still on internal medicine, Wolfe found himself making rounds with the neurologists for a week. Happy to be away from the opinionated Dr. Scott, Wolfe still had a hard time adjusting to living with the *fleas*: internists. To many of them, medicine was an intellectual game only. They cared little about their patients. The game was one-upmanship of their peers, their mentors, their students, anyone in fact including Wolfe or the patient. Their biggest goal was to be *right,* to make the correct diagnosis, know the most minutiae regardless of the consequences.

Waiting for the discussion to begin, Wolfe fished a black banana wrapped in several napkins out of his white coat pocket. He peeled back the thin dark skin and began to consume the brown banana. "You should wait another day to eat that," one of the neurology residents told him.

"Why?" Wolfe asked after finishing. He wrapping the peel in the napkins and dropping the remains in a nearby trash can."

"By then you could drink it with a straw," the resident said.

"My dad stopped on an island in the Pacific Ocean on his way to the Korean War," Wolfe said. "He told me the natives there preferred their bananas very ripe, blacker than mine. Said they were sweeter. You should try it. They are."

Wolfe and the three other doctors stood in the hallway outside a private room, which Wolfe knew held an elected City of Jacksonville official. "Wolfe," the senior neurology resident, Brad Newcomb, asked, "do you know who Phineas Gage was?"

As an undergraduate student, Wolfe had once looked through a psychology book a classmate left in his dorm room. The classmate also left a bookmark in the textbook. Wolfe casually lifted the book and it fell open to the bookmarked page, facing glossy photographs of a skull with a hole in the top and one of the tamping bar that had been driven by an explosion through the man's skull. Intrigued, Wolfe read the chapter concerning the pictures. The fascinating part of the story was the man had survived the explosion and the destruction of part of his brain. The man's name was indelibly etched into Wolfe's memory: Phineas Gage.

It wasn't often that Wolfe knew the answers when pimped by the internists. Even knowing the resident would continue to ask questions until Wolfe didn't know the answer to one, he smiled. "If I remember correctly," Wolfe said, "he was a railroad worker who was tamping some dynamite down a hole with a metal rod. Somehow he set the charge off and the explosion drove the rod through his skull. He survived, but developed a weird dementia afterwards. Something about sleeping for days on end."

Surprised Wolfe knew the answer, the resident quickly thought of more questions. "Do you know how many dementias there are? Or how to tell them apart?"

Fairly certain of the answer to the second question, Wolfe tried that first. "I think an autopsy or brain biopsy is the only way to tell them apart," he said. "Have no idea how many there are. Let's see: Lewy body, Alzheimer's, prefrontal...."

"Not bad guesses," Newcomb said. "Don't forget about vascular, neoplastic, psychiatric, hydrocephalus, or Parkinson's. Our next patient has an old age dementia of some kind. Family hasn't agreed to allowing a biopsy, yet." He opened the door to the crowded private room. The patient lay in one of the two beds. Multiple family members sat on the second bed, in the two chairs in the room, and stood in front of the window overlooking 8th Street. A loud argument ensued.

"He gave away $3000 of Duval County's money," one family member said. "He can't be in his right mind. Dad, why did you write that check for $3000?"

"What check?" the elderly man asked, smile on his face.

"See that smile," another relative said. "He wrote that check on purpose. He knew what he was doing. He did it out of political spite. There's nothing wrong with his mind."

"Excuse me," Newcomb announced. "We have to examine the patient. I would appreciate it if everyone would leave. Those of you who have not checked in with the nurse will need to go to the nurses' station down the hall. Generally, only two visitors are allowed to visit the patient at a time. And only during the specified visiting hours."

The room quieted. Family members gathered belongings and filed out of the room silently. Some squeezed the elder man's hand. Women left him pecks on the cheek. The last man out the door said to Newcomb, "Doctor, if you can't release his medical records to us, we'll have to subpoena them or get a court ordered competency test."

Newcomb replied, "I'm sorry, sir, but the records are confidential. Before you petition the court, though, you might talk with Dr. Schafer, the neurology attending physician taking care of him. The nurse will know how to get in touch with him." He pointed a thumb down the hallway.

"Thank you, sir," the man replied.

Wolfe watched as the neurology team tested the black city councilman. Initially stone faced, he brightened up when addressed by the residents. He smiled, knew his own name, and thought the year was 1974. He had no idea who the president was, but guessed it might be Truman. Counting backward by sevens from 100 proved impossible. He remembered one of three words when asked. Drawing a clock face with the time on it was too difficult a task. He did recognize the elected officials in a photograph of a building dedication in the morning newspaper.

Finished with their exam, the small group of doctors heard a commotion outside the room. When they opened the door, they found two men restraining a third man, who repeatedly tried to punch a fourth man. Two hospital security guards had just arrived and stepped between the men. Wolfe watched them handcuff the pugilist and lead him away, followed by the others. The neurology residents retired to the nurses' break room. Finding styrofoam cups and a fresh pot of coffee, they each poured a cup and camped out around the small table.

"So, what do you think, Wolfe?" Newcomb asked, sipping his black coffee.

"I don't think he should be writing checks for the City of Jacksonville," Wolfe said, dumping his fifth packet of sugar into his cup. "He definitely won't be able to balance the account."

"Want some coffee with that sugar?" Newcomb asked, "How about driving a car? Or cooking his own meals?"

Wolfe thought for a minute. "I guess that depends on his support system. Can we prevent him from doing those things?"

"A judge can take away his driver's license, if someone can prove he is a danger to others. That's sometimes hard to establish. It might be hard to enforce, too, unless you remove the vehicle from his possession. The mechanical act of driving is like the mechanical act of riding a bicycle. It's hard to forget how."

"But making good decisions and good judgments? How quick will his reflexes be?" Wolfe asked.

"Hard to say," Newcomb said. "I think he would be putting his assets in jeopardy in today's litigious climate. If he hurts someone with his car, some lawyer might want more in compensation than his automobile insurance company is willing to pay. He might become liable for the remainder. I think some of the family feels the need to protect his assets."

"Because they are in his will?" a resident asked.

"Maybe, but also maybe because they really care about him," Newcomb said. "They might have misguided ideas about freedom of action."

"Someone disagrees?" Wolfe asked.

Newcomb tilted his chin down, staring at Wolfe. "Did you not see the two men fighting in the hallway? I'd say they had a serious difference of opinion. My guess is that it's over what to do for the old man."

"Who else would disagree?" Wolfe asked. "They'd have to be in denial not to see his mental state. It's in his best interest."

"Why did the Pharaoh hold his breath?" one of the other residents asked Wolfe, then answered his own question. "He was in de Nile."

"The patient will, for sure," Newcomb said. Having heard the joke multiple times, he tried to ignore it. "He doesn't know he has lost the ability to make good judgments. He thinks he's fine; he believes the rest of the world is screwed up. Until now, he may have been able to hide his memory loss by writing himself notes and cutting down on his interactions with others. If you don't speak with someone spontaneously, it's less likely you will have to recall something from memory. If you control the agenda, that's not so apparent."

"He's like a child. He needs protection," Wolfe said.

"Or, is he like a willful, rebellious teenager?" Newcomb asked. "You can't take someone's freedom lightly. Among others, the ACLU would be on your ass. But, I'll bet he has some family members who have strong feelings both ways. Some don't recognize his mental changes, yet, and think restricting his driving or giving the checkbook to someone else would be a great imposition. What's the dividing line between protection and freedom?"

Discussion over, the residents resumed rounds. Newcomb had been asked to consult on the 15 year-old quadriplegic from the motor vehicle accident. Some sensation had returned in her legs and abdomen. "Here's a minority any one of us could join in an instant," he said before entering the girl's room. "Be extra careful driving."

Chapter 28

Figueroa started the next M&M conference with two announcements. The first drew cheers from the Emergency Medicine residents. They would no longer be required to leave the hospital ER to pronounce people dead inside the hearses that frequented the ER parking lot. Nursing home owners and funeral home directors had established this practice in an effort to save themselves time in procuring necessary paperwork to dispose of the dead. Once they had a doctor's signature on the form, they could apply for a Florida State Death Certificate.

"From now on, any funeral home director that comes to the ER parking lot will be asked to sign in and wait in line with everyone else who is waiting to see a physician. Why should the dead have head of the line privileges?" Figueroa asked. Cheers and catcalls arose from the ER residents and everyone else who understood that the ER waiting room times hovered around five hours, on good days.

"Actually," Figueroa said, after the laughter died down, "there is a new protocol. The pathology intern or resident will be beeped. He will make the pronouncement and sign the paperwork. The new paperwork states only that the patient is not merely dead, but most sincerely dead." More laughter followed the line from the *Wizard of Oz*.

Figueroa continued, "The form also states that no resuscitation is indicated and no cause of death can determined at this time. For that the funeral home director will have to talk with the patient's family doctor and/or JSO. Suspicious deaths will still have to be investigated by the Jacksonville Sheriff's Office." Within days of the announced policy change, the funeral directors and nursing home owners had stopped coming to University Hospital altogether, to the relief of the interns on the pathology rotation.

The second announcement left all but a few residents scratching their heads. "I have noticed not a few interns and residents who seem to be congregating for no obvious reason," Figueroa said. "If you have nothing to do, please come by my office. I have lots of learning materials and assignments that I can give you."

"He's on to us," Wolfe told Iggy.

"He's just paranoid," Iggy said. "What's he going to do, break up every group of residents, or try to listen to their conversations?"

The first patient presented in the conference had arrived in the ER complaining of a headache. The case was discussed by the senior neurosurgical resident, Michael Chong. "As much as Dr. Figueroa disapproves of the use of x-rays to make diagnoses in people who have back pain or headaches, I thought this would be a good teaching case," the resident said.

The lights dimmed and an x-ray was projected on the screen in front of the auditorium. A lateral view of the skull filled the panel. Inside the skull a corona of long, thin, sharp metal objects projected into the side view of the skull. "These are nails," Chong said. "Twenty-seven nails, ranging in size from two penny to ten penny."

"Was that the cause of death?" Figueroa asked. Several residents laughed.

"He's not dead," Chong said. Another view of the skull flashed onto the projection screen. In this front to back view, it was obvious that the nails were all in the midline of the skull, like a weird, morbid reverse Mohawk haircut. "Every nail is in the Longitudinal Cerebral Fissure, the empty space between the cerebral lobes. Our first priority is to make sure he doesn't develop an infection. Then we are going to try to get a court order to grant us permission to remove the nails. He's sedated on the unit with intravenous antibiotics. His vital signs are normal."

"Why do you need a court order to remove the nails?" Figueroa asked.

"I was hoping you'd ask," the resident said smiling. "Our patient is not sane, as you might guess."

"Surely, his family would agree to the surgery if he is incompetent," Figueroa said.

"His only family is his wife," the resident explained. "She's the person who placed those nails. Every time he had a headache he came to our ER. The ER docs all gave him pain medicine, from aspirin to Darvon to Demerol. Nothing worked. Of course, they took no x-rays. M&M punishes those residents who take unnecessary x-rays. We all know the x-ray won't show anything when the patient had not had a trauma he would admit to. When the medication didn't work, he would show his wife where the pain was, and she drove a nail into that spot. Kind of a poor man's, heavy-handed acupuncture. We don't think she is sane either. They have both been Baker acted, in custody because they are a danger to themselves or others."

"Then who took the x-ray and why?" Figueroa asked.

"He showed up in neurology clinic last week complaining of a headache, of course," Chong said. "When asked where the pain was and how long he had had it, he pointed to the middle of his skull and said thirteen years. The neurology resident took the trouble to part the patient's matted hair. The patient's hygiene is not the best. That may be one of the reasons he got a minimal work-up on his visits to the ER. The neurology resident found several rusty flat pieces of metal that he could not remove from the scalp and an open sore. He ordered the x-ray."

"Fascinating," Figueroa said. "What kind of work does the man do?"

"He's on welfare and retired medically from the Marines," Chong said. "Battle fatigue during the Korean War. A Chosin Reservoir veteran. His wife sells seashells at the beach," Chong smiled, "to the antiques and dinosaurs who visit Florida." A smattering of laughter filtered from the audience.

"Thanks, Michael," Figueroa said. "Oh, and one more thing. Are you going to use a claw hammer or nail pulling tool to remove the nails?" Figueroa smiled. Some residents snickered.

"Vice-grips," Chong said. He had heard too many jokes about the patient.

Internal Medicine wanted to stress a point about taking a good look at patients' laboratory studies before they left the hospital, so they picked on a surgical intern who had been on their service the previous month. A patient had been admitted with pneumonia, treated and released after three days. He returned for a follow-up visit to the internal medicine clinic where he saw a different intern, who thought the man seemed weak, and sallow in appearance. Blood tests revealed the patient was anemic and in renal failure. He had to be admitted and started on dialysis.

The only abnormal blood test, out of the hundred or so the man had received while in the hospital for pneumonia was his serum creatinine. Initially, the result was 1.0 mg/dl. Just before discharge, it was 2.2 mg/dl.

Playing the devil's advocate, Figueroa said, "So, that's only a 1.2 mg/dl increase. How important could that be?"

"More than a fifty percent loss of kidney function," the medical resident, Hiram Myers, said.

"And what was his creatinine when he returned to clinic?" another resident asked.

Myers looked at his notes. "11.7," he said.

"Unfortunately," Figueroa said, "there are no shortcuts for knowing the acceptable ranges for blood tests. They are all different. A one milligram per deciliter change in some cases means nothing; in this case it meant kidney failure. Every test is different, has different parameters and different normal values. Until you learn the common results by rote, carry this around with you at all times." He waved a small green covered, printed booklet at the residents. All the laboratory values for all the tests performed at University Hospital were listed in the book.

"There isn't anything in here about the causes of abnormal lab values, however. You would do well to invest in a copy of this book." He held up a copy of Jacques Wallach's *Interpretation of Diagnostic Tests*, 2nd Edition. "This is my bible," he said. "If you want to know the differential diagnosis of any abnormal test, you need this book. Or one like it."

"The fleas have one in the break room," Iggy told Wolfe. "We're going to need one. I can't afford it, not with three mouths to feed."

Wolfe nodded. "If we really need it, I'll spring for it. You can invite me to dinner once a month for the rest of your life."

"Dr. Myers, were any of the patient's electrolytes, or as our patients refer to them *electric lights*, abnormal?" Figueroa asked.

"On re-admission, he did not have a single normal electrolyte value," Myers said. "After dialysis three times a week for four weeks, his kidney function returned to baseline. His antistreptolysin titer was high on readmission, so we think he had a strep pneumonia and his immune system over-reacted. Glomerulonephritis shut down his kidneys. We'll follow his ASO to make sure it drops below 200."

"He survived?"

"Yes, sir."

At the end of the conference, Figueroa gave the residents another word of advice. He said, "There are three kinds of doctors: those who learn from others' mistakes, those who learn from their own, and those who learn from both. Mistakes are inevitable, despite what the lawyers tell you. You can minimize the number of them, though."

Chapter 29

Valentine's Day, February 14, 1977 fell on a Monday. Even though the residents in the Emergency Medicine program never needed an excuse to party, the '77 Valentine's Day Party started at 8 p.m. ER residents usually partied during the week, because many of the junior and senior residents had weekend moonlighting jobs in various private hospital ERs. The exception to that was Schiffer who moonlighted 24-7, sometimes even when he was supposed to be working at University Hospital. Wolfe understood the temptation to moonlight. When a resident could earn the equivalent of an entire month's salary from University Hospital by working a single 12 hour shift in an ER, the choice to stay awake when he should be sleeping or studying was easy.

A Florida State medical license was required before a resident could moonlight. After finishing an internship, new physicians could apply for the license. The medical board usually granted such requests without question, if the physician had passed all three parts of the National Board Exam and had finished an internship satisfactorily. In fact, many physicians in Florida and other states started their own practices after only one year of post medical school education. These doctors were known as General Practitioners, because they did not specialize, i.e. they did not complete a residency or fellowship in some specialty. Being a GP would be one option open to Wolfe, if Figueroa allowed him to complete the internship.

Besides the ER residents, who else attended these blow-outs depended on who had that evening and/or the next day off. During their time in the ER, Emergency Medicine residents worked two twelve hour days on and two days off, then two twelve hour nights on and two days off. Most of the residents in other specialties considered that schedule cushy. However, no one worked harder than the ER residents while in the hospital. They evaluated, processed, treated, saved, or pronounced some 350 to 400 patients per day through Primary Care, Trauma, ICU, and Resuscitation with only four to six docs on hand at any one time.

Invited by one of the ER residents, Samantha Joiner had invited Wolfe to accompany her to the party. Reluctantly, he had accepted. He arrived in Ponte Vedra, an elegant, well-to-do, beachside community south of Jacksonville Beach located in St. Johns County, at about 10 p.m. Leaving cardiology late that evening, he knew he had to return to the hospital early the next morning to read EKGs with Dr. Delaney. Iggy had gone straight home to be with Janice and the baby. Samantha arrived long before he did. Smoking a cigarette outside the home, she met him in front of the huge carved wooden double door to the house. Already drunk, Sam slurred her words. "What's up, Wolfie?" she asked. "Oh, wait, you're not Wolfie. You're Wolfie's *handler*, if you get my drift?" She laughed. "Let me introduce you around." When she opened the door, the shock wave emanating from the stereo nearly pushed him back, into the circular cobblestone driveway.

One of the senior ER residents rented the three story mansion from the owner, a contractor who lived in Miami. The builder had found himself over-extended in the faltering economy brought on by the Arab oil boycott. Unable to sell the house or handle two mortgages without renting one residence, he chose to live in Miami and rent the Ponte Vedra mansion for peanuts. There were seven bedrooms, a four car garage with a mother-in-law suite above them, two pools and a hundred yards of beachfront sand dunes.

"How does Sandoval afford this?" Wolfe asked Sam. "The mortgage must be several thousand a month."

"Nah," Sam said. "Sandoval said the builder didn't borrow much to build it. Spent cash. He gives Sandoval a break, because he considers him to be house-sitting." She introduced him to most of the people at the party, not remembering in her inebriated state that he had met a majority of them at the hospital. There was a naked couple holding bottles of beer in the small pool; it turned out to be a very large hot tub.

More guests skinny dipped in the heated full size pool. Two people ran bare-assed or scantily dressed over the dunes and through the sea oats to the beach, disappearing from the house flood lights into the darkness. The ocean chill kept most guests out of the water, but two hardy souls held hands and walked barefoot in the surf. Wolfe saw more couples clutching each other while horizontal: on couches, the floor, the deck, even in the sand.

"Nice job if you can get it," Wolfe said, as he surveyed the rowdy behavior. "House sitting, that is." He smelled the pungent sweet odor of burning pot, slightly different than the West Coast or Philippine versions he had confiscated as Shore Patrol in the navy. Burning marijuana smelled nearly the same worldwide; at least it had to him.

Initially worried about JSO and their physical approach to drug users, Wolfe calmed down when he saw three firefighter/paramedics in uniform in the great room. The civil servants had great pull with JSO, even though police and firefighters bad-mouthed each other's departments good-naturedly at every opportunity.

The dining room table held the bar. Twenty to thirty bottles of every type of liquor he could imagine sat on the table. While in the transient barracks on Treasure Island outside of San Francisco, prior to deployment to WestPac and the Gulf of Tonkin on the carrier, Wolfe's temporary job in the navy had been to clean up the Chief Petty Officers Club on a daily basis.

Along with three other sailors, he swabbed the floors, cleaned up the tables, chairs, and bar of the club. In addition, every morning of every day of the week, he stood at the huge metal dumpster and shattered empty bottle after empty bottle of booze by throwing it into the dumpster. The navy required this protective measure so the local moonshiners could not soak the labels off the bottles or re-use the containers for their concoctions. He didn't think anyone could out-drink the CPOs. *This crowd would give them stiff competition, though,* he decided. *It's one way of letting go of all your fears: death, dying, or allowing others in your care to die.*

"I have a surprise for you," Sam told Wolfe, leading him by the hand. They were halfway across the great room, dodging individuals and couples when they ran into an impasse. Eight or nine residents had gathered around a couch.

Morty Summers, red-headed second year ER resident and owner of a wicked sense of humor, sat on the couch next to a telephone. He shouted, "Quiet!" All conversation stopped. Someone shut down the stereo. Everyone stared at Summers. "We have a patient we need to dump in the University Hospital ER. Nichols is on. He should appreciate this after what Beaches Hospital tried to pull recently."

The crowd chuckled. The residents who knew about the transfer of the raped woman explained quietly to those who didn't. Summers dialed a number on the telephone. He waited for a minute, and then said in a German accented voice, "Jah, dis is Dr. Schmidt at Memorial Hospital. I am zending you a patient." He broke out in a smile. Putting his hand over the receiver, he said, "They're getting Nichols." A chuckle wormed its way through the party-goers.

"Who's dis? Oh. Good evening, Dr. Necker. Oh, Knuckles? Nichols, jah. Zo Zorry. Dis is Doctor Schmidt at Memorial Hospital. Ve have a poor patient for you. Oh, no. Ve do not see patients who have no money here. Dat's your job, jah?" Summers held the telephone in the air. The crowd heard Nichols go ballistic on the other end of the line. The fury and rage in his voice cut through the air, although his words were indecipherable. Everyone laughed. Summers held his hand over the mouthpiece with finger to lips until quiet reigned again.

"Oh, zo zorry. I cannot contact ze ambulance," Summers told Nichols. "Dey left here ten minutes ago. Dey should be arriving at your hospital at any moment. No, I have no time to speak with your attending physician. Ve are very busy here. Jah, I have seen almost ten patients in the last four hours. Very, very busy." With those words, Summers pushed down the button on the base of the telephone cutting the connection. The room roared.

"That's just cruel," Wolfe said, as the crowd dispersed. The music again blared. He looked around. Sam had disappeared. Turning toward the bar, he thought he saw a familiar figure. The sight of the woman startled him. Immediately, he strode toward her in an effort to obtain a better look at her face, to make certain he knew her.

An empty champagne glass in one hand, she turned and looked him in the eyes. Even out of uniform, with her dark brown hair in a ponytail, wearing jeans, tennis shoes, and dark blue T-shirt under a white sweater, Wolfe knew her. "Miss Johannsen," he said, trying to appear casual, while his heart pounded so rapidly he heard it in his ears. "Nice to see you, again."

Johannsen looked at Wolfe, as if for the first time. "Do I know you?" she asked.

The hammering in Wolfe's chest stopped. His face blanched when the blood stopped flowing. When he recovered, he said, "Yeah.

I'm the doctor you saw in Primary Care a couple weeks ago. Have you recovered from your cold and barotitis media?"

"Oh," she said. "You're the *intern*. I remember now. You didn't want me to fly."

Wolfe's chin went to his chest. He inhaled a deep dejected breath through his nostrils, shaking his head. *I'm a peon to her royalty*, he thought. "Yes, sorry. Hope I didn't inconvenience you too much," he said. "Nice to see you, again. Enjoy the party."

Wolfe turned to leave, knowing he would walk directly out the front door, hop in his car, and drive back to the apartment. *I just got her out of my mind,* he thought. *Now I have to go through that, again.* She stopped him with her laugh. "Addison? Right?" she said. He turned to face her. "Samantha says they call you Addy, or Wolfie." Her smile revealed even white teeth and a sparkle in her eyes. She wore no make-up, allowing her freckles to be seen.

"Actually, only Sam calls me Wolfie, and rarely," he said. "May I refill that for you?"

Sometime after 2 a.m., Wolfe dropped Lisa Johannsen at Sam's rental house. She had a key Sam had given her. They had spent the evening talking about flying, his father's, the navy's, and hers. They also discussed Savannah, where she lived, and the I-95 detour that went through Savannah. Wolfe told her he occasionally drove I-95 north to Virginia but hated the tall, steel rickety bridge and detour through the middle of Savannah, where I-95 had not been completed through Georgia. "Welcome to Georgia," he said, "set your watch back 30 years." She had taken his criticism of her home state with good humor, agreeing with his assessment. She pointed out that she lived only a mile from that bridge and invited him to stop in next time he drove home. "Won't be until July," he said, "unless Figueroa busts my chops before then." He also had complained about the paper mills and the terrible smells from them in southern Georgia.

"My word," Johannsen said in a perfectly delightful, exaggerated, southern accent, "one would think you didn't like my beloved Peach State. I was about to ask you to visit me in the near future, but if you are that adamant about the backwardness and smelliness of my home, I may withdraw the invitation." Then she laughed a laugh that made Wolfe feel good for the first time in almost six months.

"I take back everything I said," he told her. "When should I come to Savannah?" Therein lay the rub. She had a stewardess's schedule, in fact would start flying again that weekend. His internship could not be delayed. They resolved to call one another after she returned home.

When he left her at Sam's door, she planted a kiss on his cheek. "Thank you for taking care of me in the ER," she said. "I know I was rude. For that, I apologize. My ears really hurt. The medicine helped immensely."

"I thought you tore up the prescriptions," Wolfe said, confused.

"I did. I kept the scraps, though, and that dear, dear Samantha rewrote them for me. She cleared me to fly starting Friday. That's why I have to go home. Please keep in touch."

"What about your co-pilot friend?" Wolfe asked.

She batted her eyelashes. "Guess I'm just unlucky in love," she said, again with the heavy Georgian accent. "He found love with another stewardess on that flight I missed. Apparently, he has been finding love on a lot of flights. We broke up. It's over. For good. Keep in touch, Wolfie." She closed the door. Wolfie floated to his car and drove to the apartment.

Chapter 30

In winter, the sun rises late and sets early in Jacksonville. Many a day Wolfe arrived at the hospital in darkness and left in darkness, never having seen the sun. Early one morning, oh-dark-thirty the navy had called it, Wolfe parked his car in the huge lot behind the emergency room and ambled toward the door. Just as he arrived, a Trailways bus turned the corner from 8th street and entered the parking lot. When he had spent his first two months of internship in the ER and Primary Care, he had heard numerous jokes about the arrival of *the bus*, meaning a crowd had showed up. He had also heard about the *tour director*, a guy who stationed himself at the door to the hospital and would not allow entrance until the tour group had filled out, usually ten to twenty people.

Life is about to imitate humor, he thought. When he entered the ER's double doors, he began looking for the senior ER resident in order to give him a heads up concerning the bus. If the vehicle did not have a bunch of sick or injured passengers, its presence alone would be good for a laugh the rest of the day. *Anything to lighten the load.*

Not finding any physicians in Primary Care, Wolfe turned into the hallway leading to ER ICU. A loud argument immediately assaulted his ears. "I don't care where the senior resident is, Lynch," someone shouted. "Get off your ass and start seeing patients. The waiting room is – *surprisingly* – full. As usual."

Turning the corner, Wolfe could see the nurses standing behind their tall desk. Many had grins on their faces as they watched the confrontation develop in front of them. The ER ICU appeared to be deserted. All the beds sat empty. A diminutive Asian intern, whose name Wolfe did not know, harangued Lynch, the second year ER resident. Lazy Lynch got his nickname honestly. Wolfe had had difficulty finding him when he had worked in Primary Care. The man spent more time in the cafeteria drinking coffee than most interns spent in clinic. He was bright; his skills were fair; but he hated to work.

Lynch sat in a rolling chair, Nike clad feet on the desk in front of him. He wore the uniform of an ER doc, green scrubs, short white coat with pockets overflowing with small pamphlets, gloves, tongue depressors, reflex hammer, etc. A stethoscope hung around his long neck. Lynch was easily six-foot-three. He eyed his opponent carefully before speaking, an ironic smile on his face. “Nagakawa, do you really think that if I managed to see three or four patients in the next hour, before we got busy here in the ICU, it would make any difference in the number of patients you see today?”

“You arrogant ass,” the intern screamed. He could not have been more than five-foot-one. “Of course it won’t make a difference in how many people I will see. It will make a difference in how many patients are seen, though. Some of those people have been out in the waiting room for days on end waiting for medical help. And you are sitting on your ass. Show some empathy. Show some respect for the patients.”

“After you’ve been here a little longer you will feel the same way I do,” Lynch said, turning the pages to his paper slowly. He started to read the comics.

“I want to talk to the senior ER resident,” Nagakawa said.

“I do, too,” Lynch responded. “Unfortunately his shift relief at St. Augustine General Hospital just left here. Dr. Gentry won’t get to St. Augustine for an hour. Then it will be another hour before Dr. Schiffer gets back here. That is, if he doesn’t go home to shower and shave first. He worked here yesterday, so he may have been awake for 24 hours already.”

“Why isn’t he on time?” Nagakawa asked.

“He can’t leave a private hospital, where there are paying customers and no other docs on the wards, without a doc in the ER. He’d lose his job. We’d all lose our moonlighting jobs if we did that,” Lynch explained.

"So, you're covering for him. And you're sitting on your ass?" The intern tore the paper from Lynch's hands and ripped it to shreds. He had taken a karate stance and was about to punch Lynch out when the Trailways driver blew the bus's deep throated, very loud horn. Startled, everyone in the ER including the intern pivoted toward the sound.

"Oh, yeah," Wolfe said. "I almost forgot. That bus you guys talk about all the time. It's sitting outside the back door." Nurses scrambled for a stretcher and several wheelchairs, followed by Lynch and the intern. In minutes they wheeled a middle-aged man into ER ICU and transferred him to a resuscitation bed. The patient was awake and trying to talk. He had a distorted expression on his face and his words made no sense. His right arm and leg dangled uselessly from the side of the bed.

"Looks like a left middle cerebral artery stroke," the intern said. He grabbed the patient's left arm and placed a tourniquet around it in preparation for starting an intravenous line.

"I'll take care of this, Nagakawa," Lynch said. "You get back to Primary Care. This isn't a code."

Nagakawa stared bitterly at Lynch. "I'll be back when Schiffer gets here," he said, pulling off the tourniquet and dropping the patient's arm onto the bed. Several nurses patted him on the back as he left. Lynch seemed unaware or uninterested in their support of the intern.

Wolfe turned to walk toward the bank of elevators. Dr. Figueroa stood in the hallway between him and the elevators. "Aren't you late for internal medicine chart review?" Figueroa asked him.

"Stopped to see if they needed any help. Bus arrived. Brought a stroke patient," Wolfe said. He pointed a thumb over his shoulder at the ER ICU. As the door to the elevator opened, he prayed Figueroa would not follow him into the empty metallic box.

"So your prayers were answered," Iggy said when he heard the story five minutes later outside the male medical ward. "I thought you were an atheist?"

"Today, I'm a theist," Wolfe said. "God was looking out for me, I think. Usually I'm an agnostic, although some days I'm a gnostic."

"Whatever," Iggy said. "We're all one hallucination away from being believers."

"I also think God hates religion. I know I do," Wolfe said. "What did I miss in chart review?"

"Nothing. Well, something if you also hate Pete Owens like the rest of us," Iggy said. "Know him?"

"Remind me," Wolfe said.

"Owens is that smart ass second year internal medicine resident who pimps the interns about weird diseases no one else ever heard of. He's a mean s.o.b., has no personality and…."

"…spends lunch reading arcane medical texts. Says he wants to specialize in rare tropical diseases after he does a fellowship in Infectious Disease," Wolfe finished Iggy's thought. Iggy nodded. "Got it. I remember him. He's already pimping interns about the source of Legionnaires' disease. Hell, CDC just released that information. What did he do now? Is he related to Figueroa by any chance?"

"Doubt it, unless all pricks are related. Which could be true, I guess," Iggy said, laughing. "He didn't do anything. The ER residents did it to him. Revenge is sweet. Last night he was on call. Had to admit four or five patients from the ER. While waiting for the internal medicine intern to finish her work-up of the last patient, he crawled onto an empty stretcher and fell asleep. Bob Gentry had the night shift."

"Yeah, I heard," Wolfe said. "He's now on his way to St. Augustine General to relieve Schiffer. So what did he do?"

"Very stealthily, he put the leather restraints on Owens. I mean both arms and both legs. Then he cut off Owens's white coat with the penny cutters and removed his shoes and socks."

"Owens must have been out like a light," Wolfe said.

"No different than you or me after thirty-six hours," Iggy said. "Anyway, they rolled the stretcher carefully into the closed room they use for psychos without waking him up. They locked the wheels and then woke him up by pouring water on his face. He started screaming his head off, demanding to be released."

"So what happened?" Wolfe asked.

"Gentry closed the door and went to find the new rent-a-cop. He told security that the guy in the room was psychotic and not to let him loose, no matter what happened. He asked the guard to stay in the room with Owens to prevent him from hurting himself. And the best part: he also told the cop that the patient had delusions of being a doctor and not to listen to anything he said." Iggy shook his head laughing. "Dr. Scott is livid. He is going to have a meeting with Dr. Singhal today."

"Why?" Wolfe asked. "Seems like a harmless prank."

"Well, the guard didn't know anything about restraints or how to protect patients because he's new. Owens managed to get his hands free. Apparently, he forgot his feet were also tied down. He tried to jump from the bed and ended up dangling from the stretcher with his face on the floor. Looks like he suffered a broken wrist and will need some dental work on his maxillary incisors."

"Jesus," Wolfe said, with a smile. "Couldn't have happened to a nicer guy."

"Gentry?" Iggy asked.

"Yeah, Gentry. I hope he doesn't get in too much trouble. He's the best ER resident."

"I agree," Iggy said.

Chapter 31

Wolfe lay on his back in his room in the apartment at the beach, unable to sleep. He recognized the symptoms: his infatuation with Lisa Johannsen revved up his mind into overdrive. It raced. Like the colors on the side of a spinning top that refused to slow down, ideas spun through his brain in a blur, making it impossible for him to sleep. He looked at the clock, knowing that was a bad idea: 2 a.m. Staring at the ceiling, he heard muffled footsteps in the kitchen. The fridge door opened and closed, followed by Iggy and Janice's door closing. He stared at the ceiling, counted sheep, concentrated on his breathing, and spouted anatomy minutiae. Nothing worked. He could not sleep.

Surrendering to his plight, he got out of bed and turned on the light. Deciding to study something boring he pulled a small medical manual from his white coat pocket, *The Manual of Clinical Problems in Internal Medicine* by Barnes, Verdai, and Spivak. *Figueroa would be proud of me*, he thought, *studying differential diagnosis at two in the morning. I'm not too one dimensional*. After bunching up his pillow so he could read comfortably, he laid back into bed. Almost immediately he heard a soft knock on his door. "Addy," Janice whispered. "I saw your light."

Making certain he was covered decently by the blanket, he spoke in normal tones, "I'm awake. Come on in."

The door opened slowly. Janice stood there in a thick pink

bathrobe, barefoot. "Addy, would you take a look at Nancy Rose for me?"

He sat up in the bed. "Sure, Janice," he said. "What's up?"

Janice burst into tears. "She won't wake up, Addy. She never misses a feeding. She slept through dinner and her usual nighttime feeding. I don't know what to do. Iggy's at the hospital. I can't call him."

"Give me a minute to get dressed," he said. She left the room, closing the door behind her.

He found her in her room leaning over the baby's crib, hand brushing the wisp of blonde hair from the towhead's face. Tears ran down her cheeks. Wolfe felt her shudder when he put his hands on her shoulders. "Let me see her," he said, gently moving her to one side.

Nancy Rose's face radiated heat. It felt moist to Wolfe. In the dim light, her complexion seemed redder than he remembered. "Turn on the lights," he told Janice.

When the lights came on, Wolfe had a difficult time maintaining a neutral expression. Nancy Rose's right upper and lower eyelids were very swollen and a deep purple in color. "Janice," he said, as calmly as possible, "I want you to get dressed. We have to take Nancy Rose to the hospital."

"Why, Addy? What's wrong with her?" Janice asked, sobbing.

"She has a bad eye infection, Janice. It's called periorbital cellulitis. I saw a couple of these on pediatrics. As long as it is treated quickly, it turns out okay." He didn't mention that Nancy Rose had an increased chance of losing her eye and of developing meningitis.

"What hospital are we going to?" Janice asked, taking an armload of clothing into the master bath in order to change.

"University. We can't go to a regular ER; don't know how long the wait would be. She needs intravenous antibiotics as quickly as we can get them. Besides, she'll get head of the line privileges at University being an intern's kid." He did not say that he did not trust any of the ER docs who dumped patients on University Hospital, or that the real reason for the head of the line privileges would be that Nancy Rose would likely be the sickest child in the pediatric ER that night. "And Iggy's on pediatric surgery this month, so he'll be close by."

"You think she has to stay in the hospital? Can't she take antibiotics at home?" Janice asked.

"No. This infection is pretty serious," Wolfe said. He looked at the baby's swollen right eye. *Maybe deadly,* he thought.

Wolfe carried Nancy Rose to his car. After Janice climbed into the vehicle, he handed her the baby and closed the passenger door. They drove to University Hospital in silence, too afraid to talk about the possible consequences of the infection.

At the hospital, Wolfe let Janice out at the ambulance entrance, then parked as close to the ER as possible in the staff parking lot. He got to the Pediatric ER before Iggy arrived. Finding a senior pediatric resident, Lacey Thornton, present in the pediatric ER, he told her about Nancy Rose's condition and that the baby was the daughter of one of the orthopedic interns.

Wolfe liked Dr. Thornton, even though she was part of a mixed marriage. She was smart and congenial, just the type of person Figueroa believed needed to be a pediatrician. Her husband worked across the street in Methodist Hospital as an ER (and this was the *mixed* part of the marriage) *nurse*. Wolfe knew her husband had been a navy corpsman who had served with the marines in Vietnam. He maintained a military bearing, took no crap from anyone. Wolfe wondered how a doctor could give up control of anything to a spouse. Most married physicians he knew dominated their spouses, even the women physicians. They rarely let the other make a decision. Iggy arrived while Thornton examined Nancy Rose.

"Well?" Iggy said after Thornton pulled her stethoscope from her ears and laid it over her shoulders.

"The baby's yours, right?" she asked Iggy. Distracted by Nancy Rose's infection and not having paid close attention to Wolfe, she was confused as to whether Wolfe or Iggy was the father.

Iggy pulled Janice closer to him, arm around her shoulder. "She's ours," he said. "Addy is my best friend."

"Well," Thornton said calmly, "she has a serious infection. Addy's right. It appears to be periorbital cellulitis. How long ago did it start?"

"I didn't know she had it until Addy had me turn on the lights in the room," Janice said, "less than an hour ago."

"No conjunctivitis, no drainage from the eye before you put her to bed?" the senior resident asked.

Janice shook her head. "There was a little red dot I noticed on her right upper eyelid at dinnertime," she said. "She refused the bottle at dinner. I changed her diaper and put her to bed. Then she didn't wake up for her nighttime feeding. She's never done that before. And she felt hot in the car."

"Temperature was 104," Thornton said. "We gave her some

acetaminophen. I need blood for tests to see what her white count is and to get some blood cultures. Also, I need to start an i.v. to give her intravenous antibiotics. Before I start the antibiotics, I have to do a spinal tap."

"Oh," Janice said, sucking in her breath.

"You really need the lumbar puncture?" Iggy asked.

"There's a high incidence of meningitis with periorbital infections. The cultures are useless if done after the antibiotics start," Thornton said. "I will also have to talk with tonight's attending physician, Dr. Rosenberg. The best drug to use in this situation is Chloramphenicol, but I need his permission to use it."

"Geez," Iggy said. "I don't know if I want to do that." Worried, Wolfe shook his head. He knew Chloramphenicol had a rare nasty side effect of wiping out a patient's bone marrow, thereby causing aplastic anemia and death. The complication seemed more prevalent in blonde, blue-eyed infants. Iggy was a typical Viking. His daughter had his hair, complexion, and eye color.

Thornton continued. "You also don't want her to have meningitis or lose the eye. The optic nerve is part of the brain. Any infection in the eye can have dire consequences. We'll only keep her on it until we get the blood and spinal cultures back. If another antibiotic will work as well, we'll stop the Chloramphenicol."

"Okay," Iggy said, pulling Janice closer. She sobbed, her face pressed into his chest. "Get the blood for cultures and tests, do the spinal tap, and start the i.v. But let me talk with Dr. Rosenberg about the antibiotic choice before you start it. Okay?"

"Done," the senior resident said. She turned to Wolfe. "Addy, I need a holder for the tap. Up for that?"

Wolfe looked at Iggy. Iggy nodded. "No problem," Wolfe said.

Nancy Rose opened her eyes for the first time when the pediatrician drew her blood for the first culture and blood counts. Blood cultures were done twice, once in each arm. Nancy Rose eyed Thornton carefully when she took the second culture. Never did she squawk or cry. Even when Wolfe held her tightly in a ball for the spinal tap, she did not complain, although she seemed to be awake and alert. Wolfe could not decide if Nancy Rose was tough like her father, or if her infection interfered with her feeling pain. As chunky as the baby was, Thornton had difficulty finding a vein for the intravenous. Nancy Rose whimpered a little with the repeated needle sticks. *A good sign*, Wolfe thought. He felt better about her prognosis.

By the noon the next day Nancy Rose was the darling of the pediatric ward, receiving visitors from most of the orthopedic and ER nurses and other staff. Bright eyed and alert, her appetite returned. She devoured two bottles of formula. Janice had stopped breast feeding several weeks before. Nancy Rose's pediatrician suspected Janice could not supply enough calories to the baby who had screamed nightly for more food. Once they switched her to formula, her weight blossomed and she stopped crying at night. She was the size of a four month old at two months. She had never missed a meal, except this one time. Behind Iggy's back some neighbors referred to her good naturedly as the Michelin Man. Janice's pediatrician told her that Nancy Rose would be a big girl, and, like a puppy that has to grow into its feet, she'd grow into her weight.

The cultures came back in two days, *E.coli*. When the sensitivities showed the strain of *E.coli* was sensitive to a number of other antibiotics with fewer severe side effects, the senior resident and attending physician stopped the Chloramphenicol drip and started Amoxicillin. Within three more days, Nancy Rose was on oral medication and ready for discharge. Iggy had not been home for almost a week. He had stayed in the hospital to be near his daughter even when not on call. When he finally took Janice and the baby home, he collapsed into bed and did not get up for fourteen hours.

Chapter 32

Wolfe's next short internal medicine rotation found him chasing after a wild man for a week, Lance Kennedy, MD, the Chief Pulmonologist. Kennedy carried an Emergency Medicine Services radio with him at all times. Frequently, he arrived in the ER ahead of an ambulance patient because he had heard the conversation between EMS and the ER nurse or resident. He always arrived with well thought out intentions and no patience. The ER residents never did what he would have done. When patients transferred to the floor, he frequently countermanded the orders given by the admitting intern, who usually had listened to the ER or internal medicine resident on call that day.

It wasn't normal for the intern assigned to Kennedy to be on call every third or fourth night. Every other night did not suit Kennedy, either. The intern assigned to him pulled call 24/7 for the seven days of the mini-rotation. Wolfe heard that some interns had not finished the rotation, begging off or getting sick. The ones who did finish usually took a week or two to recover.

Wolfe's first patient on pulmonology had drowned. Pulled from a lake in Interlachen, he had been transported by ambulance to the University Hospital ER. Initial resuscitation at the scene had gone well. The patient arrived in the ER sitting up, demanding to be released. Since he had been unconscious and had had no pulse when pulled from the small lake, the ER resident convinced the man to stay overnight, "Just in case. We'll let you go in the morning if everything is still okay."

Wolfe preceded the patient to the floor, after calling Kennedy to discuss the case. "You watch him carefully," Kennedy said over the telephone. "Lots of these fresh water near drownings go into delayed pulmonary edema. Keep him on oxygen and keep the ET tube and the laryngoscope by the bedside. He needs a bullet proof i.v. and a cardiac monitor. Watch him like a hawk. Understand?"

"Yes, sir," Wolfe said. He hung up the telephone in the nurses' station in time to see the patient arrive in the step-down unit. Kennedy wanted him monitored on the cardiac monitor, but there had been no room in the ICU. Wide awake and alert, the patient wanted to make several phone calls. He also made certain the television in his room was in working condition.

Wolfe followed the stretcher and the transport orderly into the patient's room. He checked that the intravenous ran properly, hooked the cardiac monitor leads to the patient, and placed the prongs of oxygen tubing into the man's nostrils. "Ah, Doc, do I really need that," the man complained.

"Attending physician's orders," Wolfe explained. "If he finds you without that on in the morning, he'll kick both our asses around the parking lot for a while."

"But it's ugly, man," the patient said, "like a long green booger hanging from my nose."

Wolfe quoted Keats, "A thing of beauty is a joy forever." Then added, "A thing of ugly is usually temporary, unless it's someone's face or hairy. Get over it." The patient laughed, pointed an index finger at Wolfe and pretended to pull the trigger.

Leaving the patient to contemplate bad poetry, Wolfe made rounds in the step down unit on all the pulmonary patients. He had finished and was sitting at the table in the nurses' empty break room leafing through his stack of patients' index cards when he heard, "Code Blue, step down unit. Code Blue, step down unit," over the PA system.

Rushing into the hallway, Wolfe followed the nurses into his patient's room. Sitting upright in the hospital bed, gasping for breath, the black man hyperventilated. His eyes were wide. He gripped the side rails of the bed, knuckles white. The cardiac monitor showed a pulse of 180 beats per minute. The last BP on the monitor read 190/120. About the time Wolfe stepped to the head of the bed and told the nurses to remove the headboard, the patient's hypoxia caught up with him and he passed out. *At least I won't have to intubate him nasally*, Wolfe thought.

Picking up the ET tube, Wolfe inserted a wire guide and bent the tube into the S shape he liked for placing the tube in a patient's trachea. After asking the nurse using an ambubag to oxygenate the patient to stop bagging the man, Wolfe placed the patient's head on a folded towel to approximate the sniffing position the anesthesiologists had instructed him to use. Immediately, he opened the man's mouth using his right index finger and thumb. Before he could look down the man's throat, a huge amount of pink, frothy foam poured out. Wolfe couldn't see a thing. "Suction," he said, excitedly.

"I'll have to hook it up," a nurse said, squeezing between Wolfe and the metallic plate on the wall at the head of the bed. She held in her hand a large, clear plastic canister with two metal prongs on it.

While waiting for the nurse to plug the suction reservoir into the wall and attach the tubing and trochar to it, Wolfe used the ambubag to hyperventilate the patient with 100% oxygen. The patient's eyelids fluttered and he started to resist being held down. Wolfe slowed down his bagging and the man became comatose again.

The second time he opened the man's mouth, Wolfe suctioned out the foam quickly and again tried to place the ET tube. Before he could drop the suction trochar and grab the ET tube, pink foam filled the man's mouth and ran out the corners of it onto the bed. "Shit," Wolfe said. "One of you guys will have to suction."

The head nurse picked up the plastic suction trochar and suctioned as best she could while peering over Wolfe's hands. Wolfe guessed at the placement of the ET tube, and jammed it down what he hoped was the trachea. He put a bite block in the man's mouth and taped the tube in place, so the patient could not chew on it or dislodge it. After ordering sedation for the patient to be given through the i.v., Wolfe had the nurse bag the patient while he listened to both lungs and over his stomach.

He could barely hear air being pushed into the patient's lungs while listening over both lateral chest walls, but he heard no toilet flush noises over the man's abdomen. He was fairly certain the ET tube had been placed in the trachea, but couldn't be positive. To find out for sure, he ordered blood gases and a portable chest x-ray. Those would take several minutes to an hour, so the best precaution was to stand at the bedside and monitor the patient's respirations and heart rate. If Wolfe had managed to misplace the ET tube into the esophagus, it should become quickly evident as the man's hypoxia increased. The patient's heart rate would go way up, as would his attempted respirations. Both were high already because of the pulmonary edema, but they would climb rapidly higher if the patient got no oxygen at all.

Wolfe also ordered the patient placed on a ventilator and transferred to the ICU as soon as a bed was available. For fifteen minutes he stood at the bedside waiting for the blood gas results. Unfortunately, they were abysmal and non-diagnostic, so he waited around for the portable chest x-ray. Twenty minutes later, the x-ray suggested the ET tube was in the correct position. The patient's vital signs had improved slightly.

An ICU bed was available immediately, being recently vacated by a dying patient. Wolfe told the respiratory tech to set up the ventilator in that room. With the transport orderly, Wolfe and one of the pulmonary nurses moved the patient in his hospital bed to the ICU, with Wolfe ventilating the man with the ambubag as they trundled through the halls and onto and off the elevator.

Wolfe spent an hour writing a progress note and checking the drowning victim's vital signs. He listened to his lungs several times, before being convinced he had the situation under control. At about 2 a.m., he had poured himself a cup of coffee in the employee cafeteria when his beeper went off. Kennedy was in the ER and wanted him to come down right away. The walk from the first floor cafeteria to the ER was short. When Wolfe arrived, Sandoval, the senior ER resident, sat in a chair with his feet on the desk reading a novel. He pointed a thumb toward the private room in the back where the psychotic patients were usually held. "Back there," he said. "It's not a pretty sight."

Wolfe found Kennedy in an agitated mood. He circled two stretchers, alternately throwing his hands in the air and dropping them to his sides. Upon each stretcher lay the corpse of a young girl, each late teens to early twenties in age. Their heads lay at unusual angles, and their limbs had too many joints. Blood had seeped from their open long bone fractures, chest and abdomen wounds, and mouths onto the hospital sheets that did not cover their naked bodies decently.

Kennedy stopped at the head of one of the beds. "Look at this," he said. "See this?" He lifted the head of one of the women by the hair. Eyes open the dead woman stared at Wolfe. "We could have had such fun with them," Kennedy continued. "Ventilators, intubations, casts, chest tubes. But, no! They had to die before we could work on them. Such a shame." With a flourish, he dropped the woman's head and pulled the sheets over the bodies. "Maybe next time, Wolfe. Let's go check on your near drowning patient."

Wolfe followed Kennedy back upstairs to ICU. The charge nurse told Kennedy that they had had to call in extra help in order to suction the drowning victim through the endotracheal tube almost continually. Because they spent so much time suctioning him, he did not get much oxygen and his O^2 saturations were very low.

"Turn up the positive end expiratory pressure," Kennedy told her. "He needs that to keep the fluid out of his lungs to improve his sats."

"PEEP's as high as the manufacturer says is safe, now, according to the respiratory tech," she replied. "I don't want to give him a tension pnuemothorax."

Kennedy smiled. "Addison, my boy, looks like this is your lucky night. The chicks downstairs could have supplied you with this opportunity had they survived, but they didn't."

"Opportunity?" Wolfe asked.

'We can't take the chance that the PEEP will blow out an emphysematous bleb and squeeze his lungs down to worthless blobs of tissue. The man needs prophylactic chest tubes," Kennedy explained. "Ever put in a chest tube?"

"No, sir," Wolfe said.

"Well, like I said tonight's your lucky night. You watch me do one, then you do the second. Tomorrow, you can show another intern how to do them." Kennedy turned to the nurse. "Two chest tube trays to go, please."

Well versed in Kennedy's volatility and willing to joke with him in order to keep him happy, the nurse asked, "Do you want your .357 Magnum tray, too?"

".357 Magnum tray?" Wolfe asked, knowing chest tubes didn't come in calibers.

Kennedy laughed. "That's the tray I use whenever the patient is being a pain in the ass. It's a joke. I unwrap a replica of a .357 caliber pistol and set it in front of him. Generally shuts them up for an extended period of time," Kennedy explained. "No thanks, my dear. I don't intend for the patient to be awake during these procedures. But thanks for asking."

Kennedy went to the chalk board and drew a simplified picture of a patient's chest wall with thick ribs for Wolfe. "There is a big nerve under each rib, so we will slide across the rib below it, in hopes of missing the nerve above. The pleural cavity is like a balloon inside a balloon. We are going to place the tubes between the balloons. Constant suction will keep his lungs expanded, no matter how many blebs we blow. We can set PEEP as high as we want. It will keep the inside oxygenated. Got that?"

Wolfe nodded. "Which ribs and where?"

"You can use any interspace you want, again because the suction works to expand the lungs. But having the tubes on the anterior chest interferes with the nurses and electrodes, so we go laterally, on the sides, mid-axillary line – in the middle between anterior and posterior chest. Too high on the side interferes with the patient using his arms. Too low might put you in a spleen or liver. So, about halfway up works the best. Never put them through the back side if possible, although I have done it on patients with multiple rib fractures. Questions?"

Wolfe shook his head. He had no questions, just doubts about his ability to absorb so much information so quickly. The two physicians spent an hour placing and testing the tubes. Sedated and paralyzed medically, the patient never gave Kennedy an excuse to brandish the .357 caliber pistol. Two weeks later, after a rocky course, the patient left the hospital, alive and well. "With squash intact," Kennedy told Wolfe in the hallway one day, meaning he had suffered no obvious brain damage despite the periods of hypoxia and anoxia.

Chapter 33

On the last night of his pulmonary rotation, Kennedy had told Wolfe to meet him in the ambulance drop off in front of the ER at midnight. Earlier in the week, Kennedy had given a lecture to the internal medicine interns and had forgotten to bring handouts for them. He had some lecture notes he wanted Wolfe to give to the interns.

As Wolfe opened the passenger door to Kennedy's four wheel drive vehicle, he heard the EMS radio squawk unintelligibly, "...leaving University now..." was all he heard that he understood.

"Get in and put on your seatbelt," Kennedy said.

"I'm on call. There's a possible pulmonary admission in the ER," Wolfe objected.

"Someone else will handle it. You wanted to be an astronaut. Think of this as an orbital mission. Get in and put on your seatbelt," Kennedy repeated, "Or I'll flunk your ass."

Wolfe pulled himself up, into the vehicle, not an easy task. The suspension had been modified so the body of the Ford Bronco sat well above the usual location. Snapping on his seatbelt, Wolfe saw a police car in front of him turn on its flashing lights and race past them toward 8th Street. "Where are we going?" he asked Kennedy.

"Yee-haw!" Kennedy yelled flooring the Bronco's accelerator. The all wheel drive vehicle spun into a left 180 degree turn, lifting the two left wheels off the ground. They accelerated toward 8th Street behind the police cruiser. "Don't know, yet," Kennedy said.

The cruiser's siren sounded at the intersection, stopping traffic as it rolled into the street. Kennedy made the same right turn tail-gating the police car, this time raising the right two wheels, while pulling a red light from between the front bucket seats. He placed the light on the dash in front of him and turned it on. It flashed quickly off and on. "They won't give me a siren," he complained.

The EMS radio buzzed, screeched, and squawked. Wolfe didn't understand a word broadcast. "Oh, boy," Kennedy interpreted. "A shooting. Two down. Shooter's on the lam."

Kennedy followed the police officer north on I-95, west on I-10, and off a ramp on the west side of town. The trail ended in a dirt road subdivision. The shanties in the subdivision each had an outhouse in the back, made visible by the spotlights on the top rear corners on the boxes of two ambulances. Otherwise the subdivision remained dark. There were no street lights.

"I'll look at the victims," Kennedy said. "You follow him." He pointed at the police officer who had led the chase. The cop emerged from his patrol car with flashlight in hand. He took the holster strap off his weapon.

"Why would I want to do that?" Wolfe asked.

"When he shoots the bad guy, you save his life," Kennedy explained.

Incredulous at the naiveté of the man, Wolfe asked, "What if the bad guy shoots him?"

Irritated by Wolfe's attempt to delay the process he had outlined, Kennedy said, "He'll be alright. He's wearing a bullet proof vest. Now, go!"

But I'm not wearing a bullet proof vest, Wolfe thought. He hopped out of the Bronco, falling to the ground when he misjudged its height above the gravel driveway. He introduced himself to the officer and the two began a search behind the nearest hovel. The officer held his flashlight and pistol in front of him as a single weapon. "Stay directly behind me," he told Wolfe. *And pray the shooter is a very bad shot,* Wolfe thought, *although it would be my luck to catch a bullet meant for the officer*.

A forty-five minute search of the area in, around, and under the shanties revealed no shooter, even though it rousted most of the itinerant black and Hispanic workers sleeping in the shacks. Wolfe rejoined Kennedy in the Bronco. "Great news, Addy," Kennedy said.

"Two more indigent patients for University Hospital and the pulmonary service, eventually. After thoracic surgery finishes with them, they'll both be on the respiratory service. Both will live although they took bullets to the chest. I have an agreement with the surgeons. I get to do the follow-up on all thoracic shootings. I'm writing a paper. Too bad you are leaving the service in the morning. I'm going to miss you. Some interns just bring excitement with them. You're one of those guys."

"Yeah," Wolfe said looking at his watch. It was 1:30 a.m. "I'm going to miss you, too." *Like a hole in my head. Five and one-half hours to go.*

When they returned to the hospital, Figueroa met them at the ER entrance. "Where have you been?" his booming voice asked Wolfe when he entered the corridor between Primary Care and the ER ICU. "The nurses have been paging you for two hours."

Stunned that Figueroa would be in the hospital at this time of night, Wolfe could only say, "With him." He pointed at Kennedy.

Kennedy glared at Figueroa. "Go see what the nurses want, Addy. I'll explain to this asshole."

Never looking back, Wolfe sprinted to the stairwell and ran to the second floor, where he exited the stairway. Catching his breath, and surprised at how out of shape he had become after only eight or nine months, he pushed the button for an up elevator.

The nurses had beeped him to report the arterial blood gases drawn at midnight. Never admitted, the pulmonary patient in the ER evidently had responded to treatment for his asthma and had gone home, or had refused admission – not unusual. There had been no crises, unless you count the one generated by Wolfe for not answering a routine page from the nurses. They had called Figueroa when Wolfe did not respond. "Why?" Wolfe asked.

"Because he told us to," one said. "And as you know, he's an unpleasant guy if you don't do what he says."

Wolfe nodded. His rotation ended at 7 a.m. when he gave the pulmonary beeper to Kervork Torrosian. "Good luck," he told Torrosian, "I hope you are caught up on your sleep."

"Just so you'll know," Torrosian said, "we raised Figueroa's LDH in clinical pathology this month." He handed Wolfe a piece of paper. "This is the list of things that cause an increased LDH. You might study it before intern reviews next week. He's likely to ask about the differential diagnosis."

"Thanks," Wolfe said folding the paper and stuffing it into his pocket, "but I think he will have other issues to discuss with me."

For seven days and nights, he had followed Kennedy in and around the hospital learning a lot and sleeping little. He heard later that one of the ER residents had played a practical joke on Kennedy. He had taken the wild man's EMS radio and hooked it to a TV rabbit ears antenna that he bolted to a construction hard hat. Someone said Kennedy actually wore the contraption outside the hospital because it extended the range of his EMS radio by twenty miles.

Chapter 34

As part of the internal medicine rotation, Wolfe took part in several educational exercises. Easily flustered, he had great difficulty being articulate and expressing what he knew. One exercise especially disconcerted him: the practice oral exam, a weekly Saturday challenge.

One of the senior internal medicine residents, Rick Prescott, gave the exam to all the available interns rotating on internal medicine over eight hours on Saturdays. Some of the interns were indisposed having worked the night before, or being on call in the ER. This Saturday was Wolfe's next to last on the rotation. The following Saturday, Advanced Cardiac Life Support certification had been scheduled for the entire intern class.

Using one of the empty medical clinic exam rooms – there were no clinic patients on weekends – an actor or actress was usually hired to play the part of a patient. The interns were expected to take a history, do a physical exam, tell Prescott what labs, x-rays and other tests they would order, and then give him a list of possible diagnoses. Prescott gave the interns the results for the exams and tests. Given enough time and information, and the responses by the actor, the intern should have been able to make the correct diagnosis. Prescott never gave hints and never gave up any extra information.

Rarely an intern would succeed in diagnosing the patient. Frequently the interns left shaking their heads wondering what they had missed. For the most part the exercises were fun and educational, although the education came later when the finer points of the case were discussed in the auditorium along with the attending physicians.

Wolfe entered the exam room. Prescott sat in the corner on a chair. "Ready?" he asked.

Wolfe looked around the room. The blinds were closed and the lights dimmed. A female in a hospital gown lay on the exam table. Her feet were bare. She actually wore two hospital gowns, one on the usual way, open in the back, and the second open in the front. "I guess," Wolfe said, already intimidated.

Prescott looked at his watch. He wrote the time down. "Okay. Begin the simulation," he said.

Before Wolfe could respond, the actress began a howling, like an injured dog, "Owwww, ahhh!" she repeated over and over.

Wolfe shook his head. He went to the woman and placed his hand on her shoulder. "Can I help you miss?" he asked, feeling like he was in a high school drama class.

Her response was to scream even more loudly. Wolfe looked at Prescott, who smiled and shrugged his shoulders, holding his hands palms up. Wolfe knew he would get no assistance. He tried to open the woman's eyes, but she clenched them tightly closed. "Is she malingering?" Wolfe asked Prescott.

Prescott shrugged again. "You have to decide," he said.

"Okay," Wolfe said loudly, "I'm going to pretend to pick her up by her pubic hair." The patient made no response to the remark. Rocking side to side, she nearly fell off the exam table.

She continued to scream, distracting Wolfe. "The patient did not respond when you pulled on her pubic hair," Prescott said.

"Okay," Wolfe said, "Next I will use my reflex hammer and slap her feet." He pulled a reflex hammer from his back pocket and grabbed one foot by the toes. Lifting her foot he reared back.

Prescott caught his hand before he hit her foot. "No need to hit her," he said. "No response. She's unresponsive to pain."

"Can I sedate her?" Wolfe asked. "Her eyes are clenched shut, her fists are balled up, and she is resisting my attempts at checking her reflexes. Not to mention she's still screaming."

"Sure," Prescott said.

Wolfe ordered a sedative, intramuscularly. He also ordered blood tests and an intravenous started, all duly noted by Prescott. The screaming continued. Wolfe increased the sedation. The intensity of the screaming lessened. He could still not open the woman's eyes or test her reflexes. He listened to her heart and lungs and he did an abdominal exam. "All normal," Prescott stated.

In an effort to end the screaming and relax the patient enough to see her eyes, Wolfe upped the sedation. "End of simulation," Prescott said, looking at his watch and noting the time on the chart. She's dead." The screaming stopped.

"She's dead?" Wolfe asked.

"Yeah. You overdosed her. She stopped breathing," Prescott said. "If it's any consolation to you, she was scheduled to die in fifteen minutes, no matter what you did. She has a ruptured cerebral berry aneurysm. Nothing you could do. She was in the process of herniating her brain stem. There's no way to see an aneurysm. This one will be found at autopsy."

"No blood tests, either?" Wolfe asked.

"The only positive test was for a near overdose of aspirin. She had been taking large amounts for her headache before her family brought her to the ER. Made her bleed that much worse. Platelets weren't working." Prescott handed Wolfe his paperwork. "Have a nice day off, Addison. Don't tell anyone the diagnosis. They all have to learn that they really aren't gods." Prescott slapped him on the back. "Sometimes we succeed; sometimes we fail. Better to fail here than in the real world."

Lisa Johannsen met Wolfe in St. Marys, Georgia at the ferry dock. The rendezvous had been her idea. The invitation surprised Wolfe, because it meant she had to drive a hundred twenty miles and he had to drive only sixty. She had proposed they have a walking picnic date on Cumberland Island, the largest barrier island off the coast of Georgia. The island was home to the ruins of two revolutionary war forts, the remains of a mansion known as the Dungeness, and Thomas Carnegie's home. No motor vehicles were allowed on the island, a National Park.

Recalling from a psychiatry lecture that picnic dreams usually were indications of sexual tension, Wolfe readily agreed. He hoped Johannsen had sexual designs on his body. He had a similar objective concerning her, provided she agreed of course.

Although the weather in southern Georgia is similar to that of northern Florida, Wolfe found it necessary to wear a warm sweater and windbreaker in March. The wind whipped through the pine tress along the paths. At the sea's edge a nor'easter pummeled the sand dunes, erosion evident. White capped waves were visible all the way to the horizon in the clear, chilled air. Pelicans glided up and down the coast propelled rapidly by the wind, flying at an angle to the beach. Efficiently, they trapped energy from the wind, rarely flapping their wings.

"Why is that bird flying in circles?" Johannsen asked, pointing at a bird off shore.

"I don't know," Wolfe said. "Maybe one wing is longer than the other." He pointed at several contrails high over head. "Navy jets," he told her, "B-1-RD, and GU-11."

The chill gave Wolfe an excuse to put his arm around Lisa. "Any warmer?" he asked.

"No," she said, "Hold me tighter." He did.

"I'd like to do this more often," he told her.

"Freeze on the beach?" she asked.

He laughed. "No, silly. Hold you close. What are you doing in two weeks? Sunday will be my last day off on internal medicine. April 1st, I start two months of surgery. Too bad that's not an April Fools' Day joke. God knows what that will be like. I don't remember Iggy having much time off, though, when he did it."

Johannsen scowled. "I think I'm working," she said. She softened the blow by adding, "I'll check my calendar when I get home tonight and call you. If I am working, I'll see if I can make a trade. Okay?"

"That would be great," Wolfe said. "Maybe I could drive to Savannah, save you some driving. I'd like to see some of the restoration that is going on."

"Oh, that would be great fun, Addy. We could go to the Davenport Museum, and then walk around downtown," she said. "I have my eyes on a row of townhouses. I'll show them to you. I can buy one for a dollar. The only problem is I would have to live in it and restore it. Right now it's in a high crime area. And the restoration would cost me more than buying a house in the suburbs." She bubbled over with enthusiasm, delighting Wolfe.

"Okay," he said walking her back to the ferry, "even if it isn't in two weeks, I'll come up to Savannah and see *your* house. Some day."

When he held the door to her car open for her, she did not give him a peck on the cheek. This time she wrapped her arms around him and kissed him full on the mouth. After sitting in the driver's seat she closed the Mustang's door and rolled down the window. Leaning out, she asked, "How attached are you to Sam?"

"We're just friends," Wolfe said, adding, "and growing more

distant all the time."

"Well, I'm glad you are not close," Lisa said. "She's strange, and very manipulative and vengeful. I don't think she and I can be friends much longer. I'm not going to stay at her place any more."

"Well, you can always stay at our place," Wolfe smiled. "There's usually an empty room or the couch, if I can't talk you into my room." Wolfe grinned most wolfishly for her.

Lisa smiled, knowing exactly what was on Wolfe's mind. "I'll think about it, Addy. Do us both a favor, though, and stay away from Samantha, Wolfe-boy. She could be big trouble for you."

Don't I know it, Wolfe thought. "No problem, Lisa." He waved as she drove out of the parking lot.

Chapter 35

Figueroa started the next M&M conference by placing a large plastic jug on the desk in front of the auditorium. The container had once held water for a bottled water dispensing system used at the hospital. The jug was filled about two thirds of the way with pills of different sizes, shapes, and colors. Figueroa let the residents gaze at the container for several minutes.

"You have to be very specific when you ask our patients questions," he said. "The owner of these medications, God rest his soul, was a patient in our medical clinic for about ten years. On every visit, a resident asked him if he was getting his prescriptions filled. The answer was always *yes*. After he passed away from congestive heart failure last year, his daughter brought this bottle to the ER. She was upset that we wanted to keep it. Her father had been allowing his neighbors to borrow anything they felt they needed from his collection and she wanted to continue that tradition. Dr. Torrosian, what should the residents have been asking the patient instead of, 'Are you getting your prescriptions?'"

"Are you taking your medications properly?" Torrosian answered.

"Precisely," Figueroa said. "This is a monument, not to stupidity, but to ignorance. We need to educate as well as treat our patients. The patient evidently felt that getting the medication was sufficient. Taking the medication might have prolonged his life, although living ten years with CHF and on no meds is no mean feat."

"Dr. Harrison," Figueroa said, "are you present?"

"Yes, sir," Iggy responded, quickly hiding a piece of paper he and Torrosian had been discussing before Figueroa called on Torrosian.

"Yes, I know you are." Figueroa stared at him for a long minute. "You and Dr. Torrosian need to pay attention to this discussion. You can finish whatever you two are doing later. Understand?"

"Yes, sir. Sorry, sir."

"Good," Figueroa said. He turned to the other side of the auditorium, facing another intern. "Dr. Nagakawa, you've spent some time in the ER recently. Tell us a little about beer bottles. As weapons, I mean."

Nagakawa stood. "I'm not sure I understand the question, Dr. Figueroa."

"Sure you do," Figueroa said. "You saw three patients in the ER last month with beer bottle injuries. Two had multiple lacerations. One had a concussion. These were all the results of fights using beer bottles as weapons. So, what did you learn?"

Unable to think of a lesson learned, Nagakawa stammered, "Sharp glass can cut people?"

Frustrated, Figueroa growled, "Sit down, Dr. Nagakawa. Pay attention. If you ever find yourself in a bar fight, Nagakawa, and this goes for the rest of you gentlemen, also. You, too, Drs. Wu, Joiner, and Marks, although I'm sure it would be more likely be Dr. Joiner in this situation than Dr. Marks or Dr. Wu." A ripple of laughter crossed the room quickly, dying in the face of Samantha Joiner's stare. "If you ever need to defend yourself and you want a sharp object, don't pick up an empty beer bottle. They are extremely difficult to break. They make good clubs for that reason, can cause concussions. But you may not want to get close to someone with a knife in his hands, or a sharp beer bottle, with a club. If you want the bottle to break, leaving you with a sharp weapon of your own, pick up a full bottle with the cap on it and hit it on the table. Why, Dr. Nagakawa?"

With the flash of insight finally ignited, Nagakawa realized the connection. He said, "Because in a full bottle, the force of the blow will be transmitted by the incompressible fluid inside, shattering the glass. In an empty bottle, the air compresses and doesn't transmit the force. It won't break."

"Not easily, anyway," Figueroa added.

"If you don't mind my asking, Dr. Figueroa," Nagakawa asked, "how do you know how many patients I have seen that have been cut with beer bottles?"

With a very serious tone, Figueroa answered, "I keep very, very close tabs on all my interns, Dr. Nagakawa."

Wolfe kicked himself in the seat of his pants, mentally. Having been on Shore Patrol in the Philippines and in San Francisco with thousands of drunk sailors and with as many drunken brawls as he had witnessed, he should have picked up this insight long before. *Especially after working so hard to break empty bottles at the CPO club,* he thought.

"On a lighter note," Figueroa said, flipping through the papers in front of him. "Is Dr. Myers here? Hiram?" There was no answer. "Senior residents avoid M&M by being too busy to attend," Figueroa said. "In any event, you can all learn from this case. Dr. Myers helped out in primary care last week when it got overloaded. Seems the senior ER resident was late for work and Dr. Lynch failed to pitch in. Those problems will be addressed, by the way.

"A family of four came into the ER. The mother accompanied the children to the Pediatric ER. The father was seen by Dr. Myers in Primary Care. Both children and the father had fevers, muscle aches, and diarrhea. They were diagnosed with gastroenteritis, and were treated with supportive care and anti-diarrheal medication. The father asked for extra medication for his wife. She had the same symptoms, but he didn't think she would be seen that day with so many people backed up in the waiting room.

"Dr. Myers instructed the nurse to find the woman in pediatrics and swap Dad for Mom so the father could watch the kids. When he examined the mother, it turned out that her complaints were similar to her husband's except she had severe right lower quadrant pain – and an acute appendicitis. The lesson to be learned here is this: Make no assumptions. Examine every patient without prejudices. Think clearly. Dr. Myers did this woman a great service. She is lucky that a senior resident, who is too busy to come to M&M, wasn't too busy to examine her."

Lastly, the senior pediatric ER resident presented a case. Another child arrived in the pediatric ER accompanied by her father. The father knew no history of the illness, just that his child had had a fever and an earache. He did not know how long she had been sick, although he thought for only one day. The intern in the ER examined the child and found two bright red, bulging ear drums, indicative of severe otitis media. Except for the high fever, the child appeared normal, alert, responsive, and well-hydrated.

The intern ordered a form of intramuscular penicillin, Bicillin, wrote a prescription for an additional oral antibiotic, and left the room to see the next patient. From this point the history became rather cloudy. The intern received a call from the mother after the father left the hospital with the child. She wanted to know why her child wouldn't wake up. The intern told her to bring the child back to the hospital as soon as possible. An hour later, the intern received a call from a pediatrician's office saying the child was experiencing a seizure. He repeated his admonition, telling the office personnel to have the child transported to University Hospital as soon as possible, this time by ambulance. About ninety minutes later another hospital called. The ambulance crew had taken the child to the nearest hospital, Baptist Hospital downtown. Later that day the child was pronounced dead, likely from meningitis. Figueroa suspected *Haemophilus influenza type b* as the cause of death, given the rapidity of the disease's progression. Posthumous cultures proved him correct.

"There is more to this story than we have presented," the senior resident stated, "but we can't reveal all of it because there is a malpractice suit involved. Apparently, the nurse who gave the Bicillin injection thought the child had passed out with the injection, but she didn't tell any of the physicians. She made no mention of the syncope in her note and discharged the patient. Just be aware that *H. flu* can be deadly and it can happen very quickly. We understand that several companies are working on vaccines, but trials and use are years away."

Figueroa dismissed the residents after the pediatrician's presentation. Wolfe, Torrosian, Samantha, and Iggy met together briefly in the last row as the crowd swarmed out of the auditorium. "Who's in pathology this month?" Wolfe asked.

"I thought we'd try something a little different this time," Iggy said.

"What's that?" Torrosian asked.

"Nagakawa is in radiology this month," Iggy explained. "Figueroa has scheduled himself for an upper GI series next week. Naggy thinks he can manage to switch names on the x-rays, and also switch reports. That will tie Figueroa up for a month or two."

"Is this getting us any closer to getting rid of the man?" Samantha asked. "Another intern was dismissed last week, Jack Greer in internal medicine."

"Really?" Torrosian said.

"Yeah," Iggy said. "Although some good news, Harville got accepted into a prime Ob-gyn residency in Miami. And Menendez got accepted into the Emergency Medicine residency in Los Angeles."

"Oh, shit," Sam, said.

"What?" asked Wolfe.

"I applied for that position, too," Sam said. "I haven't heard back, yet. Did hear from Grady in Atlanta. They only have two emergency residents per year. They said they aren't taking applications."

"Well, we have an opening here in ER, since Nick left," Iggy reminded her.

"Hey, Singhal all but offered me that position," Torrosian said, "but I turned it down for now."

"Me, too," Wolfe said.

Startled, Sam said, "Don't remind me about Nick. Which brings us back to Fig. Are we any closer to being rid of him?"

As if to answer her question, Figueroa opened the door and re-entered the auditorium. He walked quickly to the podium and retrieved a notebook and several pieces of paper. Taking no notice of the four interns who sat frozen in fear of discovery in the back row, he departed, again.

"I think he's becoming distracted," Torrosian said. Each intern left the amphitheater by a different door.

Chapter 36

Lisa Johannsen could not change her flight schedule. There were too many stewardesses down with the flu. Wolfe understood. University Hospital clientele had infected some of the interns with the same virus, increasing his workload, too. The couple had to postpone his trip to Savannah, although Johannsen did send him two photographs she had taken of *her* townhouse. “Maybe, some day,” she had written on the back of the front view.

Wolfe’s first week on surgery nearly killed him, or so he thought. Someone had given him an upper respiratory infection that progressed over ten days to a sinus infection. Remarkably, it was the first time he had been sick during the internship. Wolfe had never had a bacterial sinus infection until then. To that point, he had shown little empathy toward patients who complained of severe facial pain and headaches from infections. In the early stages, he had told patients their sinus infections were colds, viral not bacterial sinus infections. If their symptoms did not go away after ten to fourteen days, then they might need antibiotics. No one liked that approach, except the internists at University Hospital who practiced academic medicine. Every patient wanted an antibiotic on his first visit. Few people had the wherewithal to make a second visit to the hospital. Wolfe assumed that meant they got well without antibiotics. *Or died,* he thought sarcastically.

After eleven days, Iggy had given Wolfe a prescription for

amoxicillin in hopes that the broad spectrum antibiotic might help. Wolfe thought his head would explode. In fact it hurt so badly, he had convinced himself that he had meningitis. He had resigned himself to undergoing a spinal tap, although he had been on antibiotics for several days and that would play havoc with the cultures. He knew the internists would not like having an intern ruin their cultures. The morning he decided he would be late for surgical rounds and present himself to the internal medicine clinic for work-up, he ignored his alarm clock and rose late.

He stumbled into the shower, avoiding turning on lights or opening curtains, bright light causing an increase in his cheek pain and headache. Standing in the hottest shower he could tolerate, he let the water flow over his head. Unable to move his arms without moving his neck and causing pain, he could not use his washcloth to cleanse himself. Suddenly, his forehead exploded. He heard a loud crack, like a rifle shot. Fluid ran from both nostrils. His pain disappeared. *Great*, he thought, *my brain has ruptured through my cribiform plate. How long will I live?*

He opened his eyes and found to his relief that the fluid running from his nostrils was not cerebral spinal fluid but a dark green stream of snot, mixed with a small amount of blood. His sinuses had finally drained. *I don't need a spinal tap and I'm going to live!* he thought.

After nine months of training, it did not surprise Wolfe to see Figueroa waiting for him at the ER entrance when he got to the hospital. "You are a couple hours late," Figueroa said when Wolfe entered the building.

Pain free for the first time in two weeks, Wolfe smiled. "I'm going to live Dr. Figueroa," he said. He shook the older physician's hand rapidly. "I don't have meningitis, just a bad sinus infection. I feel so much better today." He continued to pump Figueroa's hand until the Director of Medical Education pulled it from his grasp.

Drolly, without a trace of sarcasm, Figueroa said, "I am so glad to hear that, Dr. Wolfe. Your surgical team is in the Pediatric ER preparing to admit a patient. Your team leader thinks it might be your turn. Maybe you should join them." He then turned smartly and walked toward the elevators.

Wolfe found the senior surgical resident who led his team, Jack Petersen, standing next to an exam table in one of the pediatric exam rooms. "Good timing," Petersen told Wolfe when he entered the room. On the bed a four or five year-old blond boy lay. His right arm lay by his side, wrapped in gauze. Wolfe could tell a long arm board held the arm rigid from shoulder to fingertips. An intravenous snaked though the gauze into the boy's arm. He whimpered softly. The child's left arm was likewise immobilized with an arm board, but it was swollen and a dusky gray. The tip of the child's left middle finger was swollen, red and blue, and wrapped loosely in gauze, also.

His mother stood at the head of the exam table holding his left arm still with one hand and patting his head lightly with the other. She could have been fifty years-old if one judged by the creases in her skin and missing teeth. In reality Wolfe knew she was much younger, just indigent. Wolfe could smell the cigarette smoke that she exuded from her skin and clothing. Dirty blonde hair in a raggedy ponytail with wisps sticking out to the side of her head, she stared at Wolfe. She wore blues jeans with holes worn in the knees and in the pocket where she kept her cigarettes and lighter. She had tied a red flannel shirt at her wait. She didn't have a belt and wore well worn sandals.

"You the intern?" she said with obvious disdain.

"Yes, ma'am," Wolfe said. "What happened to your boy?"

"Bobby likes to dig holes," she said. "Our back yard is a maze of tunnels and roadways where he plays."

"He dug up a pygmy rattler," Petersen interjected. "Bit his left third finger. Show him, Mrs. Jones."

The woman leaned over to the chair behind her and lifted her purse from where it hung on the edge of the back of the chair. She pulled a small glass coffee jar from the purse and handed it to Wolfe. The head of a pit viper with a flat nose and gray bands stared back at Wolfe. The head had been severed from the body by something very sharp. "Where's the rest of it?" Wolfe asked. "Did you see any rattles?"

"It's at home in the garden. Along with my machete," the woman said. "Didn't look for no rattles."

"My arm hurts, mommy," Bobby said. The boy's mother returned to comforting the child.

"We'll be right back," Petersen told her. He pulled Wolfe by the elbow into the hallway. "The pediatricians have given him all the anti-venom we have on hand. Unfortunately, children require huge doses of anti-venom compared to adults. Has to do with venom amount injected per body mass. They don't dilute it very well. We have a request in to all the local hospitals for more. But if we don't get more pretty quickly, we'll have to take Bobby to the operating room and do a fasciotomy on his arm. Mom's pretty upset about that."

"I can understand that," Wolfe said. He had never seen a fasciotomy, but the idea of cutting the length of the boy's arm, from the bite on his finger to his shoulder and several times, in order to allow for the massive swelling that would soon result made him nauseated. "It would save his arm and maybe his life, but he'd be badly scarred."

"And likely teased terribly by his classmates. Children can be very cruel," Petersen said. "Work him up for admission to the ward, but also for a trip to the OR if the anti-venom doesn't get here on time."

"Got it," Wolfe said. He returned to the room. When he had finished the brief physical, endeavoring not to move the child's left arm in order to minimize the spread of the snake bite venom, two more units of anti-venom had arrived. The nurse added them to the intravenous line.

Wolfe accompanied the boy to the children's ward, helping the transport orderly negotiate the hallways and the elevator. Lifting Bobby gently, he transferred him to the bed on the ward and then helped the youngster get into a hospital gown. He handed Bobby's holey underwear to his mother, who blushed as she received it. The boy's outer clothing was also well worn, but relatively clean for a five year old who spent his play time digging holes. Wolfe smiled. "What do you like to do in the holes you dig, Bobby?"

"Nuthin'," the boy said. "My trucks is building interstates, bridges, and tunnels."

"Oh. You have a lot of trucks?" Wolfe asked.

"A whole bunch," Bobby said, as his mother shook her head, no.

"He has trucks made from wood blocks, pine cones, tree branches, all sorts of them," she explained.

"And a great imagination," Wolfe added. She nodded.

Over the next twelve hours, one hundred units of pit viper anti-venom arrived at University Hospital, donated from the local hospitals and hospitals as far away as Orlando and Pensacola. Bobby needed every one of them. No hospital sent its entire supply, but they sent what they could spare and not leave themselves without a reserve. Aside from a minor set back with serum sickness, a form of allergic reaction to the anti-venom, he had done remarkably well.

The surgical residents, although mildly disappointed in not having improved their skills by learning about fasciotomies, celebrated the youngster's recovery. A week later when the transport orderly wheeled him in a wheelchair – scar free – out of the hospital, he held in his arms a big, yellow, metal Tonka Truck Wolfe had found at the

Goodwill thrift store and bought for a dollar.

Chapter 37

Surgery residents spent much more time in the ER than the internal medicine residents did. More of their admissions came to the hospital by way of ambulance. Most internal medicine admissions came through the medical clinics, where the Primary Care patients had follow-up appointments. Surgery patients arrived with bullet holes, knife wounds, ruptured appendices, collapsed lungs, and more. All needed immediate care. Follow-up appointments in the surgical clinics were usually of the post-op variety.

Frequently, the ER residents called the surgical team during their initial evaluation. As soon as it became obvious an immediate or urgent surgical intervention was needed, the ER physicians involved the surgeons. Doing so saved time and lives, although it sometimes ticked off the surgeons. They had seen the ER docs *gift wrap* internal medicine patients for the internists: all tests done, all but diagnosed, and treatment started. They wanted the same courtesy for themselves and they envied the internists to some degree. However, they shot themselves in the foot on occasion. They would complain that the ER residents had done too much, put in the chest tube, done the cutdown, placed the central intravenous lines, etc., leaving them with managing the patient only.

After surgical residents demanded to do their own procedures, the attending physicians issued general guidelines: save as many procedures for the surgeons as possible, without endangering the patient's life. As with any policy, its enforcement varied with the personalities of the people it involved. The pendulum had swung the opposite way during Wolfe's internship year. This group of surgical residents might have been described as lazy compared to previous residents. Being halfway through this year of residency, they were tired of doing procedures the ER residents could have done for them. They were too busy on the wards, they said.

The battle came to a head over a burn patient. A young truck driver involved in an MVA suffered serious burns. The fuel tank on the driver's side of his 18-wheeler ruptured during the collision with a pick-up truck. Before he could get his seat belt off and climb out of the cab, the burning pick-up ignited the diesel fuel. He had been burned over 30% of his body. He lay, writhing in pain on a stretcher in the ER ICU. The ER residents had managed to start an intravenous in an unburned portion of his right arm and had just started giving him morphine for pain when they called the surgeons. No one doubted the patient's need to be admitted to the burn unit.

Wolfe accompanied the surgical team to the ER. The plastic surgery resident, Arthur Vogel, arrived at the same time also having been paged by the ER residents. He immediately took charge of the patient. Watching the patient involuntarily shiver from a medically induced chill, he asked the ER nurses, "Why are his burns wrapped in damp gauze?"

"Because that's what Dr. Gentry wanted," one said, pouring sterile saline over the gauze as she spoke. The room temperature water lowered the patient's body temperature causing his chill and involuntary shakes.

"We're still putting out the fire," Gentry said to Vogel. "The residual heat can continue to damage tissue, even though there are no flames. It's standard protocol. Same with the intravenous. He's getting a lot of fluid because he'll lose a lot through the damaged skin."

"You should have debrided the skin first, not put Silvadine on it." The plastic surgeon said.

"You can do whatever you want once he's on the floor," Gentry said. "Again, this is our protocol for burns. We don't know how long he will stay in the ER waiting for a bed. The Silvadine helps prevent infection, as you know."

"I want him debrided in the ER," the plastic surgeon said. "It will be a while before a bed is available on the burn unit. We just discharged a patient, but the room has to be cleaned."

Gentry looked around the ER ICU. The morning had started with a rush of patients. It did not look like the numbers of admissions had slowed perceptibly. He asked the charge nurse, "Is the psyche room empty?"

"No," she said. "We have a drug overdose in there, but she's calm now. We finished lavaging her stomach. She's had her charcoal diarrhea. She's charcoal through and through. The EMTs are cleaning up the charcoal emesis while we wait for a room on psyche."

"Okay," Gentry nodded, mentally rearranging patients the way Wolfe had rearranged flat plastic airplane cut outs on the aircraft carrier flight deck and hangar deck status boards. "Bring her out here. Put the burn patient in there." He turned to the plastic surgeon, "You can use the psyche room."

"I need one of your interns to debride the patient," Vogel said. "I have several patients to see in plastic surgery clinic."

"Sorry," Gentry said, "we're too busy. You'll have to use a surgical intern or do it yourself."

"Torrosian and Wolfe," the surgical team leader said, "You guys will help Dr. Vogel. When you are finished debriding the patient, meet us on the ward." Learning to make quick, sound decisions was one of the challenges to being a senior resident. Losing two interns for several hours, instead of arguing over whom did what for the same amount of time, made sense to the team leader.

The next two hours were the most frustrating and least rewarding of Wolfe's internship. The plastic surgery resident told them to debride any and all blisters from the burned areas on the young man's body. Leaving the interns alone with the patient, he left the ER.

The patient's entire left arm, left trunk, and the outside of the left leg were blistered. Most of the blisters had ruptured. Serous fluid, clear to golden yellow, drained from the blisters or encrusted them and the sheets. The intact blisters formed large bullae filled with more of the clear yellow fluid. The thin, white oily coating of the silver-based antibiotic clung to the patient's skin and dressings.

Every movement, from unwinding a bandage to lifting a finger sent pain into the driver's brain. Eventually reduced to tears, he begged them to stop. Never having debrided a patient, Torrosian and Wolfe slowed their work, trying not to cause more pain. When the plastic surgeon returned, he bellowed, "You're not done yet? What's the hold up?"

"I've never done this before," Wolfe explained. "He's in a lot of pain."

"Then give him more morphine," the plastic surgeon ordered. "Find the nurse. You do know how to order morphine, right?"

Seeing the blank looks on Wolfe and Torrosian's faces, the surgeon pulled on a pair of sterile gloves. He picked up a forceps and scalpel and began peeling away the skin from the man's biceps. The patient howled in pain. "Find the nurse," Vogel said. "Some of this is third degree burn. He can't feel pain there, the nerves have been destroyed. Most of it is second degree burn. That's the painful part," he said, pulling off a long sheet of blistered skin. As if to accentuate the statement, the driver screamed.

Torrosian left the room and found a nurse and some morphine. Without waiting for it to take effect, the surgeon used a wad of sterile gauze and wiped the dead skin from the man's lower left arm and hand. He repeated his actions on the lower leg. Since Wolfe and Torrosian had finished debriding the man's face, they were done. Vogel had done more work in three minutes than they had done in the hour and forty-five minutes he had been out of the room.

"That's it," Vogel said, admiring his handiwork. "Put a thin coating of Silvadine on everything and rewrap all the burns. Hopefully, that will keep him sterile on the trip through the hospital to the burn unit. We'll start the definitive care when I get him upstairs." The morphine finally dulled the man's senses about the time Wolfe and Torrosian finished with the dressings.

Wolfe had never been so happy to relinquish the care of a patient as he was to leave the man in the burn unit. He felt fortunate not to have to care for burn victims on a daily basis. The plastic surgery residents had been tasked with their care. Plastic surgery was considered a super-specialty of surgery. *The residency took forever, 8-9 years*, Wolfe thought. *And it apparently turns residents into assholes.* He scratched it off his list of possible future choices. He no longer cared about boob jobs, Hollywood starlets, or the mountains of money plastic surgeons supposedly made. One burn patient and an irritable plastic surgery resident permanently discouraged him from thinking about ever wanting to be one.

Chapter 38

At times, the surgical interns were required to help the residents rotating through ER Trauma. That happened most on weekend evenings when the ER in general was usually very busy. The junior ER residents took the place of the interns on weekends, the residents needing to keep up their skills while on easy rotations elsewhere in the hospital. Still, sometimes they were overwhelmed by the rush of patients and needed assistance. The interns rotating through surgery would take care of minor lacerations that newly admitted patients needed to have sewn prior to being shipped to the wards.

Late one Saturday evening, or early Sunday morning, Wolfe sat on a rolling stool in ER Trauma. He sutured the posterior scalp of an inebriated young man who was destined to be admitted for observation following what was thought to be a concussion but what might turn out to be a serious head injury. It was sometimes difficult to tell which was the case when the person with the head injury was intoxicated.

The drunk continued to ramble about how he ended up in the ER. “Sometimes my van doesn’t shift well,” the man explained. “I didn’t want to drive all the way home to Fernandina in first gear, so I pulled off the road. It usually takes just a tap with my hammer to loosen the shift rods.”

“So you were under the van?” Wolfe asked, tying a knot in the first suture. “You can talk; you just can’t move your head. Otherwise we'll be here all night trying to sew you up."

"Okay, my man," the long-haired, unshaven white man said. Wolfe thanked the ER gods that the driver faced away from him. The smell of alcohol when he spoke sent Wolfe's memory back to some of the most intoxicated sailors he had ever met. And they knew how to drink, especially after being at sea for one to two months. The drunk started to hum off key.

"Oh, yeah," he said, finally remembering to finish his previous thought. "I was under the van, on the side of the road. I had just hit the shifter with my hammer and then I saw stars."

Wolfe knew more of the story than the van driver remembered, but not everything. So, he asked, "You hit your head on the pavement and saw stars?"

"No. No," the man explained, "my van disappeared. It is as clear as a bell out there. Not a cloud in the sky. I saw the moon and all the stars. It is a beautiful night."

Wolfe did not have the heart to tell the man what had really happened, again, for maybe the fourth or fifth time. His short term memory was not functioning, impaired by a blood alcohol level three to four times the legal limit. Wolfe continued to sew; he hoped the man would remain silent. When he heard snoring, he knew the conversation had ended.

One of the second year ER residents, Morty Summers with the wicked sense of humor, came to check on Wolfe. He picked his way through the bodies and bustle within the ER trauma room. Every bed held a patient in need of attention. The floor was covered with sheets, dressings, splinting supplies, and more. Summers had been on an easy rotation during the week. He rushed from stretcher to stretcher, ordering x-rays, suturing, and splinting. His efficiency spoke of his Emergency Medicine training. "You doing alright, Wolfe?" he asked as he swept past the stretcher where Wolfe sat, putting in the twentieth and last suture. Stopping to admire Wolfe's handiwork, he asked, "What's this guy's story? How did he get the laceration and concussion?"

Wolfe explained, "He thought he had pulled off the road, but he forgot he was on a four lane highway, so he was actually parked in the right hand lane. To fix the shifter in his van, he crawled under the vehicle and was pounding on it with a hammer. A car with two drunks in it plowed into the back of his van. As he lay in the road, their car's wheels rolled on either side of him without hitting him. Something, probably his arm when hit by the undercarriage of the car, slammed his head into the pavement. No skull fracture, though. Cops found him in the highway, just behind the car that hit his van. Apparently, it was totaled; and had stopped in the middle of the road with the front caved in just yards past him. Supposedly the engine was in the front seat. The hammer was fifty yards up the road. He just told me he saw stars, the real stars when the other car pushed his van into the drainage ditch and rolled over him."

"Jesus," Summers said. "He's lucky. The occupants of the other vehicle must be the husband and wife drunk duo in ER ICU. She had her head in her husband's lap. Now she has a broken jaw, missing teeth and a maxillary fracture, along with a concussion of course. No skull fracture, though; lucky like this guy. Neither was wearing a seat belt. EMS said she was wrapped around the engine. It took an hour to extricate her. Husband broke his sternum and ten ribs on the steering wheel. Also has a cardiac contusion."

"What's their excuse for not wearing seat belts?" Wolfe asked, putting the finishing touches on the dressing and wrapping the gauze around the head and face of the van driver.

"Aside from being drunk, you mean? She was lying across the seat, head in his lap. He says he wants to be *thrown clear*. Doesn't want to be trapped in the vehicle, or have that two tons of metal protect him from the elements or other vehicles," Summers explained.

"He'd rather have it flip and roll over him after he's thrown clear, I guess," Wolfe said.

"Code Blue, ER ICU," the speaker in the ceiling above them announced.

Wolfe threw the drunk's chart onto the stretcher near his feet. He pulled the rails up on the bed to prevent the man from rolling out on his own. Following Summers to the code, he hoped it would not turn out to be a surgical case. They arrived in time to see the EMTs unload a second stretcher onto the second resuscitation table. A man lay on the first table. His face had been flattened. Wolfe could see that his frontal skull had been caved in. He had been intubated in the field and had an intravenous in place, but the ER residents ignored him. They hovered around the second man. Remarkably, the second man seemed to have suffered from the same injuries. His face had been flattened and his frontal skull also showed a huge depression.

As Wolfe and the ER staff watched, the second man took a long agonal breath and stopped breathing. "He's been doing that for the whole twenty minutes he's been in the ambulance," one of the EMTs told the senior ER resident. "Breathes about once every forty-five seconds, unless we bag him."

Sandoval lifted the man's upper eyelids with right thumb and index finger. He shone his penlight on the patient's eyes. The pupils were fixed and dilated. Blood ran from the patient's nose, mouth, and both ears. Terribly deformed, his jaw hung to the left of his face. Most of the teeth visible had been sheared off at the gum line. Half a tongue lay on the sheet. "I think you've done everything that could have been done," Sandoval said to the EMTs. "Don't bag him any more." The patient inhaled one more time, then stopped for good. "Time of death: 2:03 a.m. Exactly five minutes after this guy," Sandoval said, pointing to the man on the first resuscitation table. "I guess that means patient number two won."

"Won what?" Wolfe asked.

One of the EMTs explained, "These guys were riding motorcycles. They were playing chicken on the beach. Neither of them is a chicken. They hit head on, probably each going about thirty-five miles per hour. Now, they are both dead. Number two lived the longest, though. I guess he wins."

Wolfe wandered back to ER Trauma shaking his head. The stupidity of some people amazed him. The stretcher where he had been suturing the drunk now held a young girl with a fishhook in her left heel. She, too, was obviously intoxicated. *Probably walking on the beach, barefoot, at night, and drunk*, Wolfe thought. He vowed never to enter another bar as long as he lived. *Nothing good ever happened in one,* he told himself. "Where's the van driver?" he asked the charge nurse. "Transport take him to the floor already? I didn't think we had an empty bed on the ward."

The nurse looked at Wolfe with a blank stare. "Oh," she said, sifting her memory for who had been in the stretcher before the fish hook. "He told us you said he could leave. He walked out the back door five minutes ago." Wolfe ran to the ER parking lot. The man was nowhere to be seen.

Wolfe went looking for Sandoval to see if he needed to fill out an incident report concerning the drunk who left against medical advice, or if writing a note addressing that fact in the chart would be sufficient. He found Sandoval standing next to the radio used to communicate with the rescue units in the field. While he waited for Sandoval to finish, he was obligated to listen to an EMT babble over the airways. Wolfe recognized the paramedic's voice. Obsessive-compulsive, Clarence Chen never gave a short report. Every vital sign, every symptom, the family history, the social history, the past medical history, everything, came to the ER by radio, needed or not. He had been admonished several times about tying up the radio and preventing others from communicating with each other or the ER, but he never changed his report format.

Sandoval leaned on the radio, sly grin on his face. He looked at his nails, the ceiling, the walls, and rolled his eyes. When he made eye contact with Wolfe, he held an index finger in the air and silently mouthed, "Wait a minute."

When Chen finished his report with, "We are ten minutes out," Sandoval got his revenge.

"University ER to Unit 42. Transmission garbled. Please say again." Chen started his fifteen minute report from the top; Sandoval walked away from the radio. "Moron," he said. "Let's see if he can finish before they get here, or if they drive around the block while he completes it." Sandoval and the tired ER staff all laughed.

Torrosian came in before rounds the next morning. He met Wolfe in the cafeteria for breakfast. Sitting at one of the small tables he told Wolfe how the harassment of Figueroa was progressing. "Nagakawa found a suitable x-ray report. He attached Figueroa's name to it. The report says Figueroa has biliary disease: gall stones with possible obstruction of the biliary tree; as suggested by the size of the liver and gall bladder shadows," Torrosian said. "Figueroa has scheduled himself for more testing. So far, he's had the urologists check his prostate, and had a sigmoidoscopy and barium enema. Also, lots of blood tests."

"I hope the urologists have enjoyed getting some measure of revenge, along with the gastroenterologists and radiologists. They must be loving this," Wolfe said.

"What's even better," Torrosian said, "is they let the exams start with the intern, and then require the junior and senior residents to check his work. As a finale, the attending physician says something like, "I'm sure this will hurt me more than you," and he does one final exam. All the exams have been normal so far, of course. I would guess that Fig is becoming a little worried about his health, if not paranoid."

"Shhh," Wolfe said, pointing to the food line. Figueroa had just entered the cafeteria. He stood in line ordering coffee and breakfast. Wolfe and Torrosian slipped out without saying good morning and unseen.

Chapter 39

The very next surgery on call night found Wolfe assisting the senior year ER resident, Bob Gentry, in placing two chest tubes in a gunshot victim. Gentry operated on the patient's right chest; Wolfe the left. Wolfe had never seen such a stoic victim. He lay on the resuscitation bed in the ER ICU gritting his teeth while Wolfe used a long needle to anesthetize his left chest. Even with the xylocaine in place, Wolfe could tell that either his injection or Gentry's, or both, had not been completely effective by the changes in the man's expression. Throughout the entire procedure, the man never said a word, or moaned, or cried out, however. Resolutely, he lay perfectly still as Wolfe made an inch and a half wide incision over the face of his seventh rib in the left mid-axillary line. Wolfe used a curved forceps to tunnel through the skin and connective tissue over the top of the rib, well below the sixth rib. Then he pushed the blunt-nosed forceps through the incision and the pleura, dividing and tearing the fibrous tissue on the inside of the ribs and entering the pleural space.

A gush of air, mixed with a small amount of bloody fluid vented from the incision when the forceps reached the pleural space. Wolfe fed the chest tube into the tunnel he had created. He sutured the wound closed and tied a suture around the three quarter inch wide plastic tube so it could not be accidentally displaced. Gentry finished the right side before Wolfe completed the left, having more experience in placing chest tubes. He helped Wolfe attach the chest tube to the collection bottles and the vacuum line.

"How's that?" Gentry asked the patient, tracking the man's heart rhythm on the cardiac monitor with his eyes.

"I can breathe a whole lot easier now," the patient said, grimacing. "It was getting tough to catch my breath."

Gentry held a chest x-ray in front of the man, so he could view it under the fluorescent lights in the ceiling. It appeared as if the man had three hearts. "This is your heart. These two larger balls are your collapsing lungs," Gentry explained using a finger to outline the shrinking lung tissue. "This dark space to the side of each lung is the air in your chest that is between the lung and your chest wall. That is what the chest tubes will suck out. Until the holes in your lungs heal, you'll need to be hooked up to the suction machines."

"How is your pain?" Wolfe asked the man, imagining how it would feel to him to have his chest cut open and tissues torn, if the anesthetic didn't work. The patient was built like a fireplug: short, compact, muscular. Wolfe had heard the man tell Gentry that he worked as a welder at the Mayport shipyard. He had a thick neck and arms that were twice the size of Wolfe's. Tattoos covered both deltoids. The one Wolfe could read said *USMC, Vietnam '67-'68*. He knew the other was a heart. Inside the heart, it said *Mom*.

"It's tolerable," the man said. "Suppose I could get a smoke now, Doc?"

"Not until the chest tubes come out," Gentry said. "I don't understand. Welders breathe smoke all day. Why do you even need cigarettes? Maybe you could quit, given the incentive."

"I've tried. The bastard who shot me had better stay far away. My old lady says nicotine withdrawal turns me into a monster." The patient turned his head and explored the ER ICU with his eyes. "Where is that bastard anyway?"

"A cop is with him in ER Trauma," Gentry said. "The officer also wants to take a statement from you. JSO doesn't understand your attacker's injuries."

"They are worried about his injuries? He's lucky to be alive," the man said. "That coward bastard came up behind me and shot me in the back." That description matched the entrance wound Wolfe had seen in the man's left posterior chest below the scapula, and the exit wound just below and lateral to his left nipple. "I spun around to find him and he shot me in the chest." Gentry had found another entrance wound above the right nipple and an exit near the right scapula. "Who cares how that cocksucker got injured? I was going to kill him with my bare hands, but I started to get dizzy. So, I took his gun away from him."

"But he has rectal injuries," Wolfe said, adjusting the nasal cannula that supplied the man with oxygen. "It looks like he will have to have surgery to repair a lacerated rectum. How did that happen?"

Sheepishly, the man admitted, "Well, I'm a mean fucker if you rile me up. My old lady says that, too. I shoved that pistol into his asshole and pulled the trigger three times. He's lucky it was empty or misfired. Otherwise he'd need a new asshole and maybe new balls and a prick, too."

Gentry ordered a portable chest x-ray and blood gases to check on the position and effectiveness of the chest tubes. He had the nurse push a small dose of morphine into the intravenous line. Wolfe left ER ICU and walked toward the elevators. While waiting for the elevator, he heard, "Code Brown, ER Trauma. Code Brown, ER Trauma," the call for security. Security officers wore white shirts and dark brown trousers. Code Red had been reserved for fires.

Wolfe had never heard a Code Brown in the almost ten months of internship. It took him a moment to remember what it stood for. Iggy had joked that just like the British Redcoats, who had worn red jackets so their fellow infantrymen and the enemy could not tell when they were shot, the University Hospital Security Staff wore brown trousers so no one could tell how scared they were in a crisis.

Having followed the police officer around the itinerant workers' camp in the dark gave Wolfe a false sense of invulnerability. He decided to see what went on in ER Trauma. Chaos ruled in the far end of trauma suite, in front of the door to the surgery room sometimes used by physicians for suturing large wounds or placing pacemakers. A blue suited JSO officer lay on the floor in front of the door, semi-conscious and obviously injured. Nurses tried to get him to his feet and move him to a safer location. Every time they approached the officer and the door to the minor surgery room, someone would pull open the door and throw a bottle or an instrument at them and the officer. The nurses retreated leaving the officer lying on the floor. His weapon was visible in its holster.

After the nurses retreated for the third time, Wolfe stepped close to the door. Letting someone take the weapon would be a disaster, he realized. He listened carefully, waiting for the assailant's footsteps to approach the door. When he was sure the man was about to open the door again, he shoved his shoulder into the door as hard as he could. He heard a loud crack when the door slammed into the man's hand and head. Not waiting to see if the bottle thrower had been seriously injured, Wolfe grabbed the officer by the foot and dragged him and his weapon away from the door, sliding him on the terrazzo floor thirty feet down the corridor.

Hospital security officers and the ER ICU staff picked up the officer and placed him on a stretcher. They wheeled him into ER ICU to have his injuries evaluated.

A large University Hospital security guard boldly opened the door to the minor surgery suite thinking Wolfe had incapacitated the assailant. He met a hail of lidocaine bottles and instruments. Broken glass sliced through his right eyebrow. Blood poured out of the wound soaking his white shirt. After he withdrew from the doorway, one of the nurses pressed gauze into the wound and walked the man to the far bed in ER Trauma. She began to set him up for sutures.

"They need to wear red shirts," Wolfe said to no one. He sidled up to the second security guard, an elderly man with white hair and no apparent death wish. "What do we do now?" Wolfe asked.

"Wait," the old man said.

"For what?" Wolfe asked.

"For that," the security officer said. Wolfe heard what sounded like a thunderous herd of wild horses. It turned out to be nine JSO officers in combat boots tramping up the hallway, in step, from the ER entrance. Each held a Billy club at chest level. They pushed their way through the curious patients standing in the hallway and the staff in the ER Trauma department.

"Where's the down officer?" the lead policeman asked Wolfe. Wolfe read the man's dark blue name tag, Campbell.

Wolfe pointed to the ER ICU. "He's being evaluated in ER ICU," Wolfe said.

"Hoskins. Check on Peters," the officer shouted. The last man in the detail turned and walked to ER ICU.

"Where the *perp*?" the lead officer then asked Wolfe.

"Perp?" Wolfe asked.

"Perpetrator. The person who injured Officer Peters," Campbell explained.

Wolfe pointed to the door behind which the assailant hid. He expected the officer to draw his weapon and enter the room. *No perp armed with small bottles of lidocaine would be dumb enough to throw one at an armed officer, would he?* "Going to use your pistol?" Wolfe asked.

"Can't," the officer replied. "I am only authorized to draw my weapon if I intend to kill the suspect. He's unarmed, correct?"

"Just has stuff to throw at you," Wolfe said. "Sharp stuff, though."

"So, what are you going to do?" the charge nurse asked. "We can't let him tie up the unit all night. We have lots of sick and injured people to take care of."

"No problem," the officer said. "Is he black or white?"

"Does it make a difference?" Wolfe asked naively.

"Only to his family, reporters, and other do-gooders who worry about police brutality," the officer said.

Wolfe did not know the answer to the question. He looked at the charge nurse. "White," she said.

"Is he psychotic, injured, or sick?" the officer asked.

"He has a rectal bleed," the charge nurse said. "He shot someone during a robbery attempt tonight. The victim took away his gun and shoved it up his rectum. He's going to need surgery to repair the tear. Other than that, he's healthy, unless Dr. Wolfe hurt him when he slammed him with the door."

The remaining police squad was composed of two black and six white officers. "Jenkins and Thomas," Campbell said. "Put on your face shields and gloves. Leave your weapons with Masters and Langley. Use your batons and go get that bastard. I want him handcuffed. I also want him conscious, so don't hit him in the head. Got it?"

Two white, burly policemen unstrapped their gun belts and holsters and handed them to two other officers. They snapped Plexiglas shields onto their helmets, pulled on heavy gloves, and positioned themselves at the door.

"What's his name?" Campbell asked the charge nurse.

She looked at the chart to make certain she had the correct patient name. "Larry Rogers," she said.

Officer Campbell leaned close to the door. "Mr. Larry Rogers, can you hear me?"

"Fuck you," came the reply.

"Two Jacksonville police officers are about to enter that room. You can save yourself at lot of discomfort if you give yourself up voluntarily and cooperate."

"Fuck you, pig."

"On three," Jenkins or Thomas said. "One, two, three."

One officer shoved the door mightily with his shoulder. It swung open with a crash, hitting a stack of Mayo stands, the stretcher, and rolling stools piled in front of it. Both officers rushed quickly into the room. Wolfe heard an *oomph* and several whacks, then silence. Seconds later the two officers dragged the *perp* from the surgery room, hands handcuffed behind him, toes barely touching the floor. They threw him face first onto a stretcher, and then handcuffed him to the metal frame of the bed. Wolfe noticed the back of the patient's khaki trousers were soaked in blood from mid-buttocks to his knees. His left wrist appeared to be deformed, swollen and blue. The right side of his face was also bruised.

Chapter 40

Sunday, in mid-April, Wolfe lounged in bed. Enjoying his only real day off so far during his first month of surgery, he stared at the ceiling. Nancy Rose wailed in Janice and Iggy's room, but Wolfe could tell her's was a healthy cry. He rolled over and looked at his alarm clock. It said a little after noon. *No reason to get up, yet*, he thought, except for the hunger that gnawed at him.

He did not hear the knock on the apartment front door, but he did hear Janice open the door and greet Samantha Joiner. *Damn*, he thought, *now I have to get up*. Sitting upright he swung his legs to the side of the bed and pulled the blanket off. He had slept in his scrub pants and scrub shirt, having adjusted to wearing them both as outer clothing and pajamas. He laughed, remembering the first time he had worn scrub clothes.

A friend of his family, a urologist who had been his father's flight surgeon during the Korean War, had pushed Wolfe to go to medical school. He wanted Wolfe to study biology in college and go to medical school afterwards. Wolfe had humored the surgeon and his father by accepting an invitation to go to George Washington University Medical Center in D.C. There he had watched a cystoscopic procedure done by Dr. Barlow. Barlow wanted him to stand in the procedure room. At the same time, he wanted Wolfe to wear scrubs to blend in and not upset the patient.

In the changing room, there were no scrubs smaller than extra large left in the bins by the time Wolfe had arrived in the early afternoon. Wolfe had been forced to wear the large scrubs over his street clothes to keep them from falling to his knees. He couldn't pull the draw string tight enough otherwise. Barlow had chuckled but tried not to embarrass Wolfe, even when Wolfe managed to touch the cystoscope with his unsterile hand while Barlow attempted to explain the procedure. He wanted Wolfe to see what he had seen through the scope. Once Wolfe touched it, the scope had to be removed and replaced with a second sterile cystoscope, which Wolfe also managed to contaminate. He was so frustrated with his performance, and so certain Barlow was, too, that he never again thought about medical school until the Forrestal fire. Wolfe laughed at himself, shaking his head. What would Barlow think of him now? The urologist had died of lung cancer, unable to quit smoking even after the surgeon general issued his report on the connections between smoking and heart disease, and cancer in 1963.

A knock sounded at Wolfe's door. He stood and looked in the mirror on the bureau. Grabbing his hair brush in an attempt to flatten his unruly hair, he said, "Come in."

The door swung open. Samantha stood in the doorway, make-up smeared, with red eyes. To Wolfe, it appeared she had been crying. She took two steps and threw her arms around Wolfe, pushing her face into his chest. "Oh, Addy," she said.

"What's wrong?" Wolfe asked, patting her blonde afro. Sam was the last person he would expect to see cry. Her toughness was legendary among the residents and staff. Some of the nurses swore she had a rock for a heart, or no heart at all.

"We had a placenta previa delivery last night. Both the mother and the baby bled out. The baby's dead. The mother is likely brain dead and on a ventilator. They have scheduled EEGs over the next two days. If she really is dead they will take her off the respirator. Figueroa will think it's my fault. He's going to want to kick me out of the internship."

"Whoa, whoa," Wolfe said. "You didn't cause a placenta previa."

"But I didn't catch it in clinic. I didn't order an ultrasound," Sam said.

"Ultrasounds are expensive and the waiting list is a mile long," Wolfe said. "They tell you not to order them unless there is a good reason."

"The mother complained of some vaginal bleeding intermittently," Sam said, pulling a Kleenex from her pocket and wiping her nose. "When Figueroa reads what I wrote on the clinic visit, he's going to be upset. He's already mad at me. This is just another nail in my coffin."

"Intermittent bleeding may or may not be caused by placenta previa," Wolfe said, trying to think of other reasons. "What did the senior resident and attending physician say?"

"They said it wasn't my fault, that they need more ultrasound machines and more money to run the department properly. They are hoping some good comes from this." Sam released her grip on Wolfe and sat on his bed. Downcast eyes stared at the floor. "Are we going to be able to get rid of Figueroa before he gets rid of me?" she finally asked.

Wolfe sat next to Joiner on the bed. He put his right hand on her left thigh, patting it slowly while he thought. The silence continued for several minutes. He could think of nothing else to say. "Thanks," Sam finally said. "You've made me feel a lot better." They sat quietly on the bed for a long time. Joiner took his hand with both of hers. She started to massage his fingers in a sensuous fashion. She placed his hand between her blue jean covered thighs and left it there. With her hands, she then turned his face toward her and kissed him on the lips.

"You know, it's been a long time since my last lube job," she said. "It's probably time for your 3000 mile check, too."

Wolfe smiled. "Let's see, three thousand miles, six inches at a time. That would take a long, long time. Does the odometer work in reverse in this case?"

Joiner reached for the pull string on Wolfe's green scrubs. "Let's find out," she said.

Wolfe stopped her by grabbing the white string. "I don't think we should, Sam," he said. He stood and moved several feet away from her.

Joiner continued to sit on the bed. "Why not?" she asked.

"Well, there's your fiancé in Boston," Wolfe said.

"That never stopped you before," Joiner pointed out.

"I know, but things are different now. With me," Wolfe said.

"You mean with you and Lisa, don't you?" Joiner asked. He nodded. "Have you had sex with her, Wolfie?" Her tone turned to one of haughty anger.

"No," Wolfe said, "but even if I had, it wouldn't be any of your business, Sam. I don't keep track of who you have sex with."

Joiner stood suddenly. The anger in her voice had dissipated. She said pleasantly, "No. You're right, Addy. I don't have any right to pry into your love life. I just thought you and I could continue with our tradition of *no strings attached* sexual liaisons. What my fiancé and Lisa don't know won't hurt them."

"I don't agree," Wolfe said standing.

"Who would know?" Joiner asked.

"I would," Wolfe said. "Sorry."

"I understand," Joiner said suddenly. She stood on tip toes and placed a light kiss on Wolfe's cheek. "See you around, Wolfie." She turned and opened the door. Leaving it open, she walked to the apartment front door and left quietly.

Several minutes later, Wolfe still stood in his room near his door, trying to figure out what he had just witnessed and women in general. *Always an impossible task*, he reminded himself.

Janice strolled by, diaper draped over her shoulder and Nancy Rose on top of that. She tapped the infant lightly on her back trying unsuccessfully to induce a burp. Nancy Rose continued her mournful wail. Looking at Wolfe, Janice said, "Sam leave already, Addy? What was she so upset about?"

"I wish I knew," Wolfe said.

Chapter 41

The M&M conference that took place during Wolfe's first month on surgery lasted only a brief time, less than an hour. The average M&Ms to that point had been two hours long at a minimum. Wolfe thought Figueroa seemed preoccupied. He made very few, and only short, comments about the cases presented.

Another hospital ER had made headlines in the newspaper with a *dump* to University Hospital. Although excluded from seeing the patient's medical records an investigative reporter managed to expose the details of the case. They made headlines in the Jacksonville daily newspaper, *The Florida Times Union*.

Wolfe suspected the facts had been leaked by the ER residents, because the article echoed their point of view: All ERs needed to take care of anyone who presented to them. That was the law. *If*, upon further investigation, the other hospital found that the patient was indigent, and *if* University Hospital had a bed for that patient, then the patient could be transferred, provided he was stable. The transfer had to be done with close cooperation between the hospitals. That, too, was the law.

The latest dump showed how far another hospital would go to skirt the regulation. A man signed in one evening to be seen at the Memorial Hospital ER in Arlington. He thought he had pneumonia, having chest pain and a cough for a week. A known asthmatic, he also smoked. His only transportation was his motorcycle. He admitted he was indigent and had no insurance, not even Medicaid, when asked how he would pay for the hospital services he needed.

JSO found him several hours later, in the dark, near midnight, on the Mathews Bridge. He had lost consciousness and fallen off his bike. Fortunately, a motorist had witnessed his collapse. He stopped his car behind the cyclist and protected him from being run over by other traffic. An ambulance rushed him to the University Hospital ER, where he was found to not only have asthma and pneumonia but a collapsed lung. After the ER residents put in a chest tube, put him on oxygen, and gave him fluids, he regained consciousness.

Asked what had happened, the patient explained he had been turned away by Memorial Hospital. He asked for his leather jacket, from which he pulled a piece of paper out of a zippered pocket. It was a free hand map to University Hospital from Memorial Hospital, drawn on Memorial Hospital stationery and given to him by a nurse at Memorial Hospital. The map made the front page of the newspaper. Memorial Hospital executives declared the map a fraud. As far as the ER residents could tell, only the overt dumping stopped. Covert dumps continued.

Less than his enthusiastic, witty, sarcastic, intellectual bullying self, Figueroa said, "This will continue to be a problem until someone actually dies and a lawyer collects several million dollars from one of those hospitals. If then. I don't want any of you talking with reporters. Leave this issue to the administrative staff and the Florida State Legislature. It won't be fixed during your tenure at University Hospital, so don't get your hopes up."

Rick Prescott presented a surgical case, unusual because he was a senior internal medicine resident. He used the case to demonstrate more his aggravation with the ER residents than to make a teaching point. The junior ER resident had called him to admit a patient. The diagnosis given was Boerhaave's Syndrome because the young man being admitted had vomited bright red blood on his one and only emesis. The blood made it suspicious that he had a tear in his esophagus, and that he might need to have an endoscopy to make a definitive diagnosis – something usually done by the internal medicine service. The ER resident had no way to rule out ulcers, esophageal bleeding from other causes, or esophageal erosions secondary to pills or infection, or caustic ingestion, in the ER.

Prescott, however, had done a much more thorough abdominal examination in the ER than had the junior ER resident. Following that exam, it was his contention the young man had appendicitis. He claimed that however rare it was, the patient had torn his esophagus on his very first emesis – indeed Boerhaave's, but due to appendicitis. He refused to admit the patient to internal medicine and called the surgeons. The surgeons agreed that the young man needed an exploratory laparotomy and took him to the operating room.

In front of God, the nation, the attending physicians, his peers, and the lesser members of the hospital physician staff, Prescott could now show proof that he was *right* – a flea's sole goal in his world. The projectionist flashed a picture of the surgical specimen removed from the patient. The very distal end of the appendix was red and swollen. With a yawn, in a monotone, Figueroa congratulated Prescott backhandedly. "Very good, Rick. But, we all make mistakes. In that the appendicitis would have manifested itself more obviously later, let's hope any mistakes you make in the future will be just as inconsequential." Red-faced Prescott re-took his seat.

In the far back row, as usual, Wolfe turned to Iggy and Samantha. "Did you hear that? 'We all make mistakes.' I think he's sick. Maybe we are getting to him. He hasn't flayed anyone, yet, today."

Sam said, "We can only hope. That he's sick, not that he'll flay anyone."

"We're getting close to the end of our internships," Iggy said. "Maybe he's just tired. Kervork, what's the next test we hit him with?"

"CEA, carcinoembryonic antigen," Torrosian said. "Looking for an occult cancer should keep him busy and off our backs for the rest of the year, don't you think?"

"Brilliant," Wolfe said.

Continuing in his monotone, Figueroa said, "We do have some kudos to bestow. Dr. Phillips, please stand."

Phillips a tall, thin, bespectacled, dishwater blond, young man, stood directly in front of Iggy. Iggy slapped him on the back. "Go, Wahoos!" he said. Turning to Wolfe, Iggy said, "Phillips played basketball at U.Va., two years ahead of my class."

Figueroa ignored Iggy. He continued with his presentation. "For those of you who don't know, Dr. Phillips is a senior ER resident. He rode with the paramedics in Rescue Unit 24 all last month. On one of their calls, they went to the Public Health Department to see about a thirty-year-old black male with asthma. The public health physician had placed an intravenous line and given the patient some epinephrine, but was afraid the patient wasn't doing well. Tell us what happened, Dr.

Phillips."

"Well, the guy had a pulmonary and cardiac arrest as we got him into the ambulance," Phillips said. "No big deal. I just intubated him, started CPR, gave him more epi and cardiac drugs per the protocol. Then transported him here. He went home three days later."

"Phillips is being more than modest," Figueroa said. "There were in the neighborhood of fifty people surrounding the ambulance at the time, including most of the patient's family. There were faces in every window according to the EMTs. Nothing like performing in front of a live audience. No pressure to succeed, right?"

"There was one slight screw-up," Phillips added.

"Oh?" Figueroa said. "What was that? I though everything went pretty well."

"When we finally got him stabilized in the ER, we wanted to give him more fluids. His initial i.v. clotted off. When we unwrapped the gauze covering his i.v., it turned out to be a butterfly needle, the smallest available. We ran an entire code via a very tiny access. Given how much fluid we pushed through it, we were very lucky it didn't blow earlier."

Figueroa nodded. "Well, all's well that ends well," he said.

Iggy looked at Wolfe. He mouthed silently, *All's well that ends well*? As stunned as Iggy, the rest of the residents and attending physicians in the auditorium sat in silence staring at Figueroa.

"Well, if you guys don't have anything else of importance," Figueroa said, "we'll call it a day." Quietly, he stood, gathered his papers, and left through the front auditorium door. Immediately the babble started.

"That's it?"

"He's the guy who tore me a new one last month? He didn't say jack shit about that i.v."

"...the same guy who wanted $1 more than any other attending physician was being paid?"

"...sick..."

Chapter 42

Standing at the sink, scrubbing his hands, Wolfe prepared for an arduous two hours in the frozen tundra of the operating room watching an appendectomy. Sometimes he held retractors for the real surgeons; sometimes he stood alone observing, shivering in the frigid air conditioning. Just starting to cleanse his nails with the plastic nail cleaner that had been jammed into the surgical scrub brush on the sponge side, Wolfe was approached by an unfamiliar surgeon.

A short, muscular, dark-skinned individual, he wore a beard, unusual for a surgeon. He spoke with a sing-song accent of a native Indian. Nodding to Wolfe he said, “So, you are Wolfe, the astronaut candidate Dr. Figueroa was telling me about, no?”

Wolfe shook his head. His application to NASA seemed to have legs of its own. *Was there no one in the hospital who did not know about it?* At least now he knew how everyone knew. Figueroa was telling them. “Yes, sir,” Wolfe said.

“I’m Choudhury,” the surgeon said, pointing three fingers of his right hand at his own chest. Reflexively, Wolfe started to shake the man’s hand. Quickly pulling his hands back and showing his palms to Wolfe, Choudhury said. “Now, you don’t want to start your scrub all over again, do you?”

Blushing, Wolfe nodded. He went back to scrubbing. Choudhury stood at the next sink. He turned on the water with a foot pedal, then adjusted the temperature with the swiveling knee control. "Not too warm, Wolfe. Heat dissolves the subcutaneous fat in your hands, also dries out the skin." Wolfe nodded. Choudhury continued, "Now then, will astronauts be doing emergency surgery in outer space?"

"Not unless they can't return to Earth," Wolfe said. He sat in on several discussions on this subject during his six weeks at NASA as a medical student. He had also helped with the preliminary design of the medical kit the astronauts would take into space on the shuttle. There were no major surgical instruments or supplies in the kit, only sample supplies for drawing blood and spinning it down. There were two scalpels, a couple hemostats, forceps, some suture, a needle holder, and some bandages, but NASA did not expect the astronauts to do anything with the instruments other than suture minor lacerations. The protocol stated anything more severe dictated a return to Earth as soon as possible.

"What would be a scenario where one might need his appendix removed in outer space?" Choudhury asked. He began his vigorous scrub. "You need to mechanically remove every single bacterium from your skin. Don't miss a spot, Wolfe."

Wolfe continued scrubbing, pushing harder, raising more yellow betadine bubbles to please Choudhury. "If the astronauts were on a short flight, like the shuttle flights," Wolfe said. "they would return to Earth on the next orbit or two. One and a half to three hours time. On longer flights, say to the moon, then the protocol calls for massive doses of antibiotics and to abort the mission. If he developed symptoms as they finished the burn to escape Earth orbit, it would take three days to get to the moon and three days to return."

"Antibiotics might prevent a rupture in that case," Choudhury stated. "How about a Mars flight?"

"I think they plan on preventive removal of the astronauts' appendices for that," Wolfe said.

"Okay, then," Choudhury sounded slightly exasperated. "Under what conditions would NASA suggest for an astronaut to remove another's appendix in space?"

Wolfe thought for a minute. "Well, maybe something like the Apollo-Soyez or Skylab missions," he said. He had been at NASA during the Apollo-Soyuz mission and had helped to medically debrief the astronauts. He had held Deke Slayton's abnormal EKG in his hands. In fact, he had left it in his copy of a text book, *Rapid Interpretation of EKGs* by Dale Dubin, while trying to interpret it. "If the return capsules could not separate from docking in Apollo-Soyuz, or if the return capsule for Skylab were damaged or inoperative, it might take NASA several weeks to prep a rocket and capsule to launch to retrieve the astronauts. But I'm guessing."

"Good enough," Choudhury said, taking his foot off the pedal. The water stopped flowing. He held his hands out, palms toward chest, in the usual, *Don't touch me, I'm sterile*, position. "Come, Wolfe," he said, backing through the swinging door to the operating room.

Another surgeon, already gowned and gloved, awaited Choudhury and Wolfe. Wolfe did not know the man's name. Thick glasses balanced on the bridge of his large nose. A piece of tape between the lenses and attached to the surgeon's forehead kept the heavy lenses from sliding down his nose. He stood with gloved hands clasped together as if praying. A middle-aged man lay sleeping on the table, intubated and monitored by the anesthesiologist. "Finally, Choudhury," the second surgeon said. "Is this the surgical intern known as Atkins?"

"No, Karimov," Choudhury said. "Dr. Atkins has been detained by our old nemesis, Dr. Figueroa. He will not be assisting us today."

"Then our bet is postponed?" Karimov asked.

"Oh, no," Choudhury said, "you don't get out of our bet that easily. Dr. Wolfe is also an intern, although rotating instead of surgical. He has even dreamed up a scenario to follow. He is an astronaut on Skylab. One of his colleagues has developed right lower quadrant pain, a fever, and nausea. It's likely he has appendicitis. NASA has aborted the mission. The crew is to return home, but the space capsule they are supposed to return in has malfunctioned. The wiring has burned up. It will be two weeks until NASA can supply a replacement."

"And the bet is a weekend in the Bahamas?" Karimov continued for Wolfe's education. "If an intern can remove an appendix without killing the patient, under direction by me, just giving instructions with my back to the patient, like I was talking over the radio. Correct?"

Wolfe's eyes got big. "Wait a minute. I didn't agree to do that," he said.

"It's okay, Wolfe," Choudhury said. "I will monitor what you do. I won't let you hurt the patient. In fact, if you do anything dangerous, I will take over. It's in my interest, because then Dr. Karimov loses the bet. Correct, Karimov?"

"Absolutely," Karimov said. The OR nurse held a green cotton gown out for Wolfe to push his arms into, and then did the same for

Choudhury. The nurse tied the gowns in the back. She held sterile gloves open in front of Choudhury. He drove his hands into them so far they almost stretched to his elbows. Wolfe was not quite that vigorous. He held his hands together in front of himself, mimicking Karimov's prayer position. He prayed silently, *Oh shit, God, what have I gotten myself into?*

Standing on the opposite side of the table, but facing away from the patient, Karimov spoke in a clear voice. "Find Dr. McBurney's point," he said. "Make a 5-6 centimeter incision parallel to the anterior superior iliac spine over McBurney's point."

Wolfe found McBurney's point in the right lower quadrant. With the #10 scalpel he cut through the skin, leaving barely a scratch.

"You'll have to cut deeper than that," Choudhury said, quietly. Wolfe traced a deeper slice. "Good," the surgeon said, blotting the wound with gauze.

Under Karimov's direction, Wolfe exposed, dissected, and divided the three layers of muscle above the peritoneum. Choudhury held retractors for Wolfe so he could see what he was doing. Sweat poured out of Wolfe's forehead. Seemingly continuously, the OR nurse dabbed him with gauze in order to keep the perspiration out of his eyes.

"External oblique, internal oblique, and transversus abdominus muscles," Choudhury reminded Wolfe of the anatomy, not seen by Wolfe since gross anatomy lab freshman year in medical school.

"Use the Metzenbaum's and cut the peritoneum in a craniocaudal direction," Karimov said. Choudhury handed the scissors to Wolfe after tracing the incision on the peritoneum for him. He also collected a small amount of fluid in a test tube for culture, something Wolfe would not have done in Skylab.

Karimov told Wolfe how to find the appendix and identify the mesoappendix, where he divided the nerve and blood supply to the appendix. He placed a double ligature the base of the appendix with 2-0 Vicryl suture. Clamping the base of the appendix he divided it from the cecum. Afterward, he cauterized the base and removed the clamp.

Closing the patient was the reverse procedure, easily done with Choudhury as an assistant. "Dr. McBurney described this operation in 1891," Choudhury told Wolfe. "It hasn't changed since, although there are some minor variations. Tie the interrupted sutures like this: the first knot is a surgeon's knot, double right over left, then left over right, then right over left, at least six knots per suture if using nylon."

Wolfe had trouble concentrating, so relieved to be finished. "I'm mad at my wife," Karimov said as they followed the stretcher into the recovery room.

"Why?" Choudhury asked. "What did you do to make her angry now?"

Karimov snorted. "Ha!" he said. "I asked her to sew on a button that fell off my shirt. She refused. She said I am a surgeon and I know how to sew. She handed it back to me."

Choudhury laughed. He pointed to Karimov's shoes. "See that Wolfe? He owns only one pair of shoes. He's a simple peasant from Uzbekistan." Wolfe stared at the beat-up, brown, laced shoes. Why owning one pair of shoes mattered to Choudhury, he didn't know – until the surgeon finished his remark. "He has spoiled his wife. She has a hundred pair of shoes, and she won't sew on a button for him. That's what he gets for marrying an American. What he really needs is a peasant like himself for a wife."

"Did you really bet a weekend in the Bahamas?" Wolfe asked Choudhury.

"No," the surgeon said, smiling. "That was just to give you an incentive to pay attention. You did well, although I don't think I would want my appendix removed in zero gravity."

No patient ever received closer follow-up from Wolfe than his appendectomy patient. Wolfe finally breathed a sigh of relief when the man left the hospital four days later.

Chapter 43

The surgery rotation never seemed to finish. Wolfe shuttled back and forth between ER, OR, and wards in a never ending cycle. He found it difficult to remember the day of the week. When exhausted, he sometimes could not remember the month or the year. Passing through the ER one morning, he heard Rescue Unit 33 talking over the radio with Gentry, the senior ER resident. Wolfe thought he heard the paramedics were having a difficult time starting an intravenous line on a multiple trauma patient from an MVA.

"Jesus," Wolfe said to Gentry, "Tell them to forget it and transport the patient. He'll bleed to death if they stay in the field too long trying to start a line."

A hand slapped Wolfe on his shoulder. "Come with me," Dr. Singhal's voice said. "Did you even hear the tone of your voice when you said that?" Singhal marched toward his office.

Wolfe followed, angry, unapologetic. "I just said what everyone else was thinking," he said.

Singhal entered his office and walked around to the far side of his desk, where he sat, then put both cowboy booted feet on the edge of his desk, ankles crossed. Wolfe stood at parade rest in front of the desk, ignoring Singhal's wave of his hand in offer to be seated. "Those guys in the field work under very difficult conditions," Singhal started. "They have a very strenuous job. We are here to support them, not belittle their efforts. You should be praising them, offering to assist, helping to educate...."

The rest of the reprimand slipped past Wolfe unheard. For the first time in years, Wolfe felt tears running down his cheeks. He could not remember the last time he had cried or understand why he did so then. Sure, he had disappointed Dr. Singhal; that might get back to Figueroa. But why tears? He shook his head, embarrassed. "Sorry, Dr. Singhal," he said. "It won't happen again." He turned and walked out of the office.

Before he closed the door, Singhal called after him, "Try to cut back on the stress, Wolfe. Get some rest." Wolfe nodded. *How?* he thought.

Wolfe returned to the ER, arriving at the same time as the ambulance crew he had derided. The man they pushed into the ER on a stretcher had not been in an MVA, however. He had been walking along the sidewalk with his wife in an animated conversation. She had just told him she was pregnant with their first child. Playfully, acting like a child himself, he had reached out and swung on a sign pole. Unfortunately, he had swung out into noisy traffic. Not being able to hear what was behind him, he did not realize a city bus was pulling to the curb at the exact same time and place as where his head and chest swung into the roadway. Pedestrians lose in confrontations with buses.

The patient had been hit from behind by the bus. The momentum transferred to his body by the collision sent him into another sign post adorned with multiple aluminum signs, each with a sharp edge. One sign had left a deep cleft in the man's face. Another had almost amputated his right arm.

During the transfer from the ambulance stretcher to the resuscitation bed, the EMT lost his grip on the man's arm. A jet of arterial blood squirted across the stretcher, drenching a nurse. "Clamp that bleeder," Gentry told Wolfe handing him the hemostat he kept clipped to his white coat. It never occurred to Wolfe that the hemostat was not sterile. He found the bleeder, a partially severed brachial artery, and clamped the side closest to the heart. When Gentry handed him a second hemostat, he clamped the opposite side of the artery.

"That might make sewing the ends together tougher, but it will save him some blood," Gentry said. He called to the unit clerk, "Get me some Type O negative blood to give this guy while we wait for the match. Make it packed cells."

Aside from the gruesome facial injury, which the plastic surgery resident claimed, wanting the practice, and the blood loss, the patient was in relatively good shape. The orthopedic surgery resident accompanied the plastic surgeon to the OR, in order to re-attach some tendons and close the arm wound. A vascular surgery resident borrowed a large vein from the patient's leg and used that to make a graft for the destroyed portion of the brachial artery. Even though the patient developed an infection, possibly from the hemostat but more likely from the street sign, he did well. By the time his first born arrived, he was whole again.

Relieved not to have to admit the patient, Wolfe returned to the ward. He knew he would be off that night, so he began his own chart review. On a 3 x 5 card, he began to list all the things the on-call intern would need to do for his patients while he was gone. After filling four cards in small print, he began to think that, maybe, he should just stay in the hospital overnight. The on-call intern would be too busy to admit patients and care for his, too. The thought made some sense in a way, until the senior resident yelled at him.

The resident dashed past the nurses' station, headed for the stairwell. "Wolfe. ER. Now," was all Wolfe heard as the stairwell door opened and then slammed closed on it own. Wolfe bolted after the resident surgeon.

Barely hanging on the stair railings, the senior resident's feet almost never touched a step and only spent microseconds on the landings. Wolfe followed as best he could, losing ground with each of the five flights. He slipped on the second floor landing, falling gracelessly onto his right hip, arm, and chest. Lying flat, he waited several seconds to see if he had severe pain anywhere. Uninjured, he pulled himself to his feet and continued the journey more slowly from that point.

By the time Wolfe made it to resuscitation, the senior resident had pulled on sterile gloves and opened the left chest of a thin young woman by cutting between her left ribs with a scalpel. Wide awake, the woman screamed while the ER residents held her as still as possible. Past a river of blood that escaped the chest incision, the senior shoved his left hand armed with a pad of gauze into her chest. He pushed down on her left clavicle with his right hand. "That's all we can do here," he said. "Let's get her to the OR. Push some morphine through that line."

"Oh, my God. Oh, my God, that hurts," the young woman gasped. Gentry placed a non-rebreathing oxygen mask over her face and turned on the oxygen tank to 15 liters per minute, giving her 100%

oxygen as fast as possible.

Wolfe, unable to assist in any way other than offering encouragement, leaned in close to the frightened girl. “You’ll be alright,” he said. “Hang in there. You’ll be alright.”

“Why did she do it? Why would she stab me?” the girl asked, eyes wide, tears steaming to the sides of her face, voice muffled by the oxygen mask. Her make-up ran sideways with the tears.

“We’ll find out later,” Wolfe tried to reassure her. “Be tough. You’ll be alright. We can fix this,” Wolfe said, helping to propel the stretcher to the elevator.

The anesthesiologist met them at the door to the operating room. The patient was asleep in just a few minutes. Without scrubbing, a thoracic surgeon finished cracking her chest. He found the subclavian artery had been punctured by the stiletto knife and held open by the surrounding connective tissue when the knife had been pulled out, just as the senior surgery resident had suspected. With two sutures, he stopped the bleeding. It took less than five minutes. She died on the table anyway. *And without damage to Big Red or Big Blue,* Wolfe thought. Most of her blood volume lay in her chest cavity or on the stretcher.

Numb, Wolfe left the operating room. He did not remember the drive home. “I told her she’d be alright,” he said to a surprised Janice when he arrived in the apartment. He went straight to his room and to bed. In the morning he woke, confused as to where he was.

At 10 a.m., Janice knocked on his door. She cradled Nancy Rose in her arms, feeding her a bottle. “Don’t you have to go to work today, Addy?” she asked.

“Yeah, I guess I do,” he said. It was noon before he made it back to the wards. No one asked him where he had been. He had not been missed. Every surgery resident assumed that another had sent him on an errand.

Chapter 44

"No," Wolfe told the young woman. "I cannot refill this prescription."

"Why not?" she shouted.

"I already told you, Ms. Scroggins. This is a narcotic. It is a controlled substance. That means it is dangerous in the wrong hands," Wolfe said, exasperated. They had been through his logic three times already. The argument only increased in volume as they talked in circles. "On physical exam I can't find any reason for you to need it. Your back is fine. It's not tender. There are no neurological deficits. Your range of motion is excellent."

"The last doctor gave it to me. So did the doctor before him. They all have," she screamed. "Why won't you? Do you think you're God, or something? I'm in serious pain. I need my medicine."

"Sorry," Wolfe said. "No."

The woman left the room suddenly. She slammed the door so hard the walls shook and dust filtered onto the desk from the fluorescent lights above the exam table. Wolfe leafed through the patient's chart. As an intern, he had inherited a panel of patients from the previous surgical intern who had been on the rotation. Many were patients who had had surgery in the past, in this case a cholecystectomy more than a year ago. On one of her recheck visits following the gall bladder surgery the woman had complained of back pain. An intern had written her a prescription for pain medicine and referred her to the orthopedic clinic.

As usual with most clinics at University Hospital, clinic appoints were hard to come by. Until the woman could be seen in orthopedic clinic for her back pain, she returned to general surgery clinic for refills of her pain medicine. Most of the five or six interns, all over worked, just wrote her a script and sent her on her way. It saved time not to have to examine the patient or delve into her history. Wolfe had been conscientious enough to exam the woman.

Maybe too conscientious, he thought. *No good deed goes unpunished.* He wished his back had been as limber as hers. When he told her he couldn't see a reason for her to be on narcotics, the argument had started. *With luck, she won't come back,* he thought. *That will save the next guy a hassle.* He finished a brief note and tossed the chart onto his finished pile. Grabbing another chart from the to-be-seen stack, he called the next patient.

The fifty-six year-old man walked slowly into the exam room and sat gingerly on the exam table. Wolfe leafed through his chart. The patient returned for a follow-up appointment for an exploratory laparotomy. He had been injured in a knife fight at a bar. Stabbed in the mid-abdomen, he had been transported to University Hospital and evaluated in the ER. Although his blood pressure and other vital signs had been good, he was taken to the OR and explored, to be certain Big Blue or Big Red had not been violated. A short segment of small intestine had been punctured and had to be resected. The patient sailed though recovery without serious infection and now was six weeks post-op.

"So Mr. Miles," Wolfe said. "How's your abdomen?"

Miles raised his head slowly, obviously in pain. "Stomach's fine, Doc. But I've developed some serious back pain."

Wolfe rolled his eyes. He began to see conspiracies where none existed. *Could this be a game patients played in order to obtain narcotics and then sell them on the street?* He kept his suspicions to himself, however. He asked, "How did the pain start?"

Miles spoke in short halting sentences. He kept both hands on the exam table as he sat, stabilizing himself. If he moved his head or body too much he winced. "I haven't been able to work since I was knifed," he said. "So I was helping a neighbor work on his car. He offered to pay me $10 if I would help him change the oil. He's an old man, maybe seventy, and he don't get around too well. I leaned over the engine to take off the oil cap. Felt a pain in my back. It keeps getting worse and worse."

Wolfe yielded to the history and set his paranoid ideas aside. "Okay. Let me check your surgical wound and abdomen, like I did last week. Then we'll check out your back."

He had just finished with the exam, in which the abdomen was fine, but the patient's range of motion of his lumbar spine was severely limited by pain, when a knock sounded at the door. "Dr. Wolfe," the unit clerk said.

Wolfe opened the door a crack, shielding his undressed patient from the clerk. "Yes, Cindy," he said.

"Dr. Figueroa is here. He wants to talk with you in the patient conference room."

Incredulous, Wolfe asked, "Now? I still have four patients to see."

"He's very upset. You better not keep him waiting," Cindy said. The phone at her desk rang. She turned to go answer it.

"Sorry, Mr. Miles, I have to talk with another physician," Wolfe said. "Get dressed. I'll be right back."

Figueroa paced the conference room like a panther tracking its next meal. "Dr. Wolfe," he said when Wolfe entered, "close the door." He launched into the attack before Wolfe finished closing the door. "There's a woman, an Anne Scroggins, in the administrative offices threatening to sue you, the hospital, anyone she can find. Seems you refused to refill her prescription for medication today in clinic. She's making a terrible scene. If I don't straighten this out, we may have to call the police to remove her from the hospital. What did you say to her son?"

Stunned, Wolfe stared at Figueroa. "She's a drug addict, sir."

"Did you tell her that?" Figueroa asked, worried look on his face.

"Not in so many words," Wolfe said, "I just refused to refill her prescription for Darvon."

"Why?"

"She doesn't need it," Wolfe said. "She complained of back pain more than a year ago on a recheck visit for a cholecystectomy. The intern who saw her gave her Darvon to get rid of her, I guess. She's been back almost every month for refills. I couldn't find anything wrong with her back."

Taking in a deep breath through his nostrils, mouth set in a frown, Figueroa said. “Get me her chart.”

After quickly retrieving the woman’s chart and handing it to Figueroa, Wolfe returned to the exam room and finished examining his latest patient’s back. “I don’t see any evidence of a blown disk, no sciatica or neurological deficits, Mr. Miles,” he said. “So I’m going to treat this like a muscle strain. I’ll give you a muscle relaxant and some pain medication. I want you to come back in next week. If you aren’t any better, I’ll get an x-ray and refer you to orthopedics and physical therapy. Is that okay with you?”

“Thank you, Doctor Wolfe,” Miles said. He shook Wolfe’s hand. “Thank you so much.”

An hour later, Wolfe finished his last surgical recheck, with no more interference from Figueroa, and no more drama from the patients. He sat next to Dean Guthrie at a table in the cafeteria and stared at his hamburger and French fries, appetite almost nil. “What’s wrong, Wolfe,” Guthrie said, “Food remind you of something unpleasant?”

“Yeah,” Wolfe said. He told Guthrie about the confrontation with the Director of Medical Education. “Fig probably had some poor schmuck write her a script for a narcotic just to keep from being sued. I don’t think he has a back bone, the coward. And now he’ll be on my case at the next review.”

“As do most interns, I agree Figueroa is a hard ass. But why didn’t you just give her the prescription?” Guthrie asked. “You could have saved yourself a lot of aggravation. You know, as physicians, one of the most rewarding things we can do is relieve a patient’s pain.”

“Jesus, Guthrie, are you nuts, too?” Wolfe exploded. “One of the worst things we can do is turn our patients into addicts. This hospital probably supplies half of the drugs found on the streets in Jacksonville. She would just sell the pills. She was either an addict or a dealer. If you’re giving away pain meds like candy, you are doing the whole community a disservice. And some of your patients, or their friends, are going to end up dead because of it.”

“I disagree,” Guthrie said, coolly.

“Fuck you,” Wolfe said, standing and leaving his food on the table, no longer even slightly hungry, and angry at himself, Guthrie, Figueroa, and the world in general.

Mr. Miles missed his next surgery clinic appointment a week later. Wolfe hardly noticed. Three more cases had been added to his schedule. One of the surgical residents had been called to assist in surgery, so the interns had to divide up his patients.

"Code Blue, surgery clinic treatment room. Code Blue, surgery clinic treatment room," Wolfe heard while writing in his last chart. He opened the exam room door and followed the nurses to the treatment room. A patient lay flat on his back on the floor with arms spread, in front of a stretcher. A nurse had positioned an ambubag over his face and was beginning to push air into his lungs. Another intern knelt next to the patient with his back to Wolfe. He appeared to be starting chest compressions.

"What happened," Wolfe asked, picking up a tourniquet and preparing to start an i.v.

"Anaphylaxis to penicillin," the nurse said. "He told me he didn't have any allergies, but just seconds after the Bicillin shot intramuscularly, he dropped like a rock. Hit his head on the stretcher and floor, but not too hard. I caught him."

"Where do I give him this epinephrine?" a nurse asked, holding a syringe with capped needle near Wolfe. "Near the injection site or in his arm? Subcu or I.M.?"

"Wait a second," Wolfe said, "I almost have this in." With the intravenous in place, Wolfe asked for the epinephrine. He pushed it through the i.v. and flushed it into the patient quickly by opening the stopcock completely. They attached the Lifepack 5 cardiac monitor leads to the man's chest. With only one jolt of electricity, his heart rhythm was restored from ventricular tachycardia to sinus rhythm. His pulse returned and he began to breathe on his own. Carefully, the staff lifted him off the floor and placed him on the stretcher. Still unconscious, he was wheeled to the ER ICU for evaluation and later shipped to the medical ICU for observation. Three days later, he walked out of the hospital, admonished never to even say the word *Penicillin*, much less take a dose in the future.

The man had had absolutely no history of any allergies, indeed had been given a course of ampicillin two years before for a sinus infection, without complications. Apparently, that was when he had become sensitized to the medicine. Wolfe learned another object lesson: people will not usually react to a medicine unless their immune system had seen it in the past. He resolved that he would never give anyone an injected antibiotic when an oral form was available. *The absorption time could not be that much different,* he reasoned. *And with the oral form, the patient might vomit, or he could be lavaged in order to remove it, if he turned out to be allergic. There was no getting the*

Bicillin back once it had been deposited inside a patient's muscles.

Chapter 45

Iggy and Wolfe had gotten to M&M conference before anyone else. They sat in the last row, their usual haunt, waiting for Torrosian and Samantha. "What's next up for Figueroa?" Wolfe asked.

"Tom Whittaker is in pathology this month. Figueroa came in last week," Iggy said. "Whittaker raised his CPK."

"Do you really think Figueroa will think he has had a silent MI?" Wolfe asked.

"Addy, there are a lot more reasons to have an elevated CPK than a heart attack," Iggy explained. "Any muscle in the body that is damaged can elevate it. Prolonged exercise alone can raise it, as can trauma. In addition..."

"But, just like a myocardial infarction, he'd know if he had any of that stuff," Wolfe interrupted.

"If you'll let me finish," Iggy said. "The real reason we picked CPK elevation is to make him chase his tail over things like Polymyositis and subtle forms of Muscular Dystrophy. Might take months to sort out."

Torrosian joined them, hearing the last of their conversation. "Acromegaly and Cushing's, too," he added, "maybe even Myasthenia Gravis. You're right. He'll be busy for months. All of those are subtle and difficult to diagnose. Where's Joiner?"

Samantha was not among the throng that gathered for the

M&M conference. Wolfe worried about her, wondered what may have happened between her and Figueroa, given his and Sam's last conversation about the placenta previa and the deaths on Ob-gyn. His thoughts were interrupted by Figueroa's voice.

"Before we start the academic portion of M&M," Figueroa said, standing at the podium, "I have a personal announcement I need to make." He paused for the words to sink in and for the auditorium to quiet. When it was perfectly silent, he smiled broadly and added, "I've never had an intern class quite like you guys. Those of you responsible for my trips to my doctors need to be congratulated. No interns before you have ever played such a successful practical joke on me. It's been a real lesson in differential diagnosis.

"In case some of you are unaware, for the last four months I have undergone a number of medical diagnostic tests in attempt to uncover a disease that may have given me some abnormal lab results. Thankfully, all those procedures have proved negative. I am healthy as a horse." A low current of moans filled the lecture hall.

Figueroa laughed heartily. "You had me going in circles, guys. I panicked. First my alkaline phosphatase was elevated, and then my upper GI was reported as abnormal. I made list after list of possible diagnoses. The last test, CPK, really threw me for a loop. That is, until I realized that no one could have this many sequentially single abnormal lab results. I went to clinical pathology and found the original results – all of which were normal.

"So. I thank you for treating me as *one of the boys* and I congratulate you on being able to pull my chain. However, if I find out who, specifically, altered those tests, I will be very harsh with him, and any colleagues who assisted. The game is over. I do not want to have to repeat myself. The game is finished." Figueroa's smile disappeared. A poker face took its place. "Now we will start the educational portion of this conference."

"Shit," Iggy said. "He thinks we want to be his bosom buddies."

"It's worse than that," Wolfe said, "he isn't going to waste any more time looking into his potential illnesses. It's back to peering over our shoulders. Or blackmailing him."

"One of our senior surgical residents, Dr. Petersen, has an interesting fact to share with us." Figueroa pointed into the audience.

Petersen stood. The lights dimmed. "The patient's face in the slide looked vaguely familiar to Wolfe. "This is a gentleman seen in the surgery clinics," Petersen said. "Turns out he was allergic to penicillin and didn't know it." He recounted the entire episode for the conference attendees.

Figueroa stood again. "Now, let's see, who resuscitated the patient, Dr. Petersen?"

"Drs. Casey and Wolfe," Petersen said.

Figueroa rubbed his hands together, as if he relished his next words. "Dr. Wolfe," he said, "if you had not been able to start that i.v. quickly what would you have done for the patient?"

Wolfe stood. He spoke clearly, "Given him some epinephrine, continued CPR, shocked him, and then hightailed it to ER ICU with him on the stretcher, I guess."

"Where would you give the epinephrine?" Figueroa asked. "Subcutaneously or intramuscularly. And if intramuscularly, in the buttocks where the Bicillin was given, or somewhere else, and why?"

Wolfe froze. His mind stopped. He had no idea. He had seen epinephrine given intracardiac, but that seemed a little harsh, and he wondered if the surgery clinic had the cardiac needles on their crash cart. "I don't know," he said.

"Well, what does epinephrine do pharmacologically?" Figueroa asked.

"Speeds up the heart. Makes the cardiac muscle squeeze harder," Wolfe said.

"Okay positive inotropic and chronotropic responses. What about peripherally?" Figueroa seemed to bore down on Wolfe.

Wolfe began to perspire. "I-I-I'm not sure," he said, tremulously.

Figueroa's face turned to mock rage. "Well this is pharmacology you should know," he said. "All interns, all physicians who run codes should know this, *Doctor* Wolfe, and I use the term loosely. Epinephrine causes vasoconstriction in the skin. If you had given it to the patient subcutaneously, the blood vessels in his skin would have gone into spasm and the epinephrine would never have reached the central circulation or the heart. Injected in a muscle, epi causes vasodilation. Had you stuck the needle into his buttock, near the injection site of the Bicillin, the blood vessels in his gluteus muscles would have dilated. Likely, more penicillin would have gone into circulation than epinephrine. As a result, the patient might have died. Are you seeing a pattern here, Dr. Wolfe? Unless you know what you are doing, you can kill people."

Another intern was foolish enough to risk Figueroa's wrath. "So, where should he have put the epi, Dr. Figueroa? Looks like he's in trouble either way if there is no i.v."

Figueroa's face became more composed. He turned toward the second intern. "Wolfe lucked out by putting it directly into the blood stream via the i.v. But he could have put it in any other muscle, where it would have caused vasodilation in that muscle and ended up in the circulation before the penicillin. Or directly into the patient's heart." Figueroa turned away from the podium. "Next," he said.

An internal medicine physician presented the sources of abnormal hemoccult results. More than blood could turn the small slides blue: meat, cantaloupe, grapefruit, figs, broccoli, cauliflower, and turnips included.

Miffed at Figueroa and himself, Wolfe paid little attention. He stared at the ceiling, daydreaming, lost in a world of screaming drill instructors and navy boot camp until he heard his name called. "Dr. Wolfe. Are you with us?" Figueroa shouted. "Someone wake him up!"

Wolfe turned his head and looked at Figueroa. "Sorry," he said.

"Dr. Petersen is presenting another interesting case, Dr. Wolfe. I'll summarize it for you so far, in case you missed anything," Figueroa said. "A Mr. Miles came into the ER two days ago with severe, debilitating back pain. He is fifty-six years-old. Yesterday he spent seven hours in the OR. Apparently, you saw him in surgery clinic about nine days ago. We want your impression of him from that visit. I have your notes in front of me. Would you like to review them?"

Stunned, Wolfe stared at Figueroa. He remembered Mr. Miles well. "No sir, I think I can reconstruct the visit." He told the physicians about the knifing and the follow-up.

"What about his back pain?" Figueroa asked.

"Looked muscular to me," Wolfe said. "He had no sciatica, no neurological deficits, range of motion was normal, but very painful."

"Do you know the number one cause of death in men over fifty who complain of their first serious back pain on a visit to a physician, Dr. Wolfe?" Figueroa asked.

"No, sir," Wolfe answered.

"I didn't think so. Did you happen to check Mr. Miles's pulses? Or listen to or palpate his abdomen?"

"I checked the wound in his abdomen, and the surgical incision, but not his pulses," Wolfe said, wondering why he would have.

"Tell him, Dr. Petersen," Figueroa said.

"The number one cause of death in that situation is an aortic aneurysm, although this patient did not have that," Petersen said. "He had a blood clot in his aorta that started at the renal arteries and filled the aorta and femoral arteries to mid-thigh. Unfortunately, he was in a hypercoagulable state. The hematologists are trying to figure out which one and why. It's a safe bet he will be on anticoagulants the rest of his life. He had no pulses in either leg: femoral, popliteal, posterior tibia, or dorsalis pedis. With the ultrasound, there was the slightest flow through the aorta with maybe high-pitched bruit over the aorta. Mr. Miles got an aortic graft. If he lives, he'll be in the hospital ICU for weeks."

"Anyone over fifty with back pain needs his abdomen and lower extremity pulses checked. Any questions?" Figueroa said. "You are all dismissed."

Wolfe sat, stunned. "Well, he's back to his old self," Iggy said, slapping Wolfe on the back. "You and that new asshole he carved for you are invited to dinner with me and Janice, if you have an appetite."

The residents and attending physicians filed out of the amphitheater, while Wolfe stared straight ahead. Figueroa left without a nod in his direction.

Chapter 46

"Jesus. Can't you shut that kid up?" Wolfe said, slamming the door to his bedroom.

Janice hushed Nancy Rose as best she could, quieting the screaming child. She went into her and Iggy's room and closed the door. The baby continued to shriek, waking Iggy. "What's up with the baby?" he asked groggily.

"Nothing. Colic. Who knows?" Janice said, breaking into tears.

"Crap. What's up with you?" Iggy asked, now wide awake.

"Nothing," Janice said, in a tone that Iggy knew meant *something*.

Iggy sat up, pulled the covers off, and swung his feet to the floor. He had been napping in his gym shorts and a white T-shirt. The two long thin scars on his right knee were still a deep purple color, but his knee was no longer swollen or painful. He could jog normally, and did occasionally. "Okay," he said, "Let's have it."

"It's Addy," Janice said.

"What about Addy?"

"He just yelled at me and the baby."

"He had a tough week," Iggy said. "Figueroa was all over his ass. He didn't mean anything. It's just stress."

"I know," Janice nodded, dabbing her tears and those of the baby with a tissue. "But he upsets the baby. She can sense his anger.

She's tense and cries. Then he screams and she cries more. It's a positive reinforcement cycle."

"You know too much psychology," Iggy said. "I'll talk with him."

"Soon?"

"Right now."

"Be gentle," Janice suggested. "I think he's fragile."

Iggy nodded. He pulled on his jogging shoes without bothering with socks. Standing, he walked out of their room and stood in front of Wolfe's door. Loudly, he banged on the door. "Hey, asshole," he said.

"Go away," Wolfe said.

Iggy opened the door and barged into the room. Wolfe lay on his bed in scrubs staring at the ceiling. "You've got five minutes to change into shorts and T-shirt," Iggy said. "Put on some running shoes, too. You and I are going to the beach."

"No, thanks." Wolfe said, not looking at Iggy.

"That was not a polite invitation," Iggy said. "I'll be back in five minutes. Be ready."

"What if I say no?" Wolfe asked.

"Then I'll carry your ass to the beach. Up and at'em, Addy." Iggy strode into the master bath, used the toilet and brushed his teeth. Looking in the closet, he found a salt-water-eaten leather football. Janice sat on the bed playing a game with Nancy Rose and her pacifier. The baby cooed, smiling at her mother. "That's better," Iggy said.

The two friends walked casually to the beach, flipping the football silently between them. For a track man, Addy had surprisingly good hands. When they reached the beach, he loped into the distance. Iggy drilled him in the gut with the football from twenty yards away.

"You mad at me?" Wolfe asked tossing the ball back to Iggy.

"Damn right," Iggy said. "If you are going to yell at my wife and kid, you'll have to find somewhere else to live."

"I'm really sorry, Iggy. I don't know why I snapped at them."

The third pass knocked Wolfe backwards, over a sand castle someone left on the beach and into the hole from which the sand for the castle had been dredged. The ball slipped through his hands and rolled slowly toward the surf. Sprinting, Iggy intercepted the ball before it got soaking wet. He jogged back to Wolfe, who lay on his back in the hole. Iggy reached down, offering his hand to Wolfe. "You alright?" he asked.

Wolfe ignored the proffered hand. "No," Wolfe said. "I'm thinking about quitting internship."

"I meant your body, asshole, not your psyche," Iggy said. "Hell, everyone is thinking about quitting internship. You are supposed to think about quitting internship. I, myself, have plans to go home to Virginia and work at McDonalds until I can get a real estate license or become a sports announcer, or maybe a sports agent for NFL football players."

"What do you know about being a real estate or sports agent?" Wolfe asked.

"I minored in business," Iggy said. "George Allen, Junior, the Redskins coach's son, and I were good friends my last year at U.Va. He introduced me to his father. That could be my foot in the door as an agent. Or I could go into politics. I think Junior is going to do that. Be better for him than football. He wasn't a great quarterback."

Wolfe studied Iggy's face. "You have really thought about quitting? Why would you quit? You are so good at it. Not a klutz or dunce like me," he said.

"We are *all* thinking about quitting, Addy," Iggy said. "It's not easy for any of us. Behind this thin veneer stands a self-conscious, less than confident, insecure, sometimes depressed intern, like yourself. I just hope no one finds my mistakes. Believe me, there have been many. I don't want to be sand blasted by Figueroa any more than you do. But, I've come too far, have too many people depending on me to fold in the face of an ambush like Figueroa pulled on you. I won't like it, but I'll smile and take my whuppin' like a man. I'm not quitting. They'll have to take me out in a pine box first. I've come too far to turn back. Knowing what I know now, I'd never go to medical school. But I've invested too much of my life, of Janice's and Nancy Rose's lives, to start over."

He sat next to Wolfe in the sand. Wolfe pulled himself up, sitting with feet in the hole. The two watched the waves run into shore, over and over again. "Sisyphus," Wolfe said. "Also, like the waves. It's going to go on forever. I don't know that I can take it."

"Five weeks, Addy," Iggy said. "Just five more weeks. Only one more M&M, the one where Figueroa introduces the new interns, like our first M&M. That's it. Finish surgery and one more rotation. Take it one day at a time." Wolfe nodded.

They walked in a deeper silence returning to the apartment, ball held tightly in Iggy's hand. "You weren't gone very long," Janice said when Iggy entered their room. Nancy Rose slept quietly, drool and milk bubbles on her lips.

"Didn't take long," Iggy said.

There was a quiet tapping at their open door. Janice and Iggy turned to see Wolfe standing in front of them. "I just wanted to apologize, Janice, to you and the baby. I'm sorry I yelled at you. You didn't deserve that. She's a wonderful kid."

Janice took Wolfe's hand with both of hers. She laid a gentle kiss on his cheek. "I know, Addy. This had been a tough year for all of us."

Wolfe held his right hand out to Iggy. Wordlessly, Iggy grasped his hand. The bigger man pulled Wolfe close to him and hugged him with his left arm. Wolfe said, "Thanks, man." He fled the room before either could see the tears welling in his eyes.

Chapter 47

Lisa Johannsen and Wolfe had spent at least an hour on the telephone Saturday night. As usual, Wolfe was exhausted. Barely awake, he listened to her recounting the flight to Jacksonville and description of the hotel near the airport in which she would spend the night. She had rented a car rather than take the short commuter flight home to Savannah. He agreed to her suggestions about their rendezvous in Neptune Beach the next day, Sunday, May 29th. Lying in bed while talking on the telephone did not help Wolfe stay awake; neither did the fact that the conversation had ended after 1:30 a.m. Five minutes after hanging up with Lisa, he was asleep.

About 10 a.m., Wolfe heard a pounding at his bedroom door. Sleepily, he rose and opened the door to find Janice and Samantha Joiner. "Sorry, Addy," Janice said. "She said it was an emergency."

Wolfe yawned, pulled up his scrub pants and retied the knot. He looked at Joiner, trying to read her face. "Is it?" he asked.

"Is it what?" Joiner asked.

"An emergency, Sam. Is it an emergency?" Wolfe asked. "Last time we talked, you left in a huff, remember?"

"I need to speak with you in private," Joiner said. "Then you can decide if it is an emergency." She stared at Janice until Janice blushed.

Wolfe also looked at Janice. Feeling sorry for the way Sam treated her, he said. "I'm sorry, Janice. Thanks for answering the door and getting me up. Sam and I need to talk." He held his arm out inviting Sam to enter the room.

Janice nodded and left without saying anything more. Wolfe saw Nancy Rose lying on her favorite blanket on the couch. She waved her tiny hands and feet in the air. Iggy sat next to her, huge hand on her stomach, tickling her, but also keeping her from rolling off the sofa. Wolfe waved at Iggy and Nancy Rose. "Hi, guys," he said. Iggy waved back silently, smile on his face.

Joiner gently pushed Wolfe backward into his room. She closed the door behind them, taking care not to slam it. "Your ex-girlfriend came by my house this morning," she said.

"Ex-girlfriend?" Wolfe asked. "I don't have an ex-girlfriend."

"The flight attendant is now your ex," Sam said. "Seems you promised to meet her at a church in Neptune Beach this morning for the early worship service. Then you were going to St. Augustine to sightsee for the day. You never showed. For some reason she thought you might be at my house."

Wolfe shook his head. He remembered something about St. Augustine. *Was there a conversation about a church? Maybe? Something?* He could not recall exactly what had been said. "I don't remember...."

"She tried to push her way into my house to look for you. We had an argument," Sam said. Wolfe imagined the cat fight that could have taken place. Knowing Sam well, but Lisa less well, he wasn't sure who would have won. "When I wouldn't let her in, she gave me a message for you. 'Tell that s.o.b. I've gone back to Savannah and don't try calling me. I won't answer the phone.' I think that's verbatim."

"Oh, shit," Wolfe said. "Jesus. What have I done to..." Another knock sounded at the door.

"Addy," Iggy said, when Wolfe cracked open the door, "a word, please."

Wolfe peered out at Iggy. "Yeah, Iggy?"

"I think your woman troubles just doubled, buddy." Iggy said. "Lisa's at the front door. Shall I let her in?"

"Of course," Wolfe said. "Tell her I'll be right out." He turned to Joiner. "Do me a favor, Sam. Stay in here and be quiet until I get her out of the apartment. Thanks for warning me about her mood, though, I really appreciate it."

A look of astonishment crossed Joiner's face, almost too quickly for Wolfe to notice. "Sure," she said. "No problem."

Wolfe slipped on his leather sandals, tucked his T-shirt into the green scrub pants and opened the door. He closed it behind himself when he left the room. "Lisa," he said, holding his arms out to her. "Are we still going to St. Augustine after lunch?"

Lisa stood just inside the apartment door. Her arms were folded tightly across her chest. Her foot tapped a hard rock rhythm on the linoleum entranceway. "Where were you?" she asked.

"When?" Wolfe asked, as innocently as he could, knowing exactly when and where.

"8 a.m. at the Central Christian Church in Neptune Beach," she said. "You said you'd try going once, just for me. I thought you meant it. Then I thought maybe you were in an accident. Or something worse, with that witch Samantha. I finally decided to find out if you just overslept." As she talked, Johannsen's features softened. Tears rolled out of her eyes and down her cheeks. "Addy, I'm sorry. I know you are probably exhausted. You didn't make much sense on the telephone last night."

She raised her head to look at him. Her eyes widened; her face darkened and hardened. "You. You bitch!"

Iggy and Janice snatched Nancy Rose from the couch and headed for the shelter of their bedroom, door slamming behind them.

Wolfe spun to see what Johannsen had seen. Samantha stood outside his door, wearing his bathrobe, and apparently not much else. The bottom was open nearly to her crotch, the top almost to her naval. No undergarments were visible. "Are you coming back to bed, Sugar?" Sam asked softly.

"Oh, shit, Sam. What are you doing?" Wolfe cried, taking three or four steps in her direction. "Why would you..." He stared at Sam, shaking his head. He threw his hands in the air, totally confused. Eventually, he spun back around, madly thinking of an explanation for Johannsen: *It's a joke. She's crazy. She's under a lot of stress. Don't believe what you see.*

Johannsen was gone. The door was open. He heard her shoes striking the cement at the bottom of the stairway. Opening the door farther, he ran after her. "Lisa, Lisa. It's not what you think." She never slowed, never acknowledged his presence. Almost running him over, she backed out of the parking lot and sped away in the Hertz rental.

Wolfe walked dejectedly back up the stairs. Samantha, fully clothed again, shoved his balled up bathrobe into his midsection when he entered the apartment. "That was fun," she said. "We should do it again sometime, Wolfie."

"Get out!" Wolfe screamed. "And don't ever come back. Do you know what you have done?"

"Of course I know what I have done, Wolfie," Joiner said. "Some day you'll thank me."

"And don't ever call me Wolfie, again," he said between clamped jaws, "or, I swear, you'll be sorry."

She laughed. He heard her skip down the steps, evil incarnate, with no care in the world. Behind him, he heard Nancy Rose wail. He slammed the apartment door behind her and marched toward his room. He couldn't go after Johannsen. He had no idea where she had gone. If he went to Savannah, he would not be back in time for rounds in the morning. *And if she weren't there, what good would the trip be? As if she would listen, anyway.*

Cautiously, Iggy opened his bedroom door. "All clear?" he asked.

Morosely, Wolfe answered, "Yeah. Sorry."

"Well," Iggy said, "I never figured you for a Romeo, Addy. How many more women are you stringing along? You must have a lot of stamina, what with women fighting over you and an internship to boot." Wolfe threw the bathrobe at him. Iggy tossed it back. "Too small. I like the color, though. Could you find one like it in Extra Large?"

Wolfe flipped him the bird and slammed his bedroom door from the inside. Nancy Rose wailed. *That's what I feel like doing, crying,* he thought. *Jesus, another one to three months of trying to get a woman out of my head. Damn!*

Chapter 48

Monday, May 30th, Wolfe pulled his last night on call for the surgery service. As usual, he spent a lot of time traipsing back and forth between the wards and the ER. His only distractions were thoughts of Lisa Johannsen and of his next rotation: psychiatry. He had chosen his elective rotation not for his interest in psychotic or neurotic patients, but the banker's hours kept by the psychiatrists. The psyche residents were never seen in the ER or hospital after normal office hours. At least Wolfe had never seen them.

He had heard stories from the ER residents about psychiatric patients: overdoses, other suicide attempts, paranoid schizophrenics, manic-depressants, and more waiting in holding cells and rooms, or restrained in beds. Not one had been admitted to the psychiatric service until he had been medically cleared. That meant all metabolic disorders, brain injuries, medication overdoses, and other reasons for abnormal behavior had to be ruled out before the psychiatrist would deem it proper to lay eyes on the patient. That always happened between 8 a.m. and 6 p.m. They never laid *hands* on the patient.

Semi-jokingly, residents on other services questioned whether the psychiatry residents were real physicians. Were not the psychiatrists capable of doing their own physical exams? They vocalized their anger by asking if the MD or DO after the psychiatry residents' names meant *Missing Doc*, or *Doctor's Off*. If anyone asked, they preferred the psychiatry residents perform the work-ups and transfer the patient back to internal medicine or surgery, if he turned out not to be psychotic. The argument raged, nearly coming to blows in the past. With input from the attending physicians on all services, University Hospital administration agreed with the psychiatrists. There was no good reason to transfer patients back and forth. The psychiatric service would not get involved until after all medical reasons for psychosis had been ruled out. The psychiatrists slept in. So would Wolfe in June.

At about 3 a.m. on May 31st , Wolfe listened to an argument between a junior ER resident, Lynch, and the junior surgical resident, a *towel head* (said with a smile, of course, by other Farsi and Arabic speaking residents) Iranian named Rajamani. The ER resident wanted to have a supposed gun shot victim admitted to the surgical service. The surgical resident could see no reason to admit him.

The patient's story on arrival to the ER was that another man had fired at him, point blank, with a *Saturday Night Special*. He heard the weapon pop and felt immediate pain in his leg. In the ER, Lynch found a wound in the patient's lateral lower leg, near the tibia. It might have been an entrance wound. No exit wound was visible. An x-ray of the leg showed no bone injury, no bullet fragments or bullet.

"Put a Band Aid on him and send him home," Rajamani told Lynch. "I doubt he was shot."

"Why would he lie?" Lynch asked. "I don't think he should go home without an x-ray survey to make the sure the bullet didn't travel elsewhere in his body."

"So do one. All ER patients lie. It's a given," the surgeon said. "Everyone has his own agenda. Maybe he wants to be admitted so whoever attacked him can't get at him. I don't know."

"What about a possible bullet emboli?" Lynch asked.

"I think that would be rare," Rajamani said. "We'll work him up and discharge him if you insist, but I'm not happy about it, Lynch. My senior resident will be also unhappy when I wake him up to get his blessing to send the patient home. Are you sure you can't discharge him, bring him back to surgery clinic in a week or something?"

"Either way, I'm referring him to you," the ER resident said. "You send him home. He's your responsibility and a surgical case now."

The surgical resident sat in the ER, angry at the waste of his time. He told Wolfe to do a quick physical, dress the wound, get the patient a tetanus shot, and set him up for a clinic appointment. Sitting at the desk, Rajamani picked up the telephone and dialed the beeper number for the senior resident. A short time later the telephone at the desk rang and Rajamani answered. He held a quiet conversation, although Wolfe thought he could hear a loud, incredulous presence on the other end of the telephone. Wolfe had written the physical and discharge notes by the time Rajamani hung up.

"Lynch," Rajamani called to the ER resident. "Consensus is that bullet emboli only happen when there are arteries and veins large enough for a bullet to enter, like Big Red and Big Blue. The vessels in the lower leg are only a quarter inch in diameter. No room for bullets. Remember that in the future. Have a good night. Come on, Addy, we have real work to do on the ward."

On their way to the elevator, they were approached by a three or four year old blond child running through the corridor, chased by the pediatric ER nurse. "Bryan, Bryan," she called. "Your mommy is looking for you." Wild-eyed, the child neared Wolfe and Rajamani as they stood in front of the elevator.

"Need a hand?" Wolfe asked the nurse, grabbing the child by one arm and sweeping him into his arms. The child laughed loudly. He pushed Wolfe's chest with both hands and kicked wildly with both feet trying to escape. Wolfe noticed blood on the child's chin.

The overweight nurse stopped in front of the physicians. She bent forward, hands on her thighs and puffed rapidly, trying to catch her breath. "Thanks," she gasped. "This rug rat got into a bottle of Dimetapp. Tastes like grape juice. He finished the little that was left in it. Fortunately, there was not enough for an overdose, but it has made him into a wild child. He used his dad's razor and tried to shave his face. She took the boy from Wolfe, wrapping her arms tightly around the squirming boy.

Wolfe watched her carry the child toward to the pediatric ER as the doors closed on the elevator. He and Rajamani exited on the surgery floor. Standing at the nurses' station was a white coated attending neurology physician, an Indian Wolfe knew as Dr. P. No one could pronounce his last name. Dr. P held an armful of x-ray jackets. "We must transfer Mrs. Wilson," Dr. P said. "On CT, there's mass."

"But Dr. P, the transfer order is to internal medicine," the nurse protested. "If she has a mass, shouldn't she be going to neurosurgery?"

Exasperated, Dr. P said, "Not *a* mass, *mass*."

Standing next to Dr. P, trying to understand what the man said through his Indian accent, Wolfe said, "Mrs. Wilson has left sided weakness and right face numbness. We sent her to Methodist for a CT,

Dr. P, because we suspect she has a brain tumor."

Dr. P turned to face Wolfe. "Yes, I know. She has mass."

"Mass?" Wolfe asked. "What kind of mass, meningioma, primary cancer or metastatic?"

Suddenly aware of why everyone was confused, Dr P said, "Oh, not *mass*, M-S, as in multiple sclerosis. She needs to be on the medical floor. She doesn't need surgery." He laughed. "It's my accent, I guess."

Wolfe spent a half hour collecting Mrs. Wilson's latest laboratory results, x-ray reports, CT report, and writing a transfer note to the internal medicine service. At about 5:15 a.m., he and Rajamani finished checking all the patients on which the nurses had questions, and rewriting fluid orders on two patients. He thought about going to the break room and taking a short nap, but decided he would feel worse after an hour of sleep.

Instead, Wolfe left Rajamani sleeping on a stretcher on the ward and went to the cafeteria where he collected a large cup of coffee. Finding a Florida Times Union from earlier in the week on one of the cafeteria tables, he spent an hour catching up on the news. The entertainment section had a big article on a new science fiction movie, *Star Wars*. Wolfe made a note to see it while on psychiatry. He had always loved science fiction. *Forbidden Planet* and *The Day the Earth Stood Still* were his all time favorite movies. Living with the cheesy special effects dulled the experience somewhat, but if *Star Wars* had a good plot, it would be worth the price of admission. He made a mental note to ask Lisa to go with him, and then remembered Lisa would not be accepting any invitations from him. *Might be worth a try, though,* he thought. *Maybe with a big bouquet of flowers and dinner, she'd forgive him for what Samantha had done.*

At the end of his last day on surgery, nearly 7 p.m., he handed his 3 x 5 cards to Rajamani. "I start psychiatry tomorrow after monthly intern review with Figueroa," Wolfe said. "Won't be here for rounds. I know you don't need these for whoever your next intern will be, but you might look through them just in case."

Rajamani shook Wolfe's hand. "Thanks, Addy. Drive carefully. Get some rest tonight. Enjoy your vacation on psychiatry."

Chapter 49

At about quarter to eight, Wolfe dragged himself up the outside stairs to the third floor apartment. Sluggishly, he found his key and let himself in the front door. He heard murmuring and then silence from the kitchen/dining room. Looking in that direction, he saw Iggy, Torrosian, Samantha Joiner, Nagakawa, and Bob Woo, an intern whom he had not seen in a long time.

Iggy stood. He beckoned Wolfe to join them at the table. “Hey, Addy, can we talk with you?”

A scowl on his face, Wolfe closed the door but did not move toward the table. “What’s she doing here?” he asked, glaring at Samantha.

Smugly, Sam smiled. “Saving your ass, Wolfie.”

“That’s it,” Wolfe said. “If you guys want me to join you, you’ll have to throw her out on her ass.”

“Sam,” Iggy said. “One more word from you in that vein and I’ll do as Addy asks. Got it?” Chastened, Sam nodded in silence. “Please sit down, Addy. We’ve got a big problem and we need your help to solve it.”

“I’ll bet,” Wolfe said. He pulled a chair from the table, spun it around and sat on it, his arms on the back of the chair. He knew he could leave quickly from that position. His made certain his colleagues were aware his presence was tentative.

"Woo, tell Addy, what you know." Iggy said.

"Okay. Wolfe, as you know, we ran a CEA on Figueroa," Woo said. Wolfe nodded. "We were going to substitute a higher value, to get him to chase his own tail looking for the reason. It turns out the value returned was really high without our changing it. Repeat tests, even on his older serum were also high. Figueroa apparently laughed off the result as a part of the joke he thinks we interns are playing on him."

"Shit," Wolfe said.

"That's not all," Nagakawa said. "I substituted another, abnormal UGI report for his upper GI report. Of course, he ignored that, too, once he figured out what we were up to. I hadn't really looked at his original report until Bob told me about the CEA. His original report suggests a possible mass in his pancreas."

"Double shit," Wolfe said. "So, what do we do? Hand him the original reports? We can't let him continue to ignore the results. He'll end up dead. And it will be our fault."

"We know," Iggy said. "Sam has a plan. We'd like your input before we put it into play, though."

Seething, Wolfe stared at Samantha. "I'll bet she has a plan," he said. "She's a manipulative..."

Iggy interrupted. "You must remember, Addy, changing the lab values was your idea. She's helping you out. If you agree."

"But we only did that to help her," Wolfe protested. "She was so scared she'd be forced out of the internship."

"We all did it," Sam said. "Not just to help me, but to help us fight that bully, to get him off our collective backs." The others agreed, nodding their heads.

Defeated by the group logic, Wolfe nodded. "Okay," he said. "What's your plan, Sam?"

She laid a sheaf of papers in front of Wolfe explaining as she did so. "These are the reports, both normal and abnormal. Every test, plus the two UGI reports." Wolfe scanned them as she placed them one at a time in front of him. She continued, "This is a letter I printed. It states what we did, why we did it, and the real possibility that he has pancreatic cancer. It points out he should have further tests. And this is an article on the differential diagnosis of an elevated CEA. It states clearly that colon cancer, pancreatic cancer, and cancer of the biliary tree are prime suspects."

"What are you going to do with this?" Wolfe asked. "Hand it to him? We'll all be out on the street looking for work."

"No," Sam said. "Figueroa is out of town this week. He's at a conference for medical educators in Atlanta until Sunday. I propose we leave it in his house. I haven't mentioned any names. He won't know exactly who has played this dirty trick on him. On the flip side, if he has an early cancer, he also won't know who saved his worthless life."

"I can live without taking that credit," Nagakawa said.

"Here, here," Iggy said, seconding the statement.

"There are two problems that I can see," Wolfe said, after thinking for a couple minutes. "There may be more, though. First, that note is obviously in Sam's handwriting. I would recognize it anywhere after reading her notes on charts all year. I think it should be typed. With no signature, obviously. And how do we get into Figueroa's house? I don't even know where the bastard lives."

"I've got the house covered," Sam said. "I'll deliver this stuff, if you know where we can find a typewriter."

Wolfe jumped up from the chair and retrieved his portable typewriter from his room. He had put on a pair of exam gloves and held a sheaf of typewriter paper he had taken from the middle of the stack.

"Why the gloves?" Iggy asked.

"No fingerprints this way," Wolfe said, "in case Figueroa gets too curious. You guys have probably never been fingerprinted. Mine are on file with the FBI since I was in the military service."

'Right," Iggy said, smiling. "They have mine, too, from the navy reserve. One can never be too paranoid."

Wolfe rolled a piece of paper into the typewriter. He pushed the machine in front of Samantha. "I don't type well. It would take me all night. You probably do. Most girls have to take typing in high school."

Sam's face clouded. She gritted her teeth, but said nothing other than, "70 words a minute; no errors."

"Speaking about being too paranoid," Wolfe told the others. "One of my jobs in the navy was to smash liquor bottles so moonshiners couldn't use the labels or the bottles. My uncle fought with the army in North Africa and Italy in WWII. He used to tell a story about GIs trying to find booze in Italy. I don't know if it's apocryphal or not, but he said he took a large wine bottle away from a private one day and sent it to the rear echelons for testing. A note came back a week later. It said, 'The man's horse has a kidney stone.'"

No one laughed. Even gallows humor had no place around the table as they waited for Sam to finish typing. Once she finished composing the short note, Wolfe pulled it from the typewriter still wearing his gloves. After Sam typed*, Ramon Figueroa, MD,* on the outside of an envelope, he folded the letter in thirds and stuck it inside. Taking a sponge from the kitchen sink, Wolfe moistened the glue on the envelope and sealed it. Still wearing his gloves, he retrieved a stapler from his room and stapled the envelope to the x-ray and laboratory reports. He handed the stack of papers to Sam. "Done," he said. "Have a nice trip."

"Addy," Iggy said, "May I speak with you in private? Do you guys mind? Addy and I have been friends for a long time. Would you mind waiting for a minute before you leave, Sam?" The others nodded. Wolfe and Iggy stepped in to Wolfe's room.

"What's up, Iggy?" Wolfe asked, after closing the door.

"I don't trust her, Addy," Iggy said. "I think she manipulated us into doing this. I don't know what her end game is, but I don't trust her to not sign your or my name to that letter and then deliver it. She's very, very manipulative."

"Oh, yeah?" Wolfe said. "What was your first clue? She'll be lucky if I don't strangle her before the internship ends. But what can we do?"

"Would you mind riding with her to Figueroa's and watching her deliver it?" Iggy asked.

"Why me?" Wolfe asked.

"It was your idea. And I've got Janice and Nancy Rose to think about," Iggy said.

"Now, who's being manipulative?" Wolfe asked.

"I'll make it up to you," Iggy said. "It's really for both of us. Listen, I'll talk to Lisa, tell her that Sam only arrived here minutes before she did. That's she staged the whole thing."

"Why didn't you do that already?" Wolfe asked.

"Didn't know if you wanted me to get involved," Iggy said, holding his hands palm up.

"Okay," Wolfe said. "We'll tell Sam I'm going along. That it's for her own protection."

Iggy dug his hands into his jeans. He pulled a mini cassette tape from his pocket. "Hang on to this," he said. "It's the tape of Figueroa and Sam. If she pulls any shenanigans, threaten to give it to the hospital administration or the cops. I'll bet there's more here than we know about."

Chapter 50

Very early in the morning of June 1st, Wolfe cut off his car's ignition at the top of the slight rise on Fort Caroline Road. In addition, he turned off the headlights. His car glided almost silently down the lonely stretch of gravel road. Figueroa's house stood isolated in what Wolfe assumed would someday be an affluent subdivision of Arlington, itself a larger neighborhood in greater Jacksonville. Beyond the house under the glare of the full moon, which shone directly overhead, Wolfe could see the reflection of the marsh that surrounded the house. The warm, humid, salt smell of the marsh permeated the air flowing through his open window.

Beyond the marsh, the St. Johns River made its last two gentle turns before emptying into the Atlantic Ocean between Huguenot Park and Mayport Naval Station. Across the river in the distance, Wolfe could see bright lights on Blount Island. Men at the Jacksonville Port Authority worked around the clock loading and unloading cargo, frequently automobiles from Europe or Japan. Two a.m. was no different to them than two p.m. The tide rose and fell continuously. Some of the ships needed high tide to enter or exit the port.

"You're sure Figueroa is not at home?" Wolfe asked Joiner for the fourth or fifth time.

"I told you, he's in Atlanta for the Medical Educators Conference," Sam reassured him, again.

The car crunched to a halt on the gravel road when Wolfe gently applied the brakes. A flare of red light lit the empty lots surrounding the home and also its façade. Wolfe quickly lifted his foot off the brake pedal dousing the red lights, and set the parking brake. Gazing at the mansion nervously, he told Sam, "You stay here." He reached under the seat and took the small pry bar he kept there and a rag he had kept in the trunk until that night.

'What are you going to do with that?" she asked.

"I doubt he left the front door unlocked," he said. He wrapped the rag around the end of the crow bar and showed it to Sam. "I thought I'd break a window in the garage door and let myself in that way."

"No. You can't do that. He has a security system. It will pick up the sound of the broken glass." She reached into her purse and pulled out a large brass key. "Use this."

"What's that?" Wolfe asked, hoping it wasn't what he thought.

"The key to the front door, silly," she said. "On the right, in the front hallway is one of the control boxes for the security system. The code is 0701. Like July 1st, the first day of internship every year."

"How do you know that?" Wolfe asked suspiciously.

"Let's don't go into that right now," Joiner said.

"No," Wolfe said, staring at her in the shadow of the full moon, streaming in through the back window. "Let's do get into that. I need to know. Have you been fucking Fig?"

Joiner's facial features hardened into an implacable mask. "Let's just say I have used one of the weapons available to me in order to even the playing field. Women sometimes have a difficult time competing with men in certain endeavors. Also, it turns out that Ramon is a remarkably capable and entertaining lover. In addition to using him for other things, I have derived a certain measure of pleasure from his adroitness, that, ahem, less experienced sexual partners can provide."

"What other things?" Wolfe asked, blushing. He knew exactly who was the least experienced sexual partner Sam had.

"What?"

"You said, 'in addition to other things.' What other things?" Wolfe asked.

"Well, now that you ask," Samantha said in slow even tones. "Even though the ER residents won't let you forget that University Hospital has one of only five ER residencies in the United Sates, you probably haven't paid much attention to that fact. This is a premier place to do an ER residency, Wolfie. The first residents to graduate in ER medicine and pass their boards will be the founding generation among ER physicians. They will be the directors of the next generation of Emergency Medicine residencies. I wanted a slot in this residency. I want to run a residency myself someday. Imagine that: a woman in charge of a residency. Ramon granted that wish, in exchange for what he thought were sexual favors."

Wolfe reached for the ignition key. She grabbed his hand. "What are you doing?" she asked.

"I'm leaving. I didn't come here to participate in one of your devious plots. I can't imagine what there is to be gained by being going in there. I'll just tell Figueroa tomorrow."

"Tell him what?" she asked. "Tell him you falsified lab reports, stole medical records? Your internship will be over. Besides, this isn't about me. This is about saving Figueroa's life. You do have the lab and x-ray results and the article on pancreatic cancer, don't you?"

Wolfe nodded. He patted his shirt pocket, where the folded reports sat over his wildly thumping heart. "Okay," he finally said. "I'll drop the report inside the front door. Then we're out of here."

"He rarely goes in through the front door; he uses the garage door. It has an automatic opener." Joiner said. "The papers might sit there for days before he sees them. Follow the hallway to the great room. On the right side, you'll see the bar. Leave it there. He won't miss that."

"I have a better idea," Wolfe said. "You know your way around inside. And you have a key and know the security code. You take it."

"I don't care if he dies," Sam said, sitting back in the car seat and staring out the front window. "We can go if you want. I also don't care if you tell him in person. It won't cost me my internship or Robinson's slot in the ER residency."

Wolfe's neck snapped, head pivoting from staring at the house to looking at her. "You," he said. "You manipulated Figueroa into firing Nick, didn't you? Damn!"

Joiner pretended to curtsey, sitting in the car. "It's hard to take a bow sitting down," she said.

Wolfe opened the car door. He almost slammed it after getting out, but he held his emotions in check. Striding quickly to the front door, he inserted the key. The security box hung precisely where Sam said it would be. A red light on the box flashed silently. When he punched in 0701, the light turned to a steady green.

Moonlight streamed through the large windows in the house. He had no difficulty seeing his way into the great room. A wall of wine bottles and decanters filled the wall space behind the wet bar on the right side of the great room. To his left was the sitting area, with a large television, a huge leather couch, and several chairs and recliners. On the far side of the great room, the kitchen looked over the marsh, with French doors that led to a large deck. Wolfe saw a hot tub and wondered how many times Sam had been in that.

Pulling the folded sheaf of papers from his breast pocket with his latex gloved hands, he laid them carefully on the bar. He turned to leave and a voice spoke to him in the moonlit room. "Good morning, Dr. Wolfe." Figueroa stood between him and the hallway to the front door. Easily visible in the moonlight, he held a pistol in his hand and pointed it at Wolfe.

"So, Dr. Wolfe," Figueroa continued. "Not only do you irritate me in the hospital, you choose to violate my privacy at home, too?"

Wolfe never liked weapons, one of the reasons he chose the navy over the army after flunking out of engineering. He raised his hands over his head. "It's not what you think, Dr. Figueroa. Please point that thing at the floor. I won't run away or try to hurt you," he said.

Slowly, Figueroa lowered the pistol until it pointed downward. "Don't try anything stupid," he warned. "It is loaded and I am not a bad shot. Now, what are you doing in my house and where did you get the key and the security code?"

"I'd rather not say." Wolfe said.

"Well, that's okay," Figueroa replied. "You can tell the police when they get here." He took several steps toward the wall phone hanging on the wall between the great room and the kitchen.

"No. Wait. Let me try to explain," Wolfe said. He held his hands in front of him, using the same gesture with which he told plane captains on the carrier that they were about to be pushed in reverse by the blue-shirted crewmen.

Figueroa stopped moving and turned to face Wolfe again. "I'm waiting," he said. "It better be good, or I will call the cops anyway."

"Okay, okay," Wolfe said, trying to piece together an explanation Figueroa would understand, and maybe appreciate. "You were right, we, uh, I manipulated your lab tests. It was an attempt to get you to think about something other than screwing me, or the other interns."

"I knew it!" Figueroa said. "But you said *we*. Who else was involved? Wasn't this a big joke? Weren't you just playing with me?"

"No, sir," Wolfe said. "It was no joke. You are such an asshole the consensus was we wanted you to take a medical leave, to leave us alone."

A look of shock registered on Figueroa's face, then slid away. "You mean all the interns took part in this? Every one of you?"

"No, sir," Wolfe said, shaking his head. "There were some we didn't include. They couldn't be trusted. We knew they curried favor with you and would give it away."

"Well, so what? I know most interns wouldn't stoop to this." The gun in his hand rose toward Wolfe, again. "But that doesn't explain why you are here tonight. What could breaking into my house have to do with that?"

"We screwed up," Wolfe said. "Without reading it carefully, we replaced your abnormal x-ray report with one that was less abnormal. I brought you the real report." He pointed to the stack of papers. "And your CEA. We repeated that four or five times with previous blood samples. It was abnormal every time. We think you may have pancreatic cancer."

"There is no early test for pancreatic cancer, Wolfe. Besides I don't feel bad...."

The explosion from the front door hallway startled Wolfe. Figueroa clutched his left chest, looked at the blood he found in his hand and collapsed to the floor. Wolfe spun and saw Sam standing in the hallway. "Jesus, Sam, what have you done? You shot Dr. Figueroa."

Joiner ignored him. She strode to Figueroa and picked up his pistol in her right hand. Holding her pistol down by her side in her left hand, she pointed Figueroa's weapon at Wolfe. She pulled the trigger as Wolfe ducked. Glass shattered behind him. He scurried behind the bar.

"What are you doing?" he yelled.

"Well, after you shot Dr. Figueroa, he managed to shoot you," she explained. "You both died. Like the shootout in the OK Corral."

Picking up two bottles from the shelf behind which he hid, Wolfe stood and threw one at Sam, then ran for the closed door in the hallway behind the wet bar. He hoped it led to the garage. Ducking the bottle as it flew by her, Sam fired wildly several times. One of the bullets hit a large vase Figueroa used as an umbrella stand near the door to the garage. It rolled under Wolfe's feet. He collapsed short of the door. Unable to get to his feet quickly, he lay perfectly still. In the moonlight a thick red liquid pooled near his body, spreading over the tile floor.

Joiner took her time. With measured stride she stepped toward Wolfe, gun pointed in his direction. Seeing him to be unconscious, she turned and retraced her steps to Figueroa. She put Figueroa's gun in his right hand, closing his fingers around it. She watched the Director of Medical Education take a few slow, shallow breaths. A pool of blood spread around him also, creeping into the white carpet. She knew he would not live long without medical help.

Returning to Wolfe she placed her gun in Wolfe's gloved right hand, then laid it gently in the pool of blood collecting under his arm. Standing, she removed the surgical gloves from her hands turning them inside out to catch any blood. She placed them in her pocket. She stepped over Wolfe's body and rinsed her hands in the sink of the wet bar.

She looked up when the lights came on to find Wolfe standing, leaning against the wall and holding her weapon pointed at her. "Surprise," he said. "Not all that red stuff is blood. He pointed the pistol at the shattered bottle of red wine on which he had been lying. His chest and abdomen were dripping with red wine. He tapped his wet shirt with the pistol. "You must have thought you hit Big Red or Big Blue."

His left hand, however, dripped real blood onto the tile floor surrounding the bar. A widening area of blood crept down his left arm from the biceps, soaking his shirt. "That full bottle did shatter more easily than an empty one would have. Did I ever tell you how difficult it is to break an empty bottle? One of my jobs in the navy was breaking empty bottles. Had to throw them really hard into the dumpster. Never mind."

He waved the gun at her, forcing her to move to the middle of the room. "Lie down, face down, arms and legs spread wide. Don't move or I'll shoot you. I won't kill you, but I'll put a bullet in each hamstring, so don't temp me."

"Addy," she said. "We can talk." She started to roll over. He fired the pistol. The bullet smacked into the carpet between her legs and buried itself in the wood subfloor.

"Down!" he said. She lay motionless. "Don't move. And don't say anything. I've heard enough of your lies to last me an internship."

Training the weapon on Sam, he dialed the operator who connected him to JSO. He reported the shooting. He told the dispatcher he was a doctor and he needed an ambulance right away, in addition to the police. After hanging up, he pulled the six foot long coiled cord from the telephone. Using that he hog-tied Joiner on the floor, face down. Then dragging his left arm, one-armed, he did his best to evaluate Figueroa and staunch the flow of blood from the director's left lower chest by putting pressure on the bullet wound. He didn't find an exit wound. Figueroa's pulse remained strong and he moaned several times. Wolfe had high hopes for Figueroa's survival.

The room began to get dim. Wolfe's vision began to cloud. He felt like he was in the altitude chamber in the air force's flight medicine facility in San Antonio. There he had learned how flight crewmen respond to the drop in oxygen pressure at high altitude without an oxygen mask. Feeling the hypoxia of anemia from blood loss, Wolfe dropped to his knees and then lay flat on the floor. He felt better. It was easier for his heart to pump blood horizontally than uphill as his blood volume diminished. The gray tunnel he saw grew larger narrowing his field of vision. He never heard JSO or the paramedics enter Figueroa's home or felt the needle they stuck in his arm to give him fluid. He was vaguely aware of Sam screaming that he was a maniac and had tried to kill her and Figueroa.

Chapter 51

The sirens and lights, so shrill and bright they could have raised the dead, woke Wolfe at times. Lifted bodily and unceremoniously onto the stretcher, he felt the handcuff bite into his wrist. "You don't understand," he tried to say. *Dr. Rubel would be upset. I think I pissed off JSO somehow*, Wolfe thought.

Someone extinguished the flashing red and blue lights. Silence. Darkness. He felt his feet being elevated. The noise returned, blaring in his ears. The lights seemed dim, far away. "Pressure's ninety over forty. Pulse 140," someone said, also from far, far away.

With a jerk, he dropped six inches. His body slammed into the stretcher. The bright lights of the University Hospital ER entrance bathed him. *Ah, shit,* Wolfe thought, *but better here than Memorial or Methodist.*

Wolfe felt pinches in both arms, then a sharp pain under his right collar bone. "O negative, then type specific. Packed cells," someone called from miles away. The gloom returned, closed in on him. Again, darkness.

Wolfe gagged when the anesthesiologist pulled the endotrachael tube from his throat. He coughed. "More awake than I thought," a voice said.

Groggy, Wolfe woke in recovery. A red intravenous bag hung over his head. He assumed it was blood. His left upper arm felt like a tractor had run over it. When he moved his left hand, fire burned from his neck to his finger tips. He tried to raise his right arm. It was chained to the bed.

"Addy, are you awake?" a familiar voice called to him, his mother.

"Be right down," Wolfe said. *He was in trouble now. Late for school.*

Wolfe opened his eyes. His father stood next to his bed. His mother sat in a chair at the foot of the bed. "Hey, guys," Wolfe said. "What are you doing here?"

Shaking his head, his father reached across the hospital bed rails and grasped Wolfe's right hand. "Good to see you son," he said. "Do you remember what happened?"

Wolfe's mother left the chair, came to the side of the bed, cradled his head to her breast. "Addy, Addy," was all she could say.

A nurse Wolfe didn't recognize came into the room. "I'm sorry," she said. "Doctor's orders. You can come back for another ten minutes in an hour."

"He just woke up," Wolfe's father protested.

"Come on, Art," his wife pulled at her husband's hand. "He'll be okay. We can come back later." The two left the room haltingly, tears in their eyes, backward glances at Wolfe. He tried to wave, but could not raise his right hand. The left arm seemed weighted down, too.

"Hey, buddy," Iggy said. "You in there? Your parents said you've been awake a couple times for up to an hour at a time."

Wolfe opened his eyes. Aside from being blurry, Iggy looked dapper, clean white coat, shaven, dress shirt and tie. "All dressed up," Wolfe said.

Iggy spun like a ballerina, index finger pointed to the top of his head. "Psychiatry dress. Bankers' hours." He curtsied.

"How long have I been out?" Wolfe asked, mouth so dry his guess would have been weeks.

"About two days," Iggy said. You lost a lot of blood. Cut your left brachial artery. You got six units of blood and several more liters of Ringers and normal saline. We've been worrying about anoxia and your squash. How are you feeling?"

"Like a Mojave Desert rat lives in my mouth. Other than that, okay I guess." He tried to lift his right arm. It floated into the air unsteadily. "I seem to remember having handcuffs on that wrist. Am I under arrest?"

"You were. You slept through that part of the excitement," Iggy said. "What do you remember? No. Wait. There's a police officer that wants to hear this, too." Iggy went to the door and opened it. "Detective Scanlan. Could you come in here, sir?"

Wolfe told the detective and Iggy what he remembered. "Why didn't she shoot you?" Scanlan asked. "There were three bullet holes in the bar and nearby walls. She must have tried,"

"She thought she had. When I tripped, I had an unopened bottle of Cabernet in my hands. I had thrown one at Sam. When I fell I smashed the bottle on the tile floor on purpose. It broke easily, being full. I pretended to be seriously wounded and unconscious hoping she would think the thick red liquid under me was blood in the moonlight. She hadn't turned on the lights. It worked, thank God. Lucky for me she didn't think of a *coup de grâce*. I didn't count on cutting my arm."

"She probably didn't have an execution in mind. That would have looked suspicious. We think she was hoping Figueroa would kill you and then he would be arrested. With you gone, she would be guaranteed a spot in the emergency medicine residency. She thought Figueroa would be relieved of duty if he shot you. Since he didn't shoot you, she changed the plan. How did you get the gun away from her?" Scanlan asked.

"She put it in my hand. She wanted me blamed for Figueroa's death, she said. What happened to Figueroa?" he asked, suddenly remembering that the Director of Medical Education might have died. "And Sam?"

Iggy looked at Scanlan. "Can I tell him what I know?"

The detective nodded. "I'm going to sit here and look over my notes. You two can chat."

Iggy pulled a chair next to the bed. He sat. "Figueroa went to the nearest hospital. He was in worse shape than you."

"Memorial?" Wolfe asked.

"Yeah," Iggy said. When he saw Wolfe roll his eyes, he quickly added, "but it turned out okay. Schiffer was moonlighting in Memorial ER that night. They did a fluid resuscitation. He got sixteen units of blood before they could stop the bleeding. He'll be there a while. They had to take him to the OR and explore his left chest and his abdomen. Bullet went through a rib and fragmented, hitting his spleen. He lost the spleen. When the bullet fragments ricocheted they went in lots of directions including his gut. While they were running the bowel looking for holes, they found a mass in the tail of his pancreas. They figured he might not be strong enough for a second surgery for a while, so they took out the tail half of his pancreas."

"Cancer?" Wolfe asked.

"Yeah. We were right," Iggy said. "Preliminary pathology report looks good, completely contained in the pancreas. Of course, the Armed Forces Institute of Pathology has to pass judgment on it, but it looks like we saved that asshole's life. Not that he'll appreciate it. He might end up a diabetic. Every time he sticks an insulin needle in his abdomen, he'll think of you. And Sam."

"Where is Sam?" Wolfe asked.

Iggy sighed. "Looks like a complete break with reality. The shrinks say she may be a paranoid schizophrenic. Not unusual to see that happen in her age group, they say. They think the stress of competing with males unequally for eight to ten years put her over the edge. She's going to be in a psychiatric hospital for several months, at a minimum."

"Hospital?" Wolfe asked. "She needs to be in a psychiatric prison. She tried to murder Figueroa and me."

"Figueroa isn't going to press charges. He thinks it's not all her fault. In fact, he's taking some of the blame. He admits to being a male chauvinistic pig." Iggy paused to let the information sink in. "You need to think about your position, too, Addy. The cops are going to want to know what you think about her mental state. No one thinks she was sane at the time she shot Figueroa."

"How did she know Figueroa would have a gun? Never mind, the same way she had the key. Did she really think he'd shoot me?" Wolfe asked.

Scanlan looked up from his notes. "She had sent anonymous notes and made anonymous phone calls to Figueroa threatening his life. His wife was a pediatrician. She was murdered by the parent of one of her patients when she reported him for child abuse. Figueroa took the threat seriously. You are lucky he didn't open fire without identifying you. That would have suited her purposes: you dead and him relieved of duty until she finished internship and started residency."

"Why did they have handcuffs on me, Iggy?" Wolfe asked. "I'm the guy who called the cops and rescue."

Detective Scanlan put down his notes. He answered for Iggy. "Officers on the scene thought you were dangerous. "Dr. Joiner said you had tried to kill her and Dr. Figueroa."

"What changed their minds?" Wolfe asked the detective.

"Iggy and some of your other friends were very helpful in filling in the blanks. The note you left helped, too – by the way, we got a subpoena to confiscate your typewriter. You'll get it back when the investigation is over. Also the front door key was in your pocket. And this," Scanlan said. He flipped the mini-cassette tape onto Wolfe's bed. "The ER docs found it in your clothing with the key while they were transfusing you in the ER. It's no use to us as evidence. There's been no verified chain of custody. It was enough to get Figueroa canned, however. After I listened to it, I knew there was more to this than the love triangle suggested by Dr. Joiner. We got warrants to search her house. I can't tell you everything we found; it's being catalogued for a possible trial. But it was enough to make us question her thoroughly. She eventually broke down and confessed. She's a very sick lady."

"Will she be okay?" Wolfe asked. "Did her fiancé come down from Boston?"

"Another lie," Iggy said. "There is no fiancé. Just like Figueroa wasn't at an educational conference. I don't know if she has told the truth about anything all year. On the bright side, the shrinks think she will recover with medication. They even think she might be able to finish the internship some day and practice medicine. She'll be on a lot of drugs for a while, though."

A knock sounded at the door. It opened slowly and a nurse escorted Wolfe's parents into the room. As they entered, Detective Scanlan and Iggy bid Wolfe and his parents good-bye.

"Good news, Addy," his mother said. "They are going to put you in a regular room. We'll be able to visit more often."

Chapter 52

Even though he knew Figueroa no longer occupied the Medical Education Office, Wolfe found it difficult to sit in the outer office. Brenda Jackson typed away, oblivious to his pacing back and forth in front of her desk. The IBM Selectric buzzed happily as her fingers danced across the keys. The frosted glass windowed door opened. It still said Ramon Figueroa, DO on it, but the face was new, at least new to the position.

"Dr. Wolfe," Dr. Rubel, the pathologist, said. "Come in, son." He met Wolfe at the door and shook his hand. "When do you get out of the sling?"

Wolfe pulled his left arm from the blue sling. He waved it in the air, over his head and in big arcs, clenching and unclenching his left fist. "Good as new, Dr. Rubel. They'll probably let me take it off today. They released me from the hospital this morning, but the attending vascular surgeon wants to see me in clinic this afternoon."

"Sit down," Rubel said, pointing to a settee by the window. He sat opposite Wolfe in a stuffed chair. Wolfe noticed all Figueroa's sports memorabilia and autographed pictures had been removed from the wall. Dusty shadows of their existence remained. Rubel watched Wolfe's eyes as they searched the room nervously. "We're going to repaint, eventually. Not much money for redecorating."

"Good," Wolfe said. "Why did you want to see me, Dr. Rubel?"

"Two things," the pathologist said. "Most importantly, this." He handed Wolfe a manila folder with his name on it. "You can read all that after you leave, but I have changed your evaluations, and those of most of the interns. I let the attending physicians' marks stand in most cases, yours included."

"Great. Thanks, Dr. Rubel," Wolfe gripped the folder, as if a lifeline. "What was the second thing?"

"You still have an internship to finish, Dr. Wolfe. I think you need to report to psychiatry. You look well enough, but you are a week late. If you don't start soon, we'll have to hold you over for a month in order for you to finish your internship." The pathologist's eyes twinkled. Wolfe knew the statement was a joke.

"I've been thinking about that," Wolfe said. "You know that psychiatry is an elective, right?"

"Yes." Rubel nodded.

"Well, I'd like to change the elective to riding with the EMTs in the field. Some day I might decide to become an ER doc," Wolfe explained. "I think that would be a good experience for an ER physician."

After ten minutes of casual conversation and Rubel's inquiries into how Wolfe's parents were recovering from the shock of learning their son had been seriously injured and initially arrested for attempted murder, Wolfe left the office. Rubel promised to look into the possibility that he could ride with an ambulance crew. "With which unit do you want to ride if I can arrange it?" Rubel asked, as Wolfe opened the door to the office.

"The guys who saved my life," Wolfe said. "Unit 33."

"I'll see what I can do, Addison," Rubel said."

"Thank you, sir," Wolfe said. The buzz saw sound of the typewriter followed him down the corridor.

***

Iggy gave Wolfe a ride home after he was dismissed by the vascular surgeon. "TGIF," Iggy said pulling his tie off with one hand while driving. "No surgeon wants to wear a monkey suit like this. I'd trade these 9 to 5 hours for a scrub shirt and twelve hour days in the operating room any time."

"Nice to have the weekends off, though, isn't it?" Wolfe asked.

"Yeah, but even that gets tedious. As you know, I love Janice, but 60 hours in a row sometimes leads to rubbing each other the wrong way. If you know what I mean," Iggy said. "There are only so many *honey dos* I can handle at one time."

"How's the baby?" Wolfe asked.

"Dangerous," Iggy laughed. "She's crawling all over the apartment, pulling up on the coffee table. That reminds me. Janice and I have rented a small house off the main drag in Neptune Beach, starting in July. She wants to continue working and the baby needs a bedroom to herself. We need more room and we didn't know your plans. There is an extra bedroom if you'd like to sublet it from us."

"Thanks, Iggy," Wolfe said. "I'll think about it. Haven't made up my mind what I'm going to do, yet. Dr. Rubel and I have another meeting Monday."

Iggy led Wolfe up the steps to the third floor apartment. Still a quart low on blood, Wolfe stopped on the second landing to catch his breath. He halted again on the landing in front of the apartment door and leaned against the wall, hands on knees. "How's your heart, Addy? Strong enough for surprises?"

Wolfe tilted his head and looked at his best friend. "Dunno," he said. "What do you have in mind? Janice pregnant again?"

"You'll see," Iggy said, opening the door. "Honeys, I'm home!"

Wolfe followed Iggy into the apartment, eager to see Janice and Nancy Rose. Iggy hugged his wife. Janice held the baby between them. Janice smiled and nodded at Wolfe. He returned the smile. "Good to see you, Janice," he said.

She handed the baby to Iggy and gave Wolfe a hug. "Welcome home, Addy."

Wolfe tickled Nancy Rose's cheek. She smiled and drooled. "Thanks, Janice. I'll be back in a minute."

Wolfe continued on, toward his room. He noticed a figure sitting on the worn hide-a-bed couch and stopped, staring. "Hello, Addy," Lisa said. She stood quickly and walked to him. Taking his left hand, she stroked it softly. "I'll go, if you are mad at me. I just wanted to... Iggy explained everything to... Just so glad you weren't hurt worse. Can you forgive me?" She threw her arms around him, buried her face in his chest and started to sob."

"Lisa. Lisa," Wolfe said, hugging her tightly. "I was never mad at you. Don't cry." He led her into the bedroom and closed the door.

"Home, sweet home," Iggy said to Janice after Wolfe and Lisa disappeared into his room. He grabbed the baby and twirled her high above his head like a helicopter rotor. "Whee! What's for dinner?" Nancy Rose laughed, arms and legs spread.

***

The Vietnam War gave an impetus to the American Emergency Medical System. The taxpaying public had a hard time understanding why guys who had been blown up and riddled with bullets survived combat, but their fathers died from heart attacks because no one could help. Among national leaders, Jacksonville established a working EMS system in the late 60s and early 70s. One driving force to do so came from a strike by private ambulance owners and funeral homes in April, 1967, over the subsidy paid by Duval County. Jacksonville EMS started with station wagons, fire chiefs, and fire fighters. In addition to training fire fighters, it eventually hired many discharged army and navy medics as a nucleus for its ambulance service. Establishing a residency for Emergency Medicine made sense once the funeral homes stopped providing ambulance service. Rumor had it that the funeral home ambulances occasionally drove crash victims around the block until the patient conveniently expired, in order to guarantee the price of a funeral. In-hospital residency training did not provide the residents with a clear picture of the circumstances in which the EMTs and paramedics found themselves. Riding in an ambulance with them did.

Wolfe wore the uniform of the day for ambulances rides: Nikes, corduroy pants, scrub shirt, and short white coat. The vascular surgeons refused to allow him to lift anything with his left arm, still concerned about Wolfe's left brachial artery forming an aneurysm at the point of repair. It would be three months before they would permit lifting anything heavier than his toothbrush.

Dr. Rubel had finagled the change in Wolfe's electives. He tailored the remainder of the month to suit the vascular surgeons, and give Wolfe a chance to rebuild his blood supply. Wolfe could ride six hours a day on a rotating schedule: 6 a.m. until noon one day; noon until 6.p.m. the next; 6 p.m. until midnight the third; and then midnight until 6 a.m. on the last night, before taking a day off and starting all over again. After three cycles he would get two days off. In that manner, Wolfe worked with each of the Unit 33's three squads who worked 24 hours on and 48 hours off, and he saw how they managed day and night work. He had a lot of time off to study. He spent most of that thinking about his future and making decisions.

Unit 33's territory covered downtown Jacksonville from the Mathews Bridge west to Main Street. The only reason they had transported him the night Figueroa had been shot was they had just left Memorial Hospital after transferring a patient there from Methodist

Hospital.

The last run on the rotation found Wolfe in a three story walk-up in the slums of downtown Jacksonville. At 5 p.m. the outside temperature hovered in the mid-nineties. Humidity checked in at 85%. Inside the building, in the third floor apartment, the electricity had been cut off. Only two windows let in sunlight, the others being covered to keep out the heat. The strategy hadn't worked. The temperature inside felt like a hundred and ten. The paramedic, EMT, and Wolfe had soaked their shirts with sweat before they even reached the third floor. They climbed the stairs. There was no elevator. Sweat continued to pour off Wolfe after entering the apartment.

"Okay," Paramedic Winters asked the thin white male who answered the door in the wife-beater T-shirt and drooping beltless pants, "Who's sick?"

The man pulled a cigarette from his toothless mouth. He pointed in a dark corner near a covered window, "Him," he said. "Overdose."

Cockroaches scattered from underfoot. Wolfe smelled human urine and feces when they gathered around the man. The black man lay on the hard floor, a rag of clothing under his head. Vomit and blood covered his unbuttoned raggedy dress shirt, missing the cuff links and button studs. His tuxedo trousers had been ripped. Bare feet revealed needle tracks.

The EMT did a brief medical survey and took the man's vital signs. Obviously in his own universe, the man mumbled incoherently. Once strapped to the stretcher, painstakingly retrieved from the ambulance by two firemen who had accompanied the paramedics on the call, the man was strapped in and an intravenous started. He was lugged carefully down two flights of stairs to the ambulance. Recovering such patients took patience and diplomacy. Heroin was a *whole 'nother country, brother*, as one of its victims told Wolfe.

Unit 33 made the short run to University Hospital. On the way, Wolfe asked Winters if the patient had a heart murmur. "I thought I heard something, but it's damned difficult to hear anything under those circumstances," Winters said. "Why do you ask?"

Wolfe told the paramedic that the overdose patient might be a stroke victim as well. "See how the right side of his face droops? And his left arm is flaccid," Wolfe said. "If he has a patent foramen ovale or a septal defect that would account for the stroke. Could have easily sent a clot or an embolus of some sort up his veins while shooting up."

"Yeah," I think you're right, Addison," Winters said. "Wish you could stick around longer. I have enjoyed talking with you about medicine. I even learned some stuff."

"Really?" Wolfe teased, "A member of the *crew without a clue* learned something?"

"More than the *clan without a plan* did," Winters said, referring to the blue crew. The three alternating crews were designated red, white, and blue. "Or the *meat without a beat*," the white crew.

Wolfe shook hands with each crewman when they had finished restocking the ambulance and prepared to return to the station. Winters looked at his watch. "It's only 5:45, Doc. You still owe us fifteen minutes."

Wolfe smiled. "Just long enough to get back to the station. I'd have to go on your next run or walk back here. Thanks, anyway," he said. "I'll risk Dr. Rubel's displeasure. It's been fun. Thanks for the memories."

Winters climbed into the passenger seat of the ambulance. The unit's radio blared; the dispatcher already had new orders for Unit 33. Leaning out the window, Winters called, "Don't be a stranger, Doc..." the remainder was drowned by the sirens. The ambulance pulled a U-turn and headed for 8th Street. Wolfe watched it leave.

Back inside, he walked toward the bank of elevators, intent on retrieving his belongings from the locker in the staff lounge. "Doc. Dr. Wolfe," Manny Navarra called after him. "Hey, Doc, are you done for the day?"

"No, Manny, I'm done for the year. Well, almost. I'm finished with this rotation, but I still have to attend the last M&M tomorrow. Then I'm done."

"Well, could I have this?" Navarra said, tapping on Wolfe's black name tag. The tag itself had seen better days. It was chipped and scratched. The white letters showing through the black top layer of plastic were stained with blood and betadine. Only *olf* could be read from any distance.

"Why would you want my name tag?" Wolfe asked. He knew he no longer needed it. He had made up his mind about his future. Baffled, he unsnapped it and handed it to Navarra.

"Come with me," Navarra said, "I'll show you." Wolfe followed the assistant charge nurse into the ER ICU. As he did, he heard clapping. Not loud, not a standing ovation of hundreds in a theater, but distinct clapping just the same. Wolfe looked around. The staff had interrupted their duties. They all faced him and clapped quietly. When Navarra reached the nurses' station, he pointed to the row of Wizards of Gauze. A new one sat with the others. It had no name tag, however. With a flourish, Navarra pinned Wolfe's name tag to the construct and held it up for all to see. The clapping went on for another minute. Then the staff returned to their jobs.

Tears welled in Wolfe's eyes. He wiped them quickly before anyone could notice. "That's it, Doc," Navarra said, slapping him on the back. "That's your fifteen seconds of fame."

"I thought Andy Warhol said it was supposed to be fifteen *minutes*." Wolfe said.

"Well, everything happens faster in the ER, Addy. You know what Charge Nurse Emilou Jones says, don't you?" Navarra asked. He answered his own question, "We ain't got time for that foolishness."

Chapter 53

Before Johannsen left to catch her late evening flight at Jacksonville International Airport, she and Wolfe took a stroll on the beach in the developing twilight. They had not gotten far before they came across Kervork Torrosian. The Armenian dragged a blanket along the beach. With the four corners of the blanket held tightly in both hands and over one shoulder, he struggled to pull the heavy object wrapped inside. "Hey, Kervork," Wolfe said.

Torrosian stopped. Panting and soaked in perspiration he squatted to catch his breath. "Addy," he gasped, "How are you feeling? And who is your friend?"

"Sorry, Ker," Wolfe said. "This is *my* girlfriend." He pulled Lisa close and kissed her lightly on her forehead. "You'll have to find your own. Unless that's her in the blanket." Wolfe pointed to the pathway the object had left by flattening the sand. "Got a body in there?"

Smiling and standing upright, Torrosian said, "How did you know?" He opened the blanket to reveal the remains of the largest sea turtle Wolfe had ever seen. The limbs and head had been removed, but the shell was still intact. A long thin fishing knife lay in the blanket next to the remains. "There was a shark next to this. Don't know if it chased the turtle onto the beach, or if their being together was just a coincidence."

"Where did you find it? And what are you going to do with it?"

Lisa asked wrinkling her nose at the decaying flesh.

"Thought I'd clean the shell up, then varnish it and hang it on the wall as a decoration," Torrosian said. "If you want to borrow my knife the shark is about a mile and a half down the beach, with what's left of this guy's body. You could clean up the teeth. They make nice souvenirs, too."

"Ewww," Lisa said, "No thanks."

"Need a hand?" Wolfe asked. "I can pull with my right arm."

"Nah, I'm almost home." Torrosian pointed to an apartment building about a quarter mile away. "Are you sure you don't want the knife?"

Had he been by himself, Wolfe would have raced down the beach and dissected the shark before anyone else took the opportunity. Holding his inner packrat in check, he held Lisa's hand and answered, "No. Thanks. See you at M&M tomorrow."

Torrosian, smiled and then grimaced. He re-gathered the ends of the blanket together and slung them over his shoulder. "Yeah, see you there. Last one. Nice to meet you, Lisa. If Wolfe and you ever split up, give me a call."

Lisa blushed. "Good-bye, Ker," she said. Slowly, they followed the trail the turtle carcass had left imprinted in the sand, in silence. An enormous shark lay in the beach near where Torrosian had left turtle parts. Vultures and seabirds nibbled at the remains, fighting over the smaller pieces. Large seabirds nibbled at the shark's eyes. The stench wrinkled their noses. Having seen enough, they reversed course and walked up the beach.

"So what are you going to do now, Addy?" Lisa asked.

Wolfe stared at the beach, then at the clouds turning red and purple behind the hotels and condos that lined the beach. "I have a job in an ER. It means I'll have to move, though."

"Oh, no," Lisa said. "Where to?"

Wolfe smiled. He stopped walking. He pulled on her arm, so that she turned in his direction. "Savannah. Georgia allows reciprocity, so as soon as my Florida license is approved, I can get a Georgia license, too. I don't start work until September, though. It will take that long to get licensed. So I have two months of vacation coming up."

Lisa put her hands on his waist. Looking into his eyes, she asked, "Can I get you to stay with me for some of that time?"

Wolfe looked at the beach, used his sandal to scratch a design in the sand. Coyly, he played with her. "Well, maybe for a day or two. I already found a place to live."

"You did? Where?" she asked.

"Actually, I found us both places to live." From his pocket, he took two Polaroid pictures. Both were of a rundown line of townhouses in Savannah. Lisa recognized one of the townhouses as the one she dreamed of restoring. The other was the end unit next to it. Someone had painted the front door yellow with a crude smiley face in green on top of that. "But since we have to live in them while we restore them, I thought maybe our first job would be to cut a walk-way between the two."

"You bought them?" she asked.

"Just call me big spender," Wolfe said. "A buck each. Two dollars, total." They stood for a long time, embracing on the sand. The sun set and they never noticed.

***

Wolfe never figured out why he went to see Figueroa. He didn't hate the man, but he certainly didn't like him. He didn't need revenge; internship was over. He had survived that and the attempted murder. Being able to say I told you so, or I saved your life never entered his mind. What he sought was closure, possibly. *I guess I want to say a final, permanent good-bye, and never have to look back and wonder about anything that might have happened,* he supposed.

No longer in the ICU, Figueroa lay in a bed in a private room. The big man had lost a lot of weight, looked thin and wan compared to their last meeting. He wore his own pajamas. A purple bathrobe hung on the edge of the adjustable bedside table. The ex-Director of Medical Education sat up in the hospital bed talking on the telephone when Wolfe knocked on the door and entered.

When Figueroa recognized his visitor, he said, "I'll call you back," and hung up the receiver. He set the telephone on the nightstand. A smile slowly crossed his face. He pointed to the stuffed chair next to the bed. "Come in, my boy. Sit."

Wolfe sat, placed his hands in his lap. Not knowing where to begin the conversation, he tentatively started, "You look better than the last time I saw you, Dr. Figueroa."

"The police say I have you to thank for that," Figueroa said. His face clouded. "Although I'm not sure if I have you to thank for putting me in that position. I also have you to thank for warning me about the pancreatic cancer. Again, though, I'm not certain I like the way that came about."

Wolfe thought about arguing, telling Figueroa that his attitude had made the confrontation a certainty, or that Samantha Joiner really had manipulated them both and had put both their lives in jeopardy. "You're welcome," Wolfe said. The two men stared at one another. "Guess I should not have come," Wolfe said, rising to his feet.

"No. No," Figueroa said. "Sit. Stay. I apologize. I do owe you my life. I *am* grateful. I just don't know how to express it, I guess. I'm still confused. Am I really that big of a jerk, Addison?"

Wolfe laughed. "Yeah, you are," he said. "And a male chauvinistic pig, to boot. You'll be lucky if more women don't take more potshots at you in the future."

Figueroa smiled, blushed. "I suppose you're right," he said. "Maybe I'll go back into surgery when I finish recovering. In private practice, I can run my office the way I want. There won't be any scrutiny by a hospital administration or all its physicians. I will no longer have to practice in a fishbowl."

"Yeah," Wolfe agreed. "If you can find some staff who will work with you, you'd be home free."

"You don't think people would work for me?" Figueroa asked. "My staff loved me."

Wolfe shrugged. He didn't know how the hospital employees in the education department felt about Figueroa. He changed the subject. "You aren't pressing charges against Sam?" he asked.

Figueroa shook his head. "She's mentally ill, Wolfe," he said. "That was her on the telephone. She doesn't realize what a fantasy world she lives in. She says she loves me. I-I-I think, it's a possibility, I may be in love with her as well. But she has a long road of recovery ahead. Years, maybe. Her recuperation would take much longer if the threat of incarceration is held over her head or actually happens. How about you? What are you going to do?"

The epiphany stunned Wolfe. He didn't need to have Samantha Joiner prosecuted for attempted murder. There was a much simpler punishment, for both her and Figueroa. "No," he said. "I'm not interested in seeing her go to jail." *I think you two deserve each other. And if there is anything I can do to help you two get together and torture one another, I'll do it.*

"Good. Good," Figueroa said.

"You look beat," Wolfe said, making an excuse to leave. He stood and shook Figueroa's hand perfunctorily. "Maybe I'll see you later." *But probably not*. He left Figueroa staring out the window.

"Good-bye, Dr. Wolfe," Figueroa said as Addison departed. "Thank you, again, for everything."

***

Dr. Rubel hosted the last M&M for Wolfe's intern class, and the first for the new interns whose internships would start in two days, Friday, July 1st, 1977. The difference in teaching styles between Rubel and Figueroa became immediately apparent to the veterans in the auditorium.

"Now, with this gentleman who has been a life long alcoholic," Rubel explained. "The redness and swelling of his legs could be a cellulitis, like Dr. Lynch thought when he presented to the ER. However, if someone gets most of his calories from alcohol, in addition to not getting enough protein he will be missing some essential vitamins. Alcoholics may have a loss of muscle mass because of protein deficiency, and Wernicke-Korsakoff syndrome from lack of B1, to name two problems. This man has scurvy, from a lack of Vitamin C. That caused the rash."

In the next case, Iggy had allowed a nurse to draw up the xylocaine anesthetic he used on a patient's finger before suturing a laceration. Mike Dixon, the senior orthopedic resident, presented pictures of the finger, swollen and starkly white. The nurse had used xylocaine with epinephrine, not realizing that was anathema in hands, feet, and ears. The epinephrine caused the blood vessels in the finger to go into spasm. Blood flow stopped, completely. Gradually, over two hours, the vessels had relaxed and the digit returned to its normal pink color. "Longest two hours of my life," Iggy said. "Had he lost the finger, I could imagine the lawsuit. The right index finger on a right hand dominant patient is probably worth a million dollars to a good lawyer."

Rubel was less doubtful about the good outcome. "I don't know that using epinephrine in xylocaine in ears, feet, or hands is as bad as they say. Unless the patient has a compromised circulatory system, that is," he explained. "It makes for scary anecdotal stories, like this one. And I'm sure Iggy will never let a nurse draw up his xylocaine in the future. But my feeling is all spasm ends eventually. The blood supply would have to stop for several more hours in order to cause necrosis. Anyone up for doing a study on this topic?" No one volunteered.

Rubel spent an hour going over the signs and symptoms of aspirin overdoses, after the presentation of just such a death. The resident who presided over the resuscitation wasn't chided or yelled at. The other residents took more away from the conference than a dislike for the presiding physician. The incoming interns felt better about having decided to come to Jacksonville and University Hospital.

"That was kind of fun," a resident said as they left the amphitheater. "Maybe Dr. Rubel could preside over a medical conference put on by the residents who graduate from here."

"Yeah," another one said. "I'd like to do that, *in about thirty years*. Suppose he'll still be around then?"

If Dr. Rubel can't cheat death, knowing everything he knows, no one can, Wolfe thought.

Iggy drove the battered VW bug back to the apartment after the conference. "Well, I – and the rest of the interns, of course – have one more day 'til we're done with internship. Most of us have a residency to complete, two to five years. You have completed your internship, but what are you going to do next, Addy?" he asked.

Wolfe sighed, relieved to have the internship over. "I finally forgot everything I learned in medical school," he said laughing. He told Iggy about the townhouses and the job in Savannah. "We'll have to see how it goes with Lisa. May turn out to be a permanent thing. Never can tell."

"You don't want to specialize?" Iggy asked. "Being a GP or an ER doc without credentials may prove sticky in the future."

"I've thought about that, too," Wolfe said. "I think I'll look for a family practice residency I can share with another physician, you know alternate months or something. I've seen a couple of those positions advertised, usually by married women who are looking for someone to share. It doesn't have to be in Savannah. I can fly to anywhere in the US, one month at a time."

"Not a bad idea, although it will take you twice as long, four more years instead of two," Iggy said.

"Thought about that, too," Wolfe said. "If Lisa and I get married, I can use the money from the ER job and some of my time off to turn one of the townhouses into a free-standing clinic. I can live next to my office."

"A *free* what?"

"It's something new. Some guy in Delaware started his own free-standing ER in 1973. Even has ambulance service. Another guy in Chicago, a Dr. Flashner, put one in a strip shopping center. He called it an *emergicenter*. Critics call them *Docs in a Box*. I think they may be the wave of the future."

"Yeah. Sure," Iggy said laughing. "Don't give up your day job,

Addy."

The End

Comments or criticisms gratefully accepted.
Email: wbyAuthor@bellsouth.net

ABOUT THE AUTHOR

Bill Yancey had the privilege of being the son of an air force officer and the grandson of an army officer. As a result, he lived all over the world, but never really grew up. He attended four high schools, a prep school, and five colleges. After bouncing out of an engineering curriculum, and spending time in Vietnam as a result, he finally obtained an undergraduate degree in general science from Virginia Tech in 1971. The Medical College of Virginia still regrets giving him an M.D. degree in 1976. He writes for his own entertainment, and hopes you see the humor in it, too.

56203028R00179

Made in the USA
Charleston, SC
15 May 2016